311 PELICAN COURT

311 PELICAN COURT

Debbie Macomber

CHIVERS

| British Library Cataloguing in Publication Data available |

This Large Print edition published by AudioGO Ltd, Bath, 2013.

Published by arrangement with Harlequin Enterprises II B.V./S à r.l.

U.K. Hardcover   ISBN   978 1 4713 4616 3
U.K. Softcover   ISBN   978 1 4713 4617 0

Printed and bound in Great Britain by TJ International Ltd

To Jo and Hayley

Because you've given so much and inspired others

Some of the Residents of Cedar Cove, Washington

Olivia Lockhart: Divorced, family court judge in Cedar Cove. Mother of Justine and James (of San Diego). Lives at 16 Lighthouse Road.

Charlotte Jefferson: Mother of Olivia, widow, lifelong resident of Cedar Cove.

Justine (Lockhart) Gunderson: Married to Seth, mother of Leif.

Seth Gunderson: Justine's husband. Co-owner, with Justine, of The Lighthouse Restaurant.

Stanley Lockhart: Olivia's ex-husband and father of James and Justine. Now lives in Seattle.

Will Jefferson: Olivia's brother, Charlotte's son. Married and lives in Atlanta.

Grace Sherman: Olivia's best friend. Widow. Librarian. Mother of Maryellen and Kelly. Lives at 204 Rosewood Lane.

Dan Sherman: Grace's deceased husband.

Maryellen Sherman: Oldest daughter of Grace

and Dan. Divorced. Manager of the Harbor Street Art Gallery. Mother of Katie.

Kelly Jordan: Maryellen's sister, married to Paul, mother of Tyler.

Jon Bowman: Local photographer and chef, father of Katie.

Jack Griffin: Newspaper reporter and editor of the *Cedar Cove Chronicle*. Recovering alcoholic. Father of Eric, who lives in Nevada with his wife, Shelly, and their twin boys.

Zachary Cox: Accountant. Divorced from Rosie. Father of Allison and Eddie Cox, aged 15 and 9, respectively. The family home is 311 Pelican Court.

Rosie Cox: Zach's ex-wife. Now working as a teacher. She and Zach share custody of their children.

Janice Lamond: Zach's assistant at his accounting firm.

Cliff Harding: Retired engineer and now horse breeder living near Cedar Cove. Divorced father of Lisa, who lives in Maryland. Has an on-again, off-again relationship with Grace Sherman. Grandson of Tom Houston (Harding), cowboy film star of the 1930s.

Cecilia Randall: Navy wife, living in Cedar Cove. Accountant. Married to Ian Randall, submariner. Lost a baby, Allison.

Bob and Peggy Beldon: Retired. Own the Thyme and Tide Bed-and-Breakfast at 44 Cranberry Point. Have two adult children.

Roy McAfee: Private investigator, retired from Seattle police force. Married to Corrie McAfee, who is also his office manager. They have two adult children and live at 50 Harbor Street.

Troy Davis: Cedar Cove sheriff. Lives at 92 Pacific Boulevard.

Louie Benson: Cedar Cove mayor and brother of Otto Benson, lawyer.

Warren Saget: Local builder, formerly involved with Justine.

Dave Flemming: Local Methodist minister. Married to Emily and has two sons. They live at 8 Sandpiper Way.

One

From the moment Rosie Cox entered Cedar Cove's divorce court, she'd felt a renewed sense of failure—not to mention betrayal. Who *wouldn't* feel that way? After seventeen years of what she'd believed to be a reasonably good marriage, Zach's infidelity was the last thing she'd expected.

He'd never openly admitted to the affair. She hadn't found her husband in a compromising situation, hadn't found any concrete evidence—no matchbooks from expensive restaurants, no jewelry receipts or motel bills—but in her heart she knew. A wife always does.

Rosie owned up to the truth—she was angry and she'd expressed that anger by making this divorce as complicated and difficult as she possibly could. Why should she go easy on Zach or walk away from their marriage without one hell of a fight? And fight she had, with both fists raised.

As she turned away from the judge, the final decree in her hand, she realized she'd made another mistake.

Rosie had *assumed* that once the divorce was granted, the anger and bitterness of these dreadful months would be lifted. Wrong again. An even heavier burden had been added.

1

When the joint custody agreement she and Zach had so carefully worked out, point by point, was presented to Judge Olivia Lockhart, the judge had rejected it.

Instead, Judge Lockhart had stated that it was emotionally detrimental to kids to shuffle them between residences every few days. Allison and Eddie needed stable lives, according to Judge Lockhart, and *they* hadn't asked for the divorce. Some people considered the judge innovative, Rosie thought, disgruntled. How about interfering? Or out of her mind? Because—of all the crazy settlements—she'd awarded the children their house. That meant Rosie and Zach would be the ones moving in and out.

Talk about ridiculous! Talk about impossible.

Now that the divorce was final, Rosie and Zach would have to figure out some kind of living arrangements. The ramifications of what they'd agreed to were starting to hit Rosie and she hadn't even left the courtroom.

'Rosie,' Sharon Castor, her attorney, said as soon as they were in the silent hallway outside the courtroom. 'We have to meet with your ex-husband.'

One look told Rosie that Sharon was as flustered as she was herself.

Otto Benson, Zach's lawyer, joined them. Although he remained outwardly calm, his face was tense. She dared not glance in Zach's

2

direction. In fact, she'd avoided looking at her ex-husband from the moment she'd walked into the courtroom.

'Let's get a conference room and discuss the details,' Zach's attorney said.

Rosie peered at Zach, standing behind his lawyer. He didn't seem any happier than she was with this decision, but she'd keel over in a dead faint before she let him know how she felt.

'Rosie and I should be able to work this out ourselves,' Zach said with an edge of irritation.

Given the way everything had gone so far, that suggestion wasn't promising. 'If you remember, it took us weeks of haggling to come up with this joint custody agreement,' she pointed out. She enjoyed reminding him what a jerk he'd been. Rosie supposed Zach was hoping to avoid more attorneys' fees. Too bad. If he ended up with less money to spend on his girlfriend, that wasn't her concern.

Fists clenched, Zach snarled something under his breath. Probably just as well she couldn't hear it, Rosie decided, proud of her own display of self-control.

'What makes you think we're capable of agreeing to anything without a mediator?' she asked sarcastically.

'Fine,' Zach muttered, with a pout reminiscent of their nine-year-old son. Staring at him now, Rosie had trouble believing she'd ever loved Zachary Cox. Not only was he smug and argumentative and self-righteous, he had no idea what it meant to be a husband and father. Granted, Zach was a handsome man; not only that, his appearance proclaimed his success as a businessman, a professional. Although, in her opinion, anyone with half a brain would instantly peg him for an accountant. He had that narrowed look about his dark eyes, as if he spent too many hours a day squinting at columns of tiny numbers. Despite that, he was appealing to the eye with his broad shoulders—which nicely set off his expensive suit—and thick, dark hair. At one time he'd been an athlete, and even now he routinely jogged and kept in shape.

Rosie had loved the firmness of his muscles as she stroked his back during lovemaking. Of course, it'd been months since they'd slept in the same bed, and much longer since they'd actually made love.

Rosie didn't even remember the last time. Had she known, she might have appreciated it more, lingered a moment longer at her husband's side, savored the feel of his arms around her. One thing was certain: Zach hadn't been interested in her from the day he'd hired Janice Lamond as his personal assistant.

The thought of him entwined with Janice nearly suffocated Rosie and she forcefully shoved the image from her mind. Anger and revulsion at her husband's—no, ex-husband's—unfaithfulness rose like bile in the back of her throat.

Zach's raised voice caught her attention; apparently he'd agreed to have their attorneys negotiate this added complication to their divorce decree. Otto was checking with the clerk for an empty conference room.

Once a private room in the law library was secured, Zach and his attorney sat at one side of the table, across from Rosie and hers.

Even the attorneys seemed perplexed by the situation. 'I can't say I've ever heard of such a decree before,' Sharon said, starting the conversation.

'Me, neither.' Otto frowned. 'This is one for the books.'

'Fine,' Zach said in a curt voice, 'it's unusual, but we're both adults. We can figure this out. I know *I* was sincere about putting the children first.' He glared at Rosie, as if to suggest she hadn't been.

'If you were sincere, you would've had second thoughts about sleeping with that slut.' Rosie hadn't intended to be argumentative, but if her ex-husband was so concerned about their children's welfare, he would never have broken his wedding vows.

'I refuse to dignify that remark by responding to it,' Zach said through gritted teeth. 'Besides, if you were home more, instead of volunteering for every cause known to mankind, every cause *except* your children, you'd—'

'Well, I refuse to allow you to blame me for what *you've* done.' Her volunteer efforts were Zach's big complaint. He had his wish; she'd had to resign from every position she held and seek paid employment. She hoped he was happy. For the first time since their children were born, Rosie wasn't a stay-at-home mom.

'I thought we were here to discuss this divorce decree?' Zach asked with a bored look, an expression that was obviously for her benefit. 'If we're going to trade insults I'd rather not pay our attorneys to listen.'

That's right, Rosie mused, deriving a small sense of satisfaction out of knowing that Zach was responsible for both sets of attorneys' fees. He was the one with the high-paying job. She was currently taking summer classes to update her teaching certificate. Classes Zach was paying for. That was another notch in her belt—another concession granted in their divorce settlement.

Her application was in with the South Kitsap School District and, considering all her connections, she shouldn't have any difficulty getting hired as a substitute teacher in September.

'Let's make a list of what we can agree on,' Sharon said briskly, ignoring the antagonism between Rosie and Zach. 'Despite the breakdown of your marriage, you both claim you want to keep the needs of your children first and foremost.'

Rosie nodded and so did Zach.

Sharon smiled. She was a no-nonsense woman who wasn't swayed by emotion. 'Okay, that gives us a place to start.'

'I want to compliment you both on your attitudes,' Otto said, removing a legal pad from his briefcase as if to prove he was earning his pay. Zach had chosen the best and, for that matter, so had Rosie. Both attorneys came with high price tags.

'Yeah,' Zach said sarcastically. 'If we got along any better, we might've stayed married.'

'You know who to blame for that,' Rosie snapped.

'Yes, I do,' he snapped right back. 'How many nights were you actually home? How many dinners did you cook? If you don't remember, I do. Damn few.'

Sharon sighed audibly. 'Okay, the kids come first, and at this point, they have the house, which means Rosie will need to find somewhere else to live for the three days a week when Zach's staying with them.'

Somewhere else to live? Rosie's head jerked up as the shock ran up and down her spine. The reality—the repercussions of the judge's edict—had just started to sink in.

'*And* pay half the mortgage on the house,' Zach added, smiling at her benignly.

'But I can't—' Rosie hadn't realized, hadn't thought that far in advance. 'I don't have a job yet—how am I supposed to afford an apartment on top of everything else?' This was grossly unfair. Surely Zach could see that such a demand was unreasonable. She had a life, too, and no way of building it if every penny she earned went into paying for two separate residences.

Rosie stared at Zach. He returned her look, unblinking.

'I have a suggestion,' Sharon said.

'Let's hear it.' Zach's lawyer sounded eager, if not desperate, for ideas.

'If Zach spends three days a week at the house with the children, then his apartment will sit empty, is that right?' She turned to Zach for verification.

Rosie studied him, too. In essence, Sharon was asking if Zach intended to move Janice into the apartment, Janice and her son, who was the same age as Eddie.

'The apartment will be empty,' Zach said emphatically.

'What if—' Sharon glanced from one to the other '—Rosie moves into the apartment during the time you're at the house? You did say it was a two-bedroom apartment, didn't you?'

Objections shot up like weeds in Rosie's fertile mind. She didn't want anything to do with Zach. She certainly didn't want to be put in a situation where she had to deal with being around him or his things—or what had been *their* things. Nor did she want to be privy to any information regarding his relationship with his girlfriend.

'No way am I letting Rosie in my apartment.' Apparently Zach shared her qualms. 'We're divorced. It took months to get that way. Rosie wanted out and she got her wish.'

'You were the one who moved out,' she reminded him scornfully.

'Correction. You kicked me out.'

'If you'll recall, *you* insisted I see an attorney.' She couldn't believe how convenient his memory was.

Zach snorted and looked at Sharon. 'More fool me.'

Rosie's attorney raised both hands in a pleading gesture. 'Listen, it's just a suggestion—a way of saving money for you both.' She turned to Rosie. 'You'll be fortunate to find a place, even a studio apartment, for less than five, six hundred dollars a month.'

'Zach will have to pay—'

'The hell I will!'

'The divorce is final,' Otto Benson stated. 'Zach isn't responsible for anything more than what's already been agreed to.'

Rosie's gaze flew to her attorney, and Sharon reluctantly nodded. All at once, this was more than Rosie could bear. Not only had she lost her husband, but now she was being

9

forced out of her home, too. Moisture welled in her eyes, and she managed to blink it away. Hell would freeze over before she let Zach know what he was doing to her.

A long moment passed before Zach finally spoke. 'Okay, I'll agree to let Rosie stay in the apartment on the days I'm at the house, as long as she's willing to split the rent.'

Rosie was well aware that she had no choice, but she did have her pride and she was determined to hold on to that. 'On one condition,' she insisted, lifting her head.

'Now what?' Zach asked with a long-suffering sigh.

'I don't want you bringing that woman into the family home. I want our house to be a safe place for the children. In other words, I don't want Allison and Eddie exposed to your women.'

'What?' Zach glared at her as though she'd spoken a foreign language.

'You heard me,' she said vehemently, meeting his angry eyes. 'This divorce has been hard enough on the kids without you parading Janice or any other woman you decide to date through my home. I want the house off-limits to your…your floozies.'

'Floozies?' Zach smirked. 'Fine, no *floozies.* And the same goes for you. I don't want you bringing any men to the house, either. No studs, no hotties, no boy toys, no—'

'Oh, that's rich,' Rosie broke in, putting an

end to his ridicule. In seventeen years she'd never so much as looked at another man. Not since the day she'd met Zach.

'Do you or don't you agree?' her ex-husband challenged.

'Of course I agree!'

'Good.'

'Perfect.'

With their attorneys present, they made decisions about a number of other issues, and Sharon quickly wrote up an agreement. Zach's attorney reviewed it, and then both Zach and Rosie signed it.

By the time she left the courthouse, Rosie felt as if she'd been pummeled by wave after wave in a stormy sea. Strange as it seemed, her heart actually ached. For weeks she'd dreaded this day and at the same time longed for it, just so the divorce would finally be over. Now she wasn't sure *what* she felt, other than this deep pain that threatened to overpower her.

Nine-year-old Eddie was shooting baskets when Rosie pulled into the driveway at 311 Pelican Court. In a little more than a month, school would start again. Perhaps then their lives would return to some semblance of routine.

Eddie caught the basketball and held it against his side as he waited for her to park the car in the garage. His sad dark eyes watched Rosie as he stepped aside so she could drive past.

11

Fifteen-year-old Allison was in the kitchen, microwaving a hot dog for lunch. She turned and stared at Rosie, eyes glittering defiantly. She resembled Zach so much just then.

'How'd it go?' Eddie asked, following Rosie into the kitchen. He continued to hold the basketball.

'All right, I guess.'

The microwave beeped and Allison removed the steaming wiener, devoid of a bun. As if it had suddenly lost its appeal, she set the plate on the countertop and studied Rosie.

'There's been a…minor complication,' Rosie announced. She didn't believe in hiding the truth from her children, especially when it involved something that would affect them.

'What kind of complication?' Eddie asked, pulling out a kitchen chair. He balanced the basketball on the table, one hand supporting it. Allison crossed her arms and leaned against the counter, pretending to be bored; still, she didn't leave the room as she so often did.

With effort Rosie managed to show a bit of enthusiasm for Judge Lockhart's decree. 'Well…you guys won't be moving in and out of the house every few days, after all.'

Allison and Eddie shared a look of surprise. Trying to sound positive, Rosie explained Judge Lockhart's decision and briefly outlined how the switch would work.

'You mean Dad's going to live *here?*' Eddie asked as if he didn't quite understand. Rosie

12

didn't blame him for being confused. She was, too. Confused and irritated by this turn of events. Add miserable to the mix, and it pretty much described the way she felt about life in general.

'Your father will be at the house part-time,' Rosie said, so there wouldn't be any misunderstanding. She'd agreed to turn what had been her sewing room into a spare bedroom for his use. The sewing machine could go in the master bedroom without a problem.

'Oh,' Eddie said. He seemed disappointed, but then his eyes lit up as he realized he'd have his father back, if only half the time. 'I think it's cool!'

'I don't,' Allison shouted. 'As far as I'm concerned, this entire divorce is bogus.' With that she stormed out of the kitchen.

Rosie watched her daughter go, wishing she knew how to reach her. She wanted to put her arms around Allison and hug her and assure her that everything would be all right, but the girl wouldn't accept any kind of closeness. At least not from her...

'Don't worry about Allison,' her nine-year-old said. 'She's really glad about Dad coming home, even if it's only for a few days at a time, but she wouldn't let you know that for anything.'

Two

Sweat dripped down Grace Sherman's face, and the intense heat of the mid-July afternoon plastered her T-shirt to her skin. She dipped her roller in the tray and smoothly spread light yellow paint across her bedroom wall. She was a librarian and, despite all the books she'd taken out on home maintenance, she wasn't much good at renovations and repairs. Dan had always insisted on looking after the house. Alone at age fifty-five, Grace found that life continued to thrust her into unfamiliar and challenging situations.

'I hope you appreciate what a good friend I am,' Olivia Lockhart said from behind her. She, too, worked at covering the dingy white walls with yellow paint. Cautiously, Olivia—her lifelong friend—moved around the furniture pushed into the middle of the bedroom, protected by old sheets.

'You volunteered,' Grace reminded her, using her forearm to wipe the perspiration from her brow. The room felt stifling and the air was still, even with the windows partially open.

After learning that her husband of thirty-four years, who'd been missing since the previous April, was dead, Grace had developed insomnia. She didn't understand

14

it. Olivia had suggested she repaint the room, thinking a different color might signify a new phase in her life. Pale yellow was a calm, optimistic color. Maybe her subconscious would get the hint. At the time it had sounded like a good idea, especially when her friend had offered to help. It was just the kind of thing Olivia would do. Over the years, they'd supported each other through everything from minor domestic crises to life-shattering events.

'I can't believe I thought we could finish this in one day.' Olivia groaned. Straightening, she planted her hands on the small of her back. 'I didn't have any idea how much work this was going to be.'

'How about a glass of iced tea?' Grace was more than ready for a break herself. The two of them had been painting for what seemed like forever but was probably only an hour or two. Still, they'd had to move the furniture and do the prep work first—laying a drop cloth on the floor and taping the windows.

Olivia set aside her roller. 'You don't need to ask twice.'

Grace wrapped both paint-coated rollers in a plastic bag, then headed into the kitchen. By the time Olivia finished washing her hands, Grace had poured the iced tea into tall glasses. Buttercup, her golden retriever, scratched at the screen door and Grace absently let her inside. Panting, the dog lumbered into the house and stretched out under the table,

15

resting her chin on the cool tile floor.

Grace slumped into the chair and released the kerchief tied at the base of her neck, shaking her damp hair free. She wore it shorter these days, since she no longer needed to worry about her husband's likes and dislikes.

After witnessing Olivia's pain years before, Grace had never wanted to go through a divorce, but when Dan disappeared she wasn't left with any options. For financial reasons, it was the only practical choice.

That had been months ago now. Afterward, even learning Dan's fate was anticlimactic. She was relieved that his body had been discovered, but she'd already endured the worst of the grief and guilt: the not knowing, the doubts, the recriminations—all of which had befallen her after Dan's disappearance. So this sudden bout of insomnia didn't make sense to her.

'This was the best idea you've had all day,' Olivia said, sinking down on the chair. 'Besides putting on a Credence Clearwater Revival CD,' she added. They'd both gotten caught up in the music of their youth and hadn't realized how hot and uncomfortable they were until the last song on the CD ended.

'We may not have the moves we did thirty years ago, but we aren't ready for walkers just yet,' Grace said, and Olivia agreed with an easy smile.

'I heard about your latest decree,' Grace said, smiling across the table at her friend. They'd been working together all afternoon, but with the music playing they'd barely had a chance to talk.

'You mean the joint custody case?' Olivia asked.

Grace nodded. 'It's all over town.' This wasn't the first time Olivia had made a controversial decision in the courtroom.

Olivia rolled her eyes. 'At least Jack didn't write about it in his column.'

So Olivia was going to bring Jack Griffin into the conversation. Good. Grace had been looking for a way to introduce the subject. He and Olivia had been seeing each other for more than a year, and Grace loved Jack for the simple reason that he'd made her friend happy. Once Olivia had started dating Jack, the local newspaper editor, she'd been… more relaxed. More lighthearted. Then, a few weeks ago, Jack and Olivia had a falling out, a difference of opinion, really—and they hadn't spoken since. Olivia was miserable, although she wasn't willing to admit it.

'Speaking of Jack,' Grace asked brightly, 'what's new with the two of you?' In her opinion Jack was exactly right for her friend. He was witty and funny and just outrageous enough to be interesting.

Olivia looked up. 'I don't want to talk about Jack.'

'Then don't. Tell me about Stan.'

Stan was Olivia's ex-husband, who now lived in Seattle with his second wife, but he'd been making regular appearances in Cedar Cove lately. Something must be up; however, Olivia had kept suspiciously quiet about it.

'You heard about Stan and Marge?' Olivia asked, her eyes rounding with surprise. 'Who told you? Mom or Justine?'

'Neither one told me anything. I'm waiting for you to enlighten me.'

Olivia took a deep swallow of her iced tea, then glanced up, an uncertain expression on her face.

'Something's bothering you,' Grace pressed.

'Stan and Marge are getting a divorce.'

Shock waves went through Grace. This was news. Big news. No wonder Stan had been coming to Cedar Cove more frequently. His visits were often under the guise of seeing his daughter, Justine, and his grandson, who'd been born a little more than two weeks ago. Grace found his sudden interest in family somewhat suspect. Especially since Stan had deserted his wife and children back in the summer of 1986. Jordan, a bright, lively thirteen-year-old, had gone swimming with friends one hot August afternoon and drowned. Justine, his twin sister, had held his lifeless body in her arms until the paramedics arrived. Everything in Olivia's life was marked by that day; it was the dividing point, the boundary between believing the world was a safe place and knowing it could be a treacherous one.

Olivia and Stan's marriage fell apart after Jordan drowned, but Grace had always wondered if Stan had been involved with Marge before Jordan's death. She'd never said this to Olivia's face, but she had her suspicions.

'You haven't got anything to say?' Olivia asked.

Grace was almost surprised that Stan and Marge's marriage had lasted this many years. The ink on the divorce papers was hardly dry when Stan had married the other woman. 'I'm sorry it didn't work out,' she mumbled, which was slightly stretching the truth.

'I am, too,' Olivia said, looking melancholy and tired.

Then it came to her. Grace should've connected the dots much sooner. She felt like slapping her palm against her forehead in cartoon fashion. 'Stan wants you back, doesn't he?'

For a moment it seemed as if Olivia wasn't going to answer, then she did with a nod of her head.

Outrage filled Grace. How dare he! How dare Stan walk back into Olivia's life after all these years and expect her to welcome him with open arms. Of all the nerve! His timing was impeccable, too, she thought wryly. Naturally Stan would reappear just when

Olivia had met Jack. He must hate the idea of his ex-wife seeing anyone else.

'I didn't tell you about Stan for exactly this reason,' Olivia muttered. 'You're so angry your eyes are about to pop out.'

'I can't *help* it,' Grace cried.

It occurred to her that Olivia might actually be considering a reconciliation with Stan. That was the worst thing she could do—and if Olivia didn't know it, Grace wasn't too shy to tell her. Stan had never appreciated his wife. He'd never seemed too concerned about what his leaving would do to her or to their remaining children. All Stan had ever cared about was himself and *his* needs, *his* wants.

'I know how you feel about Stan,' Olivia murmured.

'You're not going back to him, are you? You wouldn't really consider it, would you?' The thought was so repugnant Grace had difficulty getting the words out.

The perplexed uncertainty that came over Olivia was so unlike her that Grace had to make a conscious effort not to get up and hug her.

'I don't know,' Olivia whispered.

Grace merely nodded, arranging her features in as neutral an expression as possible.

'The day Leif was born,' Olivia said, studying the inside of her glass as if it held the answers she needed, 'Stan and I had the most wonderful time reminiscing.'

'You had three children with him,' Grace said, trying to suppress her own negative view of the situation.

'We were happy for a lot of years.'

Grace couldn't deny that, but Stan had nearly crippled her friend emotionally. She above all others knew how long it had taken Olivia to recover her equilibrium following Jordan's death and the demise of her marriage.

'What about Jack?' It was probably a mistake to introduce his name just then, but she was genuinely curious. 'Does he know?' Her guess was he did, and that was the key to their current troubles.

As Olivia nodded, her hand tightened around her glass. 'Do you want to know what he did?' Her brown eyes sparked with irritation. 'I swear every time I think about it, I get mad.'

This sounded promising.

Olivia didn't wait for an answer. 'Jack gave me an ultimatum. He claimed Stan's been after me for months and that I had to choose—either him or Stan.'

'Ye-es?' Grace said, dragging out the word. 'And your point is?'

'My point,' Olivia said with exaggerated patience, 'is that I'm not some trophy to be won. Furthermore, I'm not willing to play Jack's silly games.'

'Games,' Grace countered. 'It seems to me

21

you're the one playing games.'

'Me?' Olivia cried.

'Yes, you,' Grace said. 'Do you expect Jack to hang around and twiddle his thumbs while Stan waltzes back into your life?'

'No, but I expect him to...to show some gumption. If I'm as important to him as he says, then the least he can do is let me know how he feels.'

Grace frowned. 'You mean he *hasn't* told you?'

'Told me?' Olivia repeated. 'Oh, hardly. He stopped by the house at an inopportune moment about a month ago. Stan had spent the night—'

Grace couldn't disguise her shock. 'Stan...'

'Not you, too,' Olivia said, sounding utterly exasperated. 'If you *must* know, he slept in James's old room upstairs. It was completely innocent. I can't believe you'd think I'd let him back in my bed....'

'I don't know what to think,' Grace said, eager to learn what had taken place. 'Go on, tell me what happened.'

'Jack and I were supposed to meet the next morning, but he showed up early with coffee and doughnuts, and there was Stan in Justine's old housecoat and fuzzy slippers. He looked ridiculous, but that's beside the point.'

'And naturally Jack assumed the worst.' He'd jumped to conclusions, just as Grace almost had.

'Naturally,' Olivia echoed. 'I went after him and tried to explain, but he wouldn't listen. He said if I wanted to get back together with Stan, that was fine with him.'

Grace frowned again. 'Are you *sure* that's what he said?'

Olivia paused. 'Maybe not in so many words, but that was his message. I have to tell you it upset me that he actually thought I'd sleep with Stan when the two of us had been seriously dating.'

A picture was beginning to take shape in Grace's mind. 'You haven't heard from him since, have you?'

'No. Mom thinks I should phone him.' Slowly Olivia raised her eyes to meet Grace's. 'Is that what you think, too?'

Grace shrugged. If she was the one in this situation, she might, but then...

'The thing is,' Olivia said, biting her lower lip, 'I want Jack to show some commitment here. Proof that he cares. If he honestly loves me, I think he should fight for me.'

'Fight for you?' The image that came to Grace's mind, of Jack and Stan standing in the driveway, dukes raised, was comical. 'You mean you want him to challenge Stan to a fistfight? Or—' she grinned, imagining them in Regency-era costumes, brandishing pistols '—a duel?'

'No, of course not,' Olivia said impatiently. 'I want him to give me some indication, a sign

23

that I'm worth more to him than his stupid male pride. That's all.' She lowered her eyes. 'He's acting like a hurt little boy.'

'I imagine he *is* hurt.'

'Well, so am I. He instantly decided I'd spent the night with Stan, although we'd been seeing each other exclusively. If he really believes I'm that kind of woman, I'm better off without him.'

'Don't give up on him so quickly.'

'It's been almost a month, Grace.' Slowly, sadly, she shook her head. 'What else am I supposed to think? He's apparently content just to drop the relationship.'

'What about you?' Grace asked. 'Are you willing to walk away from Jack?'

She didn't answer immediately. 'I don't think so,' she finally said.

This was encouraging. 'What are you going to do?'

'I don't know,' she readily admitted. 'Give it time, I guess.'

Grace nodded. She drained her tea, stood and set her glass in the sink. 'Let's get back to painting.'

'Just a minute,' Olivia said, stopping her. She was still seated. 'While we're on the subject of men, tell me what's happening between you and that good-looking rancher.'

Grace wanted to groan out loud. She'd really prefer not to discuss Cliff Harding. They'd been seeing each other for nearly a

24

year; they'd met shortly after Grace had filed for divorce. She hadn't officially gone out with him until her divorce was final, but he'd let her know he was interested. Grace was interested in him, too; however, for some reason, their mutual attraction made her uncomfortable.

'What's wrong?' Olivia asked.

'I'm not really sure,' she murmured. 'That's part of the problem.'

'You mean a decent, wonderful man comes into your life and you can't figure it out?'

Grace ignored the light sarcasm. 'Dan and I got married so young,' she said, and because it was apparent that Olivia wasn't going to let her escape, she reclaimed her seat. 'We were just teenagers, and then Dan went off to Vietnam. But despite all that, despite the difficulties we had, I never looked at another man.'

'I know,' Olivia said, her voice low and soothing.

'Given the least bit of encouragement, Cliff would ask me to marry him.'

'He was so kind the day of Dan's funeral.'

Grace could only agree. Cliff had shown up at the house following the wake and tenderly looked after her. She'd been exhausted, mentally, physically, emotionally. That afternoon, Cliff had comforted her, tucked her into bed and made her dinner. Grace had never met anyone as thoughtful as Cliff Harding, and, frankly, the way that made her feel frightened her.

25

'I know Cliff wants us to be serious,' she said, her voice trembling, 'but I haven't dated anyone except him since Dan disappeared.'

'You think seeing a man exclusively—any man—is the same trap you fell into during high school?' Olivia asked. 'Is that it?'

'I didn't want to be divorced or a widow, but I'm both. I guess I don't want to limit myself to one person at this stage. I don't think I'm ready to be in a relationship.' There, she'd said it, and as soon as the words were out she understood what had been happening and why.

'Grace?' Olivia was studying her closely.

'That's it,' she breathed. The insomnia, the anxiety, it all made sense to her now. She didn't need her bedroom repainted to help release her from the memories of her dead husband. Yes, she had concerns about some information Dan had given her in the letter he'd written just before his death, information to think about, but Dan had very little to do with what had been churning inside her these last few weeks. All this angst was tied to her relationship with Cliff. What she needed was time and space and freedom to discover who she was—who she'd become—and what she wanted out of life. She needed a chance to be herself, by herself.

'Grace?'

'I adore Cliff,' she whispered. 'I truly do, but I'm not ready to be as serious as he is. Not

26

yet... I just can't.' Although she was almost in tears, Grace experienced an incredible feeling of relief, and for the first time since Dan's funeral, she knew she'd sleep through the night.

'You have to tell Cliff,' Olivia said urgently.

'I know.' She had to find a way to explain without offending him or losing his friendship. 'I'd like to continue seeing him, but I want the freedom to see other men, too.' Said out loud, it seemed so unfair and selfish, but it was the truth and that was something Grace often had a difficult time admitting, especially to herself.

Three

As the morning light cascaded into her bedroom, Maryellen Sherman rolled carefully onto her back, astounded at the determined effort it took to shift her 'nine-months-and-counting' pregnant body.

Her sister had warned her there'd be days she'd feel as big as the Goodyear blimp, and there were, but Maryellen couldn't remember a time she'd been happier.

'Any day now,' she said, rubbing her hand over her tight, round abdomen. Catherine 'Katie' Grace kicked and stretched, and Maryellen marveled as she watched her stomach extend and move. Glancing at the clock, she saw it was eight-thirty, time to get up. She struggled to sit, and with her palms braced against one side of the bed, Maryellen stared down at her feet and realized they were no longer visible. In fact, it'd been weeks since she'd last seen her toes.

She stood awkwardly and supported her back with both hands. It'd begun to ache, which was no surprise. That was what she got for sleeping on a worn-out old mattress. Once she started moving around, she'd feel better. On bare feet, she padded into the kitchen and put on water to make herself a pot of herbal tea; while she waited for it to boil, she sorted through the four maternity tops that were still decent enough to wear outside the house.

This pregnancy hadn't been planned, and she'd tried to hide the fact that she was pregnant from the father—not a smart move on her part but a desperate one. Jon Bowman, an artist whose work had been displayed at the gallery she managed, had learned about the baby on his own. He'd been adamant about having a role in his daughter's life. Maryellen didn't like it, but she didn't have any choice. It was either grant Jon visitation rights or fight him in court, something she'd rather avoid.

Maryellen was fond of him and respected his considerable talent. What she disliked most about Jon wasn't his fault at all. With barely any effort, he'd managed to awaken her sensual nature. Until that November night last year, she'd assumed the sexual part of herself had been buried for good, along with her failed marriage. Jon had deftly proved otherwise.

The biggest regret in her life had come when she was a college student. Maryellen had experienced another unplanned pregnancy. She'd allowed her boyfriend, soon-to-be-husband, to manipulate her, and at his insistence had aborted her baby. She hadn't wanted to, and she'd never been able to forgive herself for doing it.

This time around, she was determined to protect her unborn child. This time she refused to listen to anyone or anything other than her own heart. She *wanted* this child, loved this child. What had begun as a terrifying mistake had become a valued second chance.

It had been a shock to find out that Jon intended to be part of Katie's life. So much so, he'd threatened to take Maryellen to court if she excluded him from seeing his daughter. Maryellen had no grounds on which to keep him away, so she'd reluctantly agreed to his terms.

The kettle whistled as she finished laying out her clothes. Massaging her back with one hand, Maryellen poured the boiling water into the waiting teapot. 'You don't have any idea how happy I'm going to be to drink coffee again,' she muttered to her unborn daughter.

Maryellen showered and dressed, and because she was only working half days, she had a leisurely breakfast of toast and yogurt and tea. She didn't need to be at the Harbor Street Art Gallery until shortly before noon. She loved her job, and enjoyed the friendships she had with many of the local artists. Jon was a photographer, and his work, mostly nature photography, was both breathtaking and insightful. After she'd rejected him, he'd decided to take his photographs elsewhere. At the time, his decision had seemed for the best, but the truth of it was, she missed seeing him and the gallery certainly missed the revenue his work had provided.

Jon's talent was what had first attracted her, but she found the man himself intriguing. He was unpretentious and straightforward— and reticent about the details of his own life. Although she'd worked with him for more than three years, she knew nothing about his artistic training and next to nothing about his personal background. The one bit of information he'd given her was that he'd inherited a stunning piece of property from his grandfather, the property on which he'd built his house. When she asked him questions, he either walked away or changed the subject. For the most part, he declined invitations to social gatherings. She'd been surprised when he'd agreed to attend a Halloween party last year. She'd made up an excuse to invite him, never believing he'd actually show up. That night they'd shared their first kiss, which was the beginning of it all. In the days that followed, Maryellen had come to know him as well as anyone in Cedar Cove, and probably better. The baby kicked and she smiled to herself. Obviously she *did* know him better than most.

Still, she was impressed by the man who'd fathered her child. Jon had constructed his own home and worked as a chef for The Lighthouse restaurant, all while his reputation as a photographer grew in the Pacific Northwest and beyond.

'I didn't expect you until noon,' Lois Habbersmith said when Maryellen walked into the gallery at eleven-thirty, a little ahead of schedule.

Until recently, Lois had been Maryellen's assistant, but had been temporarily promoted to gallery manager during Maryellen's maternity leave. She was confident Lois would do a more-than-adequate job.

'When's your next doctor's appointment?' Lois asked.

'Tomorrow morning.' The ache in her back seemed to be getting worse. Maryellen pulled out a chair and sat down.

Lois looked concerned. 'Are you feeling all right?'

'No,' Maryellen admitted. 'The truth is, I'm having this weird backache.' She realized the ache seemed to diminish and then increase fairly regularly. It suddenly occurred to her that perhaps this *wasn't* a backache, but the

31

onset of labor.

As if she, too, had reached the same conclusion, Lois walked all the way around her. 'My labor pains always started in my back.' Then holding one finger to her lips, Lois said, 'Maryellen, you think you could be going into labor?'

'I...I should probably time these...pains, shouldn't I?'

Lois clapped her hands excitedly. 'This is so wonderful!'

'Lois, Lois, I don't know if I'm in labor. I just have this...strange feeling.'

Maryellen glanced at her watch and tried to remember when she'd last felt this odd pain that seemed to radiate from her spine.

'Your mom's your birth partner, right?'

Maryellen nodded. She vaguely remembered that her mother had mentioned she'd be attending a librarians' meeting in Seattle on Wednesday. Today was Wednesday. Grace had a cell phone, Maryellen knew, but she was constantly forgetting to turn it on, or off, in which case the battery would run low. No need to contact her mother just yet, she decided. There was plenty of time, and she wasn't convinced she was officially in labor, anyway. She wondered if maybe this was false labor, which several people had warned her about.

A few hours later, at home by herself, Maryellen was no longer wondering. She knew. There was nothing false about this. What had started out as a dull ache in her back had ultimately worked its way around, and she was having contractions at five-minute intervals. She reached for the phone and dialed her mother.

Just as she'd suspected, her mother's cell phone was off or not working or the battery was dead. Or whatever! Drawing in a deep breath, Maryellen closed her eyes. There was always her sister. Kelly had been wonderful ever since she'd learned Maryellen was pregnant. They'd grown closer than at any time since they were teenagers.

After five rings, Kelly and Paul's answering machine came on. Hoping she sounded collected and in control, Maryellen left a message. 'Kelly, hi. Listen, it looks like I'm going into labor. I haven't called Dr. Abner yet and I'm sure there's loads of time, but I thought you should know.' Then, not wanting her sister to guess how panicky she was beginning to feel, Maryellen added, 'Mom won't be back from that librarians' meeting until later, so when you're available maybe you could give me a call. I…I don't have anyone to drive me to the hospital.' Any pretense of composure vanished by the time she replaced the receiver in its cradle.

As Maryellen turned away from the phone, she felt a pain so sharp it nearly doubled her over. Almost immediately water gushed from

33

between her legs. Amniotic fluid.

Maryellen stood in a puddle of water and tried to think clearly. Fearing any movement might endanger her child, she stretched out one hand for the phone, then hesitated, not knowing whom to call.

Suddenly it became obvious. She had to get the number from directory assistance. As she punched it out, she prayed Jon was home and close to a phone.

When there was no answer at his house, she nearly wept with frustration. Panic started to set in; warding it off, she forced herself to remain calm. On the off chance that he was working, she dialed The Lighthouse restaurant.

The woman who answered was polite and friendly. Maryellen was put on hold. After an eternity, Jon came on the line, and his clipped greeting said he wasn't happy to be called away from whatever he was doing.

Frightened, near desperate, Maryellen whispered hoarsely, 'Jon…I need help—'

She wasn't allowed to finish. 'Where are you?'

'Home. My water broke.'

'I'll be there in five minutes.'

Her relief was overwhelming. She blinked rapidly to keep from breaking into grateful tears. 'Thank you,' she began, but the line had already gone dead.

Only a few minutes later she heard a car

door slam outside her small rental house. By then, she'd called Dr. Abner and learned that her instincts had been right; he wanted her to go directly to the hospital's birthing center.

Jon didn't bother to knock but came barreling in the front door. He had on his white chef's shirt and pants, both of which were stained. Obviously she'd caught him in the middle of the midday rush. She hadn't seen him in weeks. The last time had been early in the summer when they'd agreed to visitation, and despite the frantic way his gaze darted to her now, he looked wonderful. By conventional standards Jon wasn't a handsome man. His features were too sharp, his face long and narrow, his nose almost hawklike, but Maryellen had learned a harsh lesson when it came to attractive men. At first glance, Jon wasn't going to cause hearts to flutter; it was only on closer examination that she'd recognized the strength of character she found so compelling.

'Hi,' she said weakly, staring down at the floor and the watery mess she was standing in.

'So you've got yourself in a little predicament here.' His smile warmed her.

'Were you serious about wanting to see Katie's birth?' she asked. The panic was completely gone now that he was here.

'I'd like that if it's possible.'

'Looks like you've just been nominated to drive me to the hospital's birthing center.'

In three quick strides he was across the room and scooped her into his arms as if her considerable weight was of little consequence.

She wanted to protest, to suggest she was too heavy for him, but she didn't. For the first time since she'd tried to reach her mother, Maryellen felt protected. Safe. He helped her change clothes and then carried her out the door.

He carefully placed her inside his vehicle. 'Is your suitcase packed?' he asked.

She nodded. 'All except my toothbrush.'

'I'll grab that and your overnight bag and be right back.'

He left her and returned just as she was having a contraction. They'd gotten much stronger in the minutes since her water broke. Closing her eyes, she tilted her head back and exhaled, trying to remember everything she'd learned in her birthing class.

Jon was in the driver's seat beside her when she opened her eyes again.

'You okay?' he asked.

He'd gone pale, she noticed. She attempted to reassure him with a smile.

Later, Maryellen remembered almost nothing about the ride from Cedar Cove into Silverdale and the birthing center. Jon didn't speak, and she didn't, either, concentrating on the breathing techniques she'd learned while he drove, expertly weaving through traffic.

When they arrived at the center, there

seemed to be all kinds of activity going on around her. She was stripped, prepped, helped into bed and had a fetal monitor attached. Jon disappeared, and she wondered if he'd dropped her off and then left again. She supposed that made sense, since she'd clearly called him in the middle of his shift.

Then she was alone in a comfortable room with every modern device to distract her from the pain. There was soft music and a television should she care to watch, but none of that interested her.

The contractions were far more intense than anyone could have warned her. She mentally counted the seconds as each contraction came over her, working its way from her back to her front, tightening her belly.

'Maryellen?' Jon's voice was low.

Her eyes flew open and she found him standing in the doorway. Her relief and gratitude were instantaneous. Propping herself up on one elbow, she asked hopefully, 'Can you stay?'

'If that's what you want.'

She did. Until that moment, she hadn't realized how much she wanted him with her, how much she needed him. Not just anyone. *Him.*

Coming all the way into the room, he sat on the chair by her side and studied the monitor as it recorded her labor. Although he hadn't attended a single birthing class, he seemed to know exactly what to say and do to comfort her. When she moved onto her side, he rubbed her back and whispered reassurances. His voice was encouraging as he repeatedly told her what a good job she was doing.

The length and intensity of the contractions continued, and in the middle of one that lasted almost a minute—the longest minute of her life—the pain overwhelmed her. She whimpered softly.

'Do something!' Jon demanded of the nurse who happened to step into the room just then. 'She can't take this pain.'

The woman smiled benevolently. 'Maryellen has opted for a natural birth. We're simply respecting her wishes.'

'I'm okay,' Maryellen said, but she wondered how long she could hold out. 'Would it be all right if I held your hand?'

Jon was on his feet and leaning toward her. He braced his elbow against the bed and offered her his hand. From that moment on, she clung to him. When it was time to bear down, Jon was with her, his head close to her own, his arm around her shoulders. Dr. Abner arrived, and that assured her it wouldn't be much longer.

Jon introduced himself and then in a low, soothing voice, continued to offer Maryellen encouragement and support. Leaning against him, she strained, pushing this child from her body and panting wildly between pains.

With the next contraction she gripped Jon's hand and pushed, groaning with the effort. Sweat poured off her. Then all at once, her daughter slipped free. Maryellen gasped as she heard Catherine Grace's fragile cry.

Pride and love filled Maryellen and her eyes brimmed with tears. She smiled tremulously at Jon and was surprised to see that he, too, had tears rolling down his cheeks.

'Welcome, Katie,' she whispered.

Jon looked at her. 'Katie, not Catherine?'

Maryellen nodded. She'd gotten in the habit of calling her daughter that. 'Catherine seems a bit of a mouthful for such a tiny baby, don't you think?' Katie was his mother's name, too, and Maryellen wanted to do that for him—to honor the mother he'd obviously loved.

Jon studied their child's red face, contorted by angry cries. 'Thank you,' he whispered, and his arm tightened around her shoulders. Dr. Abner handed their wailing daughter to the nurse.

'You can come with me, Dad,' the delivery nurse told him. 'I'm going to weigh her and wash her up, and then you can hold your little girl.'

Jon seemed to be seeking her approval. With tears of joy and jubilation, Maryellen nodded. Nothing in the world could compare to this feeling. This wonderful sense of triumph, of joy, of love. Because Maryellen already knew that she loved her baby. The power of that love settled over her heart unlike anything she'd ever experienced.

Jon and the nurse were busy on the other side of the room. Maryellen couldn't see everything that was happening, but she saw Jon's face when the woman settled Katie in his arms. His look was one of such awe and elation, she felt profoundly moved. At just that moment, he glanced up and their eyes met.

'She's beautiful,' he mouthed, cradling her protectively in the crook of his arm.

Wanting to hold her, Maryellen stretched out her arms and Jon crossed the room and placed Katie in her waiting embrace.

This was the way it would be with them, Maryellen realized. They'd have to learn to share their daughter. To work together. To put their own wants and needs aside—to put Katie's first.

There was a knock at the door, which Maryellen ignored. Instead, she studied Catherine Grace. Her tiny face was still red and her eyes were squeezed tightly shut, as if the lights were too strong for her.

Jon offered her his finger and Katie's tiny hand wrapped around it.

A young woman, apparently a volunteer, stuck her head into the room. 'A Mrs. Sherman is outside. She says she's supposed to be your birthing partner.'

'That would be my mother,' Maryellen explained, smiling.

The volunteer smiled back. 'I'll send her in.'

A couple of minutes later, both her mother and Kelly were in the room. Maryellen was bombarded with questions. Before she was even aware of it, Jon had disappeared.

She hadn't had a chance to thank him.

*   *   *

While she waited for the city council meeting to start, Charlotte Jefferson dug out her knitting. It distressed her that more people in the community didn't concern themselves with local government. But then, this was only *her* second meeting. Until recently, she hadn't paid much attention to civic affairs herself.

'Hello, Louie,' she said, nodding politely when the mayor walked in. She sat alone in the front row.

'I understand congratulations are in order,' Louie Benson said as he strolled past her. The Bensons were an old Cedar Cove family. Louie's younger brother, Otto, was a prominent attorney in town.

'Yes, I have a great-grandson,' she confirmed. 'My first.'

'I understand Grace Sherman's a grandmother now—for the second time, I think.'

'Just last week.' Grace was as proud of her first granddaughter, Maryellen's baby, as she was of her grandson, Kelly and Paul's little

41

Tyler. Charlotte thought it had worked out nicely that her daughter, Olivia, and Olivia's best friend could be grandmothers together. Those two had always been close and a blessing to each other.

'It's unusual to see you at the council meetings,' the mayor said. 'Not that it isn't a pleasure.'

'I'm here for a reason.' Charlotte jerked fiercely on her yarn as she continued knitting.

'Anything I can do?' the mayor had the good sense to inquire.

Frankly Charlotte had hoped he'd ask. 'I want to propose that this town open a health clinic. I think it's shameful that we haven't had one before now.' At a minimum, people had to drive ten or fifteen miles to the Bremerton area for medical attention, and it often meant waiting hours in the emergency room. A town the size of Cedar Cove could easily support a clinic. But Charlotte wanted a particular kind of health facility, a place for *everyone* in Cedar Cove.

'Now, Charlotte—'

'One that'll take patients on a sliding fee scale,' she added, unwilling to listen to Louie's objections. 'I know Medicare and Medicaid patients would welcome the opportunity to avoid having to go all the way into Bremerton or Silverdale for their health needs.'

'I agree, but—'

'Too many of my friends are reluctant to see

a physician for fear of what it'll cost.'

'Yes, I realize that, but—'

'Louis Benson, you're talking like a politician.'

'Now, Charlotte, you and I both know this is strictly a figurehead position. The town's run by a hired manager. If you want to talk to Matthew Harper about setting up a low-cost health clinic, then go ahead, but I can tell you right now there's no budget for it.'

Fine, if that was what it took, she'd discuss this with the manager. 'I will.'

The mayor looked slightly uncomfortable and glanced over his shoulder. When he spoke again, he lowered his voice. 'A bit of advice.'

'Anything you can tell me would be welcome,' she assured him, staring down at her knitting as if it demanded her full concentration.

'Get all your facts together before you see Matt Harper.'

'I will,' she assured him. Harper was reputed to be a tough bargainer, scrupulous about town budgets, but he'd met his match if he thought he could roadblock her efforts. If it was the last thing she did before she died, Charlotte fully intended to see that Cedar Cove got a health facility of its own.

The door opened, and the mayor quickly straightened. 'How's everyone at the Senior Center doing?' he asked, as if making polite conversation.

'Laura's rheumatism is acting up,' Charlotte informed him. 'She says it's going to be a hard winter. Bess has had a cough all summer. I keep telling her she should see a doctor, but she's afraid of what he might tell her so she refuses to go. If there was a clinic here in town, I'd make the appointment and drag her in myself. And Evelyn...' Charlotte paused when she realized Louie was no longer listening. His attention was focused elsewhere.

When he noticed she'd stopped talking, he patted her shoulder and said, 'Good to chat with you, Charlotte. I'll see what we can do about your suggestion.'

'You do that,' she said, but she already knew her words had gone in one ear and out the other. Louie Benson had given her a bit of helpful advice, however. She needed facts and figures.

Charlotte decided to leave as soon as she finished this purl row. No one wanted to listen to a cranky old woman. Least of all this roomful of men, each one struggling to appear more important than the next. The door at the back of the room creaked open, and assuming it was another councillor, Charlotte didn't turn to look.

To her surprise, it was Ben Rhodes. He was a tall, distinguished man with a thick head of white hair. She might be in her seventies, but Charlotte had never been immune to a handsome man...and still wasn't. Some of the ladies at the Senior Center thought of Ben as a Cesar Romero look-alike. He'd recently moved to the area and she didn't know him well, but he was a popular figure at the center—for obvious reasons.

'Hello, Ben,' she said when he took a seat across the aisle from her.

He glanced in her direction; she could tell from the blank look in his eyes that he didn't recognize her.

'I'm Charlotte Jefferson from the Henry M. Jackson Senior Center.'

A warm smile transformed Ben's face as he crossed the aisle and sat one chair away from her. They hadn't been formally introduced, but she'd seen him a number of times. Ben was at the Senior Center every Monday, the same as she, only he played bridge and pinochle and she was part of the ladies' knitting group.

Ben always came alone and she'd wondered about his wife, but they'd never had an opportunity to talk. From the way the ladies fluttered around him like bees over a glass of lemonade, she guessed he was a widower.

She'd made a point of saying hello to him the afternoon Olivia was guest of honor at the once-a-month luncheons the center put on. But she'd spoken to so many people that day. It'd been glorious having her own daughter give such an impressive speech. Still, that was months ago now, and Charlotte wasn't sure Ben even remembered that Olivia was her

45

daughter.

'I didn't know you were interested in politics,' Charlotte said, starting a fresh row despite her earlier decision to leave. There was no need to rush now that Ben was here.

'I don't much care for political discussion, but I wanted to make a suggestion to the council. What about you?'

'I'm here for the same reason,' she declared. 'Cedar Cove needs a health clinic.'

Ben's deep blue eyes widened. 'That's why *I'm* here.'

'A health clinic with a sliding fee scale,' Charlotte said, 'so it's affordable to everyone, no matter what age or income.'

Ben nodded fervently. 'I couldn't agree with you more.'

They sat through the meeting with one empty chair between them. When Matthew Harper asked if there was any new business, Ben stood, resting his hands on the back of the chair in front of him.

'If I might address the council,' he said.

Harper raised his head, glanced curiously at the two of them, and nodded.

Ben spoke eloquently. He talked about people's right to quality health care and the advantages a clinic would bring to Cedar Cove. He finished with the statement, 'Let's work together to overcome the bureaucratic issues and get the approvals we need. If we can do that, we'll have done what's necessary to improve the health of everyone in our community.'

Charlotte felt like leaping to her feet and applauding. He'd spoken far more convincingly than she could have and without emotion. Ben somehow made it sound as though a clinic was eminently possible thanks to the council's leadership and influence. Charlotte marveled at his finesse.

The council, all smiles, promised to look into the matter and report back at the next meeting.

Then the meeting was dismissed, and Charlotte tucked her knitting inside her bag. 'You were wonderful,' she told Ben. 'I could never have presented the case for a health clinic nearly as well as you did.'

'Thank you.' He stood and politely stepped aside, letting her exit the row ahead of him.

They walked out into the warm air. It was Thursday evening and music could be heard coming from the waterfront park. 'I'll have you know I skipped tonight's Concert on the Cove for this,' she said, although it was no real sacrifice this evening. The organizers had hired puppeteers and the program was geared more toward youngsters.

'How about a cup of coffee?' Ben offered.

Charlotte's heart fluttered wildly. This was silly, but it wasn't every night she got such an attractive invitation. 'All right.'

'Shall we go down to The Lighthouse?' Ben

asked.

Charlotte beamed. 'That would be perfect. My granddaughter and her husband just opened it, you know.'

Ben looked suitably impressed. 'They're doing a good job.'

Charlotte agreed, but it wouldn't seem right if she bragged on and on about Justine and Seth. She was thrilled at how well the couple was doing, considering how little practical experience they had with restaurants. What they did have was a wonderful chef, good people skills and genuine business ability.

As it happened, both Seth and Justine were off for the night, which was just as well, Charlotte mused, as she sat out on the patio with a lovely view of the cove. The revolving beam from the lighthouse could be seen intermittently in the distance, and the lights from the shipyard shimmered over the dark surface of Sinclair Inlet.

They both ordered coffee and apple pie with ice cream.

'What a nice suggestion,' Charlotte said, slicing her fork into her warm pie. It was spicy with cinnamon and went perfectly with the rich vanilla taste of the ice cream. Dessert was an indulgence, but life was too short to do without the occasional treat.

'There've been times I wanted to stop by here, but it isn't any fun eating by myself,' Ben confessed. Shaking his head sadly, he told her,

'My wife died six years ago. I don't know if I'll ever get accustomed to being alone.'

'My Clyde's been gone sixteen years.'

'Then you know.'

Charlotte did understand. Even after all these years, she still felt the dull ache of a deep but long-ago grief. Clyde was her everything: her faithful friend, constant companion, her husband and lover. The empty space his death had left in her life could never be filled.

'I heard you're retired navy,' she said, changing the subject before they became too melancholy.

'Forty years,' Ben confirmed. 'I enlisted shortly after World War II, when I was eighteen, served in Korea and Vietnam. Retired as an admiral.'

'Children?'

'Two boys. They're both married and have families of their own. What about you?'

'You met Olivia, I believe.'

He nodded. 'The judge.'

So he did remember. 'I have a son, too. Will. He lives near Atlanta, Georgia. He's a nuclear engineer,' she boasted.

'Steven, my oldest boy, lives in Georgia, too. Ever hear of St. Simons Island?'

'Clyde and I visited there one summer. Let me think—it must've been back in the sixties, but I still remember how lovely it was. All those giant live oaks dripping with Spanish moss.'

49

Ben smiled. 'Joan used to love visiting the island.' At the mention of his wife's name, his eyes grew sad. Because Charlotte understood how devastating it was to lose one's life mate, she gently patted his hand.

'It does hurt less after a while,' she whispered. 'Life is never the same, but gradually we adjust. Every year's a little easier.' Perhaps it would help if he talked, she thought. 'Tell me about her.'

Ben looked surprised. 'You want me to talk about Joan?'

'Only if you'd like to.'

He did; that was soon apparent. 'Joan went with me all over the world,' he said. 'I was stationed in Europe and Asia and in a number of states. Never once did she complain. I promised her that when I retired we'd settle down in one place.'

'And you did?'

'California. We built a home there, had about ten years, but then Joan got sick. Cancer.'

'What brought you to Cedar Cove?'

He didn't answer for a long moment. Dusk was descending, the lights' reflection playing on the still waters. 'I couldn't stay in that house anymore. I moved to a condo in San Diego, but it didn't feel right. I'd been up to Washington, the Seattle area, several times. Some friends had invited me to visit after the funeral, and then I came back almost every

50

year. I took the ferry across to Bremerton a couple of years ago. On a whim, I went to Cedar Cove and walked around a bit. I liked it. The people were friendly and I was looking for somewhere new to live.'

'What about your sons?'

'David wanted me to move closer to him— he lives in Arizona—but that didn't appeal to me. He was planning to take care of me, but I don't ever want to be a burden to my family.'

'I know what you mean.' Charlotte had the same concerns. She sincerely doubted that Ben would ever be a burden to anyone. He was a proud, capable man, independent by nature.

'How long have you been here?'

'Over a year now.'

That didn't seem possible.

Ben glanced at his watch and seemed surprised by the time. 'My goodness, it's almost nine-thirty.'

'It can't be!' Charlotte was sure he'd made a mistake. They'd come here shortly after eight, since the council meeting, which started at seven, had lasted only an hour.

'You're an easy woman to talk to, Charlotte.'

She felt her heart flutter at his praise. 'Thank you.' What she didn't say was that Ben Rhodes was an easy man to listen to—an easy man to like.

Four

Rosie Cox hadn't taught grade school in years. Sixteen years, to be exact. When Allison was born, Zach and Rosie had made the decision that she'd be a stay-at-home mother. For years she proudly wore her Every Mother Is A Working Mother pin. Her views about women's role within the family had leaned toward the militant. A mother's love and care, especially in the early stages of child development, was vital. At one time, Rosie had prided herself on being the world's best mother, best wife and best housekeeper. Okay, the housekeeping part was a stretch, but as far as parenthood went, she read all the books, talked to the experts and attended the latest classes. She'd been determined to do everything right by her family.

When Allison and Eddie were both in school, Rosie had briefly toyed with the idea of rejoining the workforce as a teacher. She had the credentials, the hours were ideal and she could have summers off with the kids. There hadn't been any positions available, but she'd dipped her toe in the employment pool one autumn a few years back, when she'd worked as a cashier in a drugstore. That, however, hadn't lasted long.

When Eddie entered first grade, Rosie was

already involved in a handful of volunteer jobs, which she thoroughly enjoyed. She wanted to contribute to the community and initially Zach had encouraged this. If she wanted to volunteer her services, then it was fine by him, since they'd learned to survive quite adequately on one income. Later, her husband had come to resent the hours she gave to these organizations, and complained that she was gone far too many nights. In the end, it was apparent that Zach didn't want her working, but didn't approve of her volunteering, either. What he wanted, she realized bitterly, was an old-fashioned wife, subject to his needs and desires. A glorified housekeeper, and never mind the bedroom part because he was obviously getting *that* somewhere else.

Volunteering had fulfilled her, but that was then and this was now. With the divorce final and the joint custody agreement in place—even if it was the most unusual one on record—Rosie had to find a way of supporting herself.

Her options were limited. After a few refresher classes, which she took over the summer, she was hired by the school district as a substitute teacher. She'd been counting on that. She was in line for a full-time position once an opening became available. Being a substitute, fewer hours equaled less pay, and that worried her until she was assured she could have as many hours as she wanted.

Sure enough, yesterday, the first day of school, she'd been called in to teach a second-grade class at Evergreen Elementary. This was Wednesday, day two of her new working life.

By late afternoon, Rosie's feet were throbbing and she could feel the beginnings of a migraine. Teaching wasn't easy, but it was manageable, she told herself. Mrs. Gough, the regular teacher, had had her appendix out over the Labor Day weekend and would be out of the classroom for two to three weeks, depending on her rate of recovery. As a result, Rosie would have a steady income for much of September.

It was almost five by the time she was ready to leave the school. Most, if not all, of the other teachers had gone for the day. The janitor was pushing a broom down the deserted hallway when she walked out of her classroom.

'Good night,' she said as she strolled past him, struggling to smile.

He acknowledged her with a nod and methodically continued his task.

Climbing into her SUV, she mentally patted herself on the back. She'd been awarded the vehicle, a Ford Explorer, as part of the divorce settlement. Zach had to either give her the Explorer or buy her an equivalent replacement, since her own car was old and becoming unreliable. He chose to give up the car, but then she'd known he would.

Both of them had sunk pretty low during the negotiations that led to their divorce settlement. Rosie had been unaware of how petty she could be, how...mean. She'd actually hated Zach for what he was doing to her and to their family, and she wanted to hurt him as much as he'd hurt her. He appeared to feel the same way.

Rosie turned onto Pelican Court and pulled into their driveway, heaving a giant sigh. It was good to be home. She was eager to talk to her children and learn how their days had gone. Allison attended Cedar Cove High School and Eddie was in fifth grade at Lincoln Elementary. Exhausted though she was, Rosie longed to hear about their classes. She might even order pizza, which would be a treat in these days of tight budgets. The three of them deserved something special.

The garage door was closed and Rosie frowned when it opened and she saw Zach's new vehicle parked in her spot. What was that about? Getting out of the car, she slammed the door. The last thing she wanted to do was deal with *him,* especially after the day she'd just had.

She hesitated at the door, wondering if she should knock, then decided this was her house as much as his. Without bothering to announce her arrival, she barreled into the kitchen from the door off the garage.

Sure enough, Zach was in her kitchen

wearing a ridiculous-looking apron. Both kids were with him, which irritated her further. Eddie sat at the table doing his homework, and Allison was standing at the sink peeling potatoes. This was a sight she could hardly believe, especially since the kids seemed to be performing these tasks willingly.

'What are you doing here?' she demanded, hands on her hips.

'What do you mean?' Zach asked, glancing up. His smile faded and his eyes narrowed. His hands were buried wrist-deep in a blue ceramic bowl full of what looked like hamburger and cracker crumbs. Ah, now she understood. This was his pitiful attempt at meat loaf. A year ago they'd had a big fight over her not serving him a three-course meal every night when he came home from the office. He seemed to think she had nothing to do all day but hang around the house and watch soap operas and trashy talk shows.

'Meat loaf?' she asked, making no effort to disguise her sneer.

'It's my night with the kids,' Zach said. His hands froze as he glared malevolently at her.

The hell it was. 'I don't think so.' Rosie wasn't backing down. It was bad enough having Zach in *her* house. She hated every minute of this switching back and forth. She'd memorized the schedule: she was with the children every Sunday, Monday, Tuesday and Wednesday, and then Zach was at the house

56

Thursday, Friday and Saturday, plus holidays. She'd felt triumphant about getting that extra day, but she'd had to give up the major holidays for it. The trade-off didn't seem fair, but it was the best deal Sharon Castor had been able to get her.

'Monday was a holiday,' Zach reminded her.

Crossing her arms, Rosie gave him a slow, sardonic smile. 'So?'

'Monday was Labor Day.'

'Dad has the holidays, Mom. Remember? So he's supposed to get an extra day this week.'

Leave it to Allison to side with her father. Rosie frowned at her daughter. She'd asked her a thousand times to peel potatoes for dinner. In response Allison always gave her the beleaguered look of an overworked galley slave. But let her father ask...

'We decided last month that instead of me coming here on the less important holidays, we'd simply tack a day onto my usual week.'

'We did?' She vaguely remembered some discussion having to do with Labor Day, but it had slipped her mind with all the craziness that surrounded her first day of school. The situation would be the same for Columbus Day the following month, she realized.

'Do you want my attorney to mail you the paperwork—complete with your signature?' Zach asked.

'There's no need to get sarcastic with me,'

she replied.

Eddie slammed his book closed and covered both ears. 'Stop it!' he screamed. 'Just stop it.'

'Now look what you've done,' Rosie flared, placing her arm protectively around her son's shoulders. Eddie had always been a sensitive child.

Zach's gaze bored holes into her. 'This is *my* time with *my* children,' he said, 'and I'd appreciate it if you'd leave.'

Rosie opened her mouth, intent on arguing, but he was right. She was the one who'd made the mistake.

'Fine,' she said with as much dignity as she could muster, which at this point was very little. She sent her son and daughter a reassuring smile, then walked out of the house.

Tears burned just below the surface as she climbed back inside the Explorer. This wouldn't happen again; she'd make sure of it. From here on out, she'd have the days clearly marked on the calendar so there wouldn't be a repeat of this dreadful scene.

The apartment she shared with Zach was less than a mile away from the house. She pulled into the assigned parking slot and turned off the engine. The neighborhood wasn't as good, but the rent was reasonable.

Everything inside the apartment was neatly divided. She had her own shelf in the refrigerator and Zach had his. She kept her personal items locked inside one bedroom, and his were locked in the other—not that she cared what he did or didn't have.

The apartment was hot and, unlike the house, lacked air-conditioning. Rosie turned on the television for noise and then took two aspirin and plunked down in front of the television set. The news was on, but she had no interest in world events. It was all she could do to deal with what was happening in her own life.

She must have fallen asleep because the phone woke her. Startled, she leaped off the couch and raced into the kitchen.

'Hello,' she said breathlessly, not sounding anything like her normal self.

The person on the other end of the line hesitated. 'I think I have the wrong number,' the woman said softly.

Rosie would recognize that voice anywhere. It was Janice Lamond, the home-wrecker who'd stolen her husband. The woman who'd carefully planned to ruin Rosie's life. She seethed with anger and resentment.

'Yes, I think you've made a mistake,' she said, letting the intense dislike she felt for the other woman show in her voice. Because nothing further needed to be said, she took delight in banging down the receiver. Her hand shook, and leaning against the kitchen counter, Rosie fought back angry tears.

Zach was dating. He had been even before the divorce was final. Even before he'd moved out. *She* was the one who'd honored her wedding vows, the one who'd cared for the house and the family while her so-called husband had an affair. It hurt even now to realize that the man she'd trusted implicitly and loved beyond measure had become involved with another woman.

Rosie poured herself a cold orange juice and walked back into the tiny living room. Slouching down on the sofa, she stared up at the ceiling.

Two could play that game, she decided. Rosie didn't know why it had taken her so long to figure that out.

It was high time she found herself a boyfriend.

*   *   *

With the latest issue of the *Cedar Cove Chronicle* at the printer's, Jack Griffin had a rare free afternoon, and a beautiful September afternoon it was. Normally he'd spend the time with Olivia, but now he was at loose ends and in a hell of a mood.

He'd been playing it cool, doing his best to hide his true feelings about Olivia. He wasn't fooling anyone, least of all his best friend, Bob Beldon. Bob was more than a friend, he was Jack's AA sponsor, and between them they had almost thirty years' sobriety.

He parked his battered, fifteen-year-old

Ford Taurus outside the Beldons' B and B, Thyme and Tide. Jack paused long enough to take in the view from across the cove. It really was lovely. Breathtaking. In the distance the huge green-and-white Seattle ferry was easing into the Bremerton dock. Seagulls hovered over the water. Closer at hand, statuesque herons walked delicately along the shore, picking at the exposed seabed with thin beaks while the tide lapped at their feet. A line of foam scalloped the rocky beach.

Peggy was busy clipping herbs in her garden, wearing a large straw hat to shade her face from the late-afternoon sun. She straightened when she saw him, a basket over her arm.

'Jack,' she greeted him warmly. 'We haven't seen nearly enough of you in the last little while.' Hurrying across the lawn, she kissed him lightly on the cheek. 'Isn't it a beautiful afternoon?'

'Sure is, Peggy.' He paused. 'Is Bob around?'

'Sorry, no. He's off with Pastor Flemming. I don't know how he did it, but Dave's got Bob working with the teenagers' basketball team.'

Frankly, Jack didn't know how the minister had managed it, either. 'I didn't realize you and Bob were churchgoing people,' he said, puzzlement in his voice.

'We didn't used to be,' Peggy admitted. 'Not until...' An unknown man had died in their home the previous winter, and—

61

understandably—that had shaken them up. The circumstances were shrouded in mystery. The John Doe had arrived in the middle of a storm; he'd carried false identification and had yet to be identified. So many questions remained unanswered, and some people seemed to think Bob and Peggy might be involved. If the stranger had died at *his* house, Jack suspected he might start attending church, too.

Peggy, willowy and energetic as always, headed toward the kitchen as though she expected Jack to follow. He did so willingly. Peggy was the kind of woman who made everyone feel welcome. It was her gift and made her a natural in the bed-and-breakfast business.

She held the screen door open for Jack and set her basket on the counter. 'I just made a fresh pitcher of iced tea,' she announced, and then, without asking, automatically poured two tall glasses. She arranged several large peanut butter cookies on a plate, as well.

With Jack carrying the tray, they walked to the patio. He set it down on the table and began to make an excuse to leave as soon as politeness allowed. He changed his mind; after all, he'd come here hoping for a distraction from his thoughts about Olivia.

'When do you expect Bob?' he asked.

'Around five, I guess,' Peggy told him.

A quick glance at his watch assured Jack

that was only thirty minutes off.

'After Dan Sherman's death...' Peggy began. She hesitated. 'Bob took that hard.'

As a relative newcomer, Jack didn't remember Bob being especially close to the former lumberman. Thinking about it, though, he recalled that Grace Sherman had asked Bob to speak at the memorial service held for Dan. That had surprised Jack at the time, but he hadn't said anything.

As if reading his mind, Peggy explained. 'Bob and Dan used to be good friends in high school. Dan's death really disturbed him, and then of course there was...' She shrugged and met Jack's eyes. He knew she was talking about the stranger.

'After Dan was buried, Bob decided he'd like to start attending church services,' Peggy continued. 'I certainly didn't mind. In fact, I've wanted to go for quite a while. Funny how death tends to unnerve us, isn't it?'

'Yeah.' Jack smiled wanly, disinclined to chat. But after a few minutes, the silence became uncomfortable, so he tried to fill it with questions. 'Bob and Dan didn't see much of each other lately, did they?'

Peggy shook her head. 'Not since they got back from Vietnam, but Dan was never the same after the war. They drifted apart. I don't think Dan was much of a drinker, but Bob was...well, you know about his problems with the bottle as well as anyone.'

Jack nodded. 'Friends can do that,' he said, thinking more about himself and Olivia than Dan Sherman and Bob. 'Drift apart, I mean.' Only his relationship with Olivia hadn't exactly drifted, it had been abruptly cut off. His gut twisted, and if he didn't know better, he'd think he had the beginnings of an ulcer. When he reached for his iced tea, he noticed Peggy studying him.

'You've lost weight.'

'Have I?' If so, he was grateful. He had a bit of a paunch that had come with middle age and a demanding desk job. There wasn't much time for exercise, and meals often consisted of what he could get from a vending machine.

'I suspect it has something to do with Olivia. You're obviously miserable.'

Now, that was below the belt. Jack nearly groaned aloud. 'Unfair,' he muttered. 'And Olivia's off-limits.'

'Okay,' Peggy murmured, apparently content to abide by his wishes. 'But I do have one thing to tell you and then I'll shut up.'

'One thing?' he repeated. 'Just one?'

'Yes,' Peggy said, 'and I think you'll find this interesting. I had to go down to the courthouse the other day and everyone in the whole building was buzzing about another of Olivia's decisions.' She paused, as if waiting for him to bite.

Funny Jack hadn't already heard about it. Curiosity got the best of him and he swallowed the bait. 'What did she do this time?' he asked.

Peggy explained the controversial joint custody decision Olivia had made. 'I wish more judges would take the children's needs into consideration,' she said.

This willingness to employ common sense in her courtroom was what had first attracted Jack to Olivia. He'd been surprised—and impressed—when a year earlier, she'd basically denied a young couple a divorce.

Everyone in the courtroom could tell that Ian and Cecilia Randall were still in love. They'd lost an infant daughter, and the death of their baby had ripped them apart. Olivia had not only recognized their emotional confusion and their need for each other, she'd boldly acted upon it. The last Jack had heard, Ian and Cecilia were together again.

Peggy was staring at him.

'I haven't seen Olivia in weeks.' Jack helped himself to a cookie. Six weeks to be precise, not that he was counting. All right, all right, he knew down to the day and the hour, which he wasn't admitting to anyone.

'Jack, that's terrible!'

No kidding. Well, he didn't much like it, either, but he'd backed himself into a corner. It was an impossible situation, and his ego demanded he stay exactly where he was.

'You miss her, don't you?'

He started to say that after a while it wasn't so bad, then stopped abruptly. Hell, who did he think he was fooling? It was worse than ever, especially in the past few weeks. 'She seems to be doing okay. I hear Stan Lockhart is hanging around a lot these days.'

'Is Olivia dating her ex-husband?'

'Not according to Charlotte.' Jack nearly bit his tongue in his eagerness to close his mouth. He hadn't meant to let Peggy know he'd been commiserating with Olivia's mother. Charlotte was his biggest supporter. She'd told him that she'd nagged Olivia to mend fences with Jack; unfortunately, Olivia didn't seem inclined to admit the error of her ways.

Jack set the cookie aside, his appetite gone. 'Apparently Olivia's got some bug up her butt about how I should be making a play for her.'

'A play?'

'You know,' he said, growing impatient. 'She wants me to—in her words—show some gumption and fight for her.'

Peggy frowned. 'She wants you to *fight?*'

'Well, maybe not a knock-down, drag-out fistfight but...hell, I don't know *what* she wants.' He assumed she was expecting him to come on bended knee and beg her forgiveness. He had too much pride for that. If she was interested in him, the same way he was interested in her, then that high school, high-drama stuff shouldn't be necessary. For a woman who supposedly knew so much about human nature, Olivia had fallen decidedly short on figuring this out.

'You might send her flowers,' Peggy suggested.

Jack had already thought of that. 'I don't have a reason.'

'Reason? What do you mean, reason?' Peggy repeated.

'You know...her birthday, Christmas, whatever.'

'Jack, Jack, Jack,' Peggy said slowly. 'You *have* a reason. You want her back, don't you? This nonsense has gone on long enough. That's all she wants to hear. She's waiting for you to make the first move.'

Yeah, well, Jack was waiting, too.

'You're at a standoff,' Peggy said. 'If you don't do something fast, you'll lose her. If she intended to get together with her ex, don't you think she'd be with him by now? Good grief.' She shook her head. 'Stan must be overjoyed by all this.'

Jack scowled ferociously. He'd thought plenty about that slimy bastard who'd once been married to Olivia, and heaven knew Jack didn't want to do Stanley Lockhart any favors. 'I suppose you think I should pour my heart out on one of those dinky cards, too.'

'No,' Peggy said. 'That wouldn't be like you.'

Thankfully she knew him well enough to recognize that. 'What should I say, then?'

'Why say anything? Just write your name.'

'That's it?'

Peggy nodded. 'All Olivia needs is some

67

indication that you care.'

It was that easy? Nah—couldn't be.

'Are you going to do it?' she pressed.

'Maybe.' It sounded like good advice, and at this point, he was willing to try just about anything—especially if he could hold on to his pride at the same time.

Peggy shoved the cookie plate in his direction and Jack took the last one. 'I hope you do it,' she told him.

Peggy had certainly given him something to think about, but now he was anxious to turn the subject away from Olivia. 'I happened to run into Roy McAfee the other day,' Jack said. The retired Seattle police detective had put out his shingle as a private investigator shortly after he'd moved to Cedar Cove. Jack knew that Roy had talked to Bob and Peggy extensively about the John Doe who'd checked into their B and B—and never checked out. The medical examiner still hadn't determined the cause of death.

'Is Roy still working on our big mystery?' Peggy asked, her eyes troubled.

'He didn't mention anything, but I doubt it.'

Peggy became quiet and thoughtful. 'I wish he would,' she finally said.

'Investigate your John Doe?' Jack prodded.

'It's almost as if…as if he landed here from another planet.'

'You think Roy might be able to find out something the police can't?' he asked.

'I...I don't know.' She shifted in her seat and suddenly seemed uncomfortable. 'It's just that...' Again she hesitated.

'What?'

'It's Bob. That night, he casually said there was something familiar about our guest. But with the way he arrived, so late and without a reservation, Bob couldn't put his finger on it. I think there might be more to this than meets the eye.'

Bob and Jack were close. He knew Bob had scoured his brain looking for a connection and been unable to come up with one.

'I've been married to Bob for over thirty years...' Peggy's voice dropped to a whisper. She darted a glance at him. 'Did he ever tell you about his nightmares?'

He hadn't. 'We all have bad dreams at one time or another.' Jack hadn't gone to Vietnam himself, but he knew plenty of men who had. Nightmares weren't uncommon for a man who'd been to war.

'Twice now...' She sighed. 'Sometimes, through the years, Bob's sleepwalked.'

Jack leaned forward. 'Surely you don't think he had anything to do with your guest's death?'

'Oh, no.' Her eyes widened in horror. 'It's impossible! The bedroom door was locked from the inside.'

But Jack knew they had a key, so that wasn't a viable excuse.

'And there wasn't a scratch on him.'

69

Jack nodded. That was true.

'Besides, you know Bob. He can barely swat a fly. It just isn't in him to purposely hurt anyone or anything.'

Peggy was right. 'Then why do you want Bob to talk to a private investigator?'

'I just want Bob to talk, I guess. It doesn't matter to whom. After I saw how upset he was over Dan's death, coupled with the recurring nightmares—well, I just think it would do him good to get it off his chest. He's always so afraid that he might start walking in his sleep again.'

Jack could appreciate her concern. 'Do you want me to say anything to him?'

She shook her head. 'It might do more harm than good. If he thinks I've been talking about him—even with you—he'd just get upset.'

Jack noticed the way she clenched and unclenched her hands, and he realized that Peggy was afraid. Even though she'd denied it, she was afraid her husband might have had something to do with the stranger's death.

Was that possible? Could Bob be involved?

Five

Sunday afternoon, the day Katie turned one month old, Maryellen paced the living room floor, holding her daughter against her chest. The doorbell chimed and she froze. Jon had come for Katie, to take her home for the night. This was the first time since she'd been born that Maryellen had to surrender her to Jon. Until today, he'd visited almost daily, usually staying only an awkward few minutes. Now he'd be taking her on his rotation days off, returning the next afternoon. Already she knew that abiding by their agreement wasn't going to be easy.

Reluctantly, she set Katie back in her bassinet and opened the front door. Jon stood on the other side of the screen, dressed casually in jeans and a short-sleeved shirt. His long dark hair was pulled away from his face and tied in a ponytail.

'Hi,' he said. 'You look great—both of you.'

'Jon.' Despite her resolve not to be emotional, her voice trembled.

If he noticed her distress, he ignored it. 'Is Katie ready?'

Maryellen swallowed the lump in her throat and nodded. She held the door open for him. 'I've packed everything you'll need.' She reached for the diaper bag and pulled out

71

a container of breast milk she'd pumped and several empty bottles. 'She only takes about three ounces, sometimes four, at a time. You'll probably have to get up twice during the night, and she isn't all that accustomed to the bottle, so I don't know how she'll do.' She swallowed again, trying to hide her reservations. 'You will hear her if she cries, won't you?'

'I'm a light sleeper.'

That wasn't the way Maryellen remembered it. On their one night together she'd managed to gather her clothes and sneak halfway down the stairs before he noticed she was gone.

'I put three extra outfits in her diaper bag in case she needs a change—and extra diapers, too.'

'All right.' He walked over to the bassinet, which she'd brought into the living room this morning. 'Hey, I didn't know they still had these.'

'It was mine,' Maryellen told him. 'Mom saved it and then gave it to Kelly when she had Tyler. Kelly passed it along to me for Katie.'

Jon smiled down at his daughter; the infant seemed to smile back and started moving both arms. Jon placed his hand over her tiny stomach.

'She likes her yellow blanket best....' Maryellen said. 'My mom knit it for her and I think she sleeps better with it.' She was rambling, but she couldn't help herself.

'I'll be sure the blanket is always with her.'

72

'You'll need a car seat. State law demands that—'

'I already have one.'

Not once had his gaze wavered from their daughter, and Maryellen saw him make silly faces at her. The tenderness in his eyes made her want to weep.

'She tends to be fussy first thing in the morning,' she told him, and bit her lip to keep it from trembling.

'She must get that from you,' Jon said, briefly glancing toward her. 'As I recall, you're not much of a morning person, either.'

Apparently he was reminding her of their night together. Maryellen immediately wanted to defend herself, but she was afraid that if she said one more word, she'd burst into tears. His having Katie had sounded like a reasonable solution a couple of months ago. Katie was Jon's daughter, and it was his legal right to spend time with her. But Maryellen hadn't realized when she'd agreed to this how bereft she'd feel. How lost and unsettled...

Jon carefully bent down and scooped his daughter into his arms. It was all Maryellen could do not to rush forward at the clumsy way he handled their baby. Sheer determination kept her where she was. Jon wouldn't appreciate her intervention.

'I'll take her out and put her in the car seat,' he said.

Rather than respond verbally, Maryellen

nodded. She followed closely behind, carrying the diaper bag. While Jon fiddled with the car seat, she waited anxiously to be sure he had Katie properly secured.

'What time will you have her back?' she asked, although she already knew.

'Before five.'

Twenty-four hours.

Jon closed the back door.

'You'll phone if you need anything?'

He walked around the vehicle, a brand-new sedan, and opened the driver's side door. 'Of course. I have your number next to the phone.'

'Okay…good.' Maryellen clung to the top of the door while he climbed inside and inserted the key in the ignition. The warning bell instantly started to chime. Reluctantly she stepped back and Jon pulled the door shut.

'Everything will be fine,' he assured her through the half-open window.

'I know…it's just that we've never been apart before.'

Jon's eyes went blank as he looked past her. 'You're the one who wanted it like this. I'm only going along with your wishes.'

Her wishes, she longed to remind him, had been to keep him entirely in the dark about their daughter. She hadn't originally planned to involve him because she'd believed Jon wouldn't want anything to do with their child. But she'd been wrong.

Tears blurred her vision. Normally

Maryellen wasn't a volatile or weepy person, but the pregnancy and birth had thrown her hormones off-kilter. At the slightest excuse—a television ad, watching her beautiful daughter sleep, even folding baby clothes—Maryellen would find herself on the verge of tears.

Jon was about to drive away from the curb when he glanced at her and stopped. 'Are you all right?'

She nodded forcefully and hurriedly wiped a stray tear from her cheek. 'I've been feeling emotional lately. That's all.' Wrapping her arms protectively about her waist, she moved onto the sidewalk.

'New-mother blues,' he said knowledgeably. 'I read about it in one of the books I checked out of the library. It'll pass in a few weeks.'

'Yes, I know,' she said. Maryellen could read, too, but pointing that out just now seemed childish and petty. She didn't want to say anything to irritate him, especially when he had their baby in his vehicle.

'I'll be back tomorrow afternoon,' he assured her.

'Okay,' she whispered. She could sleep in, Maryellen told herself. After a month of getting up at all hours of the night, sometimes two and three times, she should be grateful for a single night of uninterrupted rest. All this anxiety was a by-product of too many nights walking the floor and too little sleep. Not to mention those rampant hormones…

Once inside the house, Maryellen straightened the living room. She picked up the rattle, which was a gift from Jon; it had arrived in a huge basket of flowers he'd had delivered to the hospital. The burp rag draped over the end of the couch got tossed in the washing machine.

Tidying the bassinet, Maryellen sat up the large white teddy bear Jon had given Katie before she was born. The house was full of small gifts he'd brought either before or after the birth. Everywhere she looked there was evidence that he was determined to be part of Katie's life. He was serious about it and she knew he wasn't going to let his commitment slide, so she'd better get used to it now.

That night Maryellen slept miserably. She tossed and turned, certain that Katie needed her, certain Jon wouldn't hear when she stirred in the middle of the night. A hundred regrets besieged her. She'd handed her daughter over to him without once checking to be sure he was adequately prepared to deal with an infant. Maryellen envisioned Katie crying in a wet diaper with an empty stomach while Jon slept, blissfully unaware that she needed attention.

By seven the next morning, Maryellen had worked herself into a near-frenzy. Three times she reached for the phone, but she was afraid she'd wake him, or worse, Katie. When she couldn't stand it any longer, she dressed hastily and drove to her mother's house.

Fortunately Grace was up, having coffee at her kitchen table. She opened the back door for Maryellen, and Buttercup greeted her delightedly, tail wagging. Maryellen stepped into the kitchen, took one look at her mother and burst into tears.

'Maryellen! My goodness, what's wrong?'

'Nothing… Everything. Jon has Katie. Jon Bowman. Her…dad.'

Her mother poured her a cup of coffee, without commenting that this was the first time Maryellen had openly acknowledged Jon as her baby's father. 'Sit down and we'll talk.'

Maryellen felt foolish and overemotional and everything she'd never wanted to be. This was so unlike her. 'You have to get ready for work,' she said between sobs.

'Okay, I'll get dressed, and while I do, you can talk to me.'

Dabbing her eyes, Maryellen followed her mother into the bedroom. She paused when she entered. 'You painted in here.'

Grace nodded. 'Do you like it?'

Maryellen shrugged. 'I guess… I didn't think there was anything wrong with the old color.'

'There wasn't, but I had some things I needed to work out in my mind and painting helped.'

Caught up in her own world, Maryellen feared she'd failed her mother, that she hadn't paid enough attention to the difficulties Grace was confronting. This summer had been traumatic for them both. 'Anything I can do to help?' she asked as she sat on the end of her parents' bed. Her mother pulled a blouse and jumper from her closet.

Grace shook her head. 'No, but thanks. Besides, you didn't come here at this hour to ask about me. Now, tell me what's got you so upset.'

Maryellen wasn't upset as much as she was worried. 'Jon's never had Katie before…. I'm afraid she'll miss me. It wasn't supposed to be like this.'

Her mother pulled a full-length black slip over her head. 'Wait until eight-thirty or so and then give him a call,' she advised. 'My guess is that Jon will be more than happy to hear from you.'

Maryellen hoped that was the case. She didn't want him to think she was intruding on his time with Katie, but he had to understand how difficult this was for her.

'Come on,' Grace said as she finished dressing. 'Let me put on my makeup and fuss a bit with my hair, and then I'll buy you breakfast before I go to work.'

Maryellen declined with a shake of her head. 'I can't eat.'

'Yes, you can,' her mother insisted. 'And you will. Now, come on, it isn't every day I offer to treat you to breakfast. The Pancake

Palace has an early bird special. All-you-can-eat pancakes for a buck.'

Her mother was right, Maryellen realized. She needed a meal—and a distraction.

By the time she left the Pancake Palace, Maryellen felt worlds better, although they'd done more socializing with others than talking between themselves. The restaurant obviously did a thriving breakfast business. They'd run into Charlotte Jefferson and the members of the New Knee Club who met there once a month. Everyone at the long table had gone through knee-replacement surgery. Charlotte introduced them to her friend Ben Rhodes, a distinguished-looking older man. They appeared to have a relationship that was more than friendly, at least in Maryellen's opinion. She couldn't help wondering if there was a romance in the offing. It was kind of cute.

She got home after nine and headed directly for the phone, figuring Jon would be up with Katie by now. When there was no answer, she left a short message on his machine and dejectedly replaced the receiver.

At ten she called again. Still no answer. She couldn't stand not knowing and drove to Jon's home near Olalla. Her heart pounded frantically as she parked and climbed out of her car.

Even before she reached his front door, Jon had it open. Katie was in his arms, held firmly against his shoulder. She was astonished to see her daughter raising her head and peering around.

'Maryellen,' Jon said, stepping aside. 'Come on in.'

His home was almost complete now. On her last visit, the finish work had only been partially done. But today she saw that there was a carpet in the living area—a lovely Berber rug in soft greens and grays—and the oak woodwork around the windows overlooking Puget Sound was beautifully varnished. She could see Vashon Island in the distance, and the view of Mount Rainier, majestic and serene beyond the island, was stunning enough to make her heart skip.

Now that Maryellen was here it was obvious to her that Jon had managed just fine. 'You... you didn't answer the phone,' she stammered, 'and...and I didn't know what to think.'

'You called?'

'Twice.' She gave a quick shrug. 'I was worried, but I can see that everything's gone great.'

'I must've been in the shower,' he explained, 'or on the balcony.'

He seemed so easy with Katie now. During his brief visits, he'd lifted her as if she were a bag of unwieldy potatoes, and now he was as natural with her as a...dad.

Maryellen's anxiety had been for nothing. She felt embarrassed about rushing out to rescue her daughter. Jon had everything under control.

'Would you like to see Katie's room?' he asked.

Maryellen nodded. Hindsight being what it was, she should've checked on all this *before* she handed over their daughter.

Jon led her up the open stairway. She loved the house and the fact that he'd done most of the construction work himself. There didn't seem to be anything Jon Bowman couldn't master.

His bedroom was at the top of the stairs, and the French doors leading to the balcony were open. She could imagine him sitting there at first light, holding Katie and talking to her about the panorama outside.

Maryellen glanced into the bedroom and caught sight of his unmade bed and the photograph of her, beautifully framed and positioned on the opposite wall. She'd first seen it on display in a gallery in Seattle, where the majority of his work was now sold. It had been taken on a foggy afternoon while she stood on the pier next to the marina; she'd had no idea he was there. Her back was to the camera and she'd raised her arm to toss popcorn to the seagulls. The photograph had an exciting, dynamic quality, and yet the misty air gave it a sense of whimsy, too.

Jon seemed a bit flustered that she'd noticed the photograph. 'That's one of my favorites,' he said. 'Do you mind that I

81

have it here?'

The odd thing was she didn't. It gladdened her to see that he kept it in this room, although she didn't dare analyze the reasons. 'I don't mind,' she said.

'Good.' With that, he took her down the hallway to Katie's room.

Maryellen swallowed a gasp of delight when she saw the charming room. Jon had painted a zoo scene on one wall. Giraffes and elephants, zebras and monkeys appeared in a variety of realistic poses.

'You did this?' she asked, astonished.

'I haven't quite finished.' He pointed to an area that had been drawn but not yet colored.

All the furniture was new. He'd bought an infant swing and a crib with a canopy. A high chair stood in the corner; presumably he'd move it down to the kitchen when Katie was ready for it. Maryellen's previous worry seemed even more ridiculous.

'It's wonderful,' she told him. 'I made a fool of myself coming out here like this.' She couldn't look at him. 'I'll go now.'

Jon stopped her by stretching out his arm. 'Katie and I want you to stay,' he said, his eyes holding hers.

The lump in her throat eased as she gave him a smile. She wanted very much to spend this day with Jon and Katie.

Six

Tuesday evening, as the setting sun cast golden shadows over the cove, Grace left the library. She'd spent much of the day training a new assistant, so had stayed late to deal with her own paperwork. She was tired to the point of exhaustion. Times like these, she missed Dan the most. It would've been good to go home, have a quiet supper with him, maybe relate an anecdote or two. He'd disappeared the year before last, vanished without a word and without a trace. He'd hidden in a trailer deep in the woods, where he'd eventually committed suicide. His experience in Vietnam had never left him—the guilt and the horror of it.

After his body was found, Grace had been assailed by doubts, wondering if she could've known, could've helped, could've reached him somehow. She suspected it would not have been possible, because of the agony that consumed him, an agony he'd never spoken about. To her or anyone....

Most recently there'd been this sadness, this emptiness she couldn't shake. Her husband was dead and she'd lived without him for a long while and yet she couldn't get used to his absence. That confused her. Theirs had never been a vibrant, happy marriage, but they'd made the best of it. They'd loved each other;

that much she knew. She'd been wrong to think she'd be ready for another relationship so soon. She'd assumed all the grieving was over. Now she wondered if it would ever end. What she wanted was the life she'd had before Dan disappeared.

While he'd never been an overly affectionate husband, there was a certain comfort in the routines they shared. He'd bring in the mail and the newspaper every afternoon. She cooked the meals. In the evenings, they'd sit side by side and watch television or talk, whether about their daughters or about inconsequential things—incidents at work, household concerns, local news. Once a week, she'd go off to aerobics class with Olivia. Dan hadn't liked having her gone, but he'd never asked her to stay home. He understood how important Olivia's friendship was to her. Now the evenings were silent. Lonely. Now it was Grace who dragged the garbage can out to the curb, Grace who struggled with the lawn mower and edge trimmer, Grace who read the fine print at the bottom of the car insurance policy—and she hated it.

Walking to the parking lot behind the library, she tried to shake off her depression, reminding herself—as she often did—that she had much for which to be grateful. After years of longing, she was a grandmother twice over. Her daughters were close to her and to each other. She had good friends, especially Olivia.

84

Her finances were in order, and while she was a long way from living a life of luxury, she earned enough to support herself. She had the answer about Dan's disappearance, even if she didn't like it.

Life was good, or it should be.

Buttercup greeted her happily when she got home. The dog came through the pet door at five-thirty every day to wait for her; she'd been well-trained by her previous owner and didn't budge from her appointed place until Grace arrived, even if she was late, as she was today. She collected the day's mail and the newspaper, murmuring apologies and endearments to Buttercup. She flipped through the advertisements and bills as she walked back to the house and paused midstep when she came across a letter from Atlanta. The return address told her it was from Will Jefferson, Olivia's older brother. Grace eagerly ripped open the envelope. She'd always been fond of Will.

Standing on the sidewalk, she quickly scanned the neatly typed, one-page letter. While in high school, Grace had idolized Olivia's brother from afar. He'd been a heartthrob way back then, and the years had done little to diminish his appeal. She'd seen him just recently when he'd flown home for Charlotte's surgery. Grace was amazed at how attractive she found him even now, thirty-seven years after she'd graduated from high school.

His letter was one of condolence. He told her how sorry he was about Dan, then wrote briefly about the changes he'd noticed in Cedar Cove. He said it had felt good to be home for more than just a brief visit after all these years. He added that he'd enjoyed seeing her. Since his return to Atlanta, he'd been talking to his wife about retiring in a few years and said he'd like to consider moving back to Cedar Cove.

Grace knew Olivia and Charlotte must be thrilled at the prospect. Then she saw that under his signature, Will had included his e-mail address. He didn't ask her to write, but there it was, like an open invitation.

On her way into the house, Grace went through Will's letter a second time, trying to read between the lines. There didn't seem to be anything out of the ordinary, nothing beyond his sincere sympathy and a bit of chatty news about his future plans.

She replaced the letter inside the envelope, fed Buttercup and then turned on the television. These days her TV was more for companionship than entertainment. The evening was unseasonably warm and she dug around her refrigerator, deciding she'd just have a salad. She found herself humming as she shuffled the milk carton around two small yogurt containers.

Grace stopped abruptly and straightened.

When she'd left the library, she'd been feeling melancholy, but now her spirits were soaring. A feeling of happy anticipation filled her. The only thing she could attribute this change to was Will's letter. Was she so fickle, she wondered with some dismay, that a letter from an old friend—a high school crush—could improve her mood so radically?

She didn't get the opportunity to consider that. Buttercup barked once and trotted to the front door just seconds before the bell rang.

Grace walked over to answer it and discovered Olivia standing on the other side of her screen.

'Do you have a minute?' her friend asked. She looked upset, which shocked Grace, since Olivia was normally so composed.

'Olivia! Of course. What's happened?'

Her friend gestured hopelessly as if she didn't know where to start. 'I can't *believe* this.'

'Believe what?'

'First I hear from Stan, and then after weeks of silence, from Jack, too. This was within a few hours of each other—it's as if those two have radar and know exactly what the other is doing.'

This was fabulous news as far as Grace was concerned. 'Jack? You heard from Jack?' She sat down on the sofa.

Olivia nodded. 'The man is a weasel, that's what he is.'

'Jack?' Grace asked, puzzled. 'What did he

do this time?'

Olivia flopped down next to Grace. 'He had flowers delivered to the house. They're gorgeous and the colors are incredible. It must've cost him a fortune, but that's not the half of it.'

'Jack sent you flowers?' Grace cried as though outraged. 'Why, that low-down, dirty rat.'

'I called to thank him.'

'A mistake for sure,' Grace said. She enjoyed seeing her friend so obviously in love with Jack—and so confused by him—although she wished Olivia could sort out her feelings. Naturally Stan was eager to distract her, eager to have her back, and feeling as unsettled as she did, Olivia might weaken and return to him.

Grace would say one thing for Olivia's ex-husband: his timing was impeccable. The minute Olivia got involved in another relationship—up popped a repentant Stan, hoping to lure her back.

'You won't believe what he said to me.'

'Jack or Stan?' Grace was losing track.

'Both of them,' Olivia cried.

'Start with Stan.' If Olivia was ready to have Jack arrested for sending her flowers, Grace could only imagine what her ex-husband had done.

'Stan phoned and wanted to take me to dinner.'

'He didn't,' Grace said, feigning a gasp. 'Lock him up and throw away the key!'

Olivia glared at her, eyes glittering with irritation. 'You're making fun of me, Grace Sherman.'

Grace laughed. She couldn't help herself. 'No one's sending *me* flowers and asking me to dinner these days. There's got to be some other reason you're so annoyed. Are they trying to outdo each other?' That made sense—but on the other hand, it seemed to be what Olivia wanted, judging by her earlier complaints.

Olivia unfolded her arms and stroked Buttercup's silky head. 'Actually, Stan started it. He wants me to have dinner with him in Seattle on Friday night.'

Grace arched her eyebrows. 'Why Seattle?'

'He's got a corporate dinner he's required to attend and he didn't want to go alone. He has a hotel room and—'

'One room?'

Olivia rolled her eyes. 'He seems to think I'm too naive to know what he's got in mind. Oh sure, the room will have two beds, but I wasn't born yesterday and I know Stanley Lockhart. He has plans.'

'What about Jack?'

'The flowers arrived,' she said dreamily. 'Grace, after all these weeks, I have to tell you I was so pleased to get them.'

Grace was equally thrilled. Although it had

taken Jack long enough.... 'What did the card say?'

Olivia dropped her gaze. 'He signed his name. That's all.'

Smart man. 'In other words, he made the first move and the rest is up to you?'

'Exactly.'

'You phoned him?'

She nodded. 'I did, and he answered on the first ring—almost as if he'd been sitting there waiting for me to call. It felt wonderful to talk to him again. We were getting along famously until—' Her eyes narrowed and she heaved a deep sigh.

'Until what?'

'He asked me to dinner on Friday night, and I made the mistake of saying there must be something in the air because I was getting dinner invitations right and left.'

Not the most brilliant comment, Grace agreed, but Olivia already knew that.

'It took Jack about two seconds to realize the other invitation came from Stan. Then he got all weird on me and said he was busy on Friday, after all. He wished me a lovely evening with Stan, and before I could say another word, he made some excuse and was off the phone.'

Grace wanted to groan out loud.

Olivia's shoulders sank. 'Now you know why I'm upset.'

'You aren't going to dinner with Stan, are

you?' Grace asked, just to be sure.

'Not hardly,' Olivia muttered.

'I'm free Friday night. Want to go to the movies?'

Olivia laughed. 'You're on, my friend. Who needs men, anyway?'

Maybe, Grace decided, she'd find a way to get Jack Griffin to the theater on Friday evening. Apparently there were times when romance could use a helping hand.

*   *   *

Rosie finished writing out the words her second-graders had to copy. She set the worn chalk down on the blackboard ledge and brushed the dust from her hands.

The bell rang, indicating class was dismissed for the day. 'Don't forget to remind your parents that the Open House is tonight,' she told the students. The Open House introduced the teacher to the parents, and it usually occurred in the third week of September.

The children leaped up from their desks, grabbed their bags and backpacks, then dashed out. All except Jolene Peyton. The little girl with the long dark pigtails wore a forlorn look as she walked, head bowed, to the front of the room.

'Can I help you, Jolene?' Rosie asked gently.

The little girl kept her eyes lowered. 'Only

my daddy can come tonight.'

'That's wonderful. I look forward to meeting him.'

Jolene slowly raised her head until her eyes met Rosie's. 'My mommy died in a car accident.'

'I know, sweetheart, and I'm so sorry.' Rosie's heart went out to the motherless little girl.

'Every week Daddy and I put flowers by the road where she died.'

Rosie knew that, too. The flowers and balloons often caught her eye at the busy intersection.

'Well, I'm glad your father's coming to the Open House,' Rosie said.

Jolene nodded. 'He said it was one of those things Mommy would do if she was still here.'

Rosie tucked her arm around the seven-year-old's shoulder. It was apparent even now, almost two years after the accident, that Jolene missed her mother.

'I told my daddy that I need a mommy, and he said he'd think about it.' She sighed deeply. 'He says that a lot.'

So did she, Rosie thought with a grin. 'I'll think about it,' was in every parent repertoire.

That evening as the classroom started to fill with parents, Rosie made it a point to seek out Jolene's father. The little girl led him into the classroom, then rushed to bring him juice and cookies from the table set up at the front.

While he waited for his daughter, Bruce Peyton stood in the background, not mingling with the other parents. He was nice-looking, but he had a somber air about him, a remoteness, which was perfectly understandable. School events such as this evening's must be a painful reminder that he was alone. He was of average height and on the thin side. His clothes hung loose on him. Rosie could only assume this was due to a recent weight loss. His eyes were an intense blue, compelling her to steal glances in his direction.

It'd been many years—decades—since Rosie had really looked at another man. Her flirting skills had rusted from lack of use, although she was confident Janice Lamond could teach her a thing or two.

When Rosie was free she made her way toward Bruce. She smiled and held out her hand. 'Hello, I'm Rosie Cox, Jolene's teacher. I just want to say I'm very sorry about your wife.'

'Thank you.' The widower's smile was fleeting and he clasped her hand for only a few seconds. 'I'm pleased to meet you.'

'Mrs. Cox is a good teacher, but she's not my real teacher,' Jolene told him earnestly.

'I'm taking over until Mrs. Gough recovers from surgery,' Rosie explained. 'This is my first time back in the classroom after, uh, several years. I was recently—divorced.' The word nearly choked her. To Rosie's horror, tears filled her eyes and she had to turn away before she embarrassed them both.

Through sheer force of will, Rosie managed to hold on to her composure. While she talked to several other parents, Bruce lingered; Jolene showed him her desk and led him to the play area at the back of the room.

By eight o'clock, just a few parents and children remained. Rosie carried the empty punch bowl and cookie plate to the cafeteria kitchen, and when she returned, Bruce and Jolene were the only two left.

'If Jolene needs extra help with her reading or spelling, please let me know,' he said.

'I'll be happy to,' Rosie assured him. 'It was nice meeting you.'

'You, too.' He reached for his little girl's hand, then hesitated. His gaze briefly sought hers. 'I'm sorry about your divorce.'

Rosie looked down and nodded. 'I...am, too.'

He left after that, and not a moment too soon. Once again Rosie found herself blinking back tears.

It wasn't supposed to be like this. To all outward appearances, Zach was having the time of his life. When Allison and Eddie were with him they cooked together; the three of them got along famously. It didn't work that way on the nights Rosie spent with her children. Allison and Eddie bickered incessantly and her teenage daughter challenged Rosie's authority at every turn. She'd clearly taken Zach's side in the divorce.

Feet dragging, Rosie entered the small apartment she shared with Zach. He was with the children this evening, and she doubted Eddie had made a fuss at bedtime. Those bouts of temper were reserved for the nights Rosie spent with the children. Allison had probably volunteered to wash the dinner dishes. Rosie had given up asking her daughter to perform even the most routine household tasks. It just wasn't worth the argument.

Oh, yes, she was a real catch, Rosie thought wryly. She was a recent divorcée with two rebellious children. It wouldn't be long before dozens of eager men lined up at the door, all eager to date her.

Yeah, sure!

Seven

As a Seattle police detective, Roy McAfee had always had a hard time letting go of a case, no matter how cold. That hadn't changed, although he was now retired and living in Cedar Cove, where he'd become a private investigator. His dogged determination served him well in his new job. He liked his work, liked the diversity of cases that came across his desk. He was good at what he did, and he knew it. Roy had discovered through his years of police work that if he was patient enough and lucky, he eventually discovered what he needed to know. However, things didn't always turn out exactly the way he expected.

The disappearance of Dan Sherman was a prime example of that.

Grace had come to him shortly after her husband had disappeared. She was a strong woman. In his experience as a private detective, Roy had been hired by several women looking for answers regarding their husbands' activities or whereabouts. Twice he'd been asked to track down errant spouses. In one case, he'd started the investigation on a missing husband and had only gotten a week into the search when his client told him to quit looking. She'd claimed that in retrospect she was better off without the bastard. She didn't want to know where the hell he was. If he'd taken off with another woman, as she suspected, then the other woman was welcome to him.

From the little bit he'd learned about the missing husband, Roy figured his client had made a good choice.

It surprised him that Grace Sherman had contacted him again. Dan had been found, dead from a self-inflicted gunshot wound, and laid to rest. Roy assumed the case was closed. She had the answers she needed, but not necessarily the ones she wanted.

He heard the outside door open and glanced at the small clock on the corner of his desk. Twenty-five after twelve. A minute later Corrie, his wife and business manager, stepped into his office.

'Grace Sherman is here for her twelve-thirty appointment.'

She ushered Grace into the room. Corrie's eyes met his, and she shrugged as though to say she was as much in the dark about this meeting as he was.

'Have a seat,' Roy said, gesturing to the upholstered chair across from his desk.

'Would you care for a cup of coffee?' Corrie asked.

Grace declined, and Corrie left, closing the door behind her.

'What can I do for you?' Roy began. He leaned back in his chair and waited.

Grace held her purse in her lap, her hands nervously gripping the clasp. 'I came because I wasn't sure where else to turn,' she said, gazing down at the floor. 'It has to do with Dan.'

'Unfinished business?'

She nodded. 'Before he—before he killed himself, he wrote me a letter. Sheriff Davis gave it to me.' She opened her purse. 'The letter has some…information and I don't know what to do with it.'

Roy didn't remember hearing anything about a letter. 'What kind of information?'

Grace reached inside her purse for the envelope and handed it across the desk to Roy. 'No one else has read this. Not even my daughters.'

'What about Sheriff Davis?' Roy asked.

'I...I think he might've started reading it and then realized it was personal, and out of respect for Dan and me, he...' She paused, then shook her head. 'I don't know if he read it or not. I doubt it.'

Roy slid the letter out of the envelope. The writing in the first few lines was even and precise, as though Dan had carefully considered each word. Halfway down the second page the writing grew large, slanting downward. At the bottom, where Dan had signed his name, it was barely legible.

Roy turned back to the first page and began to read. Dan Sherman apologized to his wife for killing himself, and for the hell he'd put her through during their marriage.

Then Dan relayed the details of an incident that had happened in Vietnam when he'd walked into a village and killed a woman and her child. He'd mowed them down with bullets, murdered them out of instinctive fear. In the desperation of a young man willing to do anything to get out of the war alive, he'd killed innocents. Others had, too. How many had died in the village that day might never be known.

When he'd finished, Roy looked up and

discovered Grace staring into the distance. She was pale but seemed composed.

'Dan was never the same after he came back from the war,' she said in a hoarse whisper. 'Now I know why.'

'It was a long time ago,' Roy said reassuringly.

Dan hadn't indicated the number of people killed, but it appeared to have been a free-for-all. 'The shooting just never seemed to stop,' he'd written. He'd lived with that guilt all these years. Sometime back, Roy remembered reading that as many Vietnam vets had died by their own hand in the years that followed as were lost in the war. The causes were varied, although plainly it was guilt that had driven Dan to such drastic action.

'Was this incident ever reported?' he asked.

'Reported?' Grace repeated. 'That I wouldn't know, but I doubt it.'

'What would you like me to do?'

'That's just it. I...I don't know what should be done with this information.' She studied him, clearly hoping he'd offer a solution. He had none to give her.

'Should I hand the letter over to the army brass and let them deal with it?' she asked.

He didn't respond, merely raising one shoulder in a shrug.

'Or should I give it to Sheriff Davis and leave it up to him?' Her voice rose in agitation. 'Here's an idea,' she cried. 'Maybe I should put the letter away and pretend I never read it. Better yet, I should destroy it completely.'

Roy understood her dilemma, and didn't envy her. 'I can't tell you what to do, Grace.'

'Dan didn't want Maryellen or Kelly to know. They've just buried their father. That was hard enough without asking them to deal with this, too.'

Roy agreed, but unfortunately this was a decision Grace had to make on her own.

'It happened almost forty years ago. It was a horrible time in our country's history. We sacrificed fifty thousand men.... No one wants to uncover another My Lai.' She shook her head. 'He didn't say how many others were involved.' Her voice was soft, and Roy had to strain to hear. 'I want to know what's happened to the other men in the patrol. How have they managed to live with what they did? Have their lives been a living hell, too?' Her voice throbbed with emotion. 'Did they walk the floors at night the way my husband did? Have their souls been tormented?' Her eyes held his. 'Tell me what to do, Roy. You're the only one I can ask. You're the only one I trust enough to point me in the right direction.'

Roy leaned toward her. He wished he could supply the answer, but he couldn't. From the dark circles under her eyes, he knew she'd been tormented by the responsibility Dan had imposed on her.

'It's as though he couldn't deal with it any

longer and he laid the problem at my feet.' Her words confirmed his own feeling about the situation.

'For weeks—ever since Dan was found—I couldn't sleep. I thought it was because of... something else, and it was better for a while, but it's begun again. The insomnia.'

So she was the one walking the floors now.

'I've always been an easygoing sort of person, but lately...lately I've been depressed.'

'Have you been to see a physician?' he asked.

'What am I supposed to tell a doctor? That my husband was a mass murderer who recently committed suicide? Oh, by the way, this murder happened thirty-six years ago and has the potential to tear our country apart all over again?'

Roy sighed. She had a point. 'Like I said, Grace, I can't advise you what to do.'

'What if I decide to destroy the letter? The only people who'll ever know what it said are you and me.' She challenged him with a narrowed look.

'Then so be it.'

'That's not what I came to hear.'

He heard the desperation in her voice, but there was nothing more he could say.

'I'm paying you to help me figure out what I should do.'

'Do you want me to track down the other men?' he asked.

Grace shrugged. 'I wouldn't know where to start. Dan never spoke about his war experiences and he never mentioned who those other men were.'

Suddenly Roy wasn't so sure Grace *did* want the truth.

'I could find that out for you.' He had connections in the Department of Defense; it would be a simple matter of a phone call or two.

Grace hesitated, closing her eyes. 'I'll think about it and let you know.'

'All right.' Roy knew that Grace wanted an answer but not the one that would rip apart her own life—or those of others. He'd wait to hear from her.

*   *   *

The morning Katie turned six weeks old, Maryellen bathed her, the way she usually did. She watched joyfully as her daughter flung out her arms, splashing and cooing with unrestrained delight. Katie sent a spray of water toward her, hitting Maryellen in the face.

Katie smelled of baby lotion and shampoo as Maryellen dressed her in a soft pink sleeper. Six weeks ago, Maryellen's entire life had changed. Her daughter had given her purpose and such profound joy, it was all she could do not to close her eyes and thank God for this precious gift.

The doorbell rang, and Maryellen held Katie against her shoulder as she walked through the living room to answer it. The leaves on the oak tree were turning deep autumn shades and had started to litter the front lawn.

To her surprise Jon stood there, looking self-conscious. His eyes immediately went to Katie and a slow smile crossed his face.

'I developed some new pictures,' he announced. 'I realize this isn't my day to have Katie, but I wanted you to see them.'

'Nonsense, you're welcome anytime.' Maryellen had been overwhelmed by the number of pictures Jon had already taken of their daughter.

'To be honest, I was having withdrawal symptoms. I figured this was a good excuse to see my little girl.' He held out a large envelope. 'Trade you?'

He knew how much she loved his photographs. 'Deal,' she said, giving him Katie and taking the envelope. While Maryellen sat on one end of the sofa and examined these latest pictures, Jon cooed at his daughter. It was difficult to pay attention to the photographs, drawn as she was to the sight of Jon with Katie. Letting him drive away with their daughter twice a week hadn't become any easier, but she could never doubt his love.

As she reviewed the pictures, one in

particular caught her interest. It was taken the morning Maryellen had gone to his house. She'd sat in the rocking chair in Katie's nursery, breastfeeding their daughter. Her back was to the window and light spilled in around her. The cheerfully painted wall blurred in the background and only Maryellen and Katie were clear and vivid. Somehow Jon had captured the tenderness and love Maryellen felt for her daughter. Her focus was entirely on Katie, her smile a private one, for their baby alone. It was a classic image of mother and child, reminding her of paintings by Botticelli and Rembrandt.

She recalled that he'd had his camera with him that morning. She'd clowned around for him and he'd snapped picture after picture, but she hadn't expected anything like this.

'I see you found it,' he said, watching her as she studied the photograph.

'How do you do it?' she asked softly. 'How do you know the precise moment to catch a woman's heart?'

He frowned as if he didn't understand the question. For that matter, Maryellen wasn't sure she understood it, either. She loved her daughter. Loved Katie so much that just the sight of her made Maryellen's heart stop beating for a second or two. That was the love Jon had revealed so perfectly on film.

'I thought you didn't take photographs of people,' she said. 'Other than Katie, of course.'

But she couldn't help remembering the picture in his bedroom....

'Only you.' Jon kissed Katie on the forehead. 'If it bothers you, I won't again.'

That *wasn't* what she wanted, but then Maryellen no longer knew what was right or wrong as far as Jon was concerned. He made everything so much more complicated.

'I...love this picture, Jon. I really love it.'

'Then it's yours.'

To make matters worse, tears filled her eyes and she turned away as they ran down her cheeks.

'Maryellen?'

'What?'

'Why are you crying?'

'I don't know, but it's all your fault.' Her words, rash and illogical, escaped on a sob.

Jon stood and placed Katie in her bassinet. He paced back and forth a couple of times, then sat down next to Maryellen. She refused to face him as she tried to stem these ridiculous tears. Baby blues or not, she hated being out of control.

He touched her shoulder, so lightly she almost didn't feel it. 'Can you tell me why you're crying?' he whispered.

'No,' she murmured.

Slowly he ran his hand down the length of her arm.

'Why do you have to be so wonderful?' she sobbed.

105

His hand paused. 'Would you rather I was unreasonable and short-tempered?'

'I've treated you terribly. I hid the fact that I was pregnant, tried to keep you out of our baby's life and all...all you've been is patient and wonderful. I could hate you for it.'

'Hate me?' He turned her shoulders so she was forced to face him.

'I don't, though. I thought I would, but I don't.'

He stroked the sides of her neck in a leisurely, hypnotic massage. Maryellen half closed her eyes and swayed toward him. Jon wove his fingers deep into her long hair and brought her mouth within a fraction of his own.

'After the way I've treated you, you should detest me,' she told him.

'I don't, Maryellen,' he whispered, and his breath mingled with hers.

She parted her lips, anticipating his kiss. The tip of his tongue, moist and warm, outlined her mouth, and Maryellen moaned at the pure sensuality of it. Her lips parted further and Jon brushed his mouth against hers. His fingers tightened in her thick hair as he continued the kiss.

Maryellen tasted the salt of her tears and realized that she was weeping even as he kissed her. She heard him whisper, but couldn't make out the words. Whatever he was saying didn't seem nearly as important as what

106

he was doing and what he was making her feel.

With her arms wrapped around him, she pressed against his hard, muscular strength. They were both panting, their shoulders heaving with the intensity of their desire.

A discordant sound made its way into her clouded mind. She groaned, not knowing where this lovemaking would take them, unwilling to stop. His hands cupped her breasts, and sensation bolted through her. With his mouth against hers, he unfastened her blouse and bra, and she felt his hands tremble as he eased his thumb over her swollen nipple. This latest invasion made her whimper as she tilted back her head.

The cry came again and Maryellen's eyes flew open. 'Katie,' she whispered. 'It's Katie.'

Jon drew back. They momentarily leaned against each other, trying to regain their equilibrium.

'You—I almost forgot the baby,' she said.

Jon laughed softly. 'What baby? Oh, you mean our baby.'

'The very one.'

Maryellen stood up to check on Katie, who was fussing in earnest now. She punched the air with her arms and feet and screamed as though the world were ending. Maryellen supposed that for a baby, feeding time was about that important.

As discreetly as possible, Maryellen fastened her bra and blouse. It occurred to her that this was a bit silly, since she'd be unfastening them again in a minute. 'Do you think we've warped her mind forever?' she asked, hoping to make light of what had happened between them.

'I can't speak for Katie, but I know what you've done to me.'

'Are you…uncomfortable?' she asked, not knowing how to phrase the question any more delicately. Even when her intentions were good, she managed to hurt him—to reject him, either physically or emotionally. She assumed there'd been painful rejections in his past; all the signs were there. Her own life was colored with anguish he knew nothing about, distress that was impossible to share.

'I've been uncomfortable, as you put it, since the first night we kissed.'

She remembered that kiss. Halloween night a year ago. He'd walked her to her car after a party during which she'd introduced him to a friend. Her plan had been to foist him off on someone else in a pitiful attempt to get him out of her mind. That scheme had failed miserably, just like every other one she'd plotted in their bewildering relationship.

'I have to feed Katie,' she told him. Her feet felt unsteady as she reached for her daughter and positioned the infant in the crook of her arm. She sat down in her rocker, unfastened shirt and bra, and gave the baby her breast. Katie's tiny mouth latched eagerly onto her nipple.

'I take it this is my cue to leave,' Jon said.

She nodded, unable to meet his gaze.

Jon stood only a few feet away. 'I'll leave the photos with you.'

'Thank you,' she whispered. She found it hard to believe that only moments earlier they'd practically been rolling around on the floor, kissing and groping with abandon. She was embarrassed, somehow, by the juxtaposition of maternal and sexual feelings.

'Keep the pictures you like for Katie's baby book and I'll get the rest on Sunday.'

'Thank you...I appreciate it.' He'd be back then, of course, to collect Katie. Her hold tightened around their daughter.

'I'll see you Sunday.'

'Katie and I will be here.' She kept her eyes lowered.

She heard him walk over to the door. He opened it. 'Maryellen?'

She glanced up and saw that his mouth was twitching with a barely suppressed smile. 'You can hate me anytime you want.'

*   *   *

Zach Cox looked down at his watch. It was one of his nights with Allison and Eddie, and he needed to leave the office precisely at five. Frustrated, he closed a file and set it aside. He'd have to finish calculating the employment taxes for the Tulips and Things

Craft Store tomorrow morning. Just as he was about to leave, Janice Lamond appeared in his doorway.

'Mr. Cox,' she said in a low voice. 'I was wondering if you had a moment to review the Jackson quarterly tax statement with me?' Her look implored him.

It seemed she routinely required his help at closing time. Most nights Zach didn't have a problem checking her figures, but on the evenings he spent with the kids, he simply didn't have the extra minutes to spare.

'Can it wait until morning?' he asked as he stood.

Janice wore a short skirt. It rose up mid-thigh and exposed long, shapely legs. The skirt was too short and too tight. He'd never really noticed the way Janice dressed until recently. He glanced outside his office and realized the other women employed by the accounting firm were far more conservative in their clothing.

'Of course it can wait,' she assured him. 'I forgot you're with your children tonight.'

He nodded and reached for his briefcase.

'How is that arrangement working?' Janice moved all the way inside his office.

'About as well as can be expected.' Actually it was about as inconvenient as could be imagined. Half the time he didn't know where he was sleeping—the apartment or the house. A week ago he'd arrived with clothes but no underwear. He now left a spare set in the trunk of his car. He didn't feel inclined to tell Janice any of this, however.

As he prepared to leave the office, he placed several business magazines he hadn't had time to read inside the leather case. Rosie had given him the briefcase for Christmas three years earlier and he'd used it every day since. He rarely had time for reading anymore. No time for golf, either, or jogging or any of the activities he'd once enjoyed.

'I won't keep you, then,' Janice said with obvious reluctance.

'See you in the morning,' he said, and snapped his briefcase shut. 'I can look at those figures then.'

'Figures?' she repeated. 'Oh, yes, I almost forgot.'

He removed his suit jacket from the small closet and slipped his arms into the sleeves. Janice continued to linger. 'Was there anything else?' he asked.

'Do you sometimes get lonely?' She fluttered her lashes and for some reason they reminded Zach of spiders.

'Lonely?' he asked.

'I mean, I did, after my divorce. It was such a hard time emotionally and I wanted you to know that I understand those feelings. If you ever need to talk to someone, I'm a good listener.'

'I'll keep that in mind.' Zach had no intention of combining business with pleasure.

He'd made the mistake of letting the lines blur earlier. It had started out innocently—she'd joined him for lunch one day when Rosie had to cancel at the last moment. Later, when he realized how unreasonable Rosie had become, he'd asked Janice to help him look for an apartment. He'd hoped to shake up his wife, get her to recognize what she was doing. His attempt had failed, to say the least. Rosie had taken his leaving seriously and seemed more than happy to have him out of the house. Janice had found him an apartment, all right, and the lines had blurred even further when he'd accepted a housewarming gift from her and taken her and her son to lunch.

Janice hesitated. 'I was thinking we could have dinner one night. My treat.'

Dinner? Her treat? No way. 'I appreciate the invitation, but I don't think it's a good idea that we be seen together outside the office.' He wasn't handing Rosie any ammunition or giving her one more excuse to toss accusations in his face. Unfortunately, living the way they did, moving in and out of the house, made confronting each other inevitable. Zach wasn't happy about it and he suspected Rosie wasn't, either.

'Maybe some other time,' Janice said, sounding hopeful.

'Maybe,' Zach agreed, but it wasn't going to happen.

Rosie had claimed months earlier that

Janice and Zach were having an affair. She was being ridiculous and had refused to believe him when he said they weren't. Now he was beginning to wonder if Janice *had* been chasing after him. He hated the thought that he'd been played for a fool. If that was the case, then it was Rosie's doing. She was the one so ready to leap to conclusions, so eager to find fault with him—so willing to abandon him to Janice's attentions. Rosie had acted like a jealous shrew when she had no reason. It irritated him whenever he thought about it. Not that he was blaming Janice for their divorce. His marriage had been ailing for a long time before his assistant appeared on the scene.

Frowning as he walked out of the office, Zach refused to let his mind wander down the familiar paths of guilt and blame. His marriage was dead, and rehashing unresolved issues between him and Rosie would do no good.

Fifteen minutes later, Zach drove into the garage at 311 Pelican Court, the custom-built house he'd helped design. Together he and Rosie had pored over house plans for months on end. Despite this inconvenient arrangement, he felt grateful to the judge for her unconventional edict, since it meant he didn't have to completely give up a place he loved.

To Zach's surprise, the house was quiet when he came in through the kitchen door.

'Where is everyone?' he called as he set his briefcase on the counter.

'Here, Dad,' Eddie shouted from the family room. He was lying in front of the television on his stomach, manipulating the joystick to his video game. 'Allison's got a visitor in her bedroom,' he said, looking up at Zach. 'It's a boy.'

'*What?*' The word exploded out of Zach before he could stop it. He'd see about this. Allison knew the rules, and Rule Number One was no kids at the house without an adult present. No boys in her room, either. *Ever.*

Eddie nodded in the direction of the hallway. 'Check it out.'

Zach didn't need a second invitation. He practically ran to Allison's bedroom; it was the fastest he'd moved in weeks. He pounded on the closed door, then flung it open. His daughter sat on the edge of her bed with her arms entwined around the neck of a skinny boy with long stringy hair badly in need of washing. He wore a black leather jacket and motorcycle boots that laced up to his knees. A studded leather dog collar circled his neck.

'Dad.' Allison's eyes grew huge. 'What are *you* doing here?'

'I live here three days a week. Who's this?' He narrowed his gaze on the pimply-faced youth.

'This is Ryan Wilson. Ryan, this is my dad.'

'Ryan,' Zach said. He reached for the boy's

114

arm and jerked him to an upright position. 'Nice to meet you.' Without taking a breath, he continued. 'However, we have rules in this house and that includes no boys in my daughter's bedroom.' He loomed over the teenager, who blinked up at him, face paling.

'Daddy,' Allison cried.

Zach ignored her. 'If you want to see my daughter again, I suggest you abide by my rules. Do we understand each other, Ryan?' he asked pointedly.

Ryan nodded.

'Good.' He held out his hand. 'Well, goodbye, Ryan. I assume you know your way to the front door?'

Ryan made a beeline out of the bedroom.

Allison was on her feet now, too, her expression one of outrage. 'How dare you!'

'Oh, I dare, Allison, and I'll dare a whole lot more. What the hell do you think you're doing bringing a boy into this house without an adult present?'

'*I'm* an adult.'

Zach nearly laughed out loud. 'When you're living on your own, paying your own expenses, we'll revisit that issue. As it stands now, you live in my house.' He paused, because technically this wasn't his house. It belonged to Rosie and him jointly and to the kids.

'I can invite anyone I want into my room.'

Zach glared at her. 'Don't go there, little girl.'

'Little girl?' Indignation shone from her eyes, and her cheeks reddened as she clenched her fists at her sides.

Zach could see this argument was getting out of hand. He was angry and so was Allison. Difficult as it was, they both needed to step back and take a deep breath. 'We'll talk about this after dinner.' He turned and left the room, and heard the door slam a couple of seconds later.

By the time Zach entered the kitchen, he was shaking. He dragged several calming breaths into his lungs and forced his heart to settle down to a normal beat.

'What's for dinner?' Eddie asked, following him inside.

'Hot dogs,' Zach said. It was convenient, quick and he was in no mood to mess with a casserole. He'd discovered he was quite good at tossing a few ingredients together. He had his failures—notably the ground turkey baked with peas and rice—and his successes. Eddie didn't seem to care one way or the other. Of the two, Allison was the picky eater.

'We had hot dogs last night.'

Leave it to Rosie to beat him to the punch. 'What would you like?' he asked.

Without hesitation, Eddie said, 'Spaghetti.'

'Okay.' He searched the refrigerator's freezer section for hamburger and realized there was none. It was his week to buy groceries, which he should've done before he got home. More than likely, that was why Allison had Ryan in her room. She'd expected him to arrive later than normal, but he'd forgotten it was his turn to do the shopping.

'Has Ryan been here before?' he asked. He hated to use his son as a snitch, but he was beginning to think Ryan might be a routine visitor. If so, that was about to stop right now.

Eddie glanced over his shoulder and then nodded.

'Does your mother know?'

Eddie shook his head. 'No one did until now.'

Zach patted his son on the back. 'What about macaroni and cheese?'

Eddie shrugged. 'Are you going to cook the real kind or the kind that comes out of a box?'

'What do we have?' Zach asked, examining the contents of various cupboards. He needed something easy while he decided what to do about Allison. It was clear he'd have to talk to her, and much as he dreaded the idea of calling Rosie, he should probably get her advice before he initiated the big discussion.

'We've got grated mozzarella cheese,' Eddie said, peering inside the refrigerator. 'That makes the best kind 'cause it melts in the macaroni.'

'Done,' Zach said.

Eddie removed the container of cheese and set it on the counter. 'You aren't going to make me eat green beans with this, are you?

Mom does. She's on this kick about eating vegetables and fresh fruit. It's disgusting. She won't let us order pizza, either.'

Zach smiled wanly. 'I might let you off just this once.'

Eddie looked appreciative.

'I think I should call your mother,' Zach said, putting a pot of water on the stove.

'She's not home.'

His son was a fount of information. 'She isn't?'

Eddie beamed him a big smile. 'She's got a date.'

Rosie was out on a date? If so, he wanted to know who with. No one had said anything to *him* about this. 'On a school night?' he asked, hoping for more facts.

Eddie nodded. 'That was all she talked about last night. Dad, I've got problems with my math homework. Can you help?'

'Sure,' he said absently. This was great. Just great! Zach was struggling to find something edible to feed his kids. He was the one dealing with his teenage daughter's rebellion. Eddie needed help with his homework. And his ex-wife was enjoying a night on the town with her new love interest.

There was definitely something wrong with this picture.

Eight

It was a lovely Saturday morning, and the blustery winds of October blew orange and yellow leaves around the waterfront and the Cedar Cove Farmers' Market. Grace and Olivia meandered down the row between a series of festive booths.

'So, what time do you want to go to the movie?' Olivia asked.

'I was thinking I'd pass this afternoon,' Grace said nonchalantly.

'Oh—' Olivia couldn't help being disappointed. 'How come?'

Grace suddenly became flustered. 'Oh, for heaven's sake, just go to the movie without me,' she cried.

Olivia knew that look. Her friend was up to something and Olivia probably wasn't going to like it. She stopped at a booth and purchased a loaf of homemade raisin bread, which she tucked into her large straw bag.

'All right, all right, I'll tell you,' Grace said as though the truth had been tortured out of her.

Olivia didn't bother to point out that she hadn't asked.

'Jack's going to be there.'

That got Olivia's attention. 'Jack?'

'Jack. Remember Jack? He called and asked

me to set it up.'

Now, this was downright ridiculous. Jack had phoned her best friend and not her?

'Remember last month when you turned down Stan's dinner invitation?'

Olivia wasn't likely to forget. It had caused a rift between her and Stan, but she wasn't nearly as concerned about her relationship with her ex-husband as she was about her continuing disagreement with Jack.

'Jack was supposed to meet us at the theater the Friday night we went to the movies last month, but at the last minute he couldn't make it.'

'What's going on here?' Olivia demanded, although she wasn't really upset. It was increasingly obvious that she needed all the assistance she could get in the romance department. Not that her friend was any great expert. Grace had her own difficulties, but unfortunately they weren't the kind that intervention would help.

'Jack covers the Friday-night football games,' Grace reminded her. 'Gordie was supposed to go instead, but something came up.'

They continued to stroll through the market, mouths watering at the enticing scent of popping kettle corn carried on the wind. 'Jack wasn't happy about it.' Grace sighed. 'Ever since then, he's been driving me nuts, trying to get me to set up another movie outing, but between your

120

schedule, his and mine—well, it's getting too crazy to work it all out. I figured I'd just tell you.'

'It's about time he and I settled this, isn't it?' Olivia said, eager to patch up her differences with Jack. They'd let their quarrel drag on weeks longer than it should have. She didn't understand why he hadn't simply called *her,* but...well, trust a man to do things the hard way.

'Absolutely,' Grace said emphatically. 'You're both stubborn and headstrong. Now fix it.'

Olivia couldn't believe her ears. This was *Grace* speaking? Grace never ordered people about. Obviously she felt strongly about this, and that made Olivia feel good.

Leaves billowed past and leaden gray clouds had begun to darken the sky. It would rain within the hour, she predicted.

'You're going, aren't you?'

'How will he know which movie?' Olivia hadn't even decided what she wanted to see.

'Jack's a smart man, he'll figure it out.'

'If he was so smart, he'd—'

'Olivia, are you going to argue with me, or are you going to accept some heartfelt advice and do what I suggest?'

Before she answered, Olivia had a question or two of her own. 'What's happening with you and Cliff?'

Grace sighed again. 'Not a whole lot. After Dan was found, I told him I needed time to grieve for my husband. He understood.'

Olivia nodded; that much she knew. 'You haven't seen him in a while.'

'We talk every week. Cliff's been doing a lot of traveling lately and he's building a new barn.'

'Why? Is he expanding?'

'Yes. He's serious about raising quarter horses and he's increasing his herd. When we spoke last Saturday, he said he's thinking of hiring a full-time hand.' She began to say something else and stopped, obviously aware of her friend's ploy. She turned to stare Olivia in the eye. 'Are you going to the movies this afternoon or not?'

Olivia shrugged one shoulder.

Grace laughed softly. 'You're going, and judging by the smile on your face, you can hardly wait.'

That was the truth. Olivia wasn't sure how Jack was supposed to know what showing she planned to attend or which movie, but as Grace had informed her, he'd figure it out.

And Grace, it turned out, knew what she was talking about. No more than five minutes after Olivia had chosen her seat, munching popcorn and waiting for the movie to start, Jack Griffin entered the theater. He looked exactly the same as the last time she'd seen him. He wore his long dark raincoat over beige slacks and a black turtleneck sweater. He walked past her down the aisle as if he hadn't seen her and took a seat three rows up, directly in front of her.

If he expected her to talk to him first, he had a lengthy wait ahead of him. Then, as though he'd forgotten something, he stood and marched toward the door. He was two steps up the aisle when he did a double-take, as if he'd just noticed her.

'As I live and breathe, it's Judge Lockhart.'

'Jack Griffin, this is a pleasant surprise.' She played along, flushing with pleasure. It was so damned good to see her friend again, and the instant she did, she realized how much she'd missed him. Even more than she'd thought...

'What brings you to a movie all alone in the middle of a Saturday afternoon?' he asked—as if he didn't already know.

It was time for the truth. No more games, just the truth. 'You haven't figured it out?' She grinned sheepishly up at him. 'I came because of you.'

'Me?' He gave an award-winning look of surprise.

'Grace told me you were going to be here,' Olivia confessed.

Jack snorted. 'She told me you'd be here, too.'

The theater darkened and Jack moved toward her row. 'Do you mind if I join you?'

'I was hoping you would.'

He didn't need to be invited twice, nearly leaping over her in his eagerness to get into

123

the adjacent seat. As soon as he was settled, he tried to help himself to a handful of her popcorn.

Olivia playfully slapped his wrist. 'Kindly wait until I offer.'

Jack sent her a hurt look, and when she slanted the bucket in his direction, he dug right in. 'You couldn't possibly eat all this by yourself, anyway.'

'I might.'

He snickered softly. 'Are you always this bossy?'

'Yes, and if you haven't figured *that* out by now, you haven't been paying attention.'

'Are there makeup classes?' he asked, as he scooted down in his seat.

Olivia smiled. 'That can be arranged.'

Jack reached for another handful of popcorn. 'I've missed you.'

Her throat tightened. 'I've missed you, too.'

The woman sitting in front of them and off to one side twisted around. Her lips were pursed in annoyance. 'I hate to interrupt your reunion, but I'd like to hear the movie.'

'Sorry,' Olivia whispered, mortified that someone had to shush her in the theater. She hoped the lights were too dim for anyone to recognize her.

Jack straightened and leaned across the back of the seat closest to the woman who'd complained. 'It's actually all Olivia's fault,' he said conversationally. 'You see, it's been four months since we've seen each other and—'

'Jack!' Olivia tugged at the sleeve of his raincoat. 'I don't think it's necessary that she hear the details of our misunderstanding.'

He continued chatting as if this woman was his long-lost friend. Olivia sank down as far in the seat as she could.

After several minutes, just as the previews finished, Jack turned around again. 'Marion, this is Olivia. Olivia, Marion.'

'Hi.' Olivia lifted one hand in greeting and offered the woman a half smile.

Marion cheerfully waved back. 'I'm just so glad you two are together again and that your dear, dear friend lived.'

'What?' Surely Olivia had misunderstood something.

'Enjoy the movie,' Jack said as he shifted back in his seat.

'What was *that* all about?' Olivia asked, although she already knew. Jack had told another of his outrageous stories; he should've been writing fiction, not newspaper columns. She poked him in the ribs with her elbow when he chose to ignore her.

'Shh,' Jack said, staring at the screen. He glanced away long enough to scoop up more popcorn.

Olivia relaxed, and after a few moments released a pent-up sigh. It felt so good to have him back in her life. They hadn't settled anything, hadn't discussed any of the once-important issues. And Olivia wasn't even sure that was necessary.

She was so caught up in her thoughts, she didn't notice that Jack had taken the entire bucket of popcorn—until she tried to get some.

'Hey,' she protested.

'You shouldn't eat any more,' he asserted.

'Why not?'

'Because you won't be hungry when I take you out to dinner after the movie.'

'Oh.' That answered that, but didn't explain why *he* continued to eat, munching down as if he hadn't had a decent meal in weeks. 'What about you?'

He shrugged. 'I'm always hungry.'

Olivia rested her head on his shoulder and Jack put the bucket down and slid his arm around her. Like high school sweethearts, they leaned their heads against each other, holding hands. Olivia hadn't felt this contented in months.

She had no idea what the movie was about.

*   *   *

Sunday morning, Rosie was awakened by the sound of rain beating incessantly against the apartment window. She closed her eyes and tried to go back to sleep, without success. She was awake. Wide awake. It'd taken her hours to fall asleep, and now this.

Weekends were the worst for her. During the week, she was in the classroom every day, and the whole issue of the divorce and this ridiculous joint custody arrangement was easy enough to shove aside. But weekends were dreadful. She hated that Zach was at the house on Friday and Saturday nights. When she'd agreed to give him weekends, she'd thought it was poetic justice. With the children constantly underfoot, he wouldn't be able to date much. If he realized her intention, he didn't let on, but it gave Rosie a sense of satisfaction to thwart him at every turn, especially when it came to his relationship with Janice Lamond.

Wearing her thin housecoat, Rosie wandered into the kitchen and started a pot of coffee. She wasn't scheduled to be back at the house until five that afternoon. What they were doing made no sense—the way they were living, moving in and out of the house every few days. She couldn't imagine what that judge was thinking.

The rain continued and a chill raced up her arms. The housecoat she wore now was a summer one, inadequate to protect her against the chill of these autumn mornings. This was crazy! One set of clothes hung in her closet here and another at the house. Half the time she didn't know what was where.

The morning stretched before her, empty and bleak. A year earlier, she'd been so busy with her volunteer work that she couldn't squeeze in time to cook her family dinner. Her charity work, along with so much else, had gone by the wayside with the divorce. She'd been forced to resign from every volunteer position—positions she'd willingly accepted. She wasn't even missed. All her responsibilities, which were once so important, had been transferred to other people. Now she moved from school to school. Her days were filled with teaching, and when she wasn't with the children, her nights were lonely. Her entire life had changed at the sound of a judge's gavel.

Her friends, most of whom were married, no longer seemed to have time for her. A year ago, Rosie had people to see, appointments every day, plans every night. Now there was nothing but guilt and doubts and an abundance of pain.

When she finished her coffee, Rosie showered, then read the weekend editions of the *Bremerton Sun* and the local paper, but few of the articles held her interest. The *Cedar Cove Chronicle* had a brief piece about the mysterious man who'd turned up dead at the Thyme and Tide, but there didn't seem to be any additional details. Closing her eyes, she tried to remember what it had been like before...before their marital troubles. Before the divorce.

Sunday mornings had always been hectic, getting everyone ready for church and out the door in time for worship service. Until recently, she'd sung in the choir, but she'd stopped attending church once she filed for divorce. She was afraid of facing her friends and having to confess what a lie she'd been living.

If she missed church services so badly, then perhaps she should go back. Not to the same church, of course, but someplace new, where she could make a fresh start. She'd been hearing good things about the pastor at the Methodist church, Dave Flemming, if she remembered his name correctly. Maybe she should think about attending there. It just might help her deal with the upheaval in her life. God knew she needed something...and fast.

Decision made, Rosie quickly checked the telephone book for the times of the worship services and realized that if she left right away, she'd make the one scheduled for nine o'clock.

The parking lot was nearly full when she arrived. She saw several people she knew, including Bob and Peggy Beldon from the bed-and-breakfast, and a number of parents she'd met at the Open House. Seeing Bruce Peyton and his daughter might have cheered her up, but apparently they attended elsewhere. She liked Bruce and they'd talked a couple of times, meeting for dinner once when Jolene was asleep and watched over by a neighbor. Their pain was a common bond—perhaps their only bond.

The music had already started when Rosie slipped into a pew near the back of the church. Gone were the days when she proudly marched up the center aisle with her husband and children. Like so much else, her respectability had vanished with the divorce.

The music was wonderful, and even in her depressed state, it lifted her spirits. She listened carefully to the sermon, but about halfway through the service she felt someone's eyes on her. Hoping she wasn't being obvious, she looked over her shoulder and immediately froze.

It couldn't be! Of all the coincidences in this world, why here? Why now?

Two rows behind her sat Zach and Eddie. There must be fifteen churches in Cedar Cove, and she and Zach just happened to choose the same one on the same Sunday. Rosie wanted to groan with frustration. No place was safe for her. She couldn't even walk into church and not be reminded of her past.

When the service ended, Zach waited for her outside the building.

'I didn't follow you here if that's what you think,' he told her, his voice defensive.

'I didn't follow you, either. Listen, Zach, we're divorced. You have your life and I have mine. This is the first time I've attended this church, and I can easily go elsewhere. It's no big deal.'

'Hi, Mom. Hi, Dad,' Eddie said, racing up to join his parents. 'My friend Joel comes here. He invited me to his house for lunch. I can go, can't I, Dad?' He looked expectantly toward Zach and then Rosie. 'You don't mind, do you, Mom?'

Seeing that Eddie was under his father's jurisdiction until five, she left the decision to him.

'I'll need their address and phone number,' Zach said.

'You want to meet his parents?' Eddie asked.

'Sure. I'll be there in just a minute. I want to talk to your mother first.'

Eddie gave him a bright smile. 'Okay.' With that, the nine-year-old tore across the parking lot, where a small group of parents and children had gathered.

As if reading her mind, Zach said, 'I'll make sure he's home before you get there.'

She nodded. 'As I was saying about this morning—'

'It's not a problem,' Zach interrupted. 'This was our first Sunday here, too.'

'I'll change churches. It looks like Eddie's already got a friend here.' Allison, however, was nowhere to be seen. 'Where's Allison?' Rosie looked around, thinking their daughter was probably with her friends, as well. When they'd attended church as a family, Allison made a habit of sitting in any pew her family

131

wasn't.

'She didn't come.'

Now Rosie was getting irritated. Allison had been in a horrible mood ever since Zach had kicked her boyfriend out of her bedroom. 'You let her stay home?'

Zach wore a guilty look. 'She refused to come, and I figured forcing her would only make matters worse.' Zach didn't seem any too pleased about it, either. From the way he stiffened, he obviously expected Rosie to chastise him.

Actually, she was pleased Zach had to deal with their daughter's temper for once. 'Are you still having problems with Allison?' she asked, hoping he'd admit it.

'Some. What about you?'

She shrugged. 'A little.'

'Maybe we should get together and discuss what's happening with her,' Zach suggested, surprising Rosie.

'When?'

'Whenever it's convenient.'

'You mean there's more than her bringing Ryan into her bedroom?' she asked.

'I don't know, but I think it's important that the two of us communicate regularly.'

Rosie agreed, although with some reluctance. The sooner they got this over with, the better, she decided. 'How about now?'

Zach nodded. 'Okay.'

Fifteen minutes later, Zach and Rosie sat

across from each other at the Pancake Palace. Eddie was with his friend Joel, and Zach would be picking him up later.

Since the two of them were taking up a table and the place was busy with the Sunday breakfast crowd, Rosie felt obliged to order something more than coffee.

When the waitress came, she asked for coffee, two eggs and toast, plus a separate bill. Zach ordered the same thing and also asked for his own check. Once it was understood that they'd each pay for breakfast, Zach turned his attention back to Rosie.

'What do you know about Ryan?'

'Not much. His parents are divorced and he lives with his mother.'

'She lets him pierce various body parts,' Zach said, frowning.

Rosie wasn't impressed with that, either. 'Apparently so.' There were six safety pins clipped through Ryan's ear, and a small steel ball was attached to the end of his tongue. The thought of this boy kissing their daughter made her queasy.

'He hasn't been over to the house since I talked to him,' Zach added with some satisfaction.

Rosie wasn't convinced that was true, but didn't want to say anything that would threaten their fragile peace.

'I talked to his mother last week.'

That piqued Zach's interest. 'What's she

like?'

From their brief conversation, it seemed Ryan's mother didn't exactly see the situation in the same light as Rosie did. 'She...was defensive. I told her we preferred that an adult be in the house if Ryan visited. She accused me of being overprotective.'

'Is it any of her business?' Zach demanded.

'No, but I don't think we're going to get a lot of cooperation from her.'

'Seems that way.' Zach was frowning.

Rosie was so grateful to talk to him about this. It dawned on her now why she'd been so restless and uneasy—it was largely due to her daughter's behavior.

'Do you remember last year when I told you about the Harrison girl?' she asked.

Zach shook his head.

'She was in junior high and pregnant with twins.'

The color seemed to rush from Zach's face. 'You don't think—' He couldn't bring himself to say it.

'I don't know, Zach, and we might not know for sure until it's too late.'

Her words had the shock value she'd intended. Allison's anger and resentment grew more acute every week. This boy in her life was trouble, and their daughter's future could well be at stake.

'I'm worried about Allison,' Zach said, his voice low.

'I am, too,' Rosie agreed. 'She didn't take the divorce well, and she's lashing out at both of us. I'm not sure what she'd do.... I hardly know her anymore.'

Nine

Olivia was happy. She woke early on Sunday morning—her birthday—and luxuriated in bed while the last dregs of sleep left her. It occurred to her that she should be adding up the years, which now totaled a rather shocking number. Better yet, she should review her accomplishments and align them with her goals, which was what she did every birthday.

Yes, she should probably be doing that. Birthdays were a good opportunity to assess one's life. Instead, she was grinning to herself and mulling over the way she'd 'run into' Jack at the theater, all the silly subterfuge they'd indulged in. But they'd had such a good time together. Jack possessed the ability to make her laugh, and she valued that, more than almost anything. All pretense between them was gone now. It was clear how genuinely glad he'd been to see her again, and the truth was, she felt equally delighted.

They'd spent all afternoon together and all evening. After the movie, they'd had dinner at the Taco Shack and lingered for hours over coffee, talking about every subject except one. Stan. He didn't ask, and Olivia certainly didn't bring her ex-husband's name into the conversation. It was as though neither of them wanted to say or do anything that might set back their relationship.

They parted reluctantly and talked for another thirty minutes in the parking lot.

Even though Jack had bought her a birthday gift the year before, she was sure he'd forgotten the date. She could've mentioned it, probably should have. Another *should*...but she had no intention of informing him that she was about to turn a whole year older.

Charlotte insisted on cooking her breakfast, so after church services, Olivia went to her mother's place.

'Come in, come in,' Charlotte called from the kitchen when Olivia let herself in the house. Harry, her guard cat, sprawled in the front window, basking in the autumn sunshine. The scent of cinnamon rolls fresh from the oven made Olivia's mouth water.

'Happy birthday, sweetheart,' her mother said warmly, coming out of the kitchen wearing an apron. She enveloped Olivia in a tight hug. 'You look wonderful.'

'Thanks, Mom.' Olivia wasn't ready to admit that Jack was responsible for the sparkle in her eyes. Not when her mother was guaranteed to give her a hearty 'I told you so' in return.

'Everything's ready,' Charlotte said. The

136

dining table was set with her mother's best china, the orange juice poured in tall crystal goblets. Humming something Olivia didn't recognize, Charlotte bustled back to the kitchen. Come to think of it, her mother seemed to be in a mighty cheerful mood herself.

'Can I help?' Olivia asked, following her.

'All I need to do is bring everything to the table,' Charlotte assured her. 'I baked your favorite breakfast casserole and cinnamon rolls.'

Olivia swallowed a smile. The breakfast casserole was her *mother's* favorite, but far be it from Charlotte to cook it just for herself, so she always took advantage of a convenient excuse—like her daughter's birthday.

'This looks *so* good.' Olivia pulled out the chair across from her and surveyed the feast.

They bowed their heads and her mother said grace before she served the casserole, made up of bacon, onions, hash browns and lots of cheese. 'Shall I tell you about the day you were born?' Charlotte asked.

'Mother, I'm fifty-five years old! I've heard the story for fifty-four of those years. I know everything there is to know about that day.' Every minute detail had been conveyed countless times. 'I know how Daddy had to rush you to the hospital at nine in the evening and how you were in labor for twenty hours. I know there was a big storm the very next day

137

and nobody could visit until the day after. And I know I screamed for three solid hours—or so you say.'

'It's the truth.' Charlotte nodded stubbornly.

Olivia laughed. As silly as it was, she found herself passing on this tradition of her mother's to her own children. On the morning of her son James's last birthday, Olivia had phoned long distance to describe the day he was born. James had listened politely and then informed her she'd told him the same thing, almost word for word, the year before.

Through breakfast, they chatted about family and friends and then her mother casually said, 'I invited Ben Rhodes to join us, but he had other plans this morning.'

Ben, Olivia mused. She vaguely remembered hearing her mother mention Ben. It might seem peculiar that Charlotte would want to include a stranger in Olivia's birthday breakfast. But her mother was like that. She collected people the way some women collected china cups or brooches. For instance, Tom Harding, Cliff's grandfather, a man in his nineties.

She'd befriended him a couple of years back. The old man had been a stroke victim and had lost the ability to speak, but he didn't appear to have any problem communicating with her mother. It was Charlotte's gift, Olivia decided, to seek out those who needed her attention most.

'Justine and Seth invited me over for dinner,' she said, purposely turning the subject away from her mother's latest charity project.

'So I heard.'

'And Grace and I are taking the ferry to Seattle to have lunch on the waterfront next weekend.'

Her mother nodded, but seemed a bit hurt at Olivia's decided lack of interest in her new friend. 'Ben's stopping by later and we're going to visit the pumpkin patch.'

Olivia considered it a bit odd that two elderly people would want to do something traditionally reserved for young families, but she didn't say anything. More than likely, her mother's friend was senile and had reverted to childhood memories and this was an activity he'd enjoy.

'Have a wonderful time,' she said.

'Oh, we intend to,' Charlotte murmured.

If she didn't know better, Olivia would've thought she'd seen her mother blushing.

Later the same day, she asked her daughter about it. 'Have you noticed anything different about your grandmother lately?'

Justine, who was busy stirring gravy, glanced up. 'Grandma? What makes you ask?'

Olivia held her infant grandson and paced the small kitchen, gently patting his back. Leif cooed at her, and for a moment, she was caught up in the sheer wonder of holding this baby close to her heart. When she realized

Justine was waiting for her answer, she returned to the subject of her mother. 'Oh—we had breakfast this morning and, well, your grandmother seemed…oh, I don't know, secretive.'

'Secretive? How?'

Olivia shrugged.

'Mom, I've been so busy with the restaurant and with Leif that I haven't had a chance to notice.'

'It's nothing, I'm sure, but after last year's cancer scare I want to keep an eye on her.'

'I do, too. It's just that I have so much going on right now.' Justine, always responsible, was far too willing to accept blame for her shortcomings, imagined or real.

'Sweetheart, it's not your job to be your grandmother's guardian. Just pay attention when you do see her and we'll compare notes.'

Justine removed the pan from the stove top and poured the contents into a gravy boat just as the doorbell chimed. Seth, who'd been putting the finishing touches on the table, answered it.

Stan stood in the doorway, holding a bouquet of flowers and a bottle of wine. 'I'm not late, am I?' he asked as he breezed into the small house. 'Happy birthday, Olivia,' he said, kissing her on the cheek.

'Dad?' From Justine's blank look, Olivia could tell that Stan's visit was a surprise to her daughter, too.

'I thought I'd crash the birthday party. You don't mind, do you?' He smiled at Justine and Olivia.

'Of course not,' Justine said, recovering first. Seth quickly added another place setting.

'Hello, Stan.' Olivia's response was polite and cool. She hadn't talked to him since his less-than-subtle invitation to dinner in Seattle—dinner that included a night in a hotel room.

Justine took the flowers and arranged them artfully in a vase, which she set in the middle of the table. With Leif asleep, Olivia settled her grandson in his crib and joined everyone at the table.

Dinner—roast chicken and gravy, roasted root vegetables and salad—was wonderful, although Olivia felt slightly on edge. That passed, however, as the meal progressed. Perhaps the wine relaxed her. Whatever it was, she was soon laughing and joking with her family and it seemed...so natural. She could almost believe that she and Stan had never been divorced. Stan was his warm, ingratiating self. Funny, witty, clever in ways that Olivia had all but forgotten.

'So,' Stan said as Seth and Justine went into the kitchen to prepare coffee. 'Are you going to forgive me?'

Olivia saw no point in pretending she didn't know what he was talking about. 'There's nothing to forgive.'

He shrugged. 'I was a little too pushy, I think.'

'Your problem is that you need a woman who adores you.'

He chuckled and saluted her with his empty wineglass. 'You once did, and I'm hoping you will again. I adore you, you know.'

It flattered her to hear it, but Olivia was older and wiser these days. She'd once loved Stan with all of her being, but their marriage hadn't survived the loss of their son. The divorce had battered her emotionally, and it had taken her years to recover. Even now, she couldn't reflect on the summer of 1986 without sadness.

'I was wrong,' Stan said, lowering his voice. 'I want to make it up to you.'

Make it up to her? Olivia nearly laughed but held on to her composure. 'There are other women for you out there.'

'Don't tell me you're interested in that... that newspaper guy. Olivia, no! Anyone can see Griffin's all wrong for you.'

'I think I'm the best judge of that.'

Stan sat back in his chair and crossed his arms. Slowly he shook his head, intimating that he just couldn't imagine her with Jack. 'He's a loose cannon,' Stan muttered. 'You realize that, don't you?'

Olivia disagreed, but she had no intention of arguing with Stan over her relationship with another man. So she said nothing. Thankfully

Seth and Justine returned with the coffee and birthday cake, and the matter was dropped.

Later that evening, when she got home after a full day of celebrating, she discovered two messages on her machine. One was from James and Selina, his wife, who'd phoned with birthday greetings. The second message was from Jack.

Olivia returned his call first. He answered immediately, as though he'd been sitting by the phone waiting for her. It was a pleasant thought.

'Hi,' he said, and he sounded thrilled to hear from her. 'Where were you all day?'

'Out.'

'Yes, I know. I called six times and drove by once.'

'Jack!'

'I wanted to see you. I don't suppose it's proper etiquette to tell you that, but I did.... I still do.'

'It's too late now.'

'I know.' He groaned the words. 'Where *were* you?'

'If you must know, it's my birthday, and I was at dinner with Justine and Seth.'

'Your birthday! Damn, Olivia, I forgot. You'll forgive me, won't you?'

'As long as you don't ask me how old I am.'

He chuckled. 'Don't ask, don't tell?'

'You got it.'

'Anybody else there?' The question was a

blatant request regarding her ex-husband.

Olivia had the option of lying and avoiding any chance of another dragged-out misunderstanding. She hated to risk upsetting him just when they'd reconciled, but she couldn't, *wouldn't* deceive him. 'Yes,' she admitted reluctantly. 'Stan showed up. Unexpectedly.'

'Bearing gifts, no doubt?'

'A few.'

'Flowers?'

'Not as pretty as the ones you sent a while back.' Olivia had left Stan's bouquet with her daughter.

'Candy, too?'

'No candy.'

'Wine, then?'

'Wine,' she confirmed.

He growled something under his breath. 'You still want me to put on a pair of boxing gloves and fight him?'

Olivia smiled. 'I never wanted you to get into a fistfight,' she said. 'I just wanted you to prove you cared about me.'

'Okay,' he said. 'Should I call him or do you want to do it?'

'Call Stan?' Jack wasn't making any sense.

'I think we should duke it out, just the two of us. Man to man.'

'Jack Griffin, that's ridiculous! Tell me you're not serious.'

He paused, and she thought she could hear

144

him shadow-boxing in the background. He was definitely moving around.

'You could simply declare me the winner,' Jack suggested hopefully.

'I could,' she agreed, 'but first you'd have to win my favor.'

Jack groaned again. 'And exactly how am I supposed to do *that?*'

'You don't know?' She feigned surprise.

'Apparently not, but I'll study on it.'

'You do that.' Olivia gave a full-throated laugh. 'I have a feeling you'll find a way.'

Oh, yes, it was good to have him back in her life.

Ten

Maryellen was going back to work. She dropped her ten-week-old daughter off at her sister's on Monday morning, the last week of October. She'd resumed a nine-to-five schedule at the gallery.

'She'll be fine,' Kelly assured her, as Maryellen lingered anxiously at the front door.

'You'll phone if there's a problem?' Leaving her daughter was harder than Maryellen had dreamed possible. It was difficult enough to let Jon take Katie for his regular visitation. She'd assumed that leaving Katie with her own sister would be easier than this. Tears filled her eyes at the prospect of being away from her baby for more than eight hours a day.

'Every new mother goes through this,' Kelly assured her. 'It's hard leaving our babies, even when we know they're getting the best care in the world.'

'She usually needs to be fed around ten,' Maryellen said, although she'd gone over Katie's schedule twice already. She'd expressed the milk earlier and had filled several bottles.

'I know, I know. Now, get out of here before you're late for work.'

Her sister was right, but still Maryellen hovered there in the doorway. Then, before she could change her mind about the whole thing, she turned and hurried to her car. Within a few days, dropping the baby off would become part of her daily routine. She'd considered bringing Katie to the gallery with her, but an infant would be distracting. While not openly forbidding it, the owners had been discouraging.

She hated being away from her baby for a large part of every day, hated the sick sensation it left in the pit of her stomach. Doubts haunted her, fears that she was a bad mother. She couldn't help feeling that while Kelly was Katie's aunt, she couldn't possibly love her as much as Maryellen did. Despite her regrets, she knew this was necessary, and she had to face these demons sooner or later.

By ten that morning, Maryellen had phoned her sister no less than three times. Katie had slept for most of the morning, just as she normally did. During her last phone call, Kelly had told her she was warming Katie's bottle and would be feeding her right on schedule. Maryellen trusted her sister, but she worried that Kelly might not hold the baby the same way Maryellen did. Worried that the strange environment might disrupt her routine. Worried that Katie would intuitively know she wasn't in her own home, her own bed.

The bell chimed above the gallery door just as Maryellen replaced the receiver. Taking a moment to calm her pounding heart, she made an effort to look friendly and professional. As she stepped into the gallery's main room to meet her first customer of the day, she managed to smile.

Her business facade crumbled the instant she saw it was Jon. She was so pleased to see him, so glad to have someone to talk to about Katie.

He took one look at her and frowned. 'I thought so.'

'Thought what?' Her hackles immediately rose. Her pleasure at seeing him vanished. The last thing she needed was a lecture.

'I figured I should check up on you your first day back to work. It was hard to leave Katie, wasn't it?'

She wanted to pretend he'd completely

misread her, but she wasn't sure she could pull it off. She found it increasingly difficult to disguise her feelings from Jon. Before Katie, she'd been adept at fooling her mother and sister about her thoughts and emotions. But Jon had the innate ability to see straight through her.

'It was awful,' she admitted.

'Did she put up a fuss?'

Maryellen shook her head, and to her horror, tears sprang to her eyes. This was mortifying.

With his hand at her elbow, Jon led her to the back room. Turning her so she faced him, he placed his hands on her shoulders. 'Katie will be perfectly fine with your sister.'

Maryellen nodded. 'It's just that I hate not being with her.'

Jon expelled a sigh, and slowly, as if against his will, he drew Maryellen into his embrace. 'I know...'

'How can you possibly know?' she challenged, needing his comfort and yet resenting the fact that she did. She closed her eyes and welcomed the feel of his arms, savored his warmth, his masculine scent. She didn't want him to realize how weak his nearness made her. The only way she could combat these feelings was to react defensively.

'I know, Maryellen,' he said evenly, 'because every week I have to leave my daughter with you and then walk away.'

'Oh.' It couldn't *possibly* be this hard on him, she reasoned. He couldn't suffer the same regrets and doubts she did. Could he?

'I...I must be a terrible mother.' Being this close to Jon was intoxicating; there was no other word for it. She needed to escape that intoxication, to ease away from him, and she needed to do it now.

This emotional hold was exactly what she'd been afraid of ever since the day they'd kissed. He made it far too easy to rely on him. If she didn't break away now, he'd become a permanent part of her life. And that was something she couldn't risk. That wasn't part of the deal. He was Katie's father—not Maryellen's husband.

'You're not a bad mother, you're just a new mother,' Jon told her confidently. 'You have a lot to learn. We both do.' He stroked her hair with such tenderness that she could hardly move out of his arms.

With a wrenching effort, she put some distance between them. Crossing her arms, she leaned her hip against the desk. 'I'll be fine now.'

'You sure?'

Not making eye contact, she gave a slight nod. 'I...it's just the first day. It's bound to be the most difficult.'

'That's what the books say.'

She managed a weak smile. 'It was... thoughtful of you to stop by.'

Jon slipped his hands in his pockets. He did that, she'd noticed, whenever he was unsure of himself. She sensed that he didn't want to be here and at the same time couldn't stay away. She understood perfectly. She'd prefer to keep Jon out of her life—she couldn't keep him out of Katie's—but he was there. And wonderful. The day Katie was born, they'd formed a bond, as parents and as friends, and neither of them knew how to deal with emotions beyond that. Kissing him a few weeks ago had only complicated matters.

'You're on your way to work?' she asked, eager now for him to go.

Jon took the hint. 'Yeah. I should be off.'

They both seemed to relax at that. 'Well, thank you for coming.'

He headed for the door, then abruptly, without warning, turned back. He grasped her by the shoulders and kissed her. A brief, urgent kiss.

The bell chimed as he walked out. Something had to be done and quickly. Jon was becoming far too important to her.

*   *   *

Wednesday night, both Allison and Eddie were in their bedrooms doing homework, or so Rosie assumed. There was nothing she could stand to watch on television, so she threw a load of wash in the machine. She

150

preferred to do her laundry at the house. The washer in the apartment was at least twenty years old and had already ruined one good blouse. With money so tight, she didn't want to risk destroying any more of her limited professional wardrobe.

The phone rang, but Rosie knew better than to answer it. Allison considered it her right to grab all calls. Not only that, she couldn't let the phone go unanswered, as Rosie was often inclined to do these days, especially in the evenings.

Five seconds after the first ring, her daughter stuck her head out the bedroom door. 'It's for you,' she said in an incredulous tone. 'It's Dad.'

Wonderful! Rosie could only imagine what Zach had to complain about *this* time.

'Don't be long,' Allison said tartly. 'I'm expecting a call.'

This was a less-than-subtle reminder that the eccentric judge who'd set up this joint custody arrangement had more or less awarded the house to Allison and Eddie. So the phone belonged to the children—or that was the way Allison seemed to look at it.

'I can't imagine we'll talk long,' Rosie assured her.

Allison closed her bedroom door without comment.

Rosie took the call in the kitchen, thinking this was the room where they were least likely to be overheard. She took a deep breath before lifting the receiver. 'Hello,' she said cheerfully. She wanted to give the impression that she'd been having the time of her life and his call was an interruption.

'It's Zach,' he said stiffly. 'I thought you'd want to know your boyfriend phoned.'

Her boyfriend? It was news to Rosie that she even *had* a boyfriend. Oh, he must mean Bruce. Good grief, she'd only seen him that one night. One date was all it'd taken for both of them to realize that the only thing they had in common was loss. They were friendly, and they chatted now and then, but that was it.

'I thought you should know,' he said again.

'I'm sorry if the call disturbed you,' Rosie said, forcing a light tone into her voice. 'I'm sure he forgot which nights I'm at the house.' She purposely allowed Zach to think she was seeing Bruce a lot.

'Does he phone often?' Zach demanded, then paused. 'Never mind, I don't have any right to ask that.'

'No, you don't.' It felt good to tell him that. 'Thanks for letting me know. I'll get back to Bruce right away.'

'Before we hang up, can we talk,' he asked, 'just for a moment?'

'Okay, but I promised Allison I wouldn't tie up the phone. She's expecting a call.'

'She's always expecting a call,' Zach muttered. 'Speaking of Allison, how are the two of you getting along these days?'

'Really well. Why?' As long as Rosie stayed in one part of the house and Allison in another, they could cope, but there was no need to tell Zach that.

'She's got nothing but attitude with me,' he confessed reluctantly.

Rosie realized this must be hard on him. Zach and Allison had always been close. 'I'm sorry to hear that.'

'What time are you getting home from work these days?' he asked.

'Same as always—around five, sometimes five-thirty. Depends on where I'm subbing. What makes you ask?'

'Allison is home when? Two-thirty?'

'Around then.' Their daughter's interest in after-school activities had ceased following the divorce. She'd recently dropped out of volleyball, a sport she'd once loved. Allison had decided against trying out for drama club, too. That disappointed Rosie, who believed Allison had a real flair for it, but no amount of discussion could persuade her daughter to reconsider.

'I think Allison's got too much time on her hands.'

'I agree.' Rosie abandoned all pretense. She was desperately worried about her daughter and particularly about whatever might be happening with the boyfriend. Thankfully, there'd been no sign of Ryan's presence in

153

the house during the past two weeks, but that didn't mean he hadn't been there. Since Eddie's school wasn't dismissed until almost four, Allison had ample opportunity to see Ryan without anyone knowing where she was or with whom. The thought terrified Rosie.

'What should we do?' she asked Zach.

'Any suggestions?'

'None,' she admitted.

'Me, neither.'

'I guess we need to talk more about this,' Rosie said. 'Figure something out.'

Zach agreed. 'Listen,' he said next. 'Do you and this Bruce guy get along?'

She was about to remind him that her dating life was none of his concern, but changed her mind. 'We get along all right.'

'What do the kids think of him?'

'I haven't introduced him yet.' She had no intention of doing so, since it was unlikely she'd go out with him a second time.

'Oh.' Zach exhaled slowly. 'Rosie, I want you to know I wish you and Bruce well. I sincerely mean that.'

Rosie felt like weeping and she struggled to hang on to her pride. 'Thank you,' she murmured. 'If Janice makes you happy, then that's what I want for you, too.'

They were silent for half a minute or so.

'My most important job now is to be a good father to my children,' Zach said.

'The children are what's most important to

me, too,' she told him, but as she replaced the receiver, Rosie wondered if her failure as a wife and mother was what had gotten her into this predicament in the first place.

*   *   *

Pastor Dave Flemming planned to get in one last round of golf before the November rains arrived. Monday was his traditional day off, and he was prepared to take full advantage of the last bit of autumn sunshine. He stepped onto the lush green course at McDougal Woods and, to his surprise, saw Bob Beldon. Bob and his wife, Peggy, had recently started attending Cedar Cove Methodist. Peggy taught a Sunday school class and Bob had agreed to coach the youth basketball team. Dave liked Bob, and Peggy was one of the best cooks he'd ever had the privilege of knowing. The last church social, she'd brought a peach cobbler that had been the talk of the evening.

'Are you looking for a partner?' Bob asked.

'Sure,' Dave said affably; he welcomed the company.

They teed off at the first hole, then jumped into the cart. 'Actually, we didn't meet by accident this afternoon,' Bob admitted. 'I called the church, and your secretary told me you were going to be here.'

Without a pause Dave reached for his five iron. 'Something on your mind?'

'You could say that.'

Staring at the other man, Dave saw that he was pale, with dark shadows under his eyes. Bob had aged perceptibly in the last little while.

'I was hoping you might be able to give me some advice.'

'I will if I can.'

Bob's next shot was a slice that went into the trees. He muttered under his breath. 'I'm not much good at this.'

Dave was sympathetic. He had a wicked slice of his own, but he didn't comment, giving Bob the room he needed to speak his mind.

It wasn't until the fourth hole that Bob said anything more. 'I've had this recurring nightmare for thirty years—ever since I got back from Nam.'

Dave stood by the golf cart. 'Is that what you'd like to discuss?'

Bob nodded and leaned heavily against the cart. 'The event in the dream actually happened...I feel all the horror and panic, the numbing fear. I hear it and see it in graphic detail. I...live it all over again.'

He climbed into the golf cart and closed his eyes. 'After Nam, I took to the bottle to forget.' His voice was so low it was all Dave could do to make out the words.

'You started drinking?' he clarified.

Bob nodded, opening his eyes. 'After my tour of duty, I came back to Peggy. It didn't take me long to nearly destroy my marriage and my life by hiding behind an alcoholic haze. For a few years I could forget, but soon even the alcohol didn't help. That was when I went to AA. It's the only reason I'm sober today.'

Dave was growing concerned. If possible, Bob had gone even paler. 'What can I do?' he asked.

'As part of the Twelve Steps of Alcoholics Anonymous, we're asked to make amends whenever possible. I can't undo what happened that day in the jungle. Peggy's the only one who knows all the details, the only one I've ever told. Dan might've said something to Grace before he—'

'Dan Sherman?'

Bob nodded again. 'We enlisted for Nam after high school as part of the buddy plan and went all the way through together.'

'So Dan Sherman was with you in the jungle?'

'Yeah.' Bob drew one hand along his face. 'I suspect it's the reason he shot himself. God knows I was tempted to do it myself, especially in the early days when I was drinking hard. From what I understand, a lot of men have taken that way out. Truth be known, I can understand it.'

'I didn't realize you and Dan were such good friends.'

'Ever since then, we haven't been. After the war, Peggy and I moved around a lot. I worked

157

as a plumber on big construction sites. We've only been back in Cedar Cove for the last six years.' Bob leaned forward and his arms circled the steering wheel. He stared into the distance. 'I don't mean to burden you with this, but I think I might be in some kind of trouble here.'

'It's not a burden,' Dave assured him. 'Just tell me how I can help.'

Bob's hands tightened around the steering wheel. 'I need to know what I should do.'

'About what happened in the war?'

'Yes…and Dan.'

'There's nothing we can do for Dan at this point.' Perhaps Bob was thinking he should somehow help Grace, but Dave doubted that.

Bob shook his head. 'I know, I know…'

There was something Bob wasn't telling him, something he was holding back. Dave decided not to pry. Bob would tell him when he was ready.

'Did I mention that sometimes, when I have this nightmare, I've gotten out of bed and walked around the house? A couple of years ago, Peggy found me getting ready to go outside. I was still in my pajamas and I was clutching the car keys—completely and totally asleep.'

Dave nodded, hoping his lack of comment would encourage Bob to continue. A lot of this didn't add up, beginning with his talk about the dream, although that was obviously tied to whatever had happened in Nam.

Bob buried his face in his hands. 'I hit Peggy when she tried to stop me from leaving the house. I swear to God I didn't know what I was doing.'

'I'm sure that's true,' Dave said, responding to his friend's distress. 'In a sleepwalking state, you're not conscious of your actions.'

After a lengthy pause, Bob lowered his voice and whispered, 'I had the nightmare the night of that big storm, when the John Doe arrived.' His jaw was clenched tight and Dave noticed a muscle spasm.

'Did you sleepwalk?'

Bob's face twisted in torment. 'I don't know. Peggy doesn't think so, but we were both tired and she can't be sure. I can't, either.'

The confusion was starting to clear. 'Do you think you might've had something to do with that unfortunate man's death?'

Bob was silent for so long that Dave wondered if he'd heard him. 'Bob?'

'I don't know,' he answered after a moment. 'It doesn't seem likely, but...' He let the rest fade.

'Have the police questioned you?'

'They did in the beginning and one time shortly after. But I think they might want to talk to me again.'

Dave didn't ask how he'd come by that information. 'You're concerned about what they might learn?'

'I have no idea what happened that night. But it's more than not knowing. It's Dan's suicide—and the fact that the stranger seemed...familiar.'

'Familiar? How do you mean?'

Bob turned his head and stared at the fairway. 'I can't help feeling that I knew him. I've gone over it again and again in my mind, but I can't put a name with his face.'

'Have you mentioned this to Roy McAfee?' Dave asked.

Bob turned back and met his gaze. Dave could tell Bob was surprised by the suggestion.

'You think I should talk to Roy? Why would I do that?'

'Roy's an ex-cop,' Dave said. 'He'd be able to advise you a whole lot better than I can about what the police might be looking for. If you are somehow involved in this death, Roy can tell you about your rights and suggest an attorney.'

Bob's shoulders relaxed visibly. 'You really think he could help me?'

'I do,' Dave said. He slid into the golf cart next to his friend. 'But we can both do something else that will help.'

'What's that?' Bob asked.

'We can pray.'

Eleven

Grace Sherman's step was lighter than it had been in nearly two years. She pushed her grocery cart down the store aisle and sashayed a bit to the piped-in music: a golden oldie from The Mamas and the Papas.

It wasn't the music, however, that had put her in such a good mood. It was Will Jefferson, Olivia's older brother. Tall, good-looking, successful—a nuclear engineer—and just... nice. He'd recently been in Cedar Cove during Charlotte's bout with cancer, and Grace and Will had renewed their friendship then.

When Will had written her shortly after Dan's funeral, he'd added his e-mail address. At first they'd left short messages for each other once a day, but lately that had changed. Now they chatted online far longer and far more often. The night before, they'd spent almost an hour on the computer with instant messaging.

Their 'talking' had started out innocently enough. Cliff Harding had agreed to a suspension of their relationship. Once she'd learned about Dan's suicide, she'd asked for time to deal with the complex emotions surrounding it. She hadn't made a decision about his letter yet, but was inclined to leave it alone. No good could come of disrupting lives

161

now. His secret was safe with her. Cliff phoned once or twice a week; he let her know when he was going out of town, and while she was always glad to hear from him, his phone calls didn't excite her nearly as much as her online chats with Will.

She knew it was absurd to think their daily communications meant anything. Will was married—although Grace suspected he wasn't happy. Of course, he was too much of a gentleman to say anything negative about his wife, but Grace read between the lines. Olivia had mentioned Will and Georgia's marriage only a few months ago. She'd implied that there might be problems between her brother and his wife. And it did seem that if Will had this much time to spend on the computer every night, something must be lacking in his marriage.

They were friends, Grace told herself, nothing more. Friends becoming reacquainted. That was all. Still, she'd admit that 'talking' to Will had become downright addictive.

Most nights she rushed home from work and hurried to log on to the computer because she knew he'd be waiting for her. With the three-hour time difference, he'd already had dinner and was as eager to exchange messages with her as she was with him.

Grace hadn't told anyone about these daily 'chats' with Will. Her daughters wouldn't understand. They didn't know him and might put the wrong connotation on their friendship. Kelly and Maryellen worried about her, and they'd certainly disapprove of her having an online relationship, especially since Will was married. She thought about mentioning her 'Internet friend' in a casual way, then changed her mind.

Nor had Grace said anything to Olivia. It wasn't that she was hiding the truth from her best friend. It was more—well, Grace couldn't really explain *why* she hadn't said anything to Olivia. Probably because she suspected Olivia wouldn't approve, any more than her own daughters would. Grace enjoyed talking to Will so much that she didn't want to feel guilty about this one small pleasure. He seemed to enjoy chatting with her, too.

There was one other person Grace felt bad about not telling—Cliff Harding. She liked Cliff and owed him far more than she could ever repay. He'd been patient and kind during the long months after Dan's disappearance. He'd entered her life at the bleakest hour and lent her strength and emotional support when she'd needed it most.

When Cliff's marriage had fallen apart some years ago, he'd taken early retirement from Boeing and purchased acreage in the Olalla Valley, a few miles south of Cedar Cove. He'd been breeding horses and was beginning to make a name for himself. This was an occupation Grace knew nothing about, but Cliff was completely absorbed in what had once been a hobby.

Hurrying the cart down the aisle, Grace collected the remaining groceries she needed, went through the checkout and drove home. The instant she was in the door, she turned on her computer and raced around putting the perishables in the refrigerator while she waited to log on to the Internet. Buttercup followed her, and at one point Grace nearly tripped over the dog. She stopped long enough to scold her, then dumped some kibble in the golden retriever's bowl and continued with her task.

The phone rang. Balancing a quart of milk in one hand and a carton of eggs in the other, she awkwardly reached for the receiver.

'Hello,' she said, using her shoulder to press the phone to her ear. She opened the refrigerator door and thrust both items inside.

'You're home,' Cliff said.

'That's stating the obvious,' she teased. They hadn't spoken for a couple of weeks. He'd gone to California and must have returned sometime in the last few days.

'Don't you ever check your phone messages?'

'No, sorry. I haven't yet.' She'd been in such a rush that it hadn't even occurred to her. 'You've been trying to reach me?'

'For three days now, ever since I got home. I was tempted to stop at the library. I would have, if I could've squeezed an extra moment into the day.'

'I've been busy, too.'

'On the Internet again?'

'Yes,' she said, and quashed a pang of guilt. 'It's all your fault, you know.' Grace had Paul and Kelly's old computer, which Cliff had set up for her.

'You could always e-mail me,' she suggested.

Cliff groaned. 'I've created a monster.' He sounded good-natured about it, though.

'Like I said, this monster is one of your own making.'

'Don't remind me,' he muttered, chuckling. 'Say, have you got plans for Thanksgiving?'

'Uh…' It was only a few weeks away, but she hadn't given the holiday a thought. Last year she'd spent Thanksgiving with Maryellen and the two of them had been miserable. It had been her first without Dan. 'Why do you ask?'

'I want you to join me.'

'But I thought you went to your daughter's in Maryland for Thanksgiving.'

'I do,' he confirmed. 'This year I want you with me.'

Grace couldn't afford such a trip, but she hated admitting it. Since Dan's disappearance, she'd had no money for luxuries or unnecessary expenditures. And because his death was a suicide, she hadn't been able to collect any life insurance benefits.

It was as if Cliff had read her thoughts. 'Before you object, I'm buying your ticket.'

'I can't let you do that,' she protested.

'You can and you will,' he insisted sternly. 'I'm serious, Grace. It's time you met my daughter and she met you. Now, before you argue, I know you asked for a few months to deal with everything and I've given it to you, but I do want you to meet Lisa.'

'Oh, Cliff…'

'I have everything worked out, so don't argue with me. You'll sleep in the guest room and I'll bunk down on the sleeper sofa in the family room. It'll do you good to get away.'

Grace hadn't been on a plane in years. There just weren't the funds for vacations or traveling, even during the best of times. She'd last flown five years earlier to a library conference in San Antonio, Texas, and she'd loved every minute of her adventure.

'I'll need to talk to the girls,' she murmured, wondering whether she should accept Cliff's invitation or not.

'Do that and get back to me.'

'All right.' Still, she hesitated. 'You're sure about this, Cliff?'

'Very sure. You're important to me.'

'You're important to me, too,' she echoed. 'I want you to know how much I appreciate your patience with me.'

'You will come and meet Lisa, won't you?'

'I really would love to,' she said, not

bothering to hide the excitement in her voice. Grace had never spent the holiday away from her daughters. Maryellen and Kelly routinely checked up on her, despite her constant reassurances, but after all these months of living by herself, Grace had grown accustomed to her own company. Maybe, if she took this trip, her daughters would finally stop worrying and begin to acknowledge her independence.

Her only other consideration was Cliff. She shouldn't lead him on like this, but the trip sounded so good and she was so eager to get out of Cedar Cove for a few days. Of course, it meant she wouldn't be able to talk to Will online, but he was bound to be busy with the holiday, too. Besides, didn't absence make the heart grow fonder?

*   *   *

A cold chill went down Zach's spine as he read Janice Lamond's letter of resignation, which had been waiting on his desk when he arrived for work that morning. Hardly able to believe what he was reading, he went over the details a second time.

Janice was quitting. Feeling slightly sick, he sank into his high-back leather chair. So *this* was the appreciation he got for training her as his personal assistant. This was the thanks he got for being her mentor, for showing her the ropes and giving her advantage after advantage.

Janice had been invaluable to him in the early days of his separation from Rosie. She'd soothed his ego and offered him advice and encouragement.

Rosie had come up with this crazy idea that he was romantically involved with his assistant. That was utter nonsense, but there was no convincing her otherwise. For no better reason than her own jealousy, his ex-wife had insisted Zach fire the woman who'd become his right hand at the office. Zach had refused, as any reasonable man would. Rosie had flown into a temper, and shortly after that he'd moved out of the house.

In a telephone conversation a little while ago, Rosie had said she wished him and Janice well. He'd let the comment slide. If he hadn't been able to convince Rosie of his innocence before the divorce, he didn't think there was much chance now. So he'd kept silent.

Recently, though, Zach had seen his assistant with fresh eyes. He disapproved of the length of her skirts and had casually mentioned the way she dressed, as part of his latest employee review. He'd assumed she'd appreciate his continued support, as well as his advice. Perhaps he'd overstepped his bounds. He'd never mention something as personal as dress or makeup to any other employee, but he'd thought he could with Janice. They were friends, weren't they? And she'd certainly been pretty free with *her* advice when it came to his situation.

At the time she'd listened quietly to his comments. He'd been pleased by her willingness to accept constructive criticism.

Now this.

He waited for his irritation to subside and then called her into his office. A moment later, she walked in, avoiding eye contact.

'I have your letter here,' he said, figuring she'd offer an explanation.

Janice refused to raise her eyes to his.

'I didn't realize you were unhappy with your position,' he said, hoping to reason with her. In his opinion, it would be a mistake for her to quit at this point.

'I *have* been happy,' Janice admitted. She sounded a little embarrassed. 'That is, until recently.'

'Is this your way of asking for a raise?' Zach asked. No need to beat around the bush. Considering the time and cost that went into training a new employee, it was far better to retain the current employee and pay higher wages. He was willing to offer her a raise if she agreed to reconsider her resignation, but he did want it understood that he disapproved of her methods.

'I'm not looking for a pay increase,' she said, and shook her head adamantly. 'I already have another job.'

If Zach had been irritated earlier, he was

downright angry now. 'I see,' he said, working hard at concealing his reaction. Of all the ungrateful employees he'd hired over the years, this one took the prize. 'In that case, I wish you continued success.'

'I thought it best that I leave the company,' Janice said, raising her head now to boldly meet his gaze.

The anger flashing in her eyes caught him completely by surprise. Why *she* had any reason to be upset was beyond him. Zach had seen to it that she'd been well compensated for her skills. She'd advanced quickly, with routine pay hikes. In fact, there'd been some dissension in the office when Janice was given a promotion over other employees who'd been with the firm longer.

'Best that you resign?' Zach repeated.

'Yes,' she said, tilting her chin in a gesture of defiance. 'I found it highly unprofessional of you to suggest that my skirts are too short and that I wear too much makeup.'

Zach opened and closed his mouth.

'I apologize, Janice. I can see that my comments were...not well received. You're right—they were probably out of line.'

'Frankly, I think you have a lot of nerve.' She paused. 'I thought...I hoped you'd understand.'

Zach frowned. He didn't know what on earth she was talking about.

'I hoped that you and I, the two of us,' she

faltered, 'might one day be more than just employee and employer. I thought we were friends, but I also wanted you to notice me—as a woman.' She gestured down at her skirt, her high-heeled shoes. 'I can see that isn't going to happen.'

So Rosie had been right all along; Janice had been on the make. How could he have been so stupid? The signs had been there from the beginning. He tightened his jaw. 'That will be all. I'll see that your final check is drawn up immediately.'

'You're letting me go…now?'

'Two weeks' paid leave should be adequate compensation,' he said stiffly.

Without another word, Janice turned and walked out of his office. Zach was so angry he was shaking by the time she was gone. He hadn't fully recovered when his phone line buzzed.

'Yes,' he snapped.

'Line one,' Janice said. 'It's the high school.'

Zach pushed down the button and reached for the receiver. If the high school was calling, he could bet it wasn't about contributing to the latest fund-raiser.

'This is Zachary Cox,' he said in his most professional voice.

'Mr. Cox, this is LeAnn Duncan from Cedar Cove High School verifying that Allison is home sick today.'

Zach stared up at the ceiling and held

back a groan of frustration. 'No, I dropped her off myself.' It hadn't been an especially good morning. Allison had gotten up late and missed the bus and then she'd given him grief when he'd insisted on driving her to school on his way to the office.

It used to be that she sought out reasons for Zach to drop her off. They'd chat and he'd tease her about her outrageous music and she'd call him a geek. Her teasing didn't offend him because those were good times with his daughter. Now he barely recognized the girl she'd become.

For the second time that morning, a sick feeling came over him. 'I don't know where she'd be,' he said before the school secretary could ask the next obvious question. But by heaven, he'd find her. And when he did, Zach would see to it that she never pulled this kind of stunt again.

'That's your concern, Mr. Cox, not ours.'

He knew that, but he was already flustered by Janice's resignation. Now his daughter had made it her personal mission to screw up the rest of his day.

'What are the consequences of her skipping classes?' he asked.

'Is this her first offense?' Mrs. Duncan asked. She paused and seemed to be scanning a chart or a computer screen. 'Ah, I see here that it is. Has there been any upheaval in the family lately, Mr. Cox?'

172

'My wife and I were recently divorced.'

'That will do it. Well, I hope you can get the situation with Allison squared away.'

'Will she have any detentions?'

'Not for the first offense. She'll need to attend Saturday school if it happens again.'

It wouldn't; Zach would make sure of that.

'A third time means automatic suspension.'

'There won't be a second *or* a third time,' Zach assured her.

'I'm sorry, Mr. Cox.'

'So am I,' he muttered as he replaced the receiver. He didn't remove his hand and automatically dialed South Ridge Elementary, where Rosie was currently teaching fifth grade. She'd just been hired on to the permanent staff, which was both a blessing and a curse. It meant longer hours and more preparation time. He knew from Eddie's comments that Rosie was often exhausted at the end of the day.

'This is Zachary Cox. Would it be possible to speak to my wife?' he asked the school secretary, not remembering until after he'd spoken that he was no longer married to Rosie. 'It's important.'

'Please hold.'

He must have waited five minutes before Rosie picked up the extension. 'Zach,' she said, alarm in her voice. 'What is it?'

'Allison skipped school.'

'What?' Rosie was as shocked as he was.

'Today?'

'That's right. She conveniently missed the bus, but I insisted on dropping her off. I should've known something was up, because she wasn't happy with my offer to chauffeur her.'

'Where is she?'

'I don't have a clue.' His initial reaction had been anger, but now he was alarmed. Allison was fifteen years old. His mind whirled with countless possibilities, none of them pleasant.

'I'll meet you at the house as soon as I can.'

'You can leave the school?'

'I can if it's a family emergency, and if this doesn't qualify, I don't know what does.'

Zach got to the house ten minutes before Rosie did. Zach watched her pull into the driveway; the car jerked forward as she stepped hard on the brakes. The driver's door was open before the engine was completely dead.

'We need to call Hannah's mother,' she said as she rushed past him and into the house.

Zach hated letting Rosie see what a mess the house was. After all the complaints he'd made about her housekeeping skills, the state of the living room was embarrassing. Thankfully she barely noticed as she ran into the kitchen and opened the drawer below the telephone, which was mounted on the wall.

She rummaged through the drawer until she found the address book. Then she squared her shoulders and lifted the receiver from its cradle.

The transformation was truly amazing. As soon as the other woman—presumably Hannah's mother—answered the phone, it seemed Rosie didn't have a care in the world.

'Hello, Jane...yes, I know it's been ages. Good to hear your voice, too.'

Rosie caught Zach's gaze and rolled her eyes. He smiled for the first time that day. Grabbing a kitchen chair, he straddled it as Rosie did her investigative work.

'I understand Hannah and Allison are in the same algebra class. Yes, she's doing really well. She has her father's head for numbers. I think she'll probably be put in the advanced class next tri.'

If that was true, it was news to Zach. The last school papers he'd found—by accident, when Allison had left them on the kitchen table—gave every indication that she was close to flunking out of math class.

'I heard Hannah went to Homecoming with J. T. Manners. Isn't he a friend of Ryan Wilson's?'

Zach watched as Rosie made a few murmurs of agreement. Her eyes narrowed and she reached for a pencil and hurriedly wrote something down. Zach stood and looked over her shoulder. In an instant his anger flared back to life. Rosie had written: She took the ferry to Seattle.

The very thought of his daughter wandering around downtown Seattle by herself was enough to make the hair on the back of his neck stand up. A second or two later, he realized Allison probably *wasn't* alone. That no-good biker-wannabe boyfriend was most likely with her.

After a few more minutes, Rosie replaced the receiver.

'How do you know she's in Seattle?' he demanded.

'Jane sings like a canary the minute she knows she has an audience. She knew and was dying to tell me.'

'Hannah isn't with her?'

'Who knows.' Rosie was angry, too. She started suddenly for the front door.

'Where are you going?' Zach asked.

'To move my car. I want the two of us to be waiting here when she comes sneaking back.'

Zach liked the idea of lying in wait for Allison. It was the best way he could think of to prove to his rebellious daughter that she wasn't going to outsmart him.

A few minutes later, a breathless Rosie returned. She took the chair across from him and exhaled slowly. They sat in the kitchen without speaking for five minutes. Ten... The silence felt strange and awkward, as though each was afraid of bringing up the subject of their difficult daughter. Zach knew he was. If they started talking, he might have to admit the role he'd played in this mess.

Furthermore, Zach wasn't sure what to say, especially after his enlightening conversation with Janice that morning. Apparently Rosie didn't either. When he thought he couldn't sit still a moment longer, Zach stood and began straightening up the living room. Rosie tackled the kitchen, which was in even worse shape. Once he'd finished vacuuming, he moved into the kitchen. They worked side by side for an hour.

'You hungry?' Rosie asked.

Zach hadn't thought about it, but now that she asked, he realized he was. 'A little.'

'How about a ham sandwich?'

He shrugged.

'Do you want a slice of pineapple to go with it?'

'And cream cheese?' he asked hopefully. When they'd first started dating Rosie had invented the sandwich and it was his all-time favorite. He couldn't remember when he'd last had one.

As Rosie put the sandwiches on plates, he got cold sodas from the refrigerator, and they sat down across from each other again. Searching for possible topics of conversation, Zach almost mentioned that Janice had handed in her notice. He bit his tongue before he could make such a foolish mistake. Rosie would certainly gloat over that information. She was apparently dating this widower now, and the relationship must be going well. She might be stressed and tired, but he'd never seen her look better. He glanced away before she caught him staring at her.

They heard the front door open, followed by the sound of teenage laughter.

Zach and Rosie were instantly on their feet. They hurried into the living room and discovered Allison, another girl Zach didn't recognize—possibly Hannah—and Allison's so-called boyfriend. The three teens froze when they saw Zach and Rosie.

'What do you want?' Allison demanded, glaring defiantly back at them.

'I think it would be best if your friends left now,' Zach said.

'They can stay if they want.'

'I don't think so.' If she was looking for a standoff in their battle of wills, Zach figured he had the advantage. He stalked over to the front door and opened it wide. 'Nice seeing you both, don't come back again unless invited.' He raised his eyebrows. 'Do I make myself clear?'

Ryan nodded and edged toward the front door as though he couldn't get away fast enough. The other girl looked unsure, then decided leaving was probably her best option.

'Where have you been?' Zach snapped.

Rosie stepped forward. 'Don't give her the opportunity to lie, Zach,' she said, sounding perfectly calm and reasonable. He, on the other hand, was furious and not afraid to show it.

'Why should I tell you?' Allison muttered. She crossed her arms and stared angrily at them both.

'You skipped school and took the ferry over to Seattle.'

That her mother knew was clearly a shock to Allison. The girl's lips curled as if she were about to ask where Rosie had uncovered that information, but she stopped herself before the question had formed.

'You're going to have to be smarter than this if you want to fool your parents,' Rosie said smoothly.

Zach was grateful that Rosie was the one doing the talking. In his present frame of mind, he was useless. The urge to take Allison by the shoulders and give her a good shake was almost overwhelming. He'd been worried sick. Apparently she didn't know what she'd put her parents through; furthermore she didn't care. That was the crux of the matter. She didn't give a damn, and he said as much before he could censor the words.

'That was a crazy, selfish stunt you pulled, and I'm here to tell you it won't be happening again.'

Allison's eyes flared with defiance. 'I hate you!' she shouted. 'I hate you both.'

'You can hate me all you want, but you'll respect the rules of this family.'

179

'This family,' she echoed. '*What* family? You destroyed our family.' She pointed at Zach and then Rosie. '*Both* of you destroyed our family. I hate you—I hate both of you for what you did.' Whirling around, she raced toward her bedroom and slammed the door with enough force to rattle the pictures on the wall. The eight-by-ten family portrait, taken two years previously, swung violently and then crashed to the floor. The glass shattered.

Silence ensued, and Zach collected his breath. 'Well,' he murmured, 'that's that.' He wasn't proud of the way he'd lost his composure. In fact, he didn't feel proud of much at the moment.

At least Rosie had been with him when he'd confronted Allison and they'd faced her united. She was much better at this sort of thing than he was. His ex-wife knew what to say. He didn't.

After a few minutes, Rosie gathered her purse and coat and started for the front door. She seemed reluctant to leave and he was equally unwilling to let her go.

'Thanks,' he said, walking with her. 'You handled the situation ten times better than I could have. I'm grateful you were here.'

She shrugged, dismissing his praise.

The irony didn't hit him until after Rosie was gone. It seemed that they got along a whole lot better since they were divorced than they had while they were married.

Twelve

Saturday morning a week before Thanksgiving, Maryellen woke with a mission. Her nails were a mess. She was badly in need of a manicure and polish, and felt eternally grateful that she'd managed to book an appointment with Rachel at Get Nailed. Because Jon's days off changed from week to week, Maryellen was never entirely sure when to schedule an appointment. As soon as she learned he'd be taking Katie on Saturday morning, she'd phoned the salon. Rachel could do her nails but didn't have a free slot to trim her hair.

Maryellen never seemed to have time for herself anymore. Being a single mother and holding down a job was much more demanding than she'd ever envisioned. It wasn't uncommon for Katie to wake up once and sometimes twice a night. If it hadn't been for Jon taking their daughter on random evenings, Maryellen wouldn't have slept through a single night in the entire three months since Katie's birth.

As soon as she'd showered and dressed, Maryellen headed for Get Nailed, her spirits high.

Rachel was finishing with her previous client when Maryellen entered the shop. Her nail

181

appointment had gone from once a week to whenever she could fit it in. This time it'd been three weeks since she'd last seen Rachel, but that couldn't be helped.

Maryellen loved the 'girls' at Get Nailed. They were witty and a little on the wacky side. A year earlier, they'd come up with the unusual idea of a Halloween party at which they introduced their discarded boyfriends to one another in the hope that someone else might find 'true love.' In the beginning it had actually sounded like a workable idea and several of the girls had hooked up with guys. Then catastrophe struck when certain behavioral problems exhibited earlier in the discarded boyfriends resurfaced. Maryellen still smiled when she thought about it. The disastrous party was long forgotten now.

Maryellen missed the special camaraderie she'd shared with the other women now that her visits were so infrequent.

'I need a hair appointment for next week,' she told Teri, who was handling the front desk. The shop was divided into two sections: hair and nails. Rachel was the only attendant who did both, and Maryellen preferred to stay with her.

'Rachel can do it next Thursday at five if that's okay for you,' Teri said, grabbing the pencil from behind her ear.

'I may have to bring Katie with me.' It all depended on whether Katie could stay with

Kelly for an extra hour or Jon could take their daughter. Not so long ago, she didn't need to consider such things, but these days Maryellen's world revolved around Katie— Katie's schedule, Katie's needs.

Teri sighed with regret. 'I'm sorry, but we have a 'no kids' policy.' She leaned over the glass counter and lowered her voice. 'So many young mothers were bringing toddlers to their appointments that we had to do something. It just isn't a safe environment for youngsters. I know Katie's an infant, but we had to draw the line. I hope this won't be a problem for you.' She wore an apologetic expression.

Maryellen understood. As a customer, she found it distracting to have small children constantly underfoot. She bit her lower lip. 'Is there anyone who could trim my hair this morning?' It would only take a few minutes to clip off the split ends.

'I just had a cancellation,' Teri said. She cocked her head to one side as she studied Maryellen with fresh eyes. 'You want it cut, right?'

'Trimmed,' she corrected. Maryellen had worn her hair in the same easy style for years. Her dark curls fell midway down her back. She'd recently begun wearing it tied at the base of her neck, free from Katie's exploring fingers.

Teri shook her head. 'Cut. You need a change.'

183

'I do?'

With one fist on her hip, Teri nodded. 'Short, I think. How long have you had it this length?'

Maryellen had lost count of the number of years.

'Too long,' Teri answered for her. 'Yup. It's time for a change.'

Maryellen was starting to see the possibilities. 'Perhaps you're right.'

Three hours later Maryellen emerged with freshly painted fingernails and her hair in a soft straight cut that framed her face. She barely recognized herself in the mirror, but she liked the change and hoped Jon would feel the same.

She stopped herself abruptly. It didn't matter what Jon thought. He was part of Katie's life, not hers, and she'd better remember that.

Even as she reminded herself of her own small role in Jon's world, her heart pounded with anticipation as she drove out to his house to pick up Katie. He was supposed to work that afternoon, and Maryellen had an errand to run in Tacoma, so it made sense to get Katie on her way.

This was one of those rare November days in the Pacific Northwest, when the sky's a clear, bright blue and the air is crisp and cold. Driving down the now-familiar gravel driveway to Jon's house, Maryellen noticed an eagle

184

overhead. With its huge wings extended, the magnificent bird soared on an updraft, as though it reigned from its lofty height.

As Maryellen pulled her vehicle to a stop, she saw Jon with Katie strapped to his back, looking toward the sky with a camera pointed at the eagle. Their daughter was awake and happy, waving her arms and making delighted sounds, obviously enjoying the out-of-doors.

Jon must have heard Maryellen approach, because he lowered his camera and turned to face her. For a long moment he didn't say anything as he stared at the drastic change in her appearance. Self-consciously, Maryellen lifted her hand to her hair.

'What do you think?' She wanted to kick herself for asking.

He walked closer, studying her, while she stood rooted to the spot.

He cleared his throat as if searching for something to say that wouldn't hurt her feelings. 'It…takes some getting used to.'

'You don't like it?' It shouldn't matter. *It didn't.* She'd cut her hair on a whim, for herself and no one else. Jon's opinion, no matter what it was, held no weight. And yet…it did. He clearly didn't like the change and Maryellen was crushed.

To cover her disappointment, she reached for Katie, who was bundled up in a thick fleece outfit. Her daughter kicked her legs ecstatically as Maryellen freed her from the carrier.

As soon as Maryellen held the infant in her arms, Jon raised the camera once more. 'Come on,' he urged, 'give me a smile.'

Maryellen tried, but she wasn't in the mood.

He took two or three pictures. 'Again,' he insisted.

Katie was certainly a willing subject. Smiling and gurgling, she flailed her arms about from the crook of Maryellen's arm.

'Oh, sure,' Jon said, briefly lowering the camera. '*Now* you're happy. Laugh away, young lady.'

Despite her mood, Maryellen grinned. 'Did Katie keep you up last night?'

'I don't think I got more than a few hours' sleep.' He rubbed his hand over his eyes. 'Katie was in a foul mood. Nothing satisfied her. I spent most of the night sitting in the rocking chair with her.'

'I think she might be teething.' Maryellen, too, had spent many nights dozing in an upright position. Needless to say, the next workday always ended up being hectic. In an odd way, it comforted her to know that Jon was experiencing the same troubles she did.

Out of habit, Maryellen raised her hand to flip her hair to one side, but it was too short now to toss off her shoulder.

Jon took picture after picture while she stood there.

'Come inside and I'll make us a cup

of coffee,' he said when he'd finished. She wondered if he'd abandoned his art photography in favor of snapping pictures of Katie. Pictures of their daughter were all she'd seen of his work lately. Of course, he was under contract with the Seattle gallery, and she didn't know whether he'd submitted anything in the last couple of months. She did know his work continued to sell well and she was pleased for him.

Jon paused when she didn't immediately follow him into the house for coffee. 'Do you have time?' he asked.

Since their bout of kissing, Maryellen had managed to avoid spending time alone with Jon. He hadn't pressured her or questioned her reasons. 'I…can't stay,' she said.

No argument came. It was almost as if he'd expected her to decline.

'I'll get Katie's things for you,' he said.

Unsure what prompted her, Maryellen walked inside with him. 'How's everything going at The Lighthouse?' she asked, making casual conversation. She found the success of Seth and Justine's restaurant particularly gratifying, knowing Jon was employed as head chef. People raved about his innovative dishes. He was a talented, complex man.

Jon gathered up Katie's favorite blanket and stuffed it into her diaper bag. He found a toy rattle, which he also stuck in the bag.

'I heard it's impossible to get a reservation

for the weekends.'

He shrugged, then looked up, his dark gaze probing hers. 'Do you need one?'

'No, no,' she said, not understanding the change in his mood.

'No Saturday-night date?' he pried.

Maryellen laughed. 'Hardly.'

'You didn't get your hair styled to impress me, now did you?'

'I did it for *me*, Jon.'

His muscles relaxed as he slipped the strap of the diaper bag over his shoulder and gave her a brief smile. She was sure, for a moment, that he wanted to kiss her. 'That's comforting to hear,' he muttered.

His concern—was it *jealousy?*—was so endearing, she had to resist touching him. In an effort to hide her attraction, she said, 'The girls at the nail shop said how wonderful the food at The Lighthouse is.' Teri had recently dined at the restaurant. Rachel, too.

'Thank them for me,' he said in an offhand manner, as if compliments embarrassed him.

'They asked me if I knew where you got your training. I don't believe you ever mentioned it.' Teri had, in fact, asked her that, and Maryellen took advantage of her friend's interest to ask a question she herself had wondered about.

'You're right, I didn't.' His response was blunt. Clearly he didn't welcome any further inquiries.

'But you must have been formally trained to—'

'I wasn't.' He glanced pointedly at his watch. 'I need to get ready for work.'

Maryellen was stunned. Every previous time she'd been to Jon's place, he'd practically thrown himself in front of her car to detain her. Now it seemed he couldn't get rid of her fast enough.

Absently Maryellen looped a strand of hair around her ear, forgetting once again that her curls were much shorter now than they'd been a few hours earlier. This reaction of Jon's was so confusing.

Silently he walked her to the car and handed her the diaper bag. 'Do you have your work schedule for next week?' she asked.

'Not yet.' He stood beside her vehicle while she strapped Katie into her carrier in the backseat.

When she straightened, she noticed that his attention appeared to be elsewhere. 'All right,' she said, 'then I'll wait to hear from you.'

He nodded.

She hesitated, sorry to end their time on such a negative note, but she was unsure what had gone wrong or why. 'Goodbye, and... thank you.'

He stepped back from her car and Maryellen got inside and slid the key into the ignition. As she pulled away, she looked in her rearview mirror. Jon was still standing there.

Thirteen

'Are we going to have a big turkey like Mom always cooked?' Eddie asked Thanksgiving morning.

Zach wasn't fully awake yet, and already his son was demanding answers to questions he could barely comprehend. 'Sure,' he said sleepily as he sat up in bed. He glanced at the clock-radio and saw that it was only eight. Sleeping in, apparently, was not an option.

'Don't you think you should put it in the oven now?' Eddie asked.

The turkey was supposed to be in the oven? This early? Then Zach remembered he'd already solved this issue at the local grocery store. The national chain offered fully cooked Thanksgiving dinners, complete with a thirteen-pound turkey, mashed potatoes, giblet gravy, plus dressing. As a bonus, they threw in a can of cranberry sauce and a pumpkin pie.

'Mom always had the turkey in the oven early in the morning, don't you remember?' Eddie was almost bouncing on Zach's bed.

Frankly Zach *didn't* remember. What he recalled was the tension during Thanksgiving dinner last year, when he'd been fighting with Rosie. They'd barely managed to get through the day without a major blowup. This year was different. This year it was Zach and the kids and no one else.

According to the terms of the divorce, Zach had been awarded all the major holidays, including Thanksgiving, but Rosie got Christmas Day. He could have Allison and Eddie Christmas Eve, but only until midnight. Heaven forbid if he stayed here one minute past. He remembered Rosie's anger as he'd disputed those terms and suspected she'd welcome the opportunity to drag him back into court. So much for peace and goodwill, he mused darkly. During the crisis precipitated by Allison's rebellious behavior, he and Rosie had been aligned in their views and actions, but things had quickly reverted to the earlier animosity.

'Is Allison up?' Zach asked.

Eddie frowned and shook his head. 'Do you want me to set the table for dinner?'

'Can we have breakfast first?' Zach mumbled, although he was beginning to share his son's enthusiasm.

'Do we have to?' Eddie whined. 'I want stuffing. It's my favorite part of the dinner.'

'Mine, too,' Zach confided. Rosie might have her faults as a cook, but she did make the most incredible dressing. His mouth started to water before he remembered that Rosie wouldn't be stuffing the bird this year. Albertson's would.

While Zach showered, shaved and dressed, Eddie watched the Macy's Thanksgiving Day parade on television. Zach was pleasantly surprised to find Allison awake and sitting in the family room. She lounged on the sofa with her bare feet braced on the edge of the coffee table while she leafed through the newspaper.

'Morning,' Zach greeted her, uncertain what to expect in response. It was a day-to-day struggle with his daughter.

Her reply was half growl and half human. Zach had suggested a truce over the holiday, and Allison had agreed, but she'd let it be known that she was doing him a big favor and he should be grateful.

'What are you reading?' he asked, sinking down onto the sofa next to her. If Allison was willing to make an effort, then so could he. He held a cup of coffee in his hand and had half an eye on the television screen.

'The ads.'

'Advertisements?' Zach asked, her answer catching him off guard.

Eddie raced into the kitchen and returned with a huge bowl of cold cereal. Milk sloshed over the edges as he lowered himself to a cross-legged position on the floor. Zach was about to send him back to the other room, but he didn't feel right being so strict with his son on a holiday. Eddie could eat in the family room this once, despite the rules.

'Tomorrow's the biggest Christmas-shopping day of the year,' Allison informed him, continuing to turn the pages of the flyers, scanning each one with care.

These flyers didn't mean a lot to Zach. He hated shopping. Rosie was the one who purchased all the Christmas gifts. He dreaded the thought of even entering a mall. Last Christmas he'd asked Janice to buy Rosie's gifts for him; not only had she done a decent job, but she'd wrapped them, as well. His gift to Janice had been a cash bonus, a generous amount—not a personal gift but a practical one—and he'd figured that as a single mother, Janice could use the extra money at Christmas. It still rankled that she'd resigned.

'Mom and I used to read through every single ad,' Allison said absently.

This information wasn't exactly life-changing. Women enjoyed that sort of thing, he guessed.

'It was fun.'

He shrugged, not understanding the sadness he heard in his daughter's voice. This was beyond him. If she wanted to get all sentimental over a bunch of advertisements, he'd let her.

'You don't get it, do you?' Allison sobbed, her eyes swimming with tears.

'What?'

'Mom and I used to go shopping. It was our tradition. We had *fun*. I loved picking out my clothes for Christmas, and Mom was great about finding exactly what I wanted on sale.'

Zach was sorry, but he still didn't get it.

193

'You can go shopping with your mother in the morning if you want.' More power to them, as far as he was concerned. Then, thinking he'd add a bit of levity to the situation, he said. 'Eddie, your mother and Allison can go shopping tomorrow, can't they? We don't care.'

'Sure you can go,' Eddie told his sister.

In response Allison hurled down the newspaper and stormed out of the room.

'What did I say?' Eddie asked. He picked up his bowl and drank from the edge, making loud slurping noises.

'I don't know,' Zach muttered. He'd better go find out what he'd done that had warranted this reaction.

He discovered his daughter lying across her unmade bed, weeping her eyes out. Zach sighed. Sitting on the edge of her bed, he placed his hand on Allison's shoulder. She jerked away, telling him in no uncertain terms that she found his touch repugnant.

'I'm sorry, sweetheart,' he said.

Allison curled up tightly. 'Go away.'

'I can't.'

'Why can't you?' she demanded between sobs.

'Because I love you, and it hurts me to see you so unhappy.' Zach was sincere about that.

'You don't love me.'

'Allison, you're wrong. You're my princess, don't you remember?' He'd called her that for years, until she'd asked him not to when she reached thirteen. Every now and then, he forgot.

Allison rolled onto her back and stared up at him, red-faced.

'What is it about the newspaper ads that upset you so much?' he asked gently.

His daughter sat up and ran the back of her hand under her nose. 'Mom said we can't go shopping tomorrow.'

'Why not?' Zach didn't understand why Rosie was breaking such a beloved tradition, especially when it meant so much to Allison. They were looking for a way to build a bridge with their daughter, not blow it up!

'Mom said there wasn't any money for Christmas this year because of the divorce.'

Zach wanted to groan out loud. He was hurting financially himself. Maintaining two households, paying off what he owed the attorneys, plus covering the cost of Rosie's summer courses, had left him dry.

'I'm sorry,' he said, meaning it.

Allison's lower lip trembled as she nodded. 'I know you are, but that doesn't change a damn thing, does it?'

Zach had to agree she was right.

At noon, when Eddie couldn't wait a moment longer, Zach drove to the grocery store and picked up their Thanksgiving feast. Allison had all the serving plates and bowls out when he returned.

'We don't need to dirty those,' he said, thinking of all the extra dishes they would create. The dishwasher could only hold so much.

'We can't serve mashed potatoes out of a plastic container on Thanksgiving Day,' Allison protested.

'Sure we can,' Eddie insisted righteously. 'Come on, Allison, you're holding up the stuffing.'

Zach's teenage daughter rolled her eyes and surrendered.

With great ceremony Zach unloaded the box. The turkey was browned to perfection and Zach brought out the knife and fork to slice it, lifting the meat from the bird and transferring it to each of their plates. While he worked on the turkey Allison and Eddie helped themselves to the trimmings.

They waited until he'd finished dishing up his own plate and then the three of them joined hands for the prayer. Zach didn't feel much like praying so he said, 'Good food, good meat. Good God, let's eat.'

'Amen,' Eddie cried, and reached for his fork.

Allison looked at Zach, slowly shaking her head. It went without saying that if Rosie had been with them, he wouldn't have gotten away with that. Zach winked at her. She winked back. It was almost like having his daughter back.

His first bite was disappointing. The stuffing was too bland, although he supposed that made sense. The grocery store prepared huge amounts at a time and had to satisfy a lot of different tastes.

'Not bad,' Zach said, putting on a bright front.

'It doesn't taste right,' Eddie complained.

'It's not Mom's stuffing,' Allison informed them both.

No one needed to tell Eddie that. He complained with every bite and finally left the table after declining a piece of pumpkin pie.

Zach assumed his son was in front of the television, but when he went to join him and tempt him with pie, Eddie wasn't there. A search found his son sitting on his bed crying.

Eddie had been a real trouper through the divorce proceedings. It was Allison who'd acted out her anger and rejection, Allison who'd given him his first gray hairs.

'I'm sorry the stuffing was a disappointment,' Zach said, standing in the doorway.

Eddie rubbed his eyes and sniffed.

Zach walked into the room and gathered his boy in his arms. It wasn't often that Eddie crawled onto his lap anymore, but the nine-year-old came willingly now. He wrapped his arms around Zach's neck and sniffled loudly.

'I wish you and Mom had never gotten a divorce,' he said.

'I know,' Zach whispered. With all his heart he wished he'd fought harder to save his marriage. Whatever it cost him would've been worth it to avoid the pain he and Rosie had inflicted on their children. Now it was too late. They couldn't undo what they'd done.

*   *   *

Grace looked across the Thanksgiving table at Cliff and smiled, but her mind was a thousand miles away—in Georgia, where Will was spending the holiday with his wife and longtime friends.

After two days without word from him, she was suffering withdrawal symptoms. Her fingers itched for a computer keyboard so she could log on and talk to Will. When she'd inquired, Grace learned that Lisa and her husband had a computer, but it was kept in a corner of their bedroom. She felt awkward about asking to use it. Lisa hadn't offered, and Grace had been forced to drop the matter. The fact that chatting online with Will had become so important confused and bothered her. Only a few months ago he was a boy from her past, a high school crush, and suddenly he was so much more.

Then there was Cliff, and her feelings toward him were equally confusing. She was grateful to spend Thanksgiving with him and at the same time regretted accepting his invitation.

'Grace?' Cliff broke into her rambling thoughts.

She glanced at him and realized she'd missed something. She shook her head. 'I'm sorry?'

'Lisa was asking if you'd like more turkey.'

She stared down at her plate and shook her head. 'Thank you, but no, I'm stuffed.' She placed her hands on her stomach to give the impression that she'd overeaten, but she'd barely touched her dinner.

This trip to Maryland was more difficult than Grace had anticipated. They'd made the cross-country flight without problems, but sitting with Cliff for several hours the day before had been...uncomfortable. At one point early on, Cliff had reached for her hand, lacing his fingers with hers, creating a mood of intimacy she didn't want and couldn't feel.

Lisa and her husband, Rich, were at the airport when Cliff and Grace landed. Cliff's three-year-old granddaughter, April, had raced to his arms and he'd lifted her high in the air.

Thanksgiving morning, Grace had spent some time with Cliff's daughter. Grace had liked Lisa immediately. She was very close to her father, and her adoration reminded Grace of the way Kelly had felt about Dan. As far as Kelly was concerned, Dan was about as perfect as a father could be. Lisa felt protective of her father, as Kelly had, drilling Grace at every opportunity to find out more about the relationship between her and Cliff.

When they'd finished their meal, the men wandered into the living room, to watch a football game on television. April went down for her nap, and Grace helped Lisa clear off the table. During her trips from the dining room to the kitchen, Grace noticed Cliff watching her. When he realized she knew, he smiled sheepishly and looked away.

Grace's heart fell. Cliff was obviously in love with her. For a while she'd been convinced she loved him, too, but now she was no longer sure of that—or anything.

'You're the first woman my father's shown any interest in since he and my mother divorced,' Lisa said as Grace set the last of the dirty dishes on the kitchen counter. The house was cozy, and Lisa had decorated it in a kind of English-cottage style. She was a tall, lithe blonde; Grace wondered if that was how Susan, Cliff's ex-wife, had looked, too.

'I think the world of your father,' Grace told her, and it was true.

Lisa ran water into the sink, adding detergent, and slid the pans into the suds. 'Mom hurt him badly. It's taken a long time for Dad to get over the divorce. I was beginning to wonder if he ever would.'

'Some wounds go very deep,' Grace said as a niggling guilt worked on her conscience—

because it was Will who dominated her thoughts, Will who sent her pulse soaring. If she'd needed anything to prove how strongly she felt about him, these last two days had done exactly that.

Accepting Cliff's invitation had encouraged the relationship, and that had been wrong for both of them. Although Grace liked Cliff, enjoyed his company, she considered him a friend, a very dear and good friend, but nothing more.

'Dad's been so busy lately, he's worried that you've given up on him,' Lisa said. 'We talk every week, and you're the main topic of conversation.'

'Me?'

'You and the guy who turned up dead at the bed-and-breakfast,' she joked, then grew serious. 'He asks my advice. I was the one who urged him to ask you out that first time.'

'Then I should thank you.'

'He admired the fact that you refused until your divorce was final.' Those had been bleak days in Grace's life, as she'd confronted the unknown. Dan's body had yet to be found, and she'd felt certain he was with another woman. Her self-esteem had been in tatters, and then along came this handsome rancher who courted her with gentleness and humor.

'I told Dad he should hire a full-time trainer, otherwise he was going to lose you,' Lisa said. She opened the dishwasher, a model as old as Grace's, and arranged the dishes inside.

'I understand what it's like to start up a new business,' Grace hurriedly assured her. The truth was, she'd barely noticed that she hadn't heard from him much lately. Anytime she did hear from Cliff, it had seemed like an intrusion.

She hated feeling this way, but she couldn't help it. Cliff was like Buttercup. He was big and warm and friendly and there when she needed him. On the other hand, her friendship with Will was exciting and new. The two of them talking for hours every day and keeping it a secret held a hint of intrigue. They were conspirators.

'Are you in love with my father?' Lisa asked, her arms elbow-deep in dishwater.

'I...I—'

'Are you embarrassing our dinner guest?' Cliff asked as he stepped into the kitchen. He stood behind Grace, slid his arms around her waist and kissed the side of her neck. She closed her eyes—not to savor the tenderness of the moment, but in relief because she didn't have to answer Lisa's question.

This was wrong, but she couldn't say anything to Cliff. Not with his daughter and her husband so close. Not with Cliff's granddaughter napping in the other room. It would have to wait until they were back in Cedar Cove, in familiar territory.

She could have told him on the flight home, but Grace refused to do that to him, especially after the hospitality his family had shown her. That would've piled wrong on top of wrong.

The instant Grace was back in Cedar Cove, she collected Buttercup from Kelly and Paul's and headed home. Ten minutes after she walked in the front door, she was sitting in front of her computer.

'Oh, be there,' she whispered as she logged on to the Internet. She brought up the message board and hit the appropriate icons and waited an interminable few moments.

Will, are you there? she typed.

Almost immediately he responded. Welcome back. How was Thanksgiving with your boyfriend?

Wonderful. How about yours? she typed, wincing at the half lie.

All right, I guess.

I had a good time, but I missed our chats, she typed.

It seemed forever before Will answered. Grace, thank you. I hated being without you. I didn't realize how much I've come to rely on our talks to get me through the day.

I rely on you, too her fingers raced to tell him. She gnawed on her lower lip. I thought about you constantly.

Another long moment passed. You're all I thought about, too.

Grace shouldn't be this happy, but joy filled

her. She felt like a teenager all over again—a teenager head over heels in love.

Fourteen

Thick, dark clouds marred the December-morning sky over Cedar Cove. Peggy Beldon walked down the stairs, and from her view through the upper hallway window, she saw that the waters of the cove were murky and restless, churning up whitecaps.

It didn't surprise her that Bob was already awake. He'd probably been up for hours. Ever since he'd talked to Pastor Flemming, that day at the golf course, he'd been sleeping poorly. When she'd asked him about it, Bob had repeatedly shrugged off her questions. She'd pressured him until she got an answer, although it hadn't been too satisfactory.

In the beginning, their marriage had been shaky. Bob wasn't the same after Vietnam. They'd married shortly after he was discharged from the army, but he'd started drinking by then. At first it was just a few beers with his friends after work. Peggy didn't begrudge him that. Then Hollie was born, followed two years later by Marc, and Peggy had been so preoccupied with motherhood she hadn't really noticed what was happening to her husband. Soon he was out with the boys every

204

night or bringing his drinking buddies home. She and Bob had argued often and she'd grown increasingly desperate.

The summer afternoon Bob received his first DUI, she realized that his drinking was more than a few beers with friends; it had become a serious problem that dominated their marriage and their lives. Despite her tears and her pleas, he refused to acknowledge there was anything wrong.

Peggy would always be grateful to the friend who'd recommended she start attending Al-Anon meetings. Without the support and encouragement she'd received from other men and women married to alcoholics, she didn't know where she'd be today. It forever changed her life. She'd stepped back and stopped protecting Bob from the consequences of his addiction. If he drove drunk, she phoned the police; if he fell down on the floor too drunk to get up, she left him there. His drinking was *his* problem and she refused to make it hers, refused to be caught in the eye of a hurricane because he chose to hide his sorrows in booze.

Thankfully, after Bob had been fired by the third plumbing contractor in a row, gotten his car insurance canceled only to be renewed at rates that rivaled a house payment and been called before a judge, his head started to clear. Then and only then did the light dawn. He'd gone to his first AA meeting and by the grace of God, hadn't touched a drop since.

Shortly after he'd achieved three weeks of sobriety, he came to her and told her everything that had happened one terrible day in Vietnam. He'd wept bitter tears of guilt and self-recrimination as she held him and cried with him. She'd marked the date he sobbed out his story on her heart, because it was that day their lives and their marriage had changed. It was that day she knew Bob had the power to stop drinking. That had been twenty years ago now, in January 1983. He'd helped many an alcoholic through the AA program since then, and she continued to attend Al-Anon.

As Peggy came into the kitchen, Bob smiled at her. He had the Alcoholics Anonymous Big Book in one hand and a cup of coffee in the other.

'How long have you been up?' she asked. Since he was already dressed and shaved, it must've been a while.

'A few hours. I have an appointment with Roy this morning. I wouldn't mind company if you'd care to tag along.'

Although he tossed out the invitation in an offhand manner, Peggy knew her husband well enough to realize he wanted her with him. He'd been nervous for days. Ever since Troy Davis had come by the house.

The local sheriff had asked Bob a few questions regarding the John Doe who'd died in their home. As far as she could tell, they were the same questions he'd asked months earlier, when the body was discovered. Troy didn't stay long, but afterward Bob had paced the house for hours until Peggy thought she'd go mad if he didn't sit down.

'Sure, I'll go,' she told him as she poured a cup of coffee. The pot was nearly empty, and she started a fresh one. They had no guests at the moment, but extra coffee never went amiss.

'Looks like we might get snow,' her husband said, staring out the window.

Peggy sat down across from him and reached for the remote control. They kept a small TV in the kitchen, where she generally watched the morning newscast from the local Seattle station. There'd been rumors of snow all week, but only now had the temperature descended to the point that it was a possibility.

Snow in the Puget Sound area wasn't a common occurrence. Contrary to popular belief, Seattle and its outlying regions actually had a moderate climate. As long as records had been maintained, it had never gone over a hundred degrees in summer or below zero in winter.

'I hope it does snow,' Peggy said, thinking how the schoolkids would love it. As a matter of fact, so would she. The Christmas lights were up outside, the wreath hung on the door and the illuminated family of deer stood in the middle of their front yard. Snow would be the perfect complement.

Bob closed his Big Book and yawned loudly.

'What time did you get up?' she asked again.

He shrugged. 'Early.'

'Two? Three?'

'Around there,' he agreed, settling his gaze on the television screen.

Peggy suspected it might've been even earlier. Her husband couldn't get the notion out of his head that he knew the dead stranger. The John Doe had received extensive plastic surgery, which certainly complicated the process of identifying him. For a while, there'd been speculation that it might be Dan Sherman, but that had turned out not to be the case, since Dan's body was found a few weeks later. All this death in Cedar Cove—it was hard to reconcile in such a friendly, sleepy town.

'What time's your appointment?' Peggy asked.

'Ten.'

'I'll be ready,' she promised him.

A few hours later, Bob and Peggy arrived at Roy McAfee's office not far from the Harbor Street Art Gallery. Corrie, Roy's wife, acted as his secretary. Peggy liked Corrie, although she didn't know her well. Roy was a no-nonsense man, a stolid, Detective Friday kind of investigator who tracked down the facts. The similarity between Roy and Joe Friday from the old *Dragnet* TV show reassured Peggy. He was a bit distant, an observer, a man who didn't allow emotion to cloud an investigation. Corrie was just the opposite, warm and outgoing. Even though she now worked for her husband, she appeared to be the stay-at-home-and-bake-cookies type of wife and mother. Peggy suspected that was the reason she'd been drawn to Corrie. They were a lot alike.

As they sat in the reception room, Peggy picked up an old issue of *Reader's Digest* and Bob jiggled his foot incessantly. It was all she could do not to reach over and stop him.

'Roy can see you now,' Corrie announced, holding open the door.

Peggy looked at her husband, silently wondering if he wanted her to go in with him.

'Not right now.' Bob shook his head. 'I think I'd like to talk to Roy alone, if you don't mind.'

He'd gone pale, she noted. 'Of course. Whatever you want.'

Bob walked into the room and closed the door. Peggy gazed anxiously after him. She didn't know what he was going to ask Roy, or if he had anything he needed to hide.

Now it was Peggy who did the pacing.

'I've always meant to ask you about your herb garden,' Corrie said from behind her desk. 'How did you get started?'

Peggy folded her arms and looked out the office window, onto Harbor Street. 'By accident, actually. Years ago we bought a house that had a rosemary bush and I loved the scent of it. I clipped branches from it so often that I soon bought a second plant and then a third. Before I knew it, I was buying bay and sage and basil. I found out that I have a knack for growing herbs. When we decided to move back to Cedar Cove—'

'Oh, you lived here earlier?'

Peggy nodded. 'Bob and I both graduated from Cedar Cove High School. Bob was in the class of 1966 and I graduated two years later in '68.'

'We're close to the same age then,' Corrie said.

'Do you have a herb garden?' Peggy asked.

Corrie shook her head. 'No, but I'd like one. Any suggestions?'

Peggy recognized that Corrie was distracting her, but she didn't mind. The other woman seemed genuinely interested in learning about herbs. 'Come visit anytime,' Peggy invited. 'I'll give you a few plants to start off with in the spring.'

'I'd love that,' Corrie told her.

'Bob planted the blueberries.' Now that she was talking, Peggy couldn't seem to stop. 'We have our own small patch at the side of the house. They need lots of water and it's a struggle to keep the deer out of them.'

They must have talked for twenty minutes about recipes, especially ones with blueberries. Peggy stopped abruptly when the door opened and Roy stuck his head out.

'Peggy, would you join us?'

She nodded and walked into the room on shaky legs. Claiming the empty chair next to her husband, she reached for Bob's hand. His fingers tightened around hers.

'I told Roy what happened in Nam,' Bob said, his voice low and emotional. 'I told him there were four of us, all under twenty-five. We made a pact never to talk about it. I don't know if our John Doe has anything to do with this, but I've asked Roy to find out what he can.'

On the night twenty years earlier, when Bob had described that day in the jungle, he'd vowed never to speak of it again. Telling her had been a one-time thing, an act of self-preservation. The burden of carrying his secret had nearly destroyed him and their marriage.

'Dan Sherman was with me.'

'Dan?' Peggy gasped. He'd never told her his high school friend had been in that hellish fight until now.

Peggy turned her attention to Roy. 'Do you think what happened in Nam has anything to do with the man who died in our home?'

Roy leaned forward, his expression serious. 'I don't know, but I intend to find out.'

*   *   *

The festive atmosphere in the halls of Kitsap County Courthouse was contagious. Olivia looked out the window of her chamber office, delighted to see it was snowing. Snow in December was perfect. It made her want to rush home and bake gingerbread cookies and string popcorn. Instead she had to listen while lawyers stated their cases and awaited her decision.

Finishing her tea, she reluctantly went back to the courtroom. The bailiff announced her arrival and those congregated halfheartedly rose to their feet as she took her place behind the bench.

The next case was called, and the first attorney stepped forward. Olivia glanced up and to her surprise, discovered Jack Griffin sitting in the back of the room, pen and pad in hand. He was already taking notes, and she hadn't listened to a single case yet. Either he was in court on legitimate business, or he'd come to rile her. She felt her heart pound hard against her ribs.

But whatever his reason for being there, a few moments into the case, Jack stood and made his way out of the courtroom. Olivia was disappointed; they'd hardly seen each other in weeks. He was busy, she was busy, and despite effort on both their parts, their relationship hadn't returned to the closeness they used to share. Damn it all, she *missed* Jack. Missed the fun they'd had together, his merciless teasing, his potent kisses. A woman her age shouldn't be thinking about such things in the middle of a custody case, but Olivia couldn't help it.

She wanted him back in her life, and she longed for their relationship to be what it had once been. She didn't know who was the guilty party, she or Jack. A year earlier they'd had dinner together at least twice a week. Jack regularly came to the house on Tuesday nights and they'd watch crime shows on the Discovery channel. She hadn't seen him on a Tuesday night in months.

All of that was before his son had moved in with him, she remembered. Eric's presence had certainly turned Jack's world upside down, but he felt he owed this time to his son, so Olivia had graciously taken a backseat. She didn't like it, but there'd been no choice.

Eric was married now—she'd performed the ceremony herself—and the father of twins. Last summer Eric, Shelly and the babies had moved to Reno, Nevada.

Just when it looked as if life might return to normal, Stan had entered the scene. She'd give him credit; her ex-husband was persistent. He phoned her ten times more often than Jack did. She could have a date with Stan anytime if she was interested. But she wasn't.

Oh, she might've been, in the beginning. There was something so emotionally satisfying about her ex-husband admitting he'd made a terrible mistake in divorcing her. For a brief period, her ego had been comforted by it and she'd come close to letting those righteous emotions sway her. Luckily, common sense had convinced her otherwise.

Olivia was sincere in what she told her ex-husband. Stan needed a woman in his life and he wasn't afraid of a challenge. The problem was, he viewed *her* as a challenge. Of course, any woman Stan wanted would have to be adoring. Intelligence wasn't a requirement, although it was a bonus. No question, Stan Lockhart was witty and possessed a high IQ. His emotional IQ, sadly, was far lower.

The rest of the afternoon passed quickly as Olivia dealt with a series of family court cases, one after the other until they blurred in her mind. By the time court adjourned for the day, she was ready to go home and read recipes for gingerbread cookies.

As she peeled off her robe, she checked her phone messages. There was one from Stan—no real surprise—and another from her daughter. Justine was a stay-at-home mother now, although she continued to manage the finances at the restaurant. She paid the bills and took care of the payroll. But when it came to the complicated tax laws, Justine was smart enough to leave those in the hands of Zachary Cox, her capable accountant.

Olivia returned the calls, and after short conversations with both—'no, thanks' to Stan on the dinner invite, and yes, it's best to use brandy in Julia Child's fruitcake recipe with Justine—she prepared to leave the courthouse.

She pulled on her coat and gloves and

stepped out of her office to discover Jack waiting for her, leaning against the wall. He grinned sheepishly when she appeared.

'Hi,' he said, straightening.

'Hi yourself.' Her heart skipped a beat at the sight of him. Jack wasn't a handsome man at first glance, but he did manage to stir her restless heart.

'Do you have time for a walk in the snow?'

'I'd love it.' She'd been in a hurry to get home, but invitations from Jack were scarce and she wasn't about to refuse one.

He brightened, smiling that cocky off-center grin of his. 'I thought you might.'

Once outside, she noticed that the snow was coming down in large, soft flakes, the kind that floated slowly to earth.

'Let's walk down to the waterfront,' he suggested.

The hill was steep and the street was often closed when driving conditions were unsafe. The signs had already been set in place not far from the courthouse.

Jack tucked her hand in the crook of his arm. Olivia turned her face to the sky and opened her mouth to catch the falling snow on her tongue, the way she'd done as a child.

'I love when it snows,' she told him.

'I do, too,' Jack said.

'Do you want to build a snowman on the courthouse lawn?'

'I'd rather we went somewhere for a cup of

215

coffee.'

That sounded just as nice to Olivia. The lights from the marina were ablaze, the water catching their reflection as dusk settled over the cove. Boats bobbed gently on the surface, and with the snow drifting down, the scene resembled a Christmas card. The only thing missing was carolers walking by in old-fashioned winter coats or a sleigh gliding past.

Jack led her to the Pot Belly Deli on Harbor Street. The deli served a big lunch crowd, but stayed open until late afternoon. He went up to the counter while she chose a table by the window. Soon Jack returned with two thick mugs of coffee and a slice of pecan pie with two forks.

'Jack,' she protested. 'I'm watching my weight.'

'Watch it another time,' he said, and handed her a fork.

She accepted it, sighing heavily. 'You know what this means, don't you?' She didn't give him a chance to answer. 'I'm going to have to walk on the treadmill tonight.'

'I thought you did aerobics with Grace.'

'I do, but that's Wednesday nights, once a week. Everything I've read about exercise says four or five times a week is best.'

'That often, huh…?' He sliced off a section of pie with the side of his fork.

'Do you exercise, Jack?' She had helped herself to the tiniest bit of pie, avoiding the whipped cream.

'Me?' He glanced up and the guilty look he wore was answer enough.

'Oh, honestly, if you don't take care of yourself you're going to keel over from a heart attack. You need to get serious about eating right and exercising.'

'Yes, Mother,' he said, and hacked off another chunk of pie.

'Okay, I'm finished lecturing.'

'Good.' He smiled as he said it, taking the sting from his words. He reached inside his coat pocket and removed an envelope. 'I thought you might like to see these.'

Olivia took the envelope and noticed the return address. It was from Eric and Shelly. Inside was a letter wrapped around a set of pictures. Olivia unfolded the letter and studied the snapshots of Tedd and Todd, Eric's twin sons.

'Oh, Jack! Look how much they've grown.'

'Shelly wrote and said they're both walking already.'

'At nine months?' Olivia could well imagine all the mischief those boys were getting into. She didn't envy the young couple. Thankfully, Jordan and Justine hadn't walked until they were a year old. A brief sorrow, a pang of regret, came and went. She didn't think about Jordan as much anymore. Whole days would pass without her dwelling on the death of her thirteen-year-old son, Justine's twin brother.

For years she'd played a heart-wrenching game of wondering how her life would've been different if Jordan had chosen to ride his bike that fateful August afternoon instead of heading to the lake with his friends. It was a question with no answer. Jordan had gone to the lake.

'I have new pictures of Isabella,' she said, unwilling to be outdone in the grandchild department. She scooped up her purse and removed a small 'brag' book Grace had given her for pictures. 'Look at Leif, too. You won't believe how much he's changed.'

While she finished studying the snapshots of Tedd and Todd, Jack flipped through the photo book.

'Isabella and Leif are cute,' Jack agreed, 'but Tedd and Todd are cuter.'

Slowly Olivia lowered the snapshots. 'You don't want to go there, Jack Griffin. My grandchildren are the most perfect, beautiful grandchildren in the entire universe. I'd hate to slap a fine on you for denying the truth.'

He sat back and arched his eyebrows. 'Really? I could always write another article about you in the *Chronicle*,' he returned.

Olivia laughed. 'Truce, truce. Let's agree we both have the brightest, most intelligent grandchildren ever to grace the earth. Deal?'

Jack smiled and reached for his fork. Only this bite was for her.

She declined with a shake of her head, but

218

Jack was having none of it.

'I'll have to work it off later and I hate the treadmill.'

'We could always go walking.'

However, by now it'd stopped snowing and a light drizzle had started. 'In the rain?'

Jack frowned. 'How about if you take me Christmas shopping? I need to mail off gifts for Eric, Shelly and the boys, and I could use the help.'

'Deal,' she agreed, and leaned forward to accept the sliver of pie. It really did taste divine and she closed her eyes to savor this small bite.

'You ready?' he asked, sipping his coffee.

'Ready.' She stood, picking up her coat, which was draped on the chair behind her.

It wasn't until they were on their way out the door that Olivia realized this was the first time in months that Stan's silent presence hadn't loomed over them.

This was a good sign, a very good sign indeed.

*   *   *

Zach studied the young woman in the chair opposite his desk. This was the part of the job he detested most. Hiring new employees. Cecilia Randall was the last applicant of the day. He'd interviewed four others and had found some reason or other not to hire any of them.

Cecilia Randall was nervous, eager to make a good impression. She was young, but she'd come with glowing references, although none were from bookkeeping firms. Her work experience so far had been as a restaurant hostess.

A dozen questions filled his mind, but federal regulations being what they were, Zach couldn't ask them. He'd learned his lesson on that issue with Janice Lamond.

'You like accounting work, Ms. Randall?' he asked, clearing his throat.

She nodded vigorously. 'Very much. I had top marks in my class.' She leaned forward and motioned to an entry at the bottom of her résumé. 'I recently earned my accounting degree from Olympic Community College in Bremerton.'

Zach had noticed that. 'I see your husband's in the navy?'

'That's correct. He's currently out at sea.' She clasped her hands in her lap and squeezed her fingers tightly together. 'I miss him very much, but his tour of duty is almost over.' She had the wistful look of a woman in love. That was good.

Zach glanced over her résumé one final time and mentioned his main objection. 'I don't see any previous employment in this field.'

Cecilia moved to the edge of her seat.

'Yes, I know. Until recently I worked at The Captain's Galley as a hostess. That was before it was sold. It's The Lighthouse now.'

Zach nodded absently; he was certainly familiar with the restaurant, since he did their taxes.

Cecilia leaned closer. 'They offered me a job, but I turned it down. Ian and I felt it was more important for me to finish my degree and get a job in the field I've been training in for the last three years.'

He gave her an A for effort, Zach decided. She'd stuck out three years of classes and here she was.

'I'm willing to start at the bottom,' she offered. 'I'd be grateful for the experience and the chance to prove myself.'

Zach liked this young navy wife. Another good thing—she was married and from every indication the marriage was healthy. Although he'd never admit it, he didn't want to work in close proximity to a single woman again. He hadn't seen Janice for what she was until the damage was done.

'Can you start Monday morning?' he asked, making his decision. He was tired of doing interviews, and no other applicant had shown as much desire for the job as Cecilia Randall.

Her eyes grew huge. 'You mean I've got the job?'

Zach smiled. 'It's all yours.' He told her the salary and her eyes grew even bigger. He was afraid it wasn't enough when she blurted out, 'How much?' Embarrassed, she laughed and covered her mouth. 'This is just great! You won't be sorry, Mr. Cox. I'll work hard and do my very best.'

'I know you will, Ms. Randall.'

After he left the office that evening, Zach stopped at the local grocery and picked up a whole cooked chicken. It had never been one of his favorite dinners, but it was quick and easy and he didn't feel like fussing with meal preparation.

Eddie's face fell when he saw it. 'I wanted spaghetti,' he complained.

'Chicken again?' Allison said. 'Mom brought home a chicken two nights ago. Doesn't anyone in this family know how to cook?'

'Yes,' Zach said, losing his patience. '*You* do.'

'Me?' Allison snarled back at him. 'What makes you think I can cook?'

'Didn't you take home economics this trimester?'

'Yes, but we're not—'

'You get home first in the afternoon—you can put on dinner for Eddie and me.'

'You want me to cook just because I'm a girl, don't you?' Her eyes filled with fiery indignation.

Zach wasn't about to get caught in the 'My Dad is a Chauvinist' trap. 'If Eddie was home from school before you, I'd put him in change of dinner, but as it happens, you're the first one to walk in the door. Congratulations, you're elected. Your brother and I will wash the dishes.'

'I'd rather cook,' Eddie piped up.

'I'm afraid you're out of luck, sport. Allison's going to come up with a dinner plan for us.'

'A dinner plan?' She looked aghast. 'What's that?'

He wondered if she'd been sleeping through her classes. 'Make a list of what we're going to eat for the next seven days and then compile a grocery list from that.'

'Oh.'

'You can cook spaghetti every night if you want to, Allison,' Eddie said enthusiastically.

'Here, write.' Zach set a notebook on the table in front of her.

'Can we have tacos one night?' Eddie begged. 'Please, please?'

'I guess.' Allison reluctantly wrote tacos at the top of her list.

'What do we need for tacos?' Zach asked.

'Meat, cheese, tomatoes, lettuce and taco shells,' she said.

'Great,' Zach said, pointing at her. 'Write all that down on a separate shopping list.'

'We have cheese,' Eddie told him. 'Mom bought it for macaroni and cheese on Monday night.'

'Fine, but we need taco shells, tomatoes and lettuce.'

Allison dutifully listed the ingredients. They continued, with Eddie making dinner suggestions and Allison creating the list. Actually it was fun, and by the time they'd finished, the table was set and they were ready for dinner.

Eddie held a chicken leg with both hands. 'Are you really going to cook for us, Allison?' he asked his sister.

Allison shrugged. 'Only because Dad's making me.'

In an effort to bring family discussions back to the dinner table, Zach asked his two children about their days.

In typical Allison fashion, she rolled her eyes. 'All right, I guess.'

'I had a great day,' Eddie said, describing in detail every aspect of his fifth-grade life.

'What about you?' Allison asked when Eddie had finished.

'Me?' Zach replied, and then realized he didn't have anything to hide. 'I hired a new assistant this afternoon.'

'Is she pretty?' Eddie asked.

Before he could answer, the phone rang, and like a comic strip hero in a mask and cape, Allison dove for the phone. Her enthusiasm died when she discovered it was her mother.

Although Zach could only hear one side of the conversation, it was obvious from Allison's answer that Rosie had asked what they were doing.

His daughter gave a long, beleaguered sigh. 'We're just sitting around the dinner table and Dad's telling us about hiring a new assistant.'

Zach wanted to groan aloud. He'd rather Rosie didn't know that Janice had quit and left him high and dry. The fact that she'd handed in her notice was embarrassing enough. But to own up to the poor choice he'd made when he'd hired her—to Rosie of all people—would be mortifying. It'd been hard enough to admit it to himself.

His appetite gone, Zach stood and carried his plate to the kitchen. He scraped it off and set it inside the dishwasher.

Eddie talked to his mother, too, and after a few minutes, his son called him. 'Mom wants to talk to you.'

'Okay, sure.' He knew she wasn't going to let the information slide, and he was right.

The moment he was on the phone, Rosie asked the question he'd been expecting. 'You're hiring a new assistant?'

'Oh, I guess Allison told you,' he muttered. 'I'm trying to get back to family discussions over the dinner table—all of us sharing part of our day.'

'What happened to Janice Lamond?'

She was certainly persistent. 'Nothing's happened to her.'

'If that's the case, then why are you hiring

another assistant?'

'Why?' he repeated as if the answer should be obvious. 'I need one.'

'Janice got a promotion, didn't she?'

'Yes.' Zach could say that in all honesty. Janice *had* gotten a promotion—only it hadn't been with his firm. He knew very well that he should admit Janice had been everything Rosie believed. She'd had an agenda that had nothing to do with the job.

'I guess congratulations are in order, then—for Janice, that is.' Rosie sounded deflated.

'Yes...I suppose they are,' he said.

A few moments later, Zach hung up the phone. An uneasy sensation settled over him. He had an inkling that he was going to end up paying for this lie—and soon.

Fifteen

Something was wrong with Jon. Maryellen had been thinking about his strange behavior ever since he'd come to collect Katie the night before. Monday morning, as she pulled into the parking lot at the gallery, her troubled thoughts stayed with her. Harbor Street, which curved around the cove, was bright with Christmas lights arched over the street, and the traditional candy cane displays were suspended in a festive arrangement from the light posts.

Jon was wonderful with Katie, but lately he didn't linger for more than a minute or two when he was picking her up. He'd even announced that he planned to drop Katie off at Kelly's house rather than at Maryellen's.

Until recently, Jon seemed to invent excuses to spend time with her, but now everything had changed. The only reason she could imagine was that he was involved with someone else. The possibility brought with it a curious ache, an unfamiliar distress. Maryellen feared this emotion was jealousy, and she hated the way it made her feel.

By midmorning, she had to know. The first person she asked for advice was her sister. In the first free moment she had between customers she called Kelly, who answered right away.

'Hi,' Maryellen said, forcing a cheerful note into her voice. 'I just wanted to make sure Katie's with you.'

'She is. Jon dropped her off an hour ago.'

'Good.' She strove to maintain a casual tone, although her curiosity was killing her. 'How did he seem?'

'Jon? No different than any other time I've seen him. He came with Katie, spent a few minutes, exchanged high fives with Tyler and then was out the door. Any reason?'

Ten responses popped into her mind. 'He... he seems different these days.'

'Different? How do you mean?'

Maryellen pressed the phone tighter to her ear. She didn't want to admit he didn't seem interested in her anymore, especially since that wasn't even supposed to matter.

'Doesn't it seem odd that Jon wants to drop Katie off at your house instead of mine?' she asked.

'No.' Kelly was nothing if not direct. 'It makes sense. If he brings Katie back to you, he has to leave his place by seven-fifteen. If he drops Katie off at my place, he can sleep in and arrive any time he wants.'

'Oh.' Naturally her sister would say something completely reasonable and make Maryellen feel all the more ridiculous.

'Why else would he do it?' Kelly asked.

Maryellen hated to sound paranoid, but her concern had more to do with what she sensed about him than anything he'd said or done. 'He…when he came by to pick up Katie yesterday afternoon, he didn't stay a second longer than necessary.'

Kelly sighed. 'Perhaps he had plans. He does have a life, you know.'

'I realize that.' Her sister didn't understand. Jon always used to visit, sometimes for as much as an hour, but not anymore.

The sad part was that Maryellen had come to anticipate his company. She enjoyed their conversations. When he'd left so quickly on Sunday, she'd moped around the house, not knowing what to make of this sudden change in their routine.

'If you're truly bothered, you should ask him,' Kelly advised.

'I can't do that!' Her sister meant well, but Maryellen couldn't pry into Jon's life. After all, she was the one who'd spurned him.

'You can ask him indirectly,' Kelly suggested next.

Maryellen hadn't dated since her divorce; she was seriously lacking in social finesse when it came to dealing with men. She wished she didn't care.

'For heaven's sake, just ask him,' Kelly said.

Kelly was sounding impatient, so Maryellen ended the call. 'Okay, I will,' she promised.

She replaced the receiver and thought about what her sister had said—that she could find out what she needed to know by asking indirectly. That was an idea.

Of course, she *could* always talk to Justine. She and Seth owned the restaurant where Jon was employed as head chef. They were casual friends, and they'd both had babies during the summer. It would seem perfectly natural to inquire about the restaurant—and Jon. Still, it struck her as an underhanded means of acquiring information.

Perhaps Kelly was right. She should simply ask Jon.

Maryellen mulled over how to broach the subject with him and not sound paranoid or interfering. Two days later, she landed on an idea. She'd ask Jon to join her and her family for Christmas. This would be Katie's first Christmas, and it seemed a shame to be shuffling their daughter back and forth over the holiday. They could all spend the day together. It was a reasonable suggestion, and his answer would tell her everything she needed to know.

Maryellen bided her time. She waited another week, until Jon was scheduled to pick up Katie again. When he phoned to make the arrangements, she suggested they meet at the waterfront park. It was a bright, beautiful day and the small gazebo had a live Nativity scene. The local Methodist church routinely set this up; church members took turns playing the roles of Mary and Joseph, with live farm animals.

Jon was waiting for her when she arrived, standing away from the spectators, his camera around his neck. He leaned against the railing and straightened when he saw her approach.

She raised her hand and waved, and increased her pace as she pushed the stroller toward him. Katie was sound asleep, the diaper bag tucked in the rear of the stroller.

'I'm getting used to seeing you with shorter hair,' he said, and his gaze lingered on Maryellen for an extra moment, or so it seemed. 'You look nice.'

'Thank you.' This was going better than

she'd expected. She felt the warmth in his eyes and it reassured her. 'You look good yourself,' she said, recovering quickly.

He shrugged. He reached for the stroller handles; apparently he was ready to leave. Maryellen's heart dropped. It was too soon.

'Do you have a few minutes?' she asked, and started to walk slowly down the path that wandered along the waterfront toward the marina. Many of the sailboats had decorated their masts with bright Christmas lights. In the summer, this area around the waterfront was filled with booths and stands—a local farmers' market. At other times the paved area by the gazebo was a large parking lot.

'Sure,' Jon said, matching his steps to hers as he pushed the stroller.

'I was thinking,' she said, hesitating as her heart began to race. It might be silly to feel this way, but she was nervous and on edge.

At her pause, Jon turned to look at her.

'About Christmas,' she added. 'I was thinking about the two of us sharing Katie.'

'I could take her Christmas Eve and you could have her Christmas Day,' Jon suggested.

'You've certainly been flexible with the schedule,' she said appreciatively. In almost every instance, Jon had been agreeable about the schedule alterations she'd required. 'But my thought was that you might like to spend Christmas with Katie and me and my family.'

'And not have her Christmas Eve?'

'No—no, you could take her then if you wanted, but this is in addition to Christmas Eve.'

'You're asking me to join you for Christmas?' His voice was surprised.

'I'd like it very much if you could come for the day.' She smiled shyly at him. She was shocked by the depth of her desire, shocked by how badly she wanted him with her and Katie.

For a moment, it seemed as if he was pleased by her invitation. Then, for no reason she could decipher, his grin faded and he turned away from her, physically as well as emotionally. 'I appreciate the invite, but I can't.'

'You...can't?' Maryellen didn't bother to hide her disappointment, although she attempted to swallow her hurt.

'I have other plans.'

'Oh.' Well, she had her answer, but it wasn't one she liked. Jon *had* met someone else. She was sure of it now. 'I should've invited you earlier, I guess,' she said, recovering quickly. 'Perhaps we can get together next Christmas.'

'Perhaps,' he said, without committing himself.

Soon afterward, Jon made an excuse and left with Katie. Maryellen walked numbly along the waterfront. She felt rejected and dismayed and upset.

Not wanting to return to an empty house, she drove to her mother's place on Rosewood

232

Lane. This was the home where Maryellen had grown up. She loved this old house with the big dormer and the old-fashioned front porch. As a teenager, she'd spent many evenings sitting on those steps.

Her mother's car was parked in the garage, with the door left open. Buttercup was outside and barked when she eased to a stop in the driveway. As soon as the golden retriever recognized her, she wagged her tail in greeting. Maryellen stroked the dog's head and spoke a few words to her mother's companion, then knocked at the kitchen door and let herself in.

Grace sat at the computer, intently studying the screen when Maryellen entered.

'Hi, Mom,' she said in a dejected voice.

Grace spun around, her eyes wide. 'Where did you come from?'

'I just walked in. I knocked.'

'Give me a moment.' Her mother turned back to the computer and frantically typed something. Then she closed it down, stood and came into the kitchen, where Maryellen sat at the table.

'So, what brings you?' her mother asked.

She was behaving a bit strangely, Maryellen thought, frowning. It was almost as if she'd stumbled upon her mother doing something illegal. Whatever it was, Grace had *guilty* written all over her. If she hadn't been so absorbed in her own troubles, Maryellen would have pursued the matter.

'Mom, I think Jon's got a girlfriend,' she blurted out, and realized immediately how juvenile that sounded.

Her mother reached for the teakettle and filled it with tap water. 'What makes you say that?'

'I just *know*. He's avoiding me.' She tried to figure out how long this had been going on and couldn't remember. 'I invited him to spend Christmas with me and Katie and the rest of the family. He declined, said he had other plans.'

Grace sat down at the kitchen table and studied her. 'I have a question for you.'

'All right.' What Maryellen wanted just then was advice and comfort, not questions.

'Why do you care?'

'Why do I care?' she repeated, faltering over the words. 'Why do I care?' she repeated. 'Well...because I just do.'

'You were the one who insisted you didn't want Jon in your life.'

'I don't,' she blurted out, and knew it was a lie. 'I didn't,' she amended, 'but I've had a change of heart.'

'That could be the problem,' her mother said. She got up as the water started to boil.

'What do you mean?' Maryellen asked.

'Maybe Jon's had a change of heart himself.'

Sixteen

With only a few days left before Christmas, Corrie McAfee was eager to finish the last of her shopping. She'd assumed that when Roy took early retirement from the Seattle police force they'd travel. Touring Europe was something they'd talked about for years.

Retirement had sounded so liberating. No alarm clocks; a come-and-go-as-you-please kind of lifestyle. It *had* been that way at first, but Roy had gone stir-crazy within eighteen months. Shortly after their arrival in Cedar Cove, he'd hung out his shingle as a private investigator.

Linnette, their twenty-four-year-old daughter, had predicted as much. The older of their two children, she was most like her father. She shared Roy's insight into people; they both possessed an innate ability to read character and see through pretense. Linnette also had a genuine desire to help people, especially children. In fact, she was receiving her physician assistant degree in June. She'd be arriving for the holidays on Wednesday afternoon, and joining Corrie and Roy for the Christmas Eve worship service at church.

Mack was coming to Cedar Cove, too, but their son wouldn't get there until Christmas morning. Mack was a mailman in the Seattle

235

area. He'd never enjoyed school or succeeded at it the way his sister had. Corrie believed that, in time, he'd decide to further his education, but if he didn't, that was fine, too. He was generous, hard-working and honest. Roy, however, had bigger aspirations for his only son, and it had caused a rift between him and Mack. A small one they both chose to ignore, but they weren't close, and that troubled Corrie.

'Are you going out?' Roy asked as he left his office and found her wearing her coat.

'Peggy and I are meeting for lunch,' she told him. 'Then we're off to the mall.'

Her husband leaned against her desk in a relaxed pose. 'You like Peggy, don't you?'

Corrie nodded. They'd lived in Cedar Cove nearly four years now and hadn't established a lot of friendships. In the beginning, Corrie had been busy setting up their home. Later she was involved with helping Roy establish the agency. There'd been overtures of friendship from their neighbors, but Corrie and Roy tended to keep to themselves. That was how it had been in Seattle, and they'd maintained the same approach here. They waved to the neighbors, collected their mail while they were on vacation, but that was about the extent of it.

Peggy Beldon, however, was someone who genuinely interested Corrie, for a number of reasons. Corrie had a small garden space at the back of their property. Her yard in Seattle had been shaded and too small for anything other than a few flowers. After seeing Peggy's herb garden, she wanted to plant her own. But Corrie liked Peggy for more than her gardening expertise.

The day Bob came into the office and Corrie had chatted with Peggy, the other woman had graciously offered Corrie a few seedlings. That was the beginning of their friendship. Twice now, they'd met for lunch to chat, exchange recipes and get to know each other. Both times Corrie had come away with the feeling that she'd made a friend.

'You don't mind if I take the time off, do you?' she asked. Her question was a polite formality, since Roy had encouraged the friendship.

Her husband shook his head. 'By all means, tackle the mall. You're braver than I am by a long shot.'

'You don't have any appointments this afternoon?'

He looked at her absently. Corrie knew him well enough to realize his mind had drifted in another direction altogether. 'What are you thinking about?' she asked.

Roy continued to stare into space.

'Roy?'

He frowned, and it was clear he hadn't even heard her the first time. Roy was like this. His thoughts would venture off onto some case and it'd be practically impossible to get his attention.

'Is it the mystery man again?' she asked. She knew that some part of his brain refused to let this lie. He needed answers, resolution. It was one of the reasons he'd advanced quickly through the ranks of the Seattle Police Department to become a detective, a position he'd held for most of his career.

'You want my opinion?' she said.

Roy grinned. 'I have a feeling you're going to give it to me, anyway, so why not?'

'I suspect this John Doe was lost and looking for a place to stay. You and I both know there are only a couple of motels in town.'

'Both are off the Interstate,' Roy reminded her.

'So he took an early exit and got lost. That's easy enough to do,' Corrie reasoned. 'Remember the first time we drove to Cedar Cove?' If *he* didn't remember, she certainly did. They'd driven across the Narrows Bridge on a sunny Sunday afternoon, searching out areas in Puget Sound where their retirement income would match the cost of living.

Corrie had been reading the map and become confused. Consequently, Roy had exited the freeway too soon and they'd found themselves in what was primarily a rural area. They'd driven past small farms and horse ranches and then along stretches of undeveloped waterfront. They'd both grown

238

excited when they realized property values were fifty percent less than they were across the water.

'I remember,' Roy said. 'But if that was the case, the mystery man would've had to travel a long way in the dark, on unfamiliar roads, and then he just stumbled onto the Beldons' bed-and-breakfast.' He rubbed his jaw. 'I suppose it's possible. With the renaming of some streets, anyone, especially a visitor, could get confused.' Part of Lighthouse Road, on the other side of Harbor Street, was now called Cranberry Point.

'True.' Roy had a point. The Thyme and Tide wasn't on the beaten path and was miles away from the exit she'd mentioned.

'So much of his visit to town doesn't add up,' Roy muttered. 'The fact that he had plastic surgery has bothered me from the beginning.'

'I thought the coroner said it looked like the guy had some kind of accident.'

'He did,' Roy said, 'but Bob said there was something vaguely familiar about him. I keep thinking about that, too.'

'Let it go,' she urged. 'It's almost Christmas.' If Roy took a break from the case, he might free his mind to explore solutions. It often happened like that; a case would lie fallow for months and then overnight a small piece of evidence her husband had found months earlier—a bit of conversation, a previously unrelated detail—would suddenly click into

239

place. Soon afterward, he'd have the answers he needed.

'I can't do that just yet,' he mumbled. 'I've got a few feelers out.'

Corrie nearly groaned. The problem was, once Roy asked for favors, he owed just as many in return. It all depended on whom he'd contacted and why. 'What sort of feelers?'

'Not to worry, most of it can be done over the Internet.'

'It's almost Christmas,' she reminded him again. For once, she wanted him to simply enjoy the holiday and stop thinking about work.

'Yes,' he agreed mildly.

'Our children will be home soon, and it's important that we spend time as a family.'

'I agree,' he said, 'but I want you to remember there's another family somewhere who might be missing a husband and father this Christmas.'

Corrie had remained emotionally detached from the man who'd turned up dead at the Beldons' B and B. He was a stranger who'd chosen to carry false identification. Nothing was known about him or his reasons for being in town. Because of that, Corrie hadn't thought of him as a real person with a home and a wife and perhaps children.

'You're doing a missing person's search, aren't you?'

Roy shrugged, which in itself was an answer.

'Go, and have a good time with Peggy,' he told her.

'Do you want me to bring you back anything for lunch?'

Roy shook his head. 'I'll get by with peanut butter and jelly.' His favorite midday meal.

Corrie left then, and spent a pleasant afternoon with her new friend. It felt good to get out, to be part of the annual Christmas-shopping experience. They ate at the mall's food court, chatting over pizza slices and Coke as holiday tunes filled the air. Soon the two women were caught up in the crowd of shoppers.

Corrie bought Linnette new gloves and Mack a Cedar Cove sweatshirt, and Peggy chose a new golf club for Bob and a book of plays. Bob loved community theater. Roy and Corrie had recently seen him in the fall production of *Arsenic and Old Lace*. He was actually quite talented. For her husband, Corrie bought a beautiful volume of Sherlock Holmes stories.

From Peggy's comments, Corrie sensed that Bob was putting the unfortunate circumstances regarding the John Doe behind him. She knew the police had questioned him, but whatever their concern, it had apparently been laid to rest.

The two women left the mall at about three, saying goodbye in the parking lot. Vendors sold fresh-cut Christmas trees, and Corrie breathed deeply, inhaling the pungent scent of pine and fir. Nothing smelled more like Christmas.

When she returned to the office, she found Roy hunched over his computer, a plate and an empty milk glass sitting on his desk. He stared intently at the computer screen and hadn't noticed her.

'Any phone calls?' she asked.

Roy raised his head. 'Oh, hi. What? Phone calls?'

'Did the telephone go ring, ring, ring?' she teased.

He shook his head.

'Do you want to hear about my lunch?' She waited, but when he didn't respond, she continued. 'In case you're interested, Peggy and I had a great time. I was thinking maybe we could invite them over for New Year's Eve.'

Again nothing.

Corrie sighed. 'Peggy's such a good cook, I'll bet no one ever thinks to invite her to dinner. You like Bob, don't you?'

Her husband stared up at her blankly. Corrie was starting to feel irritated.

'I like the Beldons,' she said in a firm voice. 'I think all four of us could become friends.'

Roy leaned back in his chair and fixed his gaze on her. 'I don't think that would be a good idea.'

Corrie's cheerful mood evaporated. 'Why

not?' she asked.

Roy stood and walked slowly around his desk. His shoulders slouched, he ran his hand through his hair, disheveling it.

Corrie stiffened. Roy had found something in his Internet search, and whatever it was, he didn't want to tell her.

'Do you think Bob is somehow linked to the John Doe?' she asked bluntly.

Roy's eyes met hers and he nodded.

She swallowed tightly. The one friend she'd found, and now this.

'Do you think Bob had something to do with his death?' she asked next. She didn't want to believe it, didn't want to consider what that would mean for Peggy.

Roy walked back to the other side of his desk and sat down. 'I don't know, but I'm not ruling it out.'

*   *   *

Olivia's Christmas was all planned. Justine, Seth and Leif, as well as her mother, would be at her house for dinner by midafternoon. Olivia had invited Jack, too, but unfortunately he'd already made arrangements to join Eric and Shelly and the twins in Reno.

'Next year we'll be together,' Jack promised. He'd stopped at her place early Christmas morning, before he left for the airport. She gave him her gift—a first edition of H. L.

Mencken—and he set his gifts for her under the tree.

'Promise for next year?' she asked, when he'd kissed her farewell.

'Promise.' Jack gathered her in his arms and kissed her again.

Olivia felt the warmth of that kiss all the way to her toes, and when he'd finished, her head was spinning. They were only now recovering their ease and comfort with each other, although they remained a little on edge, afraid of toppling the delicate balance.

For her part, Olivia was careful. Neither of them had discussed Stan, although her ex-husband still called her often—always for what appeared to be legitimate reasons.

Stan was smart. He wanted back in her life and he was a patient man. For the moment, he was letting things slide, doing nothing overt. Olivia knew her ex-husband, though. At some point, when he figured the time was right, Stan would swoop in.

'Will you be here for New Year's Eve?' she asked, looking up at Jack. The thought of spending the night playing Scrabble with her mother held little appeal, although it'd been their tradition for almost a decade. If Jack could join them, it would turn an otherwise routine evening into something truly entertaining. Charlotte loved Jack as much as Olivia did.

'I'm sorry,' he said, 'but I already made

other plans.'

Her smile faded, and her heart thudded to an abrupt halt. 'Not with another woman, I hope?'

He chuckled and appeared to be amused by her small display of jealousy. 'It's not what you think. I volunteered to be part of a retreat for Alcoholics Anonymous. I'm sorry. If I'd thought about it, I would've cleared it with you first.'

She had no right to make that kind of demand on him. 'It's not a problem. I...I'll miss you.'

Jack kissed her one final time. 'I'm going to miss you, too.'

Olivia walked him to his car and waved as he drove off. She wouldn't see him again until after the first of the year. Sadness settled over her. And so did a measure of regret. The difficulties in their relationship had come about because she'd allowed herself to get caught up in Stan's sudden need for her and the nostalgia she'd felt for their past. A past that couldn't be retrieved...

Olivia shook off her somber mood, and Christmas was wonderful. With her mother's help, Olivia's turkey turned out golden-brown and succulent. Although he was still too young to appreciate Christmas, Leif was thoroughly spoiled by Olivia. Stan had dropped off his gifts earlier in the week.

They opened their presents after brunch,

and it was an hour full of laughter and exclamations of pleasure. The contrast between Jack's gifts to her and Stan's seemed very telling to Olivia. Jack had bought her a small framed black-and-white photograph of the Cedar Cove lighthouse, one of Jon Bowman's pictures. He'd also given her a new Cross pen, to replace the old one she'd used for years. Stan had bought her a diamond pendant, an 'any woman' sort of gift. It seemed oddly impersonal, although Justine immediately made her put it on.

At three o'clock, the small party telephoned James and Selina in San Diego and eighteen-month-old Isabella chattered away. Unfortunately, little of what her granddaughter said was decipherable to Olivia. What did come across was that this was the first Christmas her granddaughter understood that she had two grandmas. Selina assured Olivia that Isabella loved her gifts: a talking doll with its own baby carriage.

'I wish you'd invited Dad,' Justine told Olivia privately in the kitchen while scraping the dinner dishes.

'I thought about it,' Olivia confessed. She had, but she was afraid it would encourage Stan, which was the last thing she wanted to do.

'I hate it that he spent the day alone.'

Olivia swallowed down a sense of guilt, but later she reminded herself that if Stan was alone on Christmas Day, it was the result of choices he'd made sixteen years ago. *He* was the one who'd walked out on their family, on her and their two surviving children. Despite her sympathy for him, and her residual affection, she couldn't get too involved in comforting her ex-husband, even if he was in the throes of a second divorce. Knowing Stan, that would lead to willfully mistaken impressions; besides, she had other priorities now.

'Seth and I are hoping to spend New Year's Eve at the restaurant,' Justine said casually, without looking at Olivia.

If that was a hint that her daughter needed someone to watch Leif, Olivia was more than ready to volunteer. Jack had plans, so the only person she worried about upsetting was her mother.

'Let me check with your grandmother, but if she doesn't mind, I'll stay with Leif.'

'Really, Mom?' Justine was obviously relieved. 'I don't feel right leaving him with a sitter yet.'

Olivia didn't blame her. 'I'll be back in a minute.'

Her mother sat with her feet up in front of the fireplace, knitting what seemed to be a man's sweater, although she hadn't said who it was for. Possibly Seth, but that didn't seem likely. If it was, Olivia assumed her mother would've finished it before Christmas.

247

Sitting down next to Charlotte, Olivia took in the scene around her. A fire flickered in the fireplace and the Christmas stockings that had hung on the mantel were down now, empty and spread across the coffee table. Seth held his sleeping son cradled in his arms; he, too, had dozed off. Christmas music played softly from the CD player and the lights on the tree sparkled. It was about as perfect a Christmas as she could remember.

'Mom,' Olivia said, 'would you mind terribly if I didn't join you this New Year's Eve?'

'Oh, you have other plans?'

Olivia looked at her quizzically; her mother seemed *pleased* by the prospect of spending the evening alone. 'Justine asked me to watch Leif so she and Seth could be at the restaurant.'

'By all means, Olivia, you stay with Leif. Don't worry about me.'

'Would you like me to drive by and pick you up?' Olivia asked.

'Nonsense,' Charlotte returned. 'I might have a date of my own, you know.'

Olivia smiled. Charlotte had men friends, but no beaus. Her friends had encouraged her to pursue a second relationship, but Charlotte had refused. Life was simpler that way, she'd always said.

Following her divorce, well-meaning friends had tried to set Olivia up with various men. Had circumstances been different, she

248

might've been interested. But at the time, she was in no condition to get involved with anyone, and she knew it.

In addition, Justine and James had needed her. Her world and theirs had just collapsed, crushing them under the weight of their combined grief. For a long time afterward, the three of them had been emotionally crippled. They'd needed time to recover, and it hadn't happened quickly or easily.

In their own ways, they'd each succeeded. James had joined the navy and married Selina. In the military he'd found security, and Selina had offered him the unconditional love he so desperately needed.

Justine had faltered for years, and had managed to convince herself that she wanted neither a husband nor children. Thankfully, Seth Gunderson had convinced her otherwise.

For her part, Olivia had found satisfaction and joy in her position on the bench. Meeting Jack had been an unexpected bonus. He'd brought laughter and spontaneity back into her life. With him, she could relax the rigidity that she'd so carefully incorporated into her daily routine.

Her throat thickened with sudden emotion. She owed Jack so much, and she'd nearly thrown it all away. She'd nearly destroyed the relationship that gave her so much pleasure.

It dawned on her then that she hadn't heard from him all day.

Later that night, after her family had left, Jack did phone, but their conversation was brief. He was flying back the following weekend, and they arranged a dinner date at the Taco Shack, his favorite restaurant. Olivia had to admit she was growing accustomed to reading a menu on a wall.

After she talked to Jack, Olivia made a pot of tea and sat in front of the Christmas tree, reveling in a peaceful hour or so before bed. It had truly been a wonderful Christmas. The only improvement she could add to the day was Jack, and he'd already promised her they'd be together the following year.

The phone chimed in the distance, and for a moment she was tempted to let it ring. In retrospect, she wished she had.

'Merry Christmas,' she said before glancing at caller ID.

It was Stan. 'Same to you, sweetheart.' He sounded cheerful.

She resisted the urge to correct him—to tell him she wasn't his sweetheart and never would be again. 'Hello, Stan. I imagine you want to talk to Justine and Seth, but they've left.'

'No,' he said, 'I'm calling to talk to you.'

She didn't comment.

'I wanted to ask you out for New Year's Eve.' Before she could object, he added, 'Think about the two of us having dinner at the Space Needle, with champagne and ballroom dancing, just like we used to.'

Clearly he had her confused with his second wife. When she was married to Stan, they could never have afforded such extravagance. 'I'm sorry, but I already have plans.'

A momentary pause. Then he said, 'Not with that newspaper fellow. Tell me you're not serious.'

Olivia bit her tongue to keep from defending Jack. It wouldn't do any good. 'If you must know, I agreed to watch Leif for Justine and Seth.'

'You did?'

She almost confessed that Jack would be at a retreat with some of his AA friends, but quickly decided that was more information than her ex-husband needed to know.

'That's great,' Stan said, sounding jovial now. 'I'll join you. We'll put Leif down for the night, drink champagne and dance. It'll be like old times, just the two of us.'

'I don't think so.'

Stan chuckled. 'You can't keep me away from my only grandson, and it'll be the perfect opportunity for us to talk. Give me a chance to prove myself, Olivia. I made a mistake and I've paid for it. It's time to put the past behind us. I love you. I've always loved you.'

Olivia released a sigh. 'I'm sorry, Stan, but you're sixteen years too late.'

*　　　*　　　*

251

Christmas had been a miserable affair for Rosie. Allison was in a rotten mood most of the day because neither Rosie nor Zach could afford to buy her the computer she wanted. Eddie had been disappointed in his gifts, too, but he'd put on a brighter face than Allison. Rosie wondered when their children had become so terribly, terribly spoiled.

That Saturday, two days after Christmas, Rosie and Zach met to divide the monthly bills. Until the divorce, Zach had always managed the money and had done an excellent job of handling their finances; now they shared this unpleasant task. The divorce had cost them both dearly and continued to do so.

Zach had brewed a pot of coffee when she arrived at the house. The bills were spread out across the kitchen table, organized alphabetically. She noted that dishes were stacked in the sink and the living room needed to be straightened. From the look of the carpet, no one had vacuumed since before Christmas. She wasn't about to mention his failings as a housekeeper, however, considering that she wasn't much better.

'When we're finished there's something I need to discuss with you,' he said. He reached for the coffeepot and automatically filled two mugs, which he brought to the table. He set hers down, then pulled out a chair across from her.

Studying the tense look on his face, Rosie

decided she'd rather deal with whatever was bothering him first and get it over with. 'What?' she said, picking up her mug.

'It might be best if we talked about it later.'

'Where are the kids?'

'Eddie's with Jeremy and his mother at the movies, and Allison's in her room sulking.'

Nothing had changed from earlier in the week. Rosie glanced at the electric bill and nearly groaned aloud. The water bill was equally high. With both of them employed, they managed to cover expenses, but paying attorneys' fees and maintaining two residences didn't leave anything for extras.

A year ago, Rosie had been shopping the after-Christmas sales, loading up on wrapping paper and ribbon and assorted bargains. This year she couldn't afford to do that. It was a sad commentary on what her life had become.

'All right, we can talk about Allison first,' Zach said, leaning back in his chair. He folded his arms across his chest.

His body language made her feel a little wary, and she braced herself for whatever he had to say.

'For starters, Allison gave me a list I'm supposed to share with you.'

'A list?' Rosie asked, frowning.

'Apparently she's got it in her head that the judge awarded her and Eddie the house, so she's the one in charge.'

'I'm not putting up with *that* notion,' Rosie

assured him. Frankly she'd be shocked if Zach fell into line with any ultimatum their daughter presented.

His mouth quivered slightly and she could tell he was more amused than angry. 'Take a look at this,' he said. He unfolded the single sheet of paper and handed it to her.

Rosie scanned the carefully typed list of rules their fifteen-year-old daughter had given them. 'What?' she burst out incredulously. 'We're supposed to stay out of the family room if Allison has a friend over and they're watching television?'

'It gets better,' Zach told her.

Rosie's eyes widened as she continued down the sheet. 'We're not to embarrass her by asking if she has her homework done or any other personal questions.'

'She's got a rule for Eddie, too.' He pointed toward the bottom of the page.

Rosie couldn't help it, she laughed outright at the last item on the page. 'Eddie's supposed to have his hair combed at all times.'

'Apparently her little brother's unruly hair is an embarrassment to her.'

'Yeah, and neither one of us makes the grade, either,' she said, waving the sheet of rules.

Zach nodded. 'We're forbidden to enter her room, you'll notice. And we require Her Majesty's permission before cleaning in there or touching her stuff.'

'Not in this lifetime.' Zach could make his own decisions when it came to Allison's list, but for her part Rosie was planning to ignore it.

'I wish this was the only letter I had to show you,' Zach said, growing serious. 'The school wrote and said Allison's grades have dropped considerably.'

'Did they suggest counseling?' Having Allison talk to a professional would be expensive, but Rosie would do whatever was necessary to help their daughter through this difficult transition period.

'I don't think counseling's the answer, especially with her attitude. I have a better idea, but only if you agree.'

'What?' At this point Rosie was open to just about anything. They were losing Allison. Every day their daughter seemed to be drawing further and further away from them. She was angry and rebellious. Rosie knew Allison had every right to feel the things she did, but she couldn't stand by and do nothing while her daughter self-destructed.

'Allison's pretty disappointed about not getting a computer for Christmas.'

This wasn't news to Rosie; she'd already heard it, many times over.

'What if she earns it?' Zach said.

'Earns it? How?' Rosie couldn't see her daughter baby-sitting or doing the kinds of chores a typical fifteen-year-old did to earn extra cash.

'What if I bring her into the office?' Zach suggested. 'Tax time is always hectic and we could use an extra pair of hands for filing, photocopying and so on. It would be a real part-time job with a real paycheck.'

Rosie's heart started to pound with excitement. 'That way we'd be able to monitor where she is after school, and who she's with.' One of Rosie's biggest concerns was the new friends Allison had found. Where Allison went and who she was with—those were major concerns for both Zach and Rosie.

'I think it's a brilliant idea.' Rosie nodded happily. 'And Eddie's been going to his friend Nick's place in the afternoons, so that's not an issue.'

'Allison has to agree first,' Zach reminded her. 'I'm not exactly her favorite person at the moment. There are no guarantees. She could say no when she learns she'd be working at the office.'

'But,' Rosie said, 'she wants a computer.'

'Shall we mention it together?'

Rosie nodded, grateful to be included in the discussion. Zach went down the hallway that led to the bedrooms. A few minutes later, he returned with Allison, who had recently pierced her nose. Rosie cringed when she noticed, but managed to keep her opinion to herself. This new piercing was a response to not getting the computer she wanted,

256

Rosie suspected. The kids had received some Christmas money from their grandparents, and the nose ring must be what Allison had spent hers on.

'Your mother and I want to talk to you,' Zach said when Allison slouched against the counter, arms crossed, defiance radiating from every part of her body.

'I figured you would when you read my list. I'm not willing to compromise on any of my fifteen points. Since the house belongs to Eddie and me, I expect you to live up to my stipulations.'

'We can discuss that later,' Zach said, smoothly diverting her from that subject. 'What your mother and I wanted to tell you was how sorry we are that you didn't get a computer for Christmas.'

Allison glanced between them, as though she wasn't sure she should believe what Zach had said. She shrugged, implying it was no big deal, although that certainly wasn't the impression she'd given earlier.

'We can't afford it, Allison. I couldn't be sorrier.' Zach looked genuinely regretful. 'But,' he said, 'we've come up with a way for you to get a computer.'

'You have?' Her eyes brightened with hope.

'I want to hire you,' Zach said. 'Tax time's coming and my new assistant needs some additional help.'

Her eyes, which had widened just a moment

earlier, narrowed now with suspicion. 'You want me to *earn* a computer?'

'It's your decision. I'm just giving you the opportunity.'

She shrugged again, as if she wasn't sure she should admit it. 'I'd want a dollar more than minimum wage to start,' she insisted.

Zach nodded. 'That's acceptable.'

'And I should be paid overtime if I have to work extra hours.'

'That's only fair,' Zach agreed.

Allison glanced from Rosie to her father and then back. 'All right,' she said. 'I'll do it, but only because I want a new computer. Don't think you're doing me any favors.'

'I wouldn't dream of it,' Zach assured her.

'You ready to talk about my list now?' she asked, straightening abruptly.

'Let's leave that for later. All right?'

She sighed in a loud, exasperated way. 'I guess.' And with that she returned to her room.

Zach's gaze met Rosie's, and for the first time in what felt like years, they shared a smile.

Seventeen

Maryellen had been feeling anxious all morning, the first day of the new year. She'd invited Jon to dinner, and to her delight and surprise, he'd accepted. Only later did she realize that she'd offered to cook a meal for a man who was a professional chef. Her expertise in the kitchen was limited to packaged macaroni and cheese and frozen entrées. With anyone else, she would've ordered takeout, but Jon ate restaurant food every day. She felt obliged to make the effort to cook for him.

But the meal wasn't even her main concern. The important thing about this dinner was what she planned to tell him.

She wanted to change the terms of their relationship. And she wanted him to know that she treasured his Christmas gift, a photo album filled with pictures of the first four months of Katie's life.

Jon's photographs revealed hidden beauty in nature, catching an unexpected pattern or a fleeting moment. But his pictures of their daughter showed far more than the changes he documented as she grew week by week. Maryellen also saw the deep love he felt for his child.

Christmas morning when she unwrapped his

gift and slowly turned the pages of the album, tears had spilled from her eyes. Jon loved his daughter, and if she'd read him correctly, he had strong feelings for her, too. Maryellen prayed she was right.

The first picture in the album was a shot of Maryellen smiling into the camera, her belly huge with their unborn child. The next photos were of her in the hospital and then of Katie in the nursery.

Her favorite was a picture he'd taken on the autumn day she'd gone out to his property and the eagle had been soaring high above, wings spread wide. Jon had captured Maryellen holding Katie and pointing toward the bird. He'd caught their daughter's face in the sun, Katie's jubilation and the soaring eagle, all in one dramatic shot.

Naturally, with Jon's visit at hand and her insecurity about cooking, Katie was fussy all day, interrupting Maryellen at every turn. In the end, with cookbooks spread over the kitchen counters, she decided to bake a salmon, accompanied with wild rice and fresh asparagus. Meal preparation wasn't exactly rocket science, but just then it felt like it.

The table was set and dinner ready to be served when Jon rang the doorbell.

Maryellen paused for a few seconds to calm her pounding heart before she answered, arranging a welcoming smile on her face, despite her nerves.

Jon brought a bottle of white wine and a bouquet of yellow daisies.

'Thank you,' she said, ushering him in.

'Thanks for inviting me.' Jon stepped into the house and stood there for a moment, looking awkward and out of place. He seemed as nervous as Maryellen. Katie sat upright in her bassinet and obviously recognized her daddy's voice. Almost immediately she started chattering and waving her arms.

'She's really developing a personality, isn't she?' Jon said. He walked over to the bassinet, lifting Katie into his arms with familiar ease. Maryellen recalled how uncomfortable he'd seemed in the beginning. That had definitely changed.

'I'll get dinner on the table,' Maryellen told him. She'd forgotten to remove her apron, which she immediately stuffed into a kitchen drawer. Heaven forbid he should know how hard she'd worked on this meal.

Jon followed her into the kitchen and grinned when he noticed the number of open cookbooks.

Maryellen's gaze followed his. 'Mom told me that the people with the most cookbooks are the ones who cook the least. That's certainly true in my case.'

'I'm easy to please.'

Maryellen hoped that was true. 'I'm not much good at this, so if dinner isn't up to par, I hope you'll take into account that I don't do this often.' The serving dishes were already out, and she quickly transferred everything from the stove to the table.

'Katie's already eaten,' she said, standing at the table with her hands on the back of her chair, fingers clenching it tightly.

Jon put his daughter back in the bassinet and joined Maryellen. She'd placed the flowers in a crystal vase; they provided a cheery accent and perfectly complemented her pale yellow table linens. He opened the bottle and poured them each a glass as she jumped up to put on some music. When she finally sat down across from him, she offered him a shy smile. She was an emotional mess; if he said one derogatory thing about this dinner, she knew she'd burst into tears.

Jon served her and then himself, although by this time she had no appetite.

'I was surprised you came,' she said, not meeting his eyes. When she'd issued the invitation for New Year's, she wasn't at all sure he'd accept. For some reason, it seemed important to start this year off right, and for Maryellen that included a good relationship with her baby's father.

'I'm surprised I did, too,' Jon confessed.

That stung. So much for flattering her ego or reassuring her. 'Why did you?' she asked.

Jon glanced up, grinning sheepishly. 'You seemed so sincere. I guess I wanted to be with you more than I wanted to stay away.'

That was as confusing as his original comment. She thought about pressing the issue, then decided against it. 'Thank you for the photo album. I love it.'

'I liked your gift, too. No one's ever knit me socks before.'

'Did they fit?'

He nodded and pointed down at his feet with a smile. 'Wearing them now.' She smiled back. As he reached into the middle of the table for a dinner roll, Maryellen automatically passed him the butter.

'I wish you could've been with us at Christmas, but you had other plans, and I understand that,' she said, watching him for any telltale sign that would indicate where he'd been and with whom.

To her disappointment, Jon didn't comment.

They ate silently for a few moments and then Maryellen put down her fork. She couldn't swallow another bite. 'I wanted you to come tonight because...because I feel I owe you an apology—for the way I behaved when I learned I was pregnant.'

His eyes, flashing with amusement, flew up to meet hers. 'I like it when you apologize. Remember the last time?'

Maryellen had forgotten how they'd ended up kissing....

'Anyway, you *don't* owe me an apology,' he assured her.

But she did, and she had every intention of saying what needed to be said. 'Then I owe you an explanation.'

He shook his head. 'It isn't important.'

'It is to me.' Maryellen's voice trembled slightly. She should probably wait until after dinner, but the need to explain felt like a rock on her chest. She wouldn't be able to enjoy any part of their evening until she'd unburdened herself to Jon.

'I think you know that I was married while I was in college.' She set her napkin on the table and picked up the wineglass. Her hand tightened around the stem as she took a long sip of the spicy gewürztraminer— coincidentally one of her favorite wines. It had a calming effect on her. 'Clint and I got married for all the wrong reasons.'

'Everyone has regrets,' Jon said gently.

'Some people have more than others,' she whispered, unable to look at him. 'Clint and I were careful, but I was pregnant at the time.'

'So the pregnancy's the reason you married him?'

She was ashamed to admit the truth. 'I married him because I'd convinced myself I loved him and that he loved me. He didn't want the baby. He thought it best to terminate the pregnancy.'

Jon was silent as he leaned back in his chair.

Unable to remain sitting, Maryellen stood and walked into the living room, stopping by

Katie's bassinet. She peered at her sleeping baby, tears trickling down her cheeks. Impatiently she dashed them away.

There would be other pregnancies, other babies, Clint had told her, but the timing was critical. Maryellen had listened to him. She went against every dictate of her heart, and she'd regretted it from that moment on. For years she'd struggled with the guilt and the shame of what she'd done. What she'd never admitted to herself or to Clint, until it was too late, was how much she'd wanted her baby. She didn't blame her ex-husband. She was the one who walked into the clinic. The one who'd signed the consent form. She accepted full responsibility.

'Maryellen,' Jon said, coming up behind her. He placed his hands on her shoulders. 'It's all right—there's no need to say any more. I can figure out what happened.'

'Can you?'

Jon turned her and brought her into his arms.

'I didn't want you to know I was pregnant last year,' she said, her face buried in his shoulder. 'I was afraid you'd react the way Clint did.'

'I'm not Clint.'

'I know. You're nothing like him. I know that now.' What she *didn't* know was anything about his past. Even now, more than a year later, she'd learned very little—just fragments

265

of his history. Small bits of information he'd let drop now and then. Every time she pried into his life, he pulled away from her, both physically and emotionally. Maryellen had come to rely on him in so many ways, she couldn't bear to risk that withdrawal, so she kept her questions to herself.

She slowly raised her eyes to Jon's, fearing what she'd see. Instead of condemnation and repulsion, she saw understanding and love. If he'd judged her harshly, she wasn't sure what she would have done. When she saw his love, her reaction was instinctive.

She kissed him.

It'd been weeks since they'd last touched, since she'd been in his arms. Maryellen hadn't truly understood how much she'd missed him—everything about him—and the moment their mouths met, she lost control.

Jon's reaction was immediate. He splayed his fingers in her hair and their kisses became passionate, full of desperation and need. When he broke it off, he had to catch his breath. Maryellen clung to him, her own breathing labored.

'I'm not sure this is such a good idea,' he said as he disengaged her arms from around his neck. Holding both her hands in his, he retreated a step.

This was what Maryellen had dreaded. Her heart sank as she pulled her hands free. She'd waited too long to tell him, delayed explaining.

'There's someone else…isn't there?'

'Someone else?' he repeated. 'No way.' He reached for her and brought her back into his arms. Then he kissed her again, and again. Harder, deeper, longer.

He was telling her the truth; she had her answer. Although she knew almost nothing about Jon, she trusted him. He couldn't kiss her like this if he was involved with another woman. Soon, however, he eased away from her again, his reluctance obvious.

Maryellen didn't want him to stop, and when she managed to shake off the warm haze that enveloped her, she opened her eyes and stared up at him.

'Jon?' That was when she realized he planned to end their lovemaking. 'Don't stop,' she pleaded, 'please don't stop.'

'You don't know what you're asking.'

'I *do* know. You don't want me?' She hated the plea she heard in her own voice.

For just a moment, a hint of a smile touched his mouth. 'In case you haven't noticed, I want you very much.'

'But I…I want you, too.' She blushed as she said it. Until Jon, there'd only been one man in her life, so she didn't say those words lightly. If they were lovers again, he'd know she was sincere, he'd know she regretted the way she'd treated him earlier. He'd know how much she wanted him to be a permanent part of her life and Katie's.

Slowly, Jon shook his head.

Stunned and hurt, Maryellen retreated a step. She could only imagine what he must think of her, blatantly throwing herself at him like that. Perhaps this was his way of punishing her. She'd been brutal in her rejection of him and now it was her turn.

Jon frowned, and his eyes narrowed. 'I don't know what you're thinking, but whatever it is, you're wrong.'

Katie began to wake—the perfect excuse for Maryellen to turn away and recover her pride and her composure. The moment she lifted Katie from the carrier, Maryellen could tell the baby needed changing.

'She needs a fresh diaper,' she said, welcoming the excuse to leave the room.

Jon wouldn't allow her to escape. He followed her into the nursery. 'Are you on the pill?' he demanded.

'No…' There wasn't any need for her to be.

'I don't have anything to protect you.'

She was an idiot. *Of course* he was worried about birth control. They were already batting a thousand, and there was no guarantee that she couldn't, wouldn't, get pregnant a second time.

'I'm still nursing, and there's less likelihood I'd get caught.' But that sounded weak, even to her own ears. She'd been caught easily enough with Katie. 'That isn't why you refused me, though, is it?'

'No.' At least he was honest, even if the truth hurt. 'No,' he repeated. 'The fact is, Maryellen, I'm not interested in another one-night stand with you.'

'Do you seriously think that's what I wanted?' She quickly disposed of the wet diaper and exchanged it for a fresh one. 'I...I didn't *plan* to invite you into my bed, if that's what you're thinking. Dinner wasn't about that. It just sort of...went in that direction.' Although she'd hoped this meeting would be a new beginning for them—emotionally and, yes, physically.

'It doesn't matter what I believe.'

'You're right,' she said, tucking Katie against her hip. Her face was hot with anger and embarrassment. 'You're absolutely right. This entire discussion is ridiculous. I apologize for my presumption. I'm sorry....' If he didn't leave soon, she was going to humiliate herself even more.

Jon hesitated and Maryellen was afraid she'd have to ask him to leave.

Then he turned abruptly and left the room. She followed him and didn't try to stop him when he grabbed his jacket and walked out the door.

Her stomach was in knots as she held her daughter close to her heart. 'I blew it,' she told Katie. Hard as she'd tried to make this night special, she'd failed. She'd hoped so much that this evening would be the turning point for

269

her and Jon, but all she'd managed to do was alienate him.

And in the process, break her own heart.

Eighteen

What had seemed such a brilliant plan earlier was rapidly becoming a problem, Zach mused at his desk. School had resumed after Christmas vacation, and Allison had started working for Smith, Cox and Wright today. She seemed to take pride in dressing outrageously—in a manner guaranteed to embarrass him with his associates. Zach was somewhat horrified that she'd gone to school looking like she'd just climbed out of bed, complete with flannel pajama bottoms and bedroom slippers. In his day, no principal would've put up with it.

Allison arrived thirty minutes late with a chain of safety pins dangling from each ear. He'd had to fight to keep from dragging her into the parking lot and telling her the deal was off. If she wanted to work in his office, she was to show up on time and dress appropriately. He would've done it, too, but he hated to fire his own daughter her first day on the job.

Zach decided he shouldn't get directly involved. When he'd offered Allison employment, he'd told her she was to be an assistant to Cecilia Randall, and he was standing by that.

As soon as he had a free moment, Zach called Cecilia and Allison into his office.

Allison stood there, wearing an old sweater three sizes too big over the pajamas. He could only imagine where she'd gotten it. Cecilia and all the other women employed in the office wore proper business attire.

'Allison, this is Ms. Randall. You'll be working with her.'

Allison glared defiantly in Cecilia's direction.

Cecilia ignored the dirty look and smiled warmly at his daughter.

'I've offered Allison the job as your assistant, Ms. Randall,' he said, doing his best to ignore his daughter's attitude. 'I want you to treat her exactly as you would any other part-time employee.'

'I don't want any favors,' Allison announced.

Cecilia nodded. 'That's good, because it wouldn't be fair to the others if I treated you any differently.'

Zach didn't know if handing his problem child over to his assistant was going to work. Cecilia was a new employee herself. She'd fit in nicely with the staff and done an impressive job thus far. But he wasn't sure she was up to dealing with his rebellious, angry teenager.

No one could take Allison's attitude for long, and he felt guilty about thrusting her on an unsuspecting employee.

'In other words, I have to do what *she* says,' Allison muttered with a disparaging glance at Cecilia.

'Only if you want to keep the job,' Zach returned, letting Cecilia know she had firing privileges. If Allison pulled any more stunts like the ones she had this afternoon, he wouldn't be able to keep her around.

'Is that agreeable?' he asked Cecilia.

His assistant nodded.

'Allison?'

His daughter shrugged. 'Whatever.'

The two left his office, and despite a vague sense of guilt, Zach was glad to shift the responsibility elsewhere. The door started to close but not before he heard Allison taunt his assistant.

'You can fire me if you want, Ms. Randall, but remember, my dad is the one who signs your paycheck.'

Zach shut his eyes and prayed for patience.

The first week was the worst. By the middle of the month, however, Zach noticed several small changes in Allison, beginning with her timely arrival at work. And while she wasn't going to receive any fashion awards, she wore jeans and a respectable-looking sweatshirt. He was tempted to say something when he saw her, but knew it would be a mistake to call attention to the improvement in her attire.

'Would you like me to start making copies of the completed income tax forms?' Zach heard Allison ask Cecilia as he walked out of his office. His daughter completely ignored him, but he was accustomed to that.

'Please,' Cecilia told her. 'I've got a stack halfway to the ceiling.'

'I'll get on it right away.' Moving quickly and efficiently, Allison hauled the first stack of files to the copy machine.

If Zach didn't know better, he'd think... Why, it sounded as though Allison was eager to work. She actually seemed enthusiastic about her job.

Rosie noticed a change in Allison, too, and mentioned it when he saw her one Sunday afternoon toward the end of January. 'What happened?' she asked, astonished.

'I wish I knew,' Zach murmured. Allison continued to display plenty of attitude at home, but some of the more pressing problems seemed to have abated. Her boyfriend, Ryan Wilson, had apparently vanished. Zach hadn't seen the boy in weeks, for which he was profoundly grateful. Allison's questionable new friends hadn't been around all month, either. To top everything off, her geometry teacher phoned and commented on a noticeable improvement in her grades and attitude.

'I guess earning the money to buy her own

computer is exactly what Allison needed.' Rosie relaxed, leaning against the kitchen counter. 'You know what? I think what you did is absolutely inspired.'

His ex-wife's praise felt good, especially after all the tension between them in recent months. However, Zach wasn't comfortable accepting it. 'I suspect we both have someone else to thank for the changes in Allison— someone at the office. Let me find out.'

'All right.' Rosie was just as eager to learn who or what had brought about the change in Allison.

Zach knew the person to ask. Early the next morning, he called Cecilia Randall into his office. Tax season was starting and soon he'd be overwhelmed.

'Can you sit down a moment?' Zach said, gesturing her in.

'Of course.' Cecilia slipped into the chair across from his desk.

'I'd like a progress report on Allison.'

Cecilia instantly brightened. 'I'm delighted with her performance. She doesn't have any problem doing whatever I ask and her attitude is great.'

That fact hadn't escaped Zach's notice. 'How did all of this happen?' He hadn't meant to be that blunt, but he didn't have time to ask discreet questions; he needed to know.

'Happen?'

He nodded. 'You saw her that first day. She

was an inch short of belligerent.'

His assistant glanced down at the floor and Zach realized she was trying to hide a smile. 'She's a very nice girl,' Cecilia assured him. 'I'm not having any trouble with her.'

'That was the way I used to think about Allison,' Zach said. 'But everything changed after my wife and I divorced.'

'Yes, I know.'

'Allison mentioned the divorce?' As far as he knew, his daughter considered the whole matter 'bogus'—one of her current favorite words—and refused to discuss it.

'Not exactly.' Cecilia let her hand rest on the tablet she held in her lap. 'You see, my parents divorced when I was a kid. I know what it's like when a family falls apart. Allison just needed someone to talk to.'

Zach yearned to explain that tearing his family apart had never been what *he* wanted. He blamed Rosie for being jealous and unreasonable. In retrospect, he was embarrassed that he'd been so caught up in the negative emotions that had precipitated the divorce and surrounded the whole subject for months. He found it difficult to believe that he and Rosie had haggled over every aspect of the property settlement and the parenting plan. They'd each been so determined to make sure the other didn't get a 'better' deal. That was just the beginning. They were both driven by their need to prove who was right.

They'd allowed pride, ego and a sense of vindictiveness to destroy any chance of settling the divorce in a civil manner.

If he'd been able to look into the future, to witness the pain he'd brought his children—if Zach had so much as guessed how lonely and lost he'd feel without Rosie—he'd have done whatever was necessary to save his family and his marriage. Before he realized how far things had gone, it was too late.

Recently, he and Rosie had begun to communicate in a more honest and more courteous manner. He knew she was dating that widower, although they never talked about it.

However, Zach's own pride wouldn't allow him to admit that Janice Lamond no longer worked for him. He'd led Rosie to believe she'd gotten a promotion within the firm. By now, Allison had probably told her mother that Janice wasn't working there anymore. Rosie must've gloated at the news, although to her credit, she hadn't said anything.

'Will that be all, Mr. Cox?' Cecilia Randall asked.

For a moment he'd forgotten she was in the room.

'Yes, thank you.'

Later that night, Zach drove Allison home. Rosie was spending the night with the children, and the thought of walking into his dark apartment and making dinner held little appeal. Allison sat quietly beside him.

They hardly ever talked these days, and Zach missed their conversations. She'd spurned his attempts so often that after a while he'd given up trying.

'Did you know Cecilia had a baby who died?' his daughter suddenly asked him.

This was news to Zach. 'No, when?'

'Almost three years ago.'

'I'm sorry to hear that,' Zach said, completely sincere.

'She told me all about it. Her husband was at sea and she didn't have any friends here to help her. It was awful and she decided she couldn't stay married.'

'Ms. Randall's been married before?'

'*No.*' Allison's tone made him sound stupid for asking.

'So she's still married to the same man?' It wasn't any of Zach's business, but he was trying to keep Allison talking. They so rarely spoke without arguing that he didn't want their conversation to end.

'Cecilia and her husband went to divorce court, the same as you and Mom. The judge told them they needed to think it through before they rushed into a divorce.'

Zach could hardly believe any judge would say such a thing, especially in these days of no-fault divorce. 'Not in those words, I'll bet.'

'No,' his daughter agreed. 'But close. Cecilia said she was pregnant when she and Ian got

277

married and she wanted to make sure he wasn't marrying her just because of the baby.'

Zach didn't understand what that had to do with anything. He murmured a noncommittal response, hoping she'd enlighten him.

She did. 'Cecilia had him sign an agreement before she'd marry him. Then later, when they were in the court and the judge read the agreement, she wouldn't let them get rid of it.'

'So this judge gave them a reason to stop and think about what they were doing.'

'Right,' Allison said.

'Smart judge,' Zach said, wishing the one who'd been assigned his divorce suit had shown the same wisdom in dealing with him and Rosie. If someone had stepped in and talked sense to him and his ex, it might have saved his family a lot of grief.

'You know her,' Allison said next.

'Who?' Zach asked as he turned off Harbor Street and headed toward Pelican Court.

'The judge.' The look his daughter flashed him said that should be obvious. 'It's the same judge who was in court with you and Mom.'

'Judge Lockhart?' He supposed he should've known; unusual verdicts seemed to be her trademark.

'I think she must be righteous cool.'

Zach barely managed to suppress a smile. *Righteous cool* was something his daughter might've said last year. For a moment, it was almost like having her back again, the girl she'd been before the divorce.

'I like her,' she said, adjusting the seat belt strap to a more comfortable position. 'And before you ask, I'm talking about Cecilia, not Judge Lockhart.'

'I know you do.' He would be forever grateful for the way Cecilia had taken his daughter under her wing.

'I didn't in the beginning, but then she told me what it was like when her parents divorced.' Allison glanced in his direction and sighed. 'She was just a kid, too.'

'Bad, huh?'

Allison nodded. 'Her dad took off. Her mom didn't get any child support, either. Cecilia never really knew her dad when she was growing up. He's the reason she moved to Cedar Cove. She wanted to get to know him, so she got in touch with him once she finished high school. He said he could get her a job, and she came here. She did get a job at the same restaurant where her dad worked, but it wasn't what she'd expected. By then it was too late to move back home.' Cecilia's contribution to the firm was valuable—but her relationship with Allison was worth even more to him.

Whatever had brought Cecilia to Cedar Cove, he was grateful she'd come.

'It didn't work out with her and her dad, though,' Allison said absently.

'How come?'

Allison shrugged. 'Sounds like he's a real

flake.'

Zach felt his daughter's eyes on him. 'Am I a flake?'

She shook her head. 'You can be, but overall you're okay, I guess.'

Such overwhelming praise was almost more than he could bear. 'I'm glad you think so.'

'Her dad moved to California when The Captain's Galley sold. The new owners didn't offer him a job, which was probably for the best. Cecilia said her dad was drinking up the profits.'

'Oh.' That sounded like a direct quote. 'This must've been about the time her baby died.'

'Somewhere around then,' his daughter informed him. 'Ian was the one who encouraged Cecilia to take accounting classes. That's her husband, in case you forgot.'

'Good for him.'

'He was at sea, and they were e-mailing back and forth, getting to know each other again.'

'That's good.' Perhaps if he'd had the opportunity to e-mail Rosie, to correspond with her, they might've had the same chance. Somehow, putting words on paper gave a person time to think about what he or she was really saying.

'Cecilia said that the minute she met me, she knew I was special.'

'Why's that?' He didn't mean to sound skeptical, but he wanted to know what Cecilia

280

had seen in his daughter. It seemed important to find out.

'Haven't you been listening?'

Zach had. To every word. 'Yes, I have.'

'Because of her baby,' Allison said. 'Her baby's name was Allison, too.'

Nineteen

As he walked into the Cedar Cove sheriff's office, Roy McAfee looked around. The room was full of activity; several men and women sat at desks and a dispatcher handled the switchboard. There was a sense of urgency, of purpose, as deputies—uniformed and not—spoke on the phone, carried on conversations or typed at computers.

Damn it all, this was exactly the atmosphere Roy loved. He wanted to close his eyes, breathe in the scent of stale coffee, the sounds of cops at work. There was an excitement here. He'd almost forgotten what it was like to play an active role in law enforcement and he missed it. Except for the paperwork, he reminded himself. When he was on the force, he'd spent more than half his time filling out forms.

'How ya doing, Roy?' a uniformed woman asked when he approached.

Roy didn't recognize her. 'I'm good. I'm

here to see Sheriff Davis.'

She smiled. 'I'll tell him you're here.'

'I'd appreciate it.' Roy had phoned soon after the first of the year, after he'd done everything he could on his end of the investigation. Today he'd give the sheriff what he'd learned. He liked and trusted Troy Davis; the man was no one's fool. Roy was walking a tightrope, though. Officially he'd been employed by Grace Sherman and more recently Bob Beldon. His first priority was to look after his clients' interests. If a crime had been committed, his job was to do everything he could to keep his clients clear of the law.

The female deputy returned. 'Sheriff Davis will see you now.'

Roy followed her to the small office. Davis was sitting behind his desk, frowning at something on his computer screen, when Roy entered the room. Troy stood, and the two men exchanged handshakes. Roy took a seat and so did the sheriff.

'What can I do for you?' Troy Davis asked, leaning back in his chair, giving a relaxed impression.

Roy wasn't deceived. The lawman was intensely interested in his visit. 'Like I said when I called, I came to talk to you about the John Doe.'

'You know something I don't?' Davis asked.

Roy considered the question. 'I might.'

'Tell me.'

That, of course, was the reason Roy was here, although he probably wouldn't share everything he knew, and *where* he'd gotten his information would remain with him. Davis understood and accepted that, although Roy knew he'd do his best to trick him into revealing his sources.

'During your investigation, did you run into the names Max Russell or Stewart Samuels, by any chance?' Roy asked. Those were the other two men who'd been with Dan Sherman and Bob Beldon in that patrol in Vietnam. Bob had told him how the four had become separated from their squad and stumbled into the village. Four men, four lives, each marked by that afternoon. Roy had located Samuels, who'd remained in the military and had a distinguished record of service. Of the four, he seemed the least affected by the events in Nam. Russell, however, had lived a troubled life after his release from the army. Like Beldon and Dan Sherman...

'I might have.' Davis leaned across his desk, nudging a stack of files that tilted precariously.

Roy was sure Davis *couldn't* have heard about the men and had to be bluffing.

Davis riffled through the files until he found the one he wanted and flipped it open. Roy wasn't surprised that Davis kept the John Doe case file close at hand. The sheriff leafed through it, then raised his eyes to meet Roy's. 'Are you going to tell me where you came up with these names?'

Roy grinned and slid down in his chair, crossing his arms. 'No.' He had to protect Bob as much as possible. Even now, he couldn't be sure of the extent of the other man's involvement. He wanted to believe Beldon was an innocent bystander, but too many of the dots still didn't connect.

The sheriff chuckled. 'Why did I know you were going to say that?'

Roy didn't bother to answer.

'Can you tell me why I have the sneaking suspicion either Max Russell or Stewart Samuels is going to be listed as a missing person?'

Making an effort not to look self-righteous, Roy shrugged.

'Help me out a little, if you would,' Troy muttered, turning to face his computer screen. 'Can you at least give me a state?'

'I could do that, but I'd hate to see you miss out on the fun of the chase. You might want to start with Russell, though.'

Troy glanced up, frowning darkly.

'California,' Roy said.

'Not Florida?' The dead man's false ID had given a Florida address. Davis looked surprised as he punched a few keys, stared at the screen and then peered over the top of his reading glasses. 'Are you planning to tell me how you got Russell's name?'

'No.'

284

Troy exhaled slowly. 'This is our John Doe?'

Roy couldn't be sure of that, but he had his suspicions. 'Might be.'

Troy continued to study the screen. 'When did you find all this out?'

Roy gave him a halfhearted smile. 'A while back. I dug up what I could and now I've decided it's time to bring you into the investigation.'

Davis snorted. 'I appreciate that, but I wish you'd come to me sooner.'

Roy still wasn't a hundred percent sure he was doing the right thing, as far as Bob or Grace Sherman were concerned, but withholding material information put him at risk of committing a crime himself. In his view, everything revolved around what those four men had done in Vietnam.

Troy tapped his fingers on the desk. 'Before I go making an idiot of myself, did you talk to anyone in California?'

'Like who?'

His gaze went back to the computer screen. He did some more typing and glanced at Roy again. 'Hannah Russell,' he said. 'Says here she's the one who filed the missing person's report.' He scrolled down. 'Probably the wife.'

'Daughter,' Roy corrected.

'Did you talk to her?' Davis demanded. The friendly pretense was gone now.

'And step into the middle of your investigation, Sheriff?' he asked. 'Would I do that?'

'I hope to hell not, but I thought I'd better ask.'

'She's all yours,' he said. His purpose in making this visit had been achieved. He'd leave the rest in Sheriff Davis's capable hands. 'I don't suppose you'd like to thank me.'

'No,' Davis barked. 'I'd like to know how long you've been holding on to this information.'

That wasn't a question Roy wanted to answer. He'd kept it to himself as long as he dared. If possible, he wanted to keep Dan Sherman's family out of this.

'Any idea why our John Doe arrived in Cedar Cove carrying false identification?'

'That I can't tell you,' Roy said. The sheriff would talk to Hannah Russell, and would eventually check out Samuels, too. Roy's investigation had led him to the other man, who lived in the Washington, D.C., area, but Roy hadn't contacted him. He'd leave that to Davis, as well.

'What about the reconstructive surgery? I hear some people in town still think it was Dan Sherman. DNA says otherwise.'

'I'd trust what the lab tells you,' Roy said, lost in his thoughts.

'I do, but I've heard the rumors.'

Roy had, too. People liked to speculate. It *was* mighty convenient to believe the dead man could've been Dan Sherman, although

Roy hadn't heard much talk of that in recent days.

Roy stood to leave. He'd said everything he intended to and not a word more.

Davis stood, too. 'I'll thank you, then.'

Roy walked out of the office and through the department. He'd thought hard about this visit. He wouldn't betray Beldon's trust, but there was certain information he could no longer withhold. Beldon was the one who'd given him Russell's and Samuels's names—and given him permission to tell the sheriff.

Four unsuspecting soldiers had been trapped in a Southeast Asian jungle that day and walked straight into hell. What happened next had forever altered the lives of these men, whose sole desire was to come home alive. They'd seen too many of their friends and comrades leave Vietnam in body bags. To them, at that time, it was kill or be killed. War had changed them, changed their world.

Corrie was waiting when Roy returned to the office. 'How'd it go?' she asked.

Roy took off his jacket and hung it on the coat tree in the entry. 'About as well as could be expected,' he murmured.

'Does Bob know you've talked to Troy Davis?' she asked.

* * *

Jack had been looking forward to this

Friday night for two weeks. Because of some commitment Olivia had at the courthouse, she was working late today and had agreed to meet him for dinner at The Lighthouse. They hadn't had a real honest-to-goodness date since before Christmas, and he'd missed her company. Oh, there'd been lots of phone calls, a couple of quick cups of coffee, but they were both busy people with complicated lives.

The newspaper conglomerate, which had bought out the once privately owned paper a few years ago, was investigating the possibility of increasing publication from biweekly to five days a week and eventually taking it to a full seven. While the thought of those extra issues and journalistic opportunities excited him, he wasn't sure this additional responsibility would be worth the toll it would take on his personal life. A daily paper meant hiring and training extra staff, editorial meetings, more administrative duties.

There was no better way to hook a newsman than offering him more column space. His publisher was well aware of that fact and was using it to his advantage—that and a hefty pay raise. Still, Jack hesitated. As it was, he didn't see nearly as much of Olivia as he wanted to. He hoped that, someday in the near future, she'd become a permanent part of his life.

'Would you like to be seated now, Mr. Griffin?' the hostess at the restaurant asked him. 'I can show Judge Lockhart to your table once she arrives.'

'Sure,' Jack said, impressed that the young woman knew him and Olivia. But then he decided it shouldn't surprise him. Justine Gunderson and her husband, Seth, owned The Lighthouse, and Justine, after all, was Olivia's daughter. Besides, his picture appeared in the paper next to his weekly column—a rather flattering photograph if he did say so himself.

The table was one of the best, with a view that overlooked the cove. The marina lights dancing across the water's surface had a festive quality that cheered him. He could see the naval shipyard on the other side of the cove, too. Currently it housed an aircraft carrier, several destroyers and any number of diesel submarines docked there for repairs.

The waiter arrived and Jack ordered coffee, then studied the menu. Only five minutes later, Olivia showed up, breezing into the room with a smile warm enough to melt the iciest heart.

'I hope I didn't keep you waiting long?' she said, slipping into the chair across from him. She looked flustered but happy and excited.

She was so damn pretty it was hard for Jack to take his eyes off her. 'Yup. I've been waiting for hours.' Which was true; he just hadn't been sitting at the restaurant all that time.

Olivia stretched her hand across the table and Jack linked his fingers with hers. 'I've been anticipating tonight,' she said. 'Being with you...'

'Me, too.' This was a minor understatement. 'Any update on your mother's fight with City Hall?' he asked before he made a fool of himself by staring at her.

Olivia looked up from the menu. 'You didn't hear?'

'No, what?' Usually Jack was the first to pick up on local gossip. But he hadn't seen as much of Charlotte as he used to. For a while she'd written a seniors' column for the *Chronicle*, but had given it up when she was diagnosed with cancer. She'd meant to continue now that she'd recovered, but had become engrossed in her current issue, a community health clinic.

'My mother and this newfound friend of hers have decided to stage a demonstration.' Olivia frowned. 'I don't know much about this Ben character, do you?'

Jack didn't, but he wasn't going to let her sidetrack him. This was real news. 'Demonstration for what? A health clinic?'

Olivia sighed deeply. 'You know my mother! Personally I think it's Ben Rhodes who put the idea in her head. In any event, Mom's convinced this is what our community needs.'

Jack nodded; he agreed with Charlotte.

'Mom insists she tried to go through the normal channels, but no one wants to hear it, what with all the budget cuts,' Olivia went on. 'I'm afraid she's going to take matters into her own hands.' Olivia shook her head. 'In which

290

case, God help us all.'

Jack struggled not to smile. At Charlotte's urging he'd written several supportive editorials on the need for a health-care clinic.

'Jack Griffin, I swear if you plaster my mother's picture on the front page of the *Chronicle* with her holding some ridiculous sign, I may never forgive you.'

Despite himself, Jack chuckled. 'I'm not making any promises.'

Olivia set aside her menu. 'I've tried to talk sense into her, but she refuses to listen. She hasn't got a clue how potentially embarrassing this could be for me.'

Jack frowned. 'She's not thinking about you, but about the citizens of our community and their needs.'

'You're right,' Olivia agreed, and then paused and glanced up. 'I guess I sound pretty self-absorbed about this whole thing, don't I? But Mom doesn't realize how much teasing I get at the courthouse. This afternoon someone asked me what I'd do if my own mother ended up in my court. They suggested I make her sit in the corner for fifteen minutes.' Olivia rolled her eyes. 'Cute, really cute.' Then, as if she'd tired of the subject, she leaned toward him. 'Enough about my mother. How are *you*?'

'Great.' That was the way he felt, now that he had Olivia all to himself. He'd planned a romantic evening. Okay, this was about as romantic as he knew how to be. They'd have dinner, and perhaps later, if the weather cooperated, they could walk along the waterfront. If he was lucky, she'd invite him to the house for coffee. It had been far too long since he'd kissed Olivia Lockhart....

'Any more on the paper going to five issues a week?' Olivia asked.

'Nothing that I can report, but I think it's a distinct possibility.' Olivia was well aware of what that would mean, but he didn't want to waste time discussing the pros and cons of such a move.

The reason he'd accepted this job was that the *Cedar Cove Chronicle* was biweekly. The demands of a daily paper had nearly strangled his personal life. For a lot of years, he'd buried himself in his work. It was easy to do, and he'd let it happen.

That had been early in his career. He'd nearly destroyed himself, first by drowning his sorrows and fears in the bottom of a bottle, and later by working himself to a state of near-collapse. That had been Jack's attempt to deal with his son's illness. As a young boy, Eric was diagnosed with leukemia. He later recovered, but at the time Jack had believed his only child was dying and there wasn't a damn thing he could do about it, except drink and work.

During those dark years, when Jack drank, he'd functioned effectively enough at his job—usually hungover—and functioned minimally in society, as a husband, father and friend.

It was when his marriage died that he'd finally gotten the help he needed. Even then, he'd needed years to straighten himself out.

'You won't leave Cedar Cove, will you?' Olivia asked.

Jack loved the worry he heard in her voice. Another time, he might have let her assume he'd pack up his computer and head out of town, but they were beyond that. He could no more leave Olivia than he could quit being a newsman. And he couldn't play manipulative games with her, either. But being honest didn't mean he couldn't tease her a bit.

'No, I won't leave,' he assured her. Then, holding her eyes, he added, 'I could never walk away now.'

'Oh, Jack,' she sighed, gazing warmly at him.

'Yeah,' he said, 'I signed a five-year contract and these people are real sticklers when it comes to contracts.'

'Jack!'

He enjoyed her indignant expression, all the while admitting that he *wasn't* the romantic sort. He loved Olivia Lockhart, though. Perhaps he should try harder to say the right things, but he didn't have much practice in flowery language. If she wanted to hear that kind of nonsense, her ex-husband was probably an expert.

Thinking about Stan Lockhart was a mistake. Jack gritted his teeth. Stan irritated him with his pompous assumption that he could have Olivia back anytime he wanted. He made sure Jack knew it, too.

'Let's order,' he said in an effort to turn his thoughts to some other subject. As he reached for the menu, he reminded himself that *he* was the one spending the evening with Olivia, not her ex.

'I'm starving,' Olivia said happily.

Jack glanced over the specials and decided on the T-bone steak. Olivia vacillated between the scallops on the list of specials and the prime rib. In the end she decided on the scallops.

'Mom said you took her to lunch,' Olivia said when their salad with shrimp piled atop Bibb lettuce was delivered by their efficient and unobtrusive waiter.

So Olivia knew about that. Drilling her mother over Olivia's involvement with Stan hadn't been one of Jack's finer moments. His excuse was that not knowing was driving him to distraction.

What he'd learned had depressed him for days. Stan Lockhart was still making a hard play to win back his ex-wife. He had a lot going for him, too. Not only was he financially secure, cultured and sophisticated, but he had a shared history with Olivia and was the father of her children.

The first thing Charlotte had told him was that Stan and Olivia had spent New Year's Eve together. Charlotte had minimized the fact by explaining that they'd both been watching Leif so Justine and Seth could go to The Lighthouse. Still, it rankled. He could bet that when the clock struck midnight, ol' Stan was right there with the champagne and the music, ready to give Olivia a lip-lock she wouldn't soon forget. Jack's jaw flexed with anger at the thought of Stan so much as touching her.

In addition, Charlotte had let it drop that Stan occasionally stayed the night in Cedar Cove. From personal experience, Jack knew he'd slept at the house on Lighthouse Road at least once. He also knew Stan had spent the night in the guest bedroom, although Stan had let Jack assume otherwise. Now he had to wonder if Stan continued to sleep over at Olivia's.

The truth was, Jack didn't want to know. He refused to allow Stan to drive a wedge between him and Olivia. Jack had made the mistake of letting that happen once, and as far as he was concerned, history wouldn't be repeating itself. He was willing to fight for Olivia, dammit. He wasn't going to step aside—and he wanted to make that very clear—to Olivia *and* her ex-husband.

'Jack?' Olivia was giving him an odd look.

'Sorry. Did you say something?' He focused his attention on her and realized Stan had nearly gotten him a second time. Without even trying, Olivia's ex was ruining this night out.

'Did I tell you how lovely you look?' he

asked.

'No, you didn't,' Olivia told him, and propped her elbows on the table. 'But I can't wait to hear.'

*   *   *

Grace Sherman stared at the computer screen and held her breath. Excitement shot through her. New Orleans! Will wanted to meet her in New Orleans. He was traveling to Louisiana on business and had asked her to join him.

New Orleans was one of the most romantic cities in the world, and the thought of being there with Will sent her heart spinning. She imagined strolling down Bourbon Street, listening to jazz musicians with Will at her side. He'd mentioned a gambling trip down the Mississippi on a riverboat, and touring historic plantations.

I don't know she typed back. She felt as nervous as she was excited.

We should talk, and not like this. The things I want to say should be said face-to-face. His reply was instantaneous. I need you, Grace. You're all I think about.

They no longer hid their feelings from each other. Grace loved Will; it was that simple. She wanted to be with him—not just for a weekend, but forever.

Still, she lived in Cedar Cove and was employed by the town. It's hard for me to get time away from the library without several weeks' notice she typed.

Ask now. I'll send you a plane ticket.

Grace closed her eyes. The way she felt about Will, and the way he seemed to feel about her, would make it impossible for them to resist each other sexually. For weeks she'd dreamed of what it would be like. She'd created an entire fantasy about living with Will as husband and wife. For the first time in her adult life, she'd know what it was to be with a man who loved her completely. Who cherished her...

Dan had loved her; she didn't doubt his deep affection, but he'd had so little to give her. He'd struggled with such grief and guilt and misery, it was all he could do to get from one day to the next. There'd been almost no room for tenderness and joy in his life. Grace desperately needed both.

And Cliff—he was a friend. Their relationship had been about companionship more than love, at least on her part.

Now she finally had the opportunity to know real love.

There was a problem, however, and to Grace, it was a major one.

Will was married.

What about your wife? she typed back. She couldn't promise to meet him, couldn't allow this relationship to continue if he remained committed to his marriage.

I told you it was over Will typed.

Georgia's moved out?

Yes. I've already seen an attorney. The divorce is amicable. We should never have married. She understands.

She knows about us? Grace's fingers flew over the keys.

I told her there was someone else. I didn't say who it is.

Grace had kept her relationship with Will a secret, too. They spoke via e-mail every day, often more than once, and occasionally they managed a phone call. It never ceased to astonish her how much they had to talk about.

The doorbell chimed and Grace glanced irritably over her shoulder. Buttercup ambled to the door, tail wagging.

Say you'll meet me Will urged, the words flashing across the screen. I need to know as soon as possible. Promise me you'll do everything you can.

I will, I promise Grace assured him, and with regret, dragged herself away from the computer when the bell rang a second time. Determined to get rid of whoever was there, she opened her door and stared at Cliff. She had to make an effort not to groan aloud.

'Cliff,' she said, unlatching the screen and holding the door open. 'This is a pleasant surprise.'

'Surprise?' he repeated slowly. 'I called last week. We made plans to spend the afternoon together.'

Grace vaguely remembered the conversation, but all that lingered in her mind was her eagerness to get off the phone so she could get back on the computer and talk to Will.

'Of course. It just slipped my mind. I'll be ready in a minute.'

Cliff came into the living room and sat down on the sofa, frowning slightly.

'I was on the computer,' Grace explained. 'Give me a moment while I get off-line.' She pulled out her desk chair and sat down. Her fingers went to the keyboard and she quickly typed out a message to Will, telling him she'd request vacation time. She wouldn't know for another week or two if she'd get those days off, but with all her heart she hoped it would happen. Then she explained that she had company and needed to end their conversation.

When she'd finished, Grace whirled around in her chair and smiled warmly at Cliff. 'You must think I'm an empty-headed dunce,' she said brightly, hoping to disguise the fact that she'd forgotten their date.

'Not at all,' he assured her evenly. But his smile didn't quite reach his eyes. Buttercup rested contentedly at Cliff's side, and as he ran his fingers through her fur, he frowned again.

'I'll get my coat and be back in a moment,' Grace promised.

It didn't take more than a couple of minutes to grab her coat, brush her hair and apply fresh lipstick.

Cliff was still petting Buttercup when she returned. He glanced up. 'When was the last time you had Buttercup at the vet?' he asked.

Grace couldn't recall, other than the first week after she'd gotten the golden retriever. 'It's been a year or so,' she said.

'I think it might be a good idea to schedule an appointment.'

'Why?' Grace was immediately concerned. Buttercup was her constant companion and friend.

'No obvious reason, other than that she seems a bit lethargic,' Cliff said, but his brow was creased. 'There might be something wrong—she doesn't seem herself. You haven't noticed any changes in her behavior, have you?'

'None.' Grace tried to think, but nothing came to mind. The truth was, she hurried home from work every night to leap onto the computer. She realized guiltily that she hadn't paid much attention to the dog since her correspondence with Will had begun. Often she didn't bother to eat dinner until eight o'clock or later. Her time at home was precious because that was her only opportunity to connect with Will.

'Are you ready?' Grace asked, reaching for her purse.

'In a minute,' Cliff said. He continued to stroke Buttercup's back, but Grace suspected he was gathering his thoughts rather than assessing her dog's health. After a moment he stood.

'It's a lovely day, isn't it?' she said, unable to read his mood. This was the role she'd played far too often with Dan, doing whatever she could to put him in better spirits. So many times she'd failed. Seeing the same humorless expression on Cliff's face depressed her. It brought back memories of her life with Dan.

'I need to ask you something,' Cliff said after a long pause.

'Anything.' Well, almost anything, she amended silently.

Cliff walked over to the window and stared outside. 'We haven't seen much of each other lately.'

'You've been busy,' she said with a shrug.

'True, and I suppose that's the reason I didn't notice earlier.'

'Notice what?' she asked.

'How emotionally distant you've become.'

Grace shook her head, denying it. 'You're imagining things.'

Cliff rubbed the back of his neck and turned to face her. 'Funny you should use those words. That's exactly what Susan used to say to me.'

Susan was his ex-wife. Grace raised her hands in a confused, helpless gesture. 'What's this all about? I thought we were going to spend the afternoon together.'

'So did I,' Cliff murmured. He straightened, and his face was austere. 'I can't play this game, Grace.'

'What game?' She was losing patience with him.

'There's someone else. You think I don't know, but it's clear to me. I can tell what's happening—I've been there before.'

'What?' she exploded in a fit of self-righteousness. 'How can you say that? Even if it *was* true,' she continued, undaunted, 'it's my business. You don't have any claim on me.'

Cliff's smile was sad. 'You're right, of course.'

'Don't be like this,' she pleaded. Now that he was here, she was looking forward to going out with him, enjoying his company.

He shook his head as if to say he should have seen it earlier. 'At first I assumed you were pulling away from me because of Dan. I gave you time to grieve for your husband, just like you asked.'

'Cliff, please, you're making a crisis out of nothing.'

'Am I?' he asked.

He sounded resigned, and she briefly had the urge to walk into his arms, but Grace didn't like the way this conversation was going.

'You say there isn't anyone else in your life?' Cliff challenged.

She looked him straight in the eye and lied. 'That's exactly what I'm saying.' No one knew about her and Will. Not even Olivia, Will's sister and her best friend. She couldn't let word get out, especially now, when Will and Georgia were in the middle of their divorce.

'I was sure I was going to love you the first time we met,' Cliff said. 'My admiration for you grew every time we talked. You handled the situation with your missing husband honorably, refusing to get involved with me until the divorce was final. I assumed... I believed in you.'

'You don't now?'

'You're forgetting something, Grace. My wife cheated on me for years. I know all the signs—the cheerful greeting, the denial, the outrage. I lived with it and tried to ignore it. I won't again.'

Grace crossed her arms. This was getting tiresome. 'You're being ridiculous,' she said irritably.

'Am I?' he asked.

'Of course you are.'

'He's married, isn't he?'

'What are you *talking* about?'

Cliff stared hard at her. 'You're protecting him.'

'I can't believe you'd say such a thing!'

Cliff started for the door.

'Can we leave now?' she asked, relieved this inquisition was over.

His hand was on the doorknob. 'I think it would be best if we didn't see each other again.'

Grace stared at him. 'You don't mean that.' Her heart sank and she realized how deeply her lies had offended Cliff. As he walked out the door, Grace stood where she was, too paralyzed by shock to react.

She recovered quickly and hurried after him. 'Cliff,' she shouted. 'Please, let's talk about this.'

Either he didn't hear her or he chose not to listen. Without looking back, he climbed into his vehicle and started the engine, then drove down the street and out of her life.

Twenty

Katie's weak, mewling cry woke Maryellen abruptly. It was only quarter after one; she'd been asleep for barely an hour. Her eyes flew open and she got shakily out of bed. Gently lifting Katie from her crib, Maryellen held the infant over her shoulder and was instantly alarmed. Katie had been sick and fussy for two days and two tortured, sleepless nights. Now, if anything, she seemed worse.

Maryellen had stayed home from work with her the day before. The pediatrician had put Katie on antibiotics, but she was still miserable. Although she'd taken her nighttime feeding, she'd promptly vomited up the milk. Now she was burning with fever, restless and irritable.

Her eyes gritty from lack of sleep, Maryellen walked the floor, but couldn't seem to comfort Katie. With effort she managed to get the six-month-old to swallow some liquid Tylenol; even that didn't seem to lower her temperature.

By 2:00 a.m. Maryellen was exhausted and frantic. She'd already talked to the consulting nurse on the twenty-four-hour hot line, but she needed more than reassurance. She needed help. It was just too hard to do this alone. She hated to call Jon at this ungodly hour, but she simply couldn't cope by herself.

The phone rang five long rings, and disheartened, she was ready to replace the receiver. Clearly Jon wasn't home, which meant he was spending the night elsewhere. The thought so depressed her that she found tears springing to her eyes.

'Don't,' she whispered to herself. 'Forget about him.' She refused to speculate about where he was—or with whom. That would only add to her misery.

Just as she was lowering the receiver, a groggy Jon answered the phone.

'This better be good,' he grumbled.

'Jon? It's Maryellen. I'm so sorry...but I didn't know where else to turn.'

'What's wrong?'

'It's Katie. She's got quite a high fever, and is terribly congested. I took her to the pediatrician's this morning. She has bronchitis and an ear infection.'

'Is she on medication?'

'Yes, but I don't like the sound of her breathing. I already talked to the nurse on the hot line, but I'm still worried. And I'm so tired.' Her voice trembled with emotion. With only an hour's sleep, she was at the point of exhaustion and felt incapable of making the simplest decision.

'How high is the fever?'

'A hundred and three, but the nurse said that's not uncommon in infants. It's her breathing that's got me worried. She coughs so much that she starts to throw up and she can't sleep and…and consequently neither can I.' Maryellen fought back her tears. Two nights without rest, and she was an emotional wreck. 'I just don't know how much longer I can do this….'

'I'm on my way.'

'But what about work?'

'Maryellen, Katie's my daughter as well as yours.'

'Do you think I should take her into the emergency room?' That was all she really wanted him to tell her.

'Let's decide that together.'

He sounded so calm and reasonable.

Sniffling, Maryellen agreed, relieved not to be shouldering the entire responsibility for Katie's care.

Thirty minutes later, Jon rang her doorbell. He took one look at Maryellen and frowned. 'You should've called me sooner.'

Knowing she must look a sight, she handed Katie to him and self-consciously ran her fingers through her hair. It'd been a month since she'd seen Jon, other than in passing. He seemed to be avoiding her, and after the New Year's Day dinner, she'd stayed clear of him, too. Seeing him now, while she felt and looked so dreadful, worsened her dismay. But with Katie this sick, Maryellen had no choice.

'She's already on antibiotics,' she explained again as Jon lovingly attempted to comfort the baby. 'The doctor said it might be a day or two before she starts feeling better, but she's still got a fever and she can't sleep.'

Jon gently brushed his lips over Katie's brow. 'I think her fever's down a bit.'

'Thank God.'

Maryellen gauged the baby's temperature by touch, using the back of her hand. He was right; Katie's forehead felt less feverish after the Tylenol.

'What do you think? Should we take her to the emergency room?' Maryellen asked. She hated the thought of dragging Katie out in the cold and exposing her to God only knew what else, especially if it wasn't necessary. But she didn't feel confident enough to decide that on her own.

'Let's give it an hour and see,' Jon suggested.

Maryellen nodded. If Katie's fever had broken, maybe she'd be able to sleep.

'I'll stay with you,' Jon said.

Maryellen hadn't wanted to ask, but was so grateful she couldn't speak, afraid she'd burst into tears, and merely nodded.

They shuffled Katie between them while he removed his coat, then sat down in the rocking chair with his daughter.

'She breathes more easily when someone holds her,' Maryellen said, swaying with exhaustion.

'Go to bed,' Jon told her. 'There's no reason for us both to be up.'

'But...' Maryellen didn't know why she was arguing. 'You'll come and get me in an hour?'

Jon glanced up. 'Did anyone ever tell you that you're too stubborn for your own good?'

She stared at him.

'Go,' he said, pointing toward her bedroom.

Maryellen was too exhausted—and too grateful—to do anything other than nod obediently and trudge off. Being a single mother was so much more difficult than she'd thought possible. She could never have imagined what it was like to walk the floors with a sick baby, to make important decisions—decisions that affected her child's life and health—by herself. She didn't know what she would've done tonight without Jon.

Maryellen collapsed onto her bed, weak with a tiredness that attacked her very bones. Her head was spinning, and she was convinced she wouldn't be able to sleep.

She closed her eyes—and the next time she looked at the digital readout on her clock-radio, three hours had passed. Tossing aside the covers, she hurried into the living room and discovered Katie sound asleep in Jon's arms.

He opened his eyes when she walked in.

'She's asleep,' Maryellen whispered, hardly able to believe it. His arms must be aching from holding Katie so long. She reached for the infant, and as soon as she held her, Maryellen realized Katie was in a deep sleep.

'She seems to be over the worst of it,' Jon said, following Maryellen into the baby's room.

'I hope so.' Ever so gently, she placed her in the crib. When Katie turned onto her side, Maryellen pressed one hand to her daughter's back. Heat no longer radiated from the small body. 'The fever's broken,' she whispered, covering her with a light blanket.

'What time is it?' Jon asked outside Katie's room.

'Five-thirty,' she told him. 'Stay,' she urged. He looked as tired as she'd felt a few hours earlier.

Jon rubbed his face with both hands and

yawned. 'I'll take the sofa.'

'That thing is short and lumpy. You'll be miserable.'

His eyes held hers.

'We can share my bed,' she said in an offhand manner, as though his spending the night was a normal occurrence. She might have sounded calm and casual, but her heart was pounding.

Jon continued to gaze at her, apparently not sure he'd heard her correctly.

'I'll stay on my side of the bed and you stay on yours,' she added matter-of-factly. She wasn't asking him to make love to her, if that was what he thought. Without waiting for an answer, she moved silently into the darkened room.

Jon still hesitated.

'Those three hours are the most sleep I've had in two nights,' she said, sitting on the edge of the bed. 'You make your own decision, but I'm going back to sleep.' She lay down and kept her back to him. Eyes closed, she pulled the covers around her shoulders.

A minute later, the mattress on the other side of the bed shifted under his weight. 'I'll sleep on top of the covers,' he whispered. 'So you won't worry about me touching you.'

As if she'd mind! Maryellen didn't respond, pretending she was already asleep. It wasn't long before she heard the steady rhythm of his breathing and knew he'd drifted off.

Sometime later, when Maryellen woke, her bedroom was filled with light. Jon blocked her view of the clock-radio so she couldn't see the time. She lifted her head from the pillow in order to look past him. The clock told her it was almost eight. At her movement, Jon's eyes slowly opened.

'Sorry,' she whispered, and laid her head back on the pillow. 'I didn't mean to wake you.'

'I slept,' he said incredulously.

'So did Katie.' They stared at each other; neither seemed capable of moving. They'd only spent one night together, the night she'd conceived Katie, and that seemed a lifetime ago now. Maryellen had made so many mistakes in this relationship. But he'd proved to be a wonderful father to Katie and an invaluable help to Maryellen.

They'd kissed several times, and with those kisses she'd tried to tell him how much she'd learned to appreciate him—and, yes, love him—but in each instance, she'd come away hurt and disappointed. She so badly wanted to kiss him now....

'Jon.' Her voice was the slightest whisper.

'Shh.' He moved his head closer to hers and she slowly edged toward him.

Soon their lips met in a soft kiss. After a moment, Jon reluctantly eased his mouth from hers. He gazed at her, eyes narrowed, as if he wasn't sure he should continue. As if he sought her permission…

Maryellen brought her lips back to his. She'd practically thrown herself at him after Christmas, and he'd rejected her. Her heart would break if he spurned her again.

She needn't have worried. They kissed a second time, their mouths straining while they tore at each other's clothes. Maryellen's nightgown was easy to slip off. Jon, however, had remained fully clothed. While he unbuttoned his shirt, Maryellen heard Katie in the other room.

Jon froze.

Maryellen, too. 'I'll see if I can get her back to sleep.' Sometimes, if she gave Katie her pacifier, the baby would sleep for a few more minutes. Maryellen prayed she could convince their daughter to give her parents this rare opportunity.

As quickly and quietly as possible, Maryellen threw on her nightgown and tiptoed into Katie's room. Sure enough, as soon as she had her pacifier, Katie closed her eyes. Maryellen remained by her side and patted her back. All the while, she prayed the mood between her and Jon hadn't been destroyed. She so badly wanted to make love with him.

When she returned to the bedroom, Maryellen knew it was too late. Jon sat on the side of the bed, his back rigid as he faced the wall.

'Katie's asleep,' she whispered.

He didn't respond.

Kneeling on the bed, she moved behind him and wrapped her arms around his shoulders. She kissed his neck, then ran her tongue over his earlobe and felt a shiver race through him.

Jon took her hand and kissed her palm. 'It's a good thing Katie woke up when she did.'

'She's asleep, Jon,' Maryellen said.

'It isn't a good idea for us to get involved sexually,' he whispered. He got up abruptly and turned to face her.

Maryellen sank back on her heels, humiliated beyond words by his rejection.

'It would be the easiest thing in the world to make love to you now, but I'm not going to do it. The truth is, I don't trust you. You've lied to me once. You tried to keep my daughter from me—'

'That was before—'

'Before what?' he demanded.

Before I realized I could trust you, before I realized I love you. But she dared not tell him that.

'I explained why I behaved the way I did,' she said, and kept her head lowered, unable to meet his gaze. 'I was as honest as I knew how to be.'

He didn't say anything for a long moment. 'I want to be honest with you, too, Maryellen.' His voice throbbed with sincerity.

Hope flared in her and she raised her eyes. He stood with his fists clenched at his sides, his face hard. 'I don't trust you—or myself. I can't.'

'Why can't you?' she pleaded. She could see the war that raged inside him. He longed to trust her, yearned to release the burden that weighed him down. She wondered why this burden, whatever it was, hadn't troubled him a year earlier, when he'd made love to her. The reason suddenly occurred to her.

'Jon,' she whispered, and somehow managed to blurt out the question. 'Are you married?'

'Is *that* what you think?'

'I don't know what to think,' she cried.

Her raised voice must have startled Katie, whose loud wail shattered the tense moment.

'I'll get her,' Maryellen said, hurrying into the nursery. She picked up the baby and changed her diaper. Katie was in much better spirits, almost back to normal, which was encouraging.

When Maryellen returned to the bedroom, Jon had disappeared. She looked out the living room window just in time to see his car turn the corner. Judging by the way he drove, he couldn't get away from her fast enough.

*   *   *

Rosie watched Allison tackle a thick stack of pancakes at the Pancake Palace. As if aware of her mother's scrutiny, Allison glanced up and smiled. This was a chance for them to talk privately. Zach was off with Eddie on a father-son Boy Scout event and he'd suggested Rosie take Allison to dinner. It'd been a good idea.

At the time of the divorce, Rosie had thought she'd never have anything to do with Zach again. She'd known they'd have to cooperate on practical matters, but beyond that, she'd figured their relationship was over. Things had turned out differently than she'd expected. These days, they talked frequently; in fact, they were much happier divorced. It pained her to admit that, but it was true.

'All-you-can-eat pancakes for a buck,' Rosie said, reaching for the syrup dispenser once Allison had finished with it. 'You certainly can't beat the price.'

'Cecilia says they're the best in town.'

If Rosie heard the other woman's name one more time, she thought she'd scream. On the other hand, she was so grateful to have her daughter back, she knew she really didn't have cause to complain.

Two bucks for dinner was about all Rosie could afford. They still had massive legal bills—well, Zach did—and the cost of maintaining two homes. Plus, Rosie now had the additional expenses associated with working full-time. The money situation was as bad as ever, but she'd grown accustomed to stretching her pennies. 'So you like the job at your father's office?' The answer was obvious, but it opened the door to conversation.

'I didn't the first day,' Allison confessed, grabbing her water glass and gulping down several swallows. 'Dad was awful to be around. He was totally unreasonable.'

That wasn't the way Rosie had heard it, but she wasn't going to contradict Allison.

'Then he made Cecilia my boss, and it worked out much better.'

Rosie smiled, wondering what it was about Cecilia, whom she'd never met, that had influenced Allison so profoundly.

'Dad told you about Cecilia and her husband, didn't he?'

'Yes.' Zach had also mentioned the baby Cecilia had lost. 'Cecilia's baby was named Allison, too?'

Her daughter nodded. 'Would it be all right if we put flowers on her grave one day?'

'I think that would be very nice.'

'Her birthday was June 25.'

'Perhaps we should do it then,' Rosie suggested.

Allison nodded again. 'Okay! I'll pay for them myself.' She poured a generous amount of syrup on what remained of her pancakes. 'We talk, you know?' She looked up, as if she expected Rosie to object.

'I know.'

'Cecilia's really smart, but she said she didn't always realize that. Ian was the one who convinced her she could go to college and be

316

anything she wanted.'

'Didn't I hear you say that Ian's away just now?'

'The term is 'at sea,' Mom.'

Rosie hid a smile. 'Sorry.'

'Do we know anyone else who's married to someone in the navy?'

Rosie had to think about that. 'Mrs. Alman's husband is in the navy. I teach with her.'

'Oh,' Allison murmured absently.

The question Rosie had wanted to ask her daughter, and dared not, clamored within her. Zach hadn't referred to Janice Lamond in weeks, and for that matter, neither had Allison. It wasn't right to grill her children about their father's activities; Rosie had promised herself she'd never put them in a situation that would divide their loyalties. She'd never force them to defend their father—or worse, choose between their parents. The silence about the other woman confused her, but then she hadn't mentioned Bruce Peyton, either. Not that there was much to say...

'So how's everything at the office?' Rosie asked as nonchalantly as she could. She hoped Allison would bring up Janice's name without any prompting.

'Dad's really, really busy. Tax season is hard. He goes to work at six and he usually has to stay late. He has appointments all day. I hardly

317

see him anymore.'

Zach had always been an early riser. During tax season, he often left the house before dawn, usually while Rosie was still asleep. From experience, she knew how tired and cranky he could be at the end of the day, too.

'I hope he's hired the extra help he needs,' Rosie muttered.

Allison laid her fork next to her plate. 'Mom, are you trying to find out about Mrs. Lamond?'

Instant color heated Rosie's cheeks. She could deny it and almost did, but Allison was smart enough to recognize a lie. Rosie nodded. 'I apologize, sweetheart, I shouldn't be—'

'She quit,' Allison said as she leaned toward Rosie in a conspiratorial kind of way. A smile flashed in her daughter's eyes.

'Quit?' Rosie repeated. 'When?'

'Weeks ago. Before Christmas.'

Before Christmas? That was impossible. Rosie vaguely remembered Zach's saying he'd given the other woman a promotion. 'What's the matter, didn't she get a big enough pay raise?' Rosie asked. She didn't try to disguise her dislike for the other woman.

'I don't know anything about a pay raise, but the gossip is she left without notice and Dad was really upset about it.'

Rosie would just bet he was.

'The other staff members didn't like her, either.'

318

'Really?' This was interesting, and contrary to what Zach had told her. He'd made Janice sound like a paragon of efficiency and helpfulness, implying that no one could resist liking such a friendly, supportive person.

'At first Mrs. Lamond was really nice. That's what Mrs. Long said—you know, the office manager. But then later Mrs. Lamond got all uppity with the other staff. They said she manipulated Dad to do whatever she wanted.'

As if Rosie didn't already know *that*. 'I'm sure she did,' she said. 'Do you know why she quit like that?'

'No one seems to have any idea.'

Rosie would have derived real satisfaction from discovering the details.

'Do you want me to find out more?' Allison asked, obviously eager to dig up dirt.

The temptation was strong, but Rosie shook her head. 'Don't worry about it.'

She and Allison chatted easily through dinner, laughing frequently and even reminiscing about pre-divorce days. It buoyed Rosie's spirits to have this relaxed conversation with her daughter—and to learn that the Lamond woman was gone from the office.

The following afternoon, Rosie dropped by the accounting firm. She hadn't been to the office since shortly before the separation, mainly because she hadn't wanted to give Janice Lamond the opportunity to gloat.

Mary Lou Miller was at the reception desk. She looked up when Rosie stepped into the office, and her face showed surprise, followed almost immediately by genuine welcome. There'd been a time when Rosie's relationship with the office staff had been pleasant and mutually respectful.

'Mrs. Cox, it's so good to see you!' Mary Lou said.

'Hi, Mary Lou.' The sense of welcome was gratifying and helped ease her nervousness. Rosie hadn't mentioned to Zach that she planned to stop by. Classes were cut short for the day because of a teachers' seminar on new curriculum requirements in the areas of math and science. Rosie was exempted, since she'd taken the course while updating her skills. She had a rare afternoon free.

'How can I help you?' Mary Lou walked over to the counter, which acted as a partition between the waiting area and the inner office. 'Do you want me to call Mr. Cox? Unfortunately, he's with a client at the moment, but I can let him know you're here.'

'Thanks, but that won't be necessary,' Rosie told her. 'I came to meet Cecilia Randall.'

'Oh, sure,' Mary Lou said. 'I'll get her right away.'

'Cecilia's on her break,' a woman Rosie didn't recognize announced from her desk. There'd been a number of changes in the office that she knew nothing about. She and

320

Zach had often discussed office politics, but that had been BJ—before Janice.

'You can go on back to the break room, if you like,' Mary Lou suggested.

That was perfect as far as Rosie was concerned. She didn't want to interrupt Cecilia while she was on the job. Her purpose was to thank her for everything she'd done for Allison.

Rosie was as familiar with the layout of the office as she was her own home—or what had, at one time, been the home she'd lived in with Zach. These days...well, that was territory she didn't want to enter.

Just as Mary Lou had told her, Rosie found a young woman sitting at a table, reading a magazine and sipping coffee. An older woman sat at a separate table, chatting on a cell phone. Cecilia had dark curly hair that hung just above her shoulders and she didn't look more than seventeen. She glanced up when Rosie walked in.

'Hello.' Rosie smiled. 'I'm Allison's mom.'

'Oh, hi,' Cecilia said, smiling back. 'She talks about you a lot.'

Rosie pulled out a chair and sat down at the table. She was astounded that her daughter had mentioned her at all. 'I just came to introduce myself and to thank you for being Allison's friend.'

'I enjoy working with her.'

Rosie was sure she hadn't felt that way

321

in the beginning. 'I wanted you to know how much I appreciate your patience with her. She's going through a rough time, and you've made a tremendous impression on her.'

'I appreciate your telling me that.'

'It's true,' Rosie said. 'Just working with you has made a real difference to Allison.'

'Spending time with her has helped me, too,' Cecilia said. 'I was only ten when my parents divorced and I remember thinking the breakup was my fault....'

Rosie was immediately concerned. She'd repeatedly talked to both children about this very thing, but Allison and Eddie had dismissed her questions, and after a while she'd let the matter drop. Surely, Rosie prayed, her children hadn't taken on any blame for a problem that was clearly between her and Zach.

'Did Allison tell you she blames herself for what happened?' Rosie burst out. 'Because that simply isn't true.'

'No, no,' Cecilia assured her, and held up one hand. 'I just meant that talking about what happened when my parents split has helped me realize I had nothing to do with their divorce. So you see, it's been a real advantage to me to look back at that episode in my own life.'

'I see,' Rosie murmured, relieved. In retrospect, she wished she'd handled so many things differently, not only with the divorce,

ut her marriage, too. She tried not to think
bout the last twelve months. What was done
vas done. Indulging in regrets left her feeling
epressed, and she was working hard to get
ast those negative emotions.

'I hope you don't mind my coming by like
his, but I did want to thank you,' Rosie said.

'It's really sweet of you to do that.' Cecilia
losed her magazine. 'Did you enjoy your
inner with Allison?'

Rosie nodded. 'It was great, although I
lmost needed a translator. Words like *wicked*
nd *righteous* and *mad* don't seem to mean
vhat I thought they did.'

Cecilia smiled. 'I know. Teenagers have
heir own way of expressing things, don't
hey?'

'That they do.' It was important Rosie leave
efore her daughter arrived for work. She
ot up, ready to head back to the front office,
vhen Mary Lou approached her.

'Mr. Cox said he'd like to see you,' she said,
ounding apologetic as she stepped aside and
llowed Rosie to pass.

Zach's door was open. When Rosie walked
nto his office, she immediately noticed that
he family photograph was no longer on the
redenza, but he'd displayed one of Allison
nd Eddie. He stood when she entered,
rowning darkly. Without a word, he moved
rom behind his desk and shut the door, a little
arder than he needed to.

323

Ah, so that was how it was going to be. Rosie tried not to let him intimidate her, but that was difficult.

'What are you doing here?' he demanded.

She didn't understand his anger and suppressed the urge to respond in kind. 'I came to talk to Cecilia. I wanted to thank her—'

'That's a convenient excuse and we both know it.' He was back on the other side of his desk, his expression furious.

'Excuse for *what?*' she asked, equally angry.

'Finding out about Janice.'

Now she understood. Zach didn't want her to know that his 'girlfriend' had left the company. From the little Allison had said, she knew Janice's departure hadn't been amicable.

'My visit had nothing to do with Janice and everything to do with our daughter,' Rosie insisted.

'So you say.'

'Let's agree to disagree. I'm sorry if my being here is an embarrassment. I'll make sure it doesn't happen again.' Eager to escape, she turned to leave.

Zach crossed his arms over his chest and slowly exhaled. 'Did you learn what you wanted to know?' he asked.

Rosie turned back from the door. 'What I wanted to know?' she repeated. Then she realized her ex-husband was worried that she'd find out what great pains he'd taken to

324

hide the truth from her all these weeks. 'As a matter of fact, I did.'

Zach's jaw went white. 'What happened between Janice and me—'

'I learned that Cecilia Randall is a warm, generous woman who has been a wonderful friend to our daughter,' she said, interrupting him. 'And I also learned that my ex-husband can be a real jerk.' She offered him a quavering smile, which under the circumstances was the best she could do. 'No surprise there, however.'

She walked out the door.

Twenty-One

Bob Beldon was puttering around in his wood shop in the garage, cleaning tools and putting them away, when he noticed the sheriff's vehicle in the distance. The green car was making its way along Cranberry Point; Bob wondered if Sheriff Davis was headed in his direction and what it meant if he was.

It'd been a year since the John Doe had checked into Thyme and Tide and promptly gone to meet his Maker. So much of that night remained a blur in Bob's mind. Of one thing he was sure: the man, whoever he was, had evoked the recurring nightmare. As the years passed, the dream had come less and less frequently. But it had returned that night. When he woke, he'd had the same sensation he always felt following the nightmare. He'd been badly shaken; discovering their guest dead in the downstairs bedroom had heightened his anxiety beyond anything he'd experienced in years.

Considering the number of times Sheriff Davis had stopped by since that fateful morning, Bob couldn't help feeling he was somehow a suspect. It was Davis's last visit that had led him to contact Roy McAfee. He'd half expected an arrest warrant. He needed to talk to someone he trusted, someone who could help him, so—at Pastor Flemming's suggestion—he'd gone to Roy.

Retelling the story of that day in a Vietnam jungle hadn't been easy. Peggy was the only one he'd ever told. Bob didn't know what would've happened to him if not for his wife, who'd held him and wept with him as he relived those terrible memories. Since then— until now—they'd never spoken of the incident again.

He peered out at the road again. Sure enough, the sheriff's car drove through the wrought-iron gate that marked the driveway to Thyme and Tide. He recognized Troy Davis at the wheel. Bob reached in his rear pocket for a clean rag and wiped his hands free of sawdust and grime.

Davis parked in back and climbed out,

nodding in Bob's direction.

'Sheriff,' Bob said, coming out to meet him. He extended his hand, which Troy Davis shook, all the while looking him full in the face. That was encouraging. If Davis planned to arrest him, he figured there'd be some sign. Thus far, he hadn't seen any.

'How's it going, Bob?' Troy asked.

'All right.'

'Peggy around?'

'She's inside baking. She's probably almost done. Cookies, I think. Do you want to come in the house?'

Sheriff Davis nodded. 'I'd like to talk to you both.'

Bob led the way through the back door off the kitchen. As he'd predicted, Peggy's cookies were cooling on wire racks and the lingering scent of oatmeal and raisins filled the room. She must've seen Troy pull into the driveway because she'd already placed three mugs on the table and had the coffee poured. She'd set aside a plate of cookies, too.

Silently they each took a seat at the round oak table in the alcove next to the kitchen, then reached for a mug.

'You have news?' Peggy asked.

Bob admired the fact that she got straight to the point. He assumed the sheriff had learned something. The fact that he was here in uniform told Bob this wasn't a social call.

'We have the identity of our John Doe,'

Sheriff Davis said. He paused as if he expected Bob to provide the name.

Peggy gasped. 'You know who it is?'

'Maxwell Russell.' Once again, the sheriff looked at Bob.

'Max?' Bob repeated slowly. Roy had wondered about that possibility. A chill raced down his spine, and he closed his eyes as the face of his old army buddy came to him. The room felt as if it were buckling beneath his chair. In the back of his mind, for whatever reason, he'd known that the man who'd died was somehow connected to his past.

'You remember him?' Davis asked, but it was clear he already knew the answer.

'We were in the army together—that was years ago.'

Davis nodded as if waiting for more.

'Why didn't he identify himself?' Bob asked. They hadn't seen each other in nearly forty years. Max hadn't arrived on his doorstep that night by accident. He'd come for a reason— and died before he could tell Bob what it was.

'I was hoping *you* could give me the answer to that,' the sheriff murmured.

Bob couldn't. He'd never been particularly good friends with Max. They were in Vietnam together, in the jungle...in the village. Afterward all four men had gone their separate ways, desperate to put the past behind them, to forget. No one wanted a reminder of what they'd done. Least of all

328

Bob.

After the war, Bob had stayed away from Cedar Cove simply because Dan had chosen to return to their hometown. Bob did eventually move back, but the two men rarely spoke. It was as if they were strangers now, although in their youth they'd been close friends.

'He died before he could tell you anything?' The sheriff made it a question.

Bob pushed away his chair and stood. With his back to the sheriff and Peggy, he stared out the window. 'No matter how many times you ask the question, I can only answer it one way. Max came to the door without giving us so much as his name, paid for a room and said he'd fill out the paperwork in the morning.'

'But by morning he was dead.'

The sick feeling in Bob's stomach intensified. He didn't understand why Max had come to Cedar Cove in the first place. Even more of a mystery was the fact that he'd had extensive plastic surgery—and that he'd carried false identification.

'How'd you find out who he was?' Bob had a few questions of his own.

'His daughter filed a missing person's report with the police in Redding, California. I spoke to Hannah Russell earlier in the week.'

'California?' Bob repeated. The trail had first led to an investigation in Florida, but that had quickly gone cold.

'What did she tell you?' Peggy asked before

Bob could.

'Unfortunately not as much as I'd like. The last time she spoke to her father, he told her he was leaving town. He didn't give her any details. They were apparently quite close, but when she questioned him about where he was going and why, he was evasive.

'He never returned. After two weeks, she reported him as a missing person.'

'That's all she knows?' Bob turned to face the sheriff. He gripped the back of his chair and slowly released his breath. Reclaiming his seat, he mulled over the information, feeling more confused than ever.

'It seems so,' Davis told him, picking up his coffee.

'Was it a business trip?' Bob asked next.

Davis shook his head. 'He hasn't worked since the accident.'

'Accident?' Peggy echoed.

'He was in a car crash five years ago. It killed his wife and badly disfigured him. The accident was the reason for his reconstructive surgery.'

Well, that explained that....

'I didn't recognize him at all,' Bob murmured. He'd seemed vaguely familiar—his bearing, perhaps, but Bob would never have associated that stranger with the twenty-year-old he'd once known.

'In the last few years, Hannah's lost both her parents. She took the news hard.'

'That poor girl,' Peggy said sympathetically. 'She must've been beside herself when she didn't hear from her father all those months.'

'It's no wonder.' Bob didn't realize he'd spoken aloud until he heard the sound of his own voice. He leaned forward and rested his elbows on the table, splaying his fingers through his hair.

No wonder the nightmare had come that night. His subconscious had made some connection, and he'd been swept into the churning memories the nightmare induced.

'Do you know why Max would seek you out?' Sheriff Davis asked again.

'No.' Bob could only speculate.

'His daughter's coming to get the ashes.' The sheriff looked from Bob to Peggy. When there was no one to claim the body or pay burial expenses, the county cremated the remains. 'Hannah asked if she could speak to you both.'

'What did you tell her?' Bob asked.

'I told her it was up to you, but I imagined you wouldn't have a problem with it.'

Peggy nodded. 'When is she coming?'

'As soon as she can make the arrangements. She's hoping to arrive next week.'

Peggy glanced at Bob. He knew what she was asking and he knew his answer, too.

'Tell Hannah she's welcome to stop by anytime.'

The sheriff nodded. 'I'll do that.'

*   *   *

Olivia saw the huge bouquet of vibrant red roses being delivered to the courthouse when she broke for lunch. They were lovely, and in February, especially this close to Valentine's Day, they must have cost a fortune.

She followed the florist's deliveryman down the halls of the courthouse and wondered who was lucky enough to receive such gorgeous roses. When the man announced he was looking for Judge Lockhart's office, she stopped abruptly.

Someone had sent her roses?

'I'm Judge Lockhart,' she said quickly, and led the way into her office. The roses were stunning, the buds just opening, their color rich and deep.

As soon as the man left, Olivia grabbed the card, certain Jack had sent them. She tore at the envelope, then hesitated when a second thought gave her pause.

They could be from Stan.

She stared hard at the half-opened envelope, and sank into her chair. She reached for the telephone, although she didn't often call Grace at work.

It took a moment to get her best friend on the line.

'What happened?' Grace asked automatically. 'What's wrong?'

'Nothing yet.' Olivia was giddy with anticipation—and a hint of dread. 'I have the most incredible roses here and a sealed card.'

'You don't know who sent them?'

'No.'

'Open the card,' Grace urged.

'I think they're from Stan.'

'And you want it to be Jack?'

Olivia rolled her eyes toward the ceiling. 'Of course I want it to be Jack.' But he'd already sent her flowers once, and it had been completely out of character then. Twice would be too much to expect.

'When was the last time you heard from him?'

Grace always did get caught up in the details. 'We talk all the time.'

'Did he mention getting together for Valentine's?'

Olivia strained her memory. If he had, it was only a vague reference. 'Not that I recall. He's busy, I'm busy. It's harder now that the paper's going to five days a week.'

'When was the last time Stan called you?'

Olivia didn't answer. 'They must be from Stan,' she said, already disappointed. The irony was, she couldn't remember once in all the years they were married that Stan had sent her roses.

'Look at the card, would you?' Grace insisted.

'Oh, all right.' She ripped the envelope all

the way open, holding her breath.

'Well?' Grace said after a few tense seconds.

'Stan.'

'That's what you thought.'

'I know.'

'What does the card say?'

Olivia glanced down at it again, and with little enthusiasm read the few scribbled lines aloud. "Be my Valentine now and forever. Join me for a night to remember." And then it's signed Stan.'

Grace muttered something unintelligible; whatever her friend's sentiment, Olivia shared it. If Stan had loved her so much, he wouldn't have walked out on their family when he had. He wouldn't have married Marge the moment their divorce was final. He wouldn't have abandoned Olivia in the hour of her darkest pain. Love demanded more.

'You're awfully quiet,' Grace commented. 'What are you thinking?'

Olivia grinned. 'That Jack tries, but he doesn't have a romantic bone in his body.'

'So what else is new?'

These days, Stan could be counted on to bring her flowers and candy, to make all the conventional gestures, but there was no substance to him. He had a handsome face and an empty heart. He seemed more worried about losing Olivia to Jack—as if she was the object of some male competition—than about her happiness.

'What will you tell Stan?' Grace asked.

'I'm afraid he's going to be disappointed because I've already got a date.'

'You do? But you said Jack hadn't mentioned anything about Valentine's....'

Olivia's decision had been made. 'If he doesn't ask me, then I'll just ask him.'

Grace laughed, and it was the same wonderful sound Olivia remembered from when they were teenagers. It seemed only a few years ago that they *were* teenagers, talking endlessly about boys and dates and Valentine's Day. Neither of them had expected to be single at this stage of their lives.

'Just when do you plan to give him this Sadie Hawkins Valentine invitation?' Grace teased.

Olivia laughed, too. 'As soon as I'm finished here.' She was about to suggest that Grace invite Cliff, as well, but that relationship had become very complicated all of a sudden. She wasn't sure what had happened, and Grace was reluctant to discuss it. Olivia gathered they'd had some sort of falling out. If it wasn't cleared up after a while, she'd press the issue, but at the moment, Grace seemed content. After all the grief and uncertainty her friend had been through, that was good enough for now.

They spoke for a few more minutes, Olivia promising to call Grace with an update that evening. As soon as court was over for the day, she drove directly to the newspaper. The *Cedar Cove Chronicle* office was situated on Cedar Cove Drive, toward Southworth, where Washington state ferries transported cars and passengers to Vashon Island and West Seattle.

Once she'd parked, Olivia lost her nerve. She was part of a generation raised to believe that men did the inviting. Etiquette dictated certain procedures, and even though many of those rules were outdated in today's world, they were so ingrained, Olivia had a hard time ignoring them.

Well, she'd come here for a reason, and she was determined to see it through. She marched purposefully into the office, only to discover he was in a meeting.

'I'll get him if you like,' the receptionist told her.

'Ah…' Thankfully Olivia didn't have time to formulate a response.

The door to the back office opened and Jack walked out, wearing a preoccupied frown. But the instant he saw her, his eyes brightened and his step quickened. 'Olivia!'

Jack's delight at seeing her seemed to infuse him with energy, and Olivia felt gratified. He held out his hands to her. 'This is a surprise.'

'I'm looking for a Valentine,' she announced. 'Are you interested?'

Jack chuckled. 'Yeah, except…'

'What?' If he told her he already had a date, she'd hit him with her purse.

'I take it you want to go someplace other than the Taco Shack for dinner?'

'I like the Taco Shack, but…' It occurred to her then that Jack was nervous. He was afraid he wouldn't meet her expectations. She also knew he wasn't about to admit it.

'All right, the Taco Shack is out.' He paused, as though searching his limited repertoire of restaurants. 'There's always The Lighthouse, right?'

'Why don't you let me make the reservations,' she suggested.

Jack grinned slyly in her direction. 'Are you romancing me, Olivia?'

'I am.' She couldn't see any reason to deny it. 'So, are you interested or not?'

'You bet I am.' He draped his arm around her shoulder. 'Can you have dinner with me tonight, too?'

'Taco Shack?' she asked.

Jack nodded. 'They make a mean enchilada.'

'And I make a mean chicken pot pie,' she said, tempting him with her cooking. Jack ate far too many meals in restaurants. 'See you in an hour?'

Jack nodded. 'I've got some work to finish up. How about two hours?'

'That sounds great,' she said. Her spirits soared as she drove home, planning the rest of her menu.

Jack was only ten minutes late, and by then

she had salad made, the table set and the pie waiting on top of the stove. She greeted him with an enthusiastic kiss. Sliding his arms around her waist, he held her a moment longer than necessary.

'I could get used to this,' Jack said, following her into the kitchen. The chicken pie smelled savory and enticing, the crust a perfect golden-brown.

'So could I,' she confessed.

Jack had intended to go back to the office, but he stayed instead, and they cuddled up on the sofa and watched television. At eleven, Olivia reluctantly kissed him good-night at the door, then wandered into her bedroom, feeling contented and relaxed. She looked forward to another evening like this one; they'd be having dinner again soon, on Valentine's Day, and she was already thinking about possible restaurants.

When she woke the next morning, it was because she'd heard a noise. Then she heard it again. It seemed to be coming from the kitchen. Frowning, Olivia sat up in bed. Reaching for her housecoat at the end of the bed, she slipped her arms into the sleeves, then hurried downstairs.

To her dismay, she found Stan sitting at the kitchen table, drinking coffee and reading the Seattle morning paper. After the divorce, she hadn't bothered to change the locks, but she couldn't believe that, all these years later, Stan still had a key. Perhaps she'd forgotten to lock the door when she said goodbye to Jack.

'Stan!'

'Morning,' he said, as if he sat in her kitchen each and every day.

'What are you *doing* here?'

He set the coffee mug down. 'Sorry if I startled you. I was in the neighborhood.'

Olivia was so furious she could barely speak. How dared he enter her home without permission!

'Did you get my roses?' he asked.

Olivia ignored the question. 'What are you doing in *my* home?' She emphasized the fact that this house was hers; he no longer had any rights to it. Or to her...

He gave her that hurt-little-boy look she knew so well. 'You're upset, aren't you?' he said.

'I don't think it's a good idea for you to sneak into my home like...like a thief.'

'You're absolutely right,' he agreed. 'I apologize, Olivia. Now, please, don't be angry with me. You know I hate it when you're angry.'

Olivia refused to fall victim to his cajoling. 'I don't want it to happen again. Do you understand?'

'Of course,' he said, then smiled as though she was the most enthralling woman in the world. 'Now, tell me, did you receive the roses?'

'I did.'

'You'll go out with me on Valentine's, won't you?'

'No, Stan, I won't. I think it's time you finished your coffee and left.'

He shook his head. 'I think you're actually glad to see me, but you won't admit it.'

'No, Stan, I am not glad to see you. Now, would you kindly *leave.*'

Twenty-Two

Zach replaced the telephone receiver and sighed heavily. Dashing off to the grade school because Eddie had been in a fight was not how he'd planned to spend his afternoon. However, the school had phoned him, and he didn't have any choice.

He called Cecilia into his office. 'Please cancel my three o'clock appointment, apologize and reschedule as soon as possible.'

Cecilia nodded. She seemed shocked when he reached for his briefcase and collected his coat. 'You're leaving?'

'Unfortunately, yes.'

In other circumstances he would've phoned Rosie and asked her to deal with the situation. Eddie was an easygoing boy and not prone to fistfights. Whatever had caused the altercation, Zach was convinced it hadn't been Eddie's

340

ault.

Since his blowup with Rosie in the office that day, Zach hadn't been in contact with her. He felt bad about it, especially when Cecilia had told him how much she'd enjoyed meeting Rosie. Zach felt guilty for leaping to conclusions, but what else was he to think when he'd heard Rosie was busy chatting with Cecilia? Naturally enough, he'd assumed she was grilling his assistant for information about Janice.

Only later, after his outburst, did he realize he'd made an idiot of himself. It wasn't the first time and it probably wouldn't be the last. In any event, they were divorced, so it shouldn't bother him as much as it did. Still...

Zach got into his car and started the engine. He placed his hands on the steering wheel as an uneasy feeling settled in the pit of his stomach. He'd made a mistake, and that mistake had cost him his marriage. Lessons didn't come easy to him; he was still too impulsive, too ready to assume the worst—and act on it. He owed Rosie an apology, but she'd avoided him, and frankly, he was grateful.

As Zach pulled into the school parking lot, he decided he should've called Rosie and asked her to deal with this situation, after all. She was closer to the grade school, and knew the principal. Actually, he was surprised that the authorities had notified him instead of her.

The school was filled with kid noises when

he opened the main doors—classes were being released for afternoon recess. Just as Zach walked into the building, a couple of hundred students shot out the doors. He couldn't move until they'd rushed past, and found himself standing there like a rock in a fast-flowing stream. As soon as the halls had emptied, he made his way to the principal's office.

Mr. Durrell, the principal, came out of his office once his secretary had announced Zach's arrival.

The two men shook hands.

'What's the problem?' Zach asked.

Durrell brought him into the other room. A petulant Eddie sat on a sofa, his shoulders slumped forward. He stared down at the floor, glancing up briefly when Zach entered. Eddie had a bruise on the side of his face and his eyes were red from crying.

The principal sat at his desk and Zach took the seat next to his son. Eddie wasn't a fighter, and Zach couldn't imagine what had happened to bring him to blows with another student. Zach placed his arm protectively around Eddie's shoulders. His son leaned into Zach's strength for a moment, but then caught himself and stiffened.

'Eddie was involved in a fistfight earlier today,' Mr. Durrell explained. 'The other boy claims Eddie threw the first punch.'

'Eddie?' Zach asked, waiting to hear his son's version of events.

'Eddie refuses to answer my questions,' the principal said.

Zach turned to look at his boy. 'Is it true, Eddie?' he asked gently. 'Did you throw the first punch?'

Eddie sniffled and wiped his nose with one sleeve. He nodded.

'I'm sure there's a good explanation,' Zach told the principal. 'Eddie's never been in any fights before.'

'I agree,' Principal Durrell said, 'and that's what concerns me. This is out of character for Edward. I'm willing to overlook the incident this time, but I want assurances that it won't happen again.'

'Of course,' Zach said.

'The reason I phoned you, Mr. Cox, is that this is serious. I want you to know that if Edward takes part in a second fight, I won't have any choice but to expel him.'

'I understand.'

'Why don't I give you a few minutes to talk, and then the three of us can discuss the matter before I bring in Christopher Lamond.' Mr. Durrell stood and walked out of the room.

At the mention of Janice's son, Zach's head snapped up and his mouth went dry. As he sorted out his thoughts, Zach heard the sound of children's laughter drifting in from outside. A bell rang, and the thunder of feet signaled that recess was over. Suddenly the halls were quiet.

'You want to tell me what happened?' Zach asked once he'd regained his composure.

Eddie's shoulders had slumped so far forward, his forehead almost touched his knees. He sniffled again, then gradually straightened. 'Chris said...his mom used to be your girlfriend, and that's why you and Mom don't live together anymore.'

Zach felt as if he'd been hit square in the chest. The impact was so jarring he nearly placed his hand over his heart. 'You know that's not true.'

'I told Chris, but he wouldn't listen.' Eddie shook his head. 'I shouldn't have hit him, but he wouldn't shut up and he kept shouting it and finally...I had to make him stop.'

'What'll happen the next time, Eddie?'

'Next time,' Eddie repeated, 'I'm going to look him in the eye and tell him it isn't true and then I'll walk away.'

'That sounds like a good idea.' Zach ruffled his son's hair. 'You want me to beat him up for you?' he teased.

The hint of a smile touched Eddie's mouth. 'Dad!'

Zach nudged him with his elbow and Eddie nudged him back. After a couple more elbow exchanges, the door opened and Mr. Durrell returned. The three of them talked for a few minutes, and then the principal brought in the other boy. Chris refused to look at Zach. After the two boys had apologized, Mr. Durrell

344

instructed Eddie and Christopher to go back to their respective classrooms.

Zach was about to suggest Eddie come home with him, but he realized it was better that his son face his class and his friends sooner rather than later.

Zach thanked Mr. Durrell and left. He pitied Chris Lamond, suspecting that Janice had paraded a number of men through her son's life. He'd almost been one of them. Zach was halfway to the parking lot when he recognized Rosie. She was dressed in a straight skirt and matching jacket and looked…professional. Sharp and savvy. He wasn't used to seeing her like this, and it made him feel a bit odd, as though she'd somehow become someone different. When she noticed him, she paused momentarily. Then, with her chin held high, she continued toward the school.

'I've already been to see Mr. Durrell,' Zach said when their paths crossed.

She nodded. 'The school secretary called to tell me Eddie had been in a fight. I thought I'd better find out what happened. That just isn't like him.'

'Mr. Durrell phoned me.'

'I didn't know if you'd be able to come. I know how busy you are this time of year and I managed to leave a few minutes early.'

'You assumed I *wouldn't* come.' Zach was mildly offended that she'd expected him to put his work schedule ahead of his son's needs. He might be lacking in a lot of other areas, but Zach prided himself on being a good father.

'Oh, no, I knew you'd come. I just figured that it'd be later, and I didn't think it was a good idea for Eddie to sit in Mr. Durrell's office all afternoon.' She gave a quick shrug. 'I was wrong—you obviously came over here right away.'

He wondered if she'd said this just to prove she had no trouble admitting when she was at fault. Fine, he could do it, too.

'Speaking of assumptions,' Zach said, looking past his ex-wife. He owed her this, even if it meant humiliating himself in the process. 'It's easy to leap to conclusions.' He glanced at Rosie to see if she got his point.

'How do you mean?'

It should be obvious, but apparently she wanted him to spell it out. 'The way I assumed you were talking to Cecilia to pump her for information about Janice.'

Rosie stared at him. Then she frowned as if she wasn't sure she'd heard him correctly. 'Are you apologizing, Zachary Cox?'

Zach clenched his jaw and nodded. 'Yes, I'm apologizing. I was out of line that day.'

Her face relaxed, and she offered him a soft, almost shy smile. Then she said, 'Thank you, Zach.'

'For what?'

'For admitting you were wrong. I know how hard it is for you to do that.'

'Really?' He didn't think he was *that* bad, just reluctant at times. Still, he'd gotten worse once his marriage began to fall apart. Although maybe that was *why* his marriage had fallen apart—or at least a contributing factor.

'Oh, that sounded self-righteous of me, didn't it?' Rosie laughed and shook her head.

It was easy to forgive her when she was so willing to laugh at herself. He smiled in response, feeling a connection with her that he hadn't felt in nearly two years.

'I owe you an apology, too,' she told him.

'Me?' They'd waged war over a comma in their divorce papers. Their weapons had been highly paid attorneys. During the bitter months preceding the divorce, there'd been no interchange that wasn't witnessed and presided over by those same attorneys. Yet here was Rosie, standing with him in a school parking lot, and they were having one of the most important conversations of their relationship.

'I apologize for assuming you were involved with Janice,' Rosie continued. 'I convinced myself that you were having an affair and I turned into a vindictive shrew. I'm not proud of the things I said and did, and I apologize.'

Zach had never expected Rosie to do anything like this. For months she'd been filled with resentment and vicious anger. Now he saw the tears of regret in her eyes, and his own heart softened.

'Rosie…'

'You denied the affair from the beginning,' she went on, barely able to speak through her tears. 'I never had any real proof. I'd decided it was happening, felt it must be. She was obviously attractive and capable, and you spent eight hours a day with her. I was insanely jealous.'

Zach swallowed hard. He looked toward the school, sick at heart. Even now, months after his divorce, Janice haunted his life. Today his son had even fought with hers. She wasn't to blame for the death of his marriage, but she wasn't exactly a disinterested bystander. Janice's attention had flattered him; he'd liked the way she'd catered to him, liked it far more than he should have. And she'd been well aware of that….

Clearly embarrassed by her loss of control, Rosie shoved the hair away from her face. 'I apologize for the ugly things I said, for the way I behaved.'

The school bell rang, but they both ignored it.

'Rosie, listen, I was as much at fault as you. More so,' Zach confessed. 'I should never have let things go on as long as they did. I was wrong, dead wrong.'

'But—'

'Let me finish,' he said, fearing he'd lose his courage if he didn't say it now. 'I wasn't physically involved with Janice, but I did care about her. And I relied on her.'

Zach held his breath a moment. 'I didn't sleep with Janice, although it might have gone that way eventually—it was definitely what *she* wanted. But I did become emotionally dependent on her.'

He watched as the color drained from Rosie's face. He wanted to explain what he meant, but by then the school buses had rolled into the parking lot, belching smoke and diesel fumes.

'Mom,' Eddie shouted, running toward them. 'What are you doing here?'

'We'll talk later,' Zach promised, but he could see from the shock in Rosie's eyes that she wasn't ready to discuss Janice. For that matter, he wasn't eager to bring up the subject again—ever.

*   *   *

Grace was breathing hard as she followed the aerobics instructor. 'One, two, one, two, three. Come on, ladies! Pick up the pace.' She groaned at the young woman's words; she could barely keep up with the other members of her Wednesday night class as it was. She had conceded a long time ago that Olivia was far more agile than she was. The only reason she'd signed up for this class was so she could count on seeing her best friend at least once a week. By now, three years later, she'd figured

349

all these exercises would've gotten easier. Not so.

Back in the locker room, Grace felt convinced she was losing whatever ground she'd gained. The problem was, this was her only exercise program. Like it or not, she needed the class.

She used to take a brisk walk along the waterfront at lunchtime, especially on sunny days. Now she ate her lunch in front of the computer at the library. At home it was the same thing. If Will wasn't online when she logged on, he almost always had a message waiting for her. She'd come to live for his messages. She'd let so many things slide, and all because of Will. She feared their online relationship had become an obsession, but recognizing that did nothing to change the way she felt about him.

'I don't know why I do this to myself,' Grace complained as she slumped onto the bench in the locker room.

Olivia wasn't even out of breath, whereas Grace was panting. Her hair was plastered to her head and her face felt hot. This couldn't be good for her, although according to the pencil-thin group leader, she was doing wonderful things for her heart. Wanna bet?

'You're going to seed, Gracie-girl,' Olivia teased.

Grace rolled her eyes. 'And you're not?'

Olivia braced her tennis shoe against the

bench and untied it. 'Not me. Say, you never did tell me what you did on Valentine's Day.' Olivia sank down on the bench next to Grace.

'Nothing much. I stayed home.' She didn't have anything exciting to report. In fact, her night had gotten off to a slow start.

Olivia wiped her face with a towel. 'Being alone didn't bother you?'

'Not in the least.' Grace shrugged. 'I enjoy my own company.' Yes, at first she'd been a bit down, since Will hadn't been available, but eventually she was able to talk to him. He'd e-mailed her later than usual. He'd stayed at the office finishing up a report so he could leave for New Orleans the following week. Grace didn't dare think about that. After all this time, she was actually going to be in Will's arms. She'd dreamed of this in high school and only recently confessed to him how she'd felt back then.

The plane ticket he'd mailed her waited on her dresser, where she gazed at it every day, imagining the pleasures to come. For his part, Will had made her a number of promises. This first time would be as special as he could make it. Soon they'd have a life together. Will hadn't wanted to discuss the details but said they'd go over all of that once she arrived.

'Did you and Jack have a good time?' Grace asked in order to turn her thoughts from Will.

'We had a fabulous time,' Olivia said, with a long, drawn-out sigh.

'Did he get you flowers?'

'Jack?' Olivia arched her eyebrows dramatically. 'Once a year is about all I should expect from him.'

'He did buy you that tennis bracelet for your birthday last year.'

'And gave it to me weeks late,' she recalled.

Olivia loved that bracelet; she wore it almost constantly.

'If you must know, Jack bought me two tickets to the Sonics basketball game.'

'He didn't!' Grace loved the way Jack could make Olivia smile. It was just like him to buy her a gift *he* wanted.

'That's all right, I outsmarted him,' Olivia assured her. 'I bought him a facial at the health spa.'

Grace shook her head and marveled that her friend could get exactly what she wanted and do it in such a clever manner. 'You two are getting along better than ever, aren't you?'

Olivia nodded. 'I can't believe how silly I was to make demands on him. And that stupid ultimatum—I should've known better. I was such a fool to consider getting back with Stan.' She lowered her voice. 'I'm in love with Jack.'

Grace was thrilled for her. This really was good news, but it wasn't something she hadn't figured out herself. Olivia's feelings for Jack were obvious. While Grace had similar news concerning Will, she wasn't free to share it. But she would the minute his divorce was final.

Grace had told Olivia everything nearly her entire life. The urge to tell her dearest friend about her plans with Will was almost overwhelming, but she couldn't. Soon, though. Very soon. According to Will, his wife had moved out and the divorce was all but over. The legalities couldn't be settled quickly enough to suit Grace.

'Did I tell you Mom heard from Will? He's worried about this protest rally she's organizing. He's going to be out of town next week, but he's planning to call and give her his two cents' worth.'

Grace already knew he'd be in New Orleans. What Olivia didn't know was that Will would be with *her.* She was a bit surprised that Olivia avoided mentioning his divorce, but she was probably waiting until it was final before she said anything, which was understandable.

'I'd love to take a cruise one day,' Olivia said dreamily.

Grace frowned. 'A cruise. What's that got to do with anything?'

Olivia glanced at her. 'My brother. He and Georgia booked a cruise this summer in the South Pacific.'

It felt as if her heart had stopped beating. 'Will's taking a cruise with his wife?' she asked, just to be certain she'd heard Olivia correctly.

'They've gone on several over the years. Will says it's the only way to travel.'

This was a mistake; it had to be. Will and

353

Georgia were in the middle of a divorce. Will couldn't have misled Grace like this, couldn't have lied to her...not after the things he'd promised. She didn't believe it. She absolutely refused to accept it.

Somehow Grace managed to remain in one piece until she got back to the house. Buttercup was waiting for her as usual, but Grace ran past the dog and reached for the phone. Her hand trembled so badly she nearly dropped the receiver.

No, she couldn't just call him out of the blue like this. After all these months of communicating online, she didn't even know his home number. He was always the one who phoned her. With finances so tight, she couldn't afford lengthy long-distance conversations, and Will knew that. She needed to think this through before she made accusations.

Perhaps it was all a big misunderstanding. Will didn't want his family to find out about the impending divorce; that was it. Naturally, after all these years, it would be difficult for him to tell his mother and sister that his marriage was a failure.

Of course, Grace reasoned, that *had* to be it. Instantly she felt better, but no matter how hard she struggled to find reassurance, she couldn't sleep. At midnight, she got up, turned on the computer and went online; no new messages from him. At one, with a pounding headache, she took an aspirin and crawled back into bed. At two, she still couldn't sleep. Nor at three. Doubts invaded her mind. The fact that Will had insisted she not let Olivia know they were talking online, the secrecy of it, had always bothered her.

Olivia rarely mentioned her brother. He lived on the other side of the country, so his name didn't often enter the conversation. He hadn't lived in Cedar Cove since his early twenties. People changed.

She had to know.

At three-thirty, when the night was at its darkest and dawn only an unfulfilled promise, Grace picked up her bedside phone. She got Will's home phone number from directory assistance. With the time difference, he would be awake, just getting ready for the office.

The phone was answered on the first ring. A female voice, sounding depressingly cheerful.

'Good morning.'

'Is this the Will Jefferson residence?'

A short hesitation. 'Yes, this is Mrs. Jefferson. May I ask who's calling?'

'This is Grace Sherman from Cedar Cove, Washington.'

'Oh, hi. My husband's from Cedar Cove. I hope everything's all right?'

'Yes. Could I speak to Will?'

'Of course. I'll get him for you right away.'

Grace thought she was going to be physically ill. She closed her eyes and concentrated on taking deep breaths.

A moment later Will picked up the phone. 'Hello.'

'Hello, Will. It's Grace.' She paused to let the words sink in. 'You aren't getting a divorce, are you? That was your wife who answered the phone!'

'This isn't a good time to talk. I'll explain later.' He sounded annoyed with her.

'An explanation won't be necessary.'

'I—'

She didn't give him a chance to respond. 'Please don't try to contact me again.' How calm she sounded, Grace mused. And yet her heart was racing and her mouth was dry. 'I'll return the plane ticket and if you ever try to get in touch with me again, I'm going straight to Olivia and your mother. Do I make myself clear?'

Grace could hear his wife speaking in the background, worried that something was wrong with his mother. 'I understand,' he said, and then quietly replaced the receiver.

At eight o'clock, Grace phoned the library and reported that she was sick. It wasn't a stretch of the imagination. Every flu symptom she'd ever experienced hit her, all at the same time. She fell into bed, pulled the sheets over her head, trying to shut out the world.

She'd been so gullible, so trusting and naive. Will was her best friend's brother and not once did she suspect that he'd ever do anything

356

this underhanded or deceitful—especially to her. The fact that he'd lied was bad enough, but that he'd preyed on her heart was nothing short of cruel. He'd lured her to New Orleans, paid for the flight and planned an erotic, exotic weekend for the two of them. She wondered what he'd intended to do once she learned he wasn't divorcing his wife. Apparently he'd assumed he could keep her dangling like this indefinitely. And he probably could have, except for a chance remark of his sister's.

So she was stupid, too… Because it was now abundantly clear that Will had no intention of leaving his wife, especially for her. With her high school crush on him, Grace had been a willing victim.

Even though she was dizzy and sick to her stomach, Grace turned on her computer and blocked Will's name and e-mail address. Never again would he be able to contact her online. Anything he sent her would be automatically returned.

Midmorning, Grace fell into a fitful sleep. She woke in the afternoon, and found Buttercup lying on the bedroom floor. 'What is it, girl?' Grace asked. 'Do you have a broken heart, too?'

Buttercup didn't respond, didn't even wag her tail. Grace walked over to her, crouched down beside her, and immediately realized something was terribly wrong. Stroking the dog's head, she grabbed the phone and called the vet.

'I don't know what's the matter with her,' she told the receptionist. 'But please get me in as soon as possible.'

Luckily there was an appointment available that afternoon. Grace dressed in sloppy jeans, ran a brush through her hair and loaded Buttercup in the car, then drove to the animal clinic as fast as she dared.

Weeks earlier, Cliff had mentioned that there might be a problem with Buttercup's health. Why hadn't she paid more attention? Why had she ignored what was right before her eyes? The answer was too painful to examine. Grace knew why. She'd neglected her dog because of Will.

While Grace sat in the waiting area, she felt sick with guilt. She'd let her friend down. The door to the clinic opened and, to her dismay, in walked Cliff Harding. Tall, dark, ruggedly good-looking, he seemed to energize the compact waiting area. A woman with a large cat on a leash sat up straighter and smiled enticingly. An older man with a terrier grinned and exchanged a few remarks.

Grace shrank as far as she could into the corner and prayed he hadn't seen her. Looking as bad as she did, maybe he wouldn't recognize her.

'Hello, Mr. Harding.' The receptionist perked up. Cliff was obviously a favorite. 'The medication you ordered is in.'

'That's what I'm here for,' he said, sauntering to the counter. He good-naturedly teased the girl, who blushed with pleasure. One of the assistants from the back must have heard Cliff's voice, because she made an excuse to slip out front. She was about Grace's age and flirted openly with him.

Grace lowered her head and pretended to read a magazine. From the corner of her eye, she watched as Cliff paid for the worming medication he needed for his horses and turned to leave.

While he might not have recognized her, he didn't have any problem remembering Buttercup.

He shoved his wallet in his back pocket and for a moment she thought he might do them both a favor and walk away. No, that would've been entirely too easy. Instead he walked across the room and stood directly in front of her.

'Hello, Grace.'

She put down the magazine as if noticing him for the first time. 'Oh—hello, Cliff.'

'How's Buttercup?' he asked. Bending down on one knee, he gently placed his hand beneath the golden retriever's jaw and looked into her eyes. 'What does Doc Newman say?'

'I haven't been in to see her yet.'

A frown darkened his face. 'This is your first visit?'

She nodded. He didn't need to say anything

359

more; she read the censure in his eyes, felt the reprimand. She wanted to defend herself—but she couldn't.

After a moment, he stood and stared down at her. 'I hope you aren't too late.' He touched the brim of his hat in farewell and strode out the door.

Twenty-Three

It'd been three weeks since Maryellen had seen Jon, other than in passing. She'd gotten quite good at inventing reasons for him to linger when he came to collect Katie, but he always had an excuse to leave almost as soon as he arrived.

The unspoken message that he no longer wanted to be part of her life was beginning to sink into her stubborn heart. The more she obsessed over his behavior, the more convinced she became that there was someone else.

For the most part, Maryellen was able to hide her pain and disappointment from those closest to her. Her sister was busy and involved in her marriage. These days Kelly was preoccupied with getting pregnant a second time and seemed oblivious to anything outside her own small world. Not that Maryellen was complaining. If their circumstances had been reversed, she probably would've done the same.

Her mother was a different story. In the last year, Maryellen had felt closer to her mother than anyone, but that, too, had changed and for reasons she didn't understand. While Maryellen was pregnant with Katie, she'd had many wonderful talks with her mother. But lately, Grace had been distracted, and Maryellen felt excluded from her mother's life.

Oddly, the one person she could confide in was her nail tech. Rachel had been working on Maryellen's nails for three years; during that time, she'd become both confessor and counselor.

There was something liberating about sitting across from Rachel like this. The minute Rachel reached for her hands, it was as if an emotional wall lowered between them. Despite the privileged nature of their relationship, their time together was limited to these occasional appointments.

What she couldn't tell her mother and sister, she could discuss with Rachel. It was Rachel who'd first guessed that she was pregnant, although Maryellen had worked hard to keep it a secret for as long as possible. And Rachel was the first to recognize that Maryellen had fallen in love with Jon, something she'd barely acknowledged to herself. Rachel's insight and practical wisdom had been a special gift these last few weeks.

February wound to a close. Maryellen sat across from Rachel for her nail appointment; when she looked up, she found Rachel studying her intently.

'What?' Maryellen stretched out her hands.

Rachel frowned. 'I wondered, but now I know. You didn't hear from Jon, did you?'

'Is it that obvious?' Maryellen tried to make a joke of it and failed.

'Yes.' Rachel lifted Maryellen's hands for inspection. 'Look at these nails! They're a disaster. I can always tell when something's troubling you by looking at your fingernails.'

'I know, I know.' She'd chipped the polish on two nails and broken another. Rachel was right; she was a mess and in more ways than one.

Rachel nonchalantly reached for a cotton ball and polish remover. 'I saw Jon the other day, down by the waterfront with Katie. I think it's so cute the way he hauls her around on his back, all bundled up and everything. He had his camera around his neck.'

Maryellen had seen Jon with Katie in exactly that way a dozen times. She marveled at what a good father he was. She felt sure that Katie would love the outdoors with the same energy and enthusiasm as Jon.

'Speaking of Katie, how's she doing?' Rachel asked. 'Last time you were in, she'd just gotten over a cold and an ear infection. Poor little thing.'

'She's much better.' A fact for which Maryellen was eternally grateful. Katie's illness had been a nightmare for her. She was astonished by how well she'd managed to function on so little sleep. Not that she wanted to try it again anytime soon. 'Katie's crawling around like crazy. I'll bet she starts walking early.'

Rachel sighed and vigorously rubbed the Forever French polish from Maryellen's fingertips. 'I'd love to have a baby. I'm telling you, Maryellen, that biological clock of mine is getting louder than Big Ben. I'm almost thirty, and if I don't meet someone soon, I have a feeling I never will.'

Men or the lack thereof was a frequent topic between them. Rachel liked to say that her chances of meeting eligible men in a hair-and-nail shop were equivalent to losing weight on a diet of hot fudge sundaes. She'd done the bar scene, hung around at all the 'guy' places. A year ago, she'd even enrolled in a mechanics class at the community college. Not a single date had come as a result of all that effort, and Rachel was discouraged.

'Anytime you want to borrow Katie for a fix, let me know,' Maryellen told her.

'I just might.' Rachel dumped the used cotton balls in the garbage and picked up her file. 'Enough about my pathetic love life, let's talk about you and Jon.'

As if there was anything to talk about.

'Unfortunately, it all seems pretty hopeless.'

'Why?'

There was no easy way to answer that question. She hadn't intended to tell Rachel what she suspected, but the words were out before she could stop them. 'I think he's involved with someone else.'

Rachel looked up and held Maryellen's gaze. 'I don't believe it.'

Maryellen mumbled a response, her head lowered. This was humiliating enough without inviting the entire shop to listen in.

'What?' Rachel asked. 'I didn't hear you.'

Embarrassed, Maryellen said, 'I practically threw myself at him not once, but twice— and Jon turned me down both times.' She spoke in a hoarse whisper. The morning they'd awakened next to each other and he'd moved away from her had been a low point for Maryellen.

'That's what I mean,' Rachel whispered back heatedly. 'If Jon *didn't* love you, he'd have taken what you offered, and just enjoyed himself. Then he would've left without a backward glance. But, you'll notice, Jon didn't do that. He exhibited self-control.'

'But why?' Maryellen demanded. If Jon truly loved her, she'd know it; she'd feel it. If he did care for her, she wouldn't have felt so utterly devastated when he walked away.

'That I can't answer,' Rachel murmured as she continued to file Maryellen's nails.

'Maybe he's seeing one of the women he works with,' Maryellen said, and her heart grew heavy at the thought. The Lighthouse employed lots of single women who worked as waitresses. There were others in the kitchen. And his photographs were gaining more and more attention. Maryellen had been around the artists' community long enough to know how attractive women found creative men.

'There's no one else,' Rachel said, with such conviction that several heads turned in their direction.

'How can you be so sure?'

Rachel concentrated on her filing. 'I wish I could give you definite proof. I can't, but I'm convinced he loves you.'

Perhaps it was wishful thinking, but Maryellen desperately wanted to believe that, too.

'You know,' Rachel said suddenly. 'Here's a thought. You could always *ask* him if there's someone else.'

Maryellen immediately shook her head.

'Why not?'

'Well...because...' Maryellen couldn't think of a reason quickly and found herself stuttering. 'It's out of the question,' she said with finality.

Rachel paused again. 'You don't want to know, do you?'

Maryellen gaped at her.

'You're afraid of the truth,' Rachel insisted.

Maryellen started to defend herself and then admitted Rachel was right—she *was* afraid.

'What's the worst thing that can happen?' Rachel said next. 'My mother used to ask me that whenever I had a problem. It always got me thinking, you know?'

Maryellen realized she needed to do some thinking, too. This situation with Jon was making her miserable, and there was no solution in sight.

'You love him, Maryellen.'

'I know.'

'I don't understand why two people who so obviously care for each other have such a hard time finding happiness.' Rachel released a long slow sigh. 'I have to tell you, this is not encouraging to someone like me.'

'You'll find a husband,' Maryellen said. Surely a woman as lovely, practical and just plain nice as Rachel would succeed in meeting a man.

'Sure I will,' Rachel agreed, 'but I'd prefer he didn't come with a police record or an addiction to drugs or booze.'

'There's your problem, Rach,' Maryellen teased. 'You're just too darn picky.'

*   *   *

Peggy had seen changes in Bob over the last year, but the most dramatic ones had come

366

after Sheriff Davis's last visit. Her husband didn't sleep well and was often up roaming the house at all hours of the night. He'd lost interest in his wood shop, too. He used to spend much of the day there, working on a variety of projects, but now many of them were left uncompleted. Lately nothing interested him.

For the last few weeks, he'd attended his AA meetings on a daily basis: twenty-one meetings in twenty-one days. He hadn't been to that many in such quick succession since he'd first gotten involved with Alcoholics Anonymous. Bob refused to talk about his feelings and snapped at her when she pried. For now, she decided, it was best to leave him alone. They'd meet Hannah Russell later today; maybe then they'd find the answers they sought.

After spending a sleepless night herself, Peggy called Corrie McAfee. They met at least once a week, to shop, exchange recipes and talk about gardening. She was the one person Peggy could speak to about this upcoming meeting.

'It's Peggy,' she said when her friend picked up the receiver.

'Hi,' the other woman said cheerfully. 'How are you?'

'Can I ask a favor?' Peggy's stomach was in knots, and emotionally she wasn't in much better shape than Bob.

'Of course!'

'Would it be possible for you and Roy to be here this afternoon? We promised Sheriff Davis we'd see this girl, but now I'm not so sure we should.'

'Let me talk to Roy,' Corrie said, and put her on hold for a moment.

Peggy gnawed on her lower lip, leaning against the kitchen wall as she waited for Corrie. The meeting with Hannah would be hard on everyone. Peggy didn't know what they could tell Max Russell's daughter; she, too, was looking for answers and unfortunately they had none to give her.

Corrie was back. 'Roy's clearing his schedule now. We'll be there.'

Peggy mentioned the appointment time, then added. 'I...I didn't discuss this with Bob, but I'll tell him you're coming before you and Roy get here.' She felt it was only fair to let her friend know this.

'That's fine,' Corrie assured her. 'Don't worry, Peg, everything's going to be fine.'

Peggy wished she could believe that.

All afternoon, Peggy and Bob were tense and on edge with each other. He did agree to having the McAfees at the meeting, though, which was a relief to Peggy, who wanted them for emotional support.

By three o'clock when the doorbell rang, Peggy was an emotional wreck and Bob wasn't any better. Although she'd been a hostess for many years, she fussed about the kitchen with coffee cups and cookies and plates as though she'd never entertained before.

Roy and Corrie arrived first. Bob shook hands with Roy and then led the couple into the living room. Corrie and Roy sat on one of the two sofas, leaving the two wing chairs by the fireplace vacant.

Bob waited until they were seated before he said, 'Peggy told me she'd asked you to join us. Frankly I appreciate the fact that you're here.'

'I'm glad to do it,' Roy assured him.

The doorbell chimed again, and Peggy's heart instantly flew into her throat. Bob's eyes met hers and he, too, seemed momentarily paralyzed. He recovered quickly. With a determined stride he went to answer the door.

The young woman who stepped into the foyer was very tall and thin, and Peggy had a whimsical image of her as one of the great blue herons who stalked the pebble beach of the cove. Sheriff Davis entered the house behind their guest.

The woman, who appeared to be close in age to her own children, wore a full-length, tan raincoat with navy blue pants and a sweater. Her dark hair was tied with a scarf at the base of her neck.

'It's a pleasure to meet you, Hannah,' Bob said as he took her coat. 'I wish it was under more pleasant circumstances.'

'So do I.' She glanced nervously into the

room.

Roy stood for the introduction, which Peggy thought was a nice touch. He then shook hands with Sheriff Davis. If the sheriff had any questions about the McAfees' presence, he didn't voice them.

Once everyone was settled—Sheriff Davis and Hannah in the chairs by the fireplace— Peggy suggested they talk first and save the coffee and cookies for later.

'I think that would be best,' Hannah said. Her voice was soft and modulated as she leaned forward and folded her hands on her knees, almost as if she were a schoolgirl. She did look young, and so vulnerable. Peggy resisted the urge to give her shoulders a reassuring squeeze.

'I hope we can answer your questions,' Bob began.

'I hope you can, too.' Hannah inhaled loudly, obviously gathering strength.

'Earlier today I was in to see Sheriff Davis,' Hannah said, nodding at him. 'He gave me my dad's ashes. I'll take them back to California and place them in the mausoleum next to my mother.'

Peggy could only imagine how difficult this must be for someone so young. 'I hope now that your father's been found, you have some closure,' she said. The words sounded hollow and trite to her own ears.

'I don't know if closure is possible until

I discover why Dad came to Cedar Cove in the first place,' Hannah responded. 'As I was telling Sheriff Davis, we don't know anyone in Washington state. As far as I'm aware, Dad's never been to this area before...and he was acting so mysterious when he left. He didn't want me to find out where he was going—that was pretty clear. I wouldn't even have known he was leaving if I hadn't stopped in to see him that day. Can you tell me *anything?*' she pleaded.

'I wish I could,' Bob answered, 'but Peggy and I are as much at a loss as you.'

Peggy murmured agreement.

'I suppose you want to know whatever I can tell you about that night,' Bob said, leaning forward.

'Please. Anything would be helpful.'

Bob proceeded to fill in the details, describing everything he and Peggy had discussed dozens of times, together and with the police.

'Sheriff Davis said sometimes it's the minutest detail that leads to an answer,' Peggy added.

There was a brief silence after this remark.

'Would you mind answering a few questions I have?' Roy asked Hannah.

'I will if I can.'

Sheriff Davis frowned, but he didn't intrude.

'I understand your father was injured in a car accident that also killed your mother?'

Hannah's face was troubled. 'He never forgave himself for that.'

'What caused the accident?'

Her eyes widened. 'The investigation determined that my father was at fault.'

'I read the accident report,' Roy said slowly, 'and your father claimed the steering failed.'

'He did say that,' Hannah agreed, 'but the accident investigators couldn't find anything wrong with the steering system. The only thing they could suggest is the tube leading to the automatic steering system had an air pocket in it. Apparently that sometimes happens, but it's rare, and without any conclusive evidence, my father was found to be at fault.' She paused and looked at Sheriff Davis. 'I think in some ways it might've been easier on my dad if he'd died that night.'

'The guilt?' Troy asked.

'That,' she said, 'and month upon month of surgery and physical therapy.'

'What about your father's friends?' Roy asked next.

Hannah glanced down at her hands. 'Dad was pretty much a loner. He didn't have a lot of friends. Oh—there was one old army buddy who helped him get into the VA hospital where he was treated. But other than that...' She shook her head. 'Mom told me he was a different man before the war. They were just dating back then, and she saved all his letters. Some days after they'd had an argument, she would sit on their bed and read them. She said they reminded her of what Dad was like before the war.'

'Do you still have those letters?' Roy asked.

'I'd like to see them if you do,' Sheriff Davis said before Roy could ask.

'Yes, but I'd want them back.'

'Of course,' Troy Davis assured her.

'I understand you knew my father.' Hannah's question was directed at Bob.

He nodded. 'We spent a year together in Nam.'

'Can you tell me what he was like then?'

Bob leaned back in his chair and took a moment to compose his thoughts. 'What I remember most about Max is his guitar. At the end of the day, we'd sit around and he'd bring it out and strum a few songs. You can't imagine how much music can do to take the edge off, especially in the situation your dad and I were in.'

'I didn't know my father played the guitar.'

'He didn't after—' Bob stopped abruptly and faltered. 'Something happened in the war that affected both your father and me. War is like that. It can destroy your soul.'

'He never spoke of the war,' she said softly.

Bob didn't, either. When he'd first returned from Nam, Peggy had thought it would help if her husband talked about his experiences. He'd refused. Had she known what demons hounded him, she would've suggested counseling, but he kept many of his experiences hidden from her. It wasn't until he'd just about drowned in a bottle that she understood why, and by then it was almost too late.

'Is there anything else you'd like to ask us?' Peggy inquired.

Hannah shook her head. 'I appreciate that you let me come. I wondered, you know. Anyone would. He's gone...both he and my mom. I just wondered....'

Like Hannah, Peggy wondered if she and Bob would ever find peace.

*   *   *

Rosie tried not to dwell on Zach's confession that he'd relied emotionally on his personal assistant. In essence, Zach had admitted to falling in love with the other woman. She'd known in her heart that he'd been unfaithful, and he'd proved her at least partially right. Rosie could only speculate about what had happened, but—as he'd admitted—eventually Zach would have become Janice's lover.

Their divorce had been final for months, and by now she should be ready to move on. Instead, she felt as if she was falling deeper and deeper into an abyss, a place of uncertainty and sadness.

Sunday afternoon she waited until she was sure Zach would be out of the house before she arrived. Her entrance didn't cause much of a stir. Eddie was reading one of the Harry Potter books and Allison was in her bedroom with the door closed.

'What's for dinner?' Eddie asked, glancing up when she came in, carrying two plastic grocery bags.

'How about spaghetti?' she asked, knowing it was her son's favorite.

'We had that last night, and I like Dad's spaghetti sauce better than yours.'

'Thank you so much,' she muttered under her breath. Her son was nothing if not honest.

When Rosie walked into the kitchen, she set the groceries on the counter and stared around her in complete awe. The room was meticulously clean. The floor had been washed and waxed to such a bright sheen she could see her own reflection. Not only that, the countertops were cleared off and wiped down. The stove had a shine to it that had been sadly absent since the day they'd moved into the house. Rosie walked over to the wall-mounted oven and opened it. Sure enough, that, too, was spotless.

'Who cleaned the kitchen?' Rosie called out to her son.

'Dad.'

It hurt like hell to admit that her ex-husband was a better housekeeper and cook than she'd ever been. Rosie tried not to feel sorry for herself. She should be counting her blessings instead of complaining. The kitchen was immaculate. She'd wanted to clean it for weeks, but even in her heyday as a wife and mother, she'd never have managed anything close to the perfection that lay before her now.

'Hi, Mom,' Allison said, wandering into the kitchen. She opened the refrigerator and took out a can of soda.

Even without looking, Rosie knew it had been cleaned, too.

'Sloppy joes okay with you for dinner?'

'I guess.'

Such enthusiasm. 'Do you think Dad's a better cook than I am?' Rosie wasn't sure why she bothered to ask. Her daughter was bound to heap salt onto her already bleeding wounds.

'Do you want me to be honest?' Allison said, pulling the tab on the soda can.

That, on its own, was answer enough. Rosie crossed her arms and mentally prepared herself for the answer. 'Go ahead.'

Allison took a deep swallow of her soda. 'At first Dad cooked the same things you did, but then he really seemed to get into it. He doesn't have a lot of time, you know, so he does fun things like chicken salad with grapes and pineapple and lettuce. I sometimes help him,' she added proudly. 'We use bottled sauce—the gourmet stuff. It's really yummy. I'll give you the recipe if you want.'

'No, thanks.'

'His spaghetti's really good, too. He adds

376

sliced olives, and last night he threw in a can of jalapeños. It was great. Dad said that's called fusion cooking.'

'It's what?'

'Fusion. Come on, Mom, get with it.'

For reasons she didn't want to examine too closely, tears filled Rosie's eyes and spilled down her cheeks. She tried to hide them from her daughter but should have known better.

'Mom, are you crying?'

Rosie shrugged and turned her back to Allison.

'You'd better tell me what's wrong,' Allison said.

'I don't know—I'm just so glad to have you back.' She turned around and hugged her daughter. The girl was taller than Rosie—when had that happened?

'I didn't go anywhere,' Allison protested.

'But you did,' Rosie said, and cupped her daughter's beautiful face. 'I thought I'd lost you. I'm so grateful you're back.'

Allison rolled her eyes. 'It's nothing to cry about.'

'I know.' It didn't escape Rosie's notice that she wasn't the one her daughter had reached out to. Instead, a woman who was virtually a stranger had stepped into the role of mentor. Rosie could now add another failing to her list: besides being a bad wife and an inadequate housekeeper, she was a terrible mother.

It was suddenly too much for her, and

377

pulling out a chair, Rosie buried her face in her hands.

'Are you all right?' Allison asked.

'Fine...sorry, just give me a minute.'

'Tell me what's wrong,' Allison insisted.

How could she? Rosie kept her face covered and continued to cry into her hands. She could hear Allison and Eddie whispering in the background, but she was too upset to pay attention.

After about ten minutes, she stood, unloaded her grocery bags and set a pan on the stove top. She wasn't hungry, but in all likelihood the children were. She was enough of a failure without adding that to her list of sins.

The front door opened, and Rosie quickly wiped her cheeks and reached for a tissue to blow her nose. When she looked up, she discovered Zach standing in the kitchen doorway.

'What's wrong?' he asked.

Allison and Eddie crowded around their father. 'Don't be mad, Mom. We called Dad.'

'Why would you do that?' she demanded, knowing she sounded defensive. At this point she didn't care.

Allison took a step forward. 'Because you wouldn't stop crying.'

'Your father—'

Zach's jaw tightened. 'I'm right here, Rosie. There's no need to talk about me as if I wasn't

378

in the room.'

She placed her hands on her hips and glared at him. 'This is *my* time with the kids.'

'Fine, whatever. I'll just turn around and leave.'

'No.' It was Eddie who spoke first.

Allison echoed him. 'No. Dad, Mom needs you.'

'I don't,' Rosie muttered.

'You do, Mom,' Allison said. 'Now, talk, both of you, and Eddie and I'll cook dinner.'

Eddie seemed ready to protest, but at a glance from his sister, he closed his mouth.

Rosie and Zach frowned at each other for a moment before Zach gestured toward the family room. 'It looks like we have our orders.'

Rosie grabbed a second tissue and reluctantly followed her ex-husband.

They sat as far apart from each other as possible. Rosie took one end of the sofa and Zach sat on the edge of the recliner. Neither said anything for several tense minutes.

'I wanted to explain about my comment the other day,' Zach said.

Rosie wasn't up to hearing another confession. She raised her hand, stopping him. 'Please don't. Frankly, I don't want to hear it.'

Zach ignored her request. 'I felt it was only fair to tell you—'

'Didn't you hear me?' she said, losing patience.

'The least you can do is let me explain.'

'Why, so you can drag my self-esteem through the gutter again? Fine, you had an *emotional* affair. I heard you the first time. I got the message.'

Zach hung his head. 'But I was never physically involved with Janice.'

'That's not the point. You were in love with her.'

'No,' he corrected quickly. 'I had an emotional relationship with her, and there's a difference.'

Rosie wasn't sure that was true. All she knew was that her husband, the man she loved, had wanted another woman.

'When I look back on everything that led up to the divorce,' Zach continued, 'I understand how you must have felt. Instead of answering your concerns, I saw you as a jealous shrew.'

'I was,' Rosie admitted softly. She closed her eyes in shame as she remembered the things she'd said, the way she'd behaved toward her husband.

'I'm sorry, Rosie. I couldn't regret what happened any more than I already do. I hurt you, I hurt our children and in the process I hurt myself.'

She sniffled loudly. 'I'm sorry, too, but that isn't the only reason I'm crying. Oh, Zach,' she wailed, 'the kitchen is so *beautiful*.'

'You noticed,' he said, and there was a note of satisfaction in his voice. 'I wanted to do something for you and that was the only thing

I could think of.'

'You're a better housekeeper than I'll ever be,' she sobbed.

'Hey, we each have our strengths and weaknesses.'

'And a better cook.'

He shrugged, teasing her with a sexy grin. 'I disagree with you there.'

Rosie blew her nose. 'The kids don't think so. Eddie said your spaghetti sauce is better than mine.'

'You use the stuff in jars. I make it fresh.'

'See what I mean?'

'Okay,' Zach conceded, 'I make better spaghetti than you do, but no one bakes an orange cake as good as yours.'

She gave him a hopeless look. 'The recipe's from a boxed cake mix.'

'Do you think anyone cares so long as it tastes good?'

He smiled at her again and this time Rosie smiled shyly back.

Allison and Eddie marched into the room.

'Feel better, Mom?' Her teenage daughter was far too pleased with herself.

Rosie nodded. 'Much better, thank you both.' She glanced over at Zach. 'Thank you, too.'

Her ex-husband stood up, obviously ready to leave.

'Dad,' Eddie said in a stage whisper. 'Ask her.'

'Ask her what?' Zach whispered back.

'On a date.'

'What?' Rosie stared at her son.

'I think Dad should ask you on a date,' Eddie explained.

Zach frowned, not meeting Rosie's eyes. 'Your mother's going out with that widower now.'

Allison shook her head. 'No, she isn't.'

'You aren't?' Zach turned to Rosie.

'No. We only went out once and it was…not a success. Neither of us is ready for another relationship.'

'Well, then.' Zach smiled. 'Are you game for dinner?'

'Dad!' Allison groaned. 'You've got to be more romantic than *that*. Ask Mom again and this time do it right.'

With a mock-serious expression, Zach bowed. 'Rosie, would you do me the honor of having dinner with me on Thursday evening?'

'She can't,' Eddie answered. 'That's Scouting night.'

'Right,' Zach muttered.

'Take Mom out tonight,' Allison urged. 'I'll cook dinner for me and Eddie. You two talk. Okay?'

Rosie looked at Zach and he looked at her. A slow grin came over his face as he extended his hand. With barely a pause, she placed her own hand in his.

Twenty-Four

Grace sat with her morning cup of coffee. It was early Saturday, and the kitchen light caused shadows to flicker across the wall, heightening the impression of a dark and gloomy day. More than three weeks had gone by since she'd taken Buttercup to the vet. More than three weeks since she'd seen Cliff.

The dog was only now beginning to recover from cancer. Fortunately, all the tumors had been successfully removed. For a while, her prognosis had been poor and Grace had worried endlessly that she would lose her faithful companion. If Buttercup had died, Grace would've been to blame, and she would have had a hard time forgiving herself. Cliff had warned her that Buttercup didn't look well; she'd ignored him, just as she'd ignored everything else these last few months during her obsession with Will.

In retrospect, Grace saw how easily she'd fallen into this. It made her ill to think how low she'd sunk in her Internet relationship with Will Jefferson. She berated herself for being swayed by his compliments and his admiration. In truth, though, it hadn't been as one-sided as that. She knew he'd derived comfort and gratification from Grace's feelings for him; his marriage was in trouble—that much she believed—and he'd used her to salvage his ego, to bask in another woman's adoration. Caught in this web of mutual fascination, Grace had ignored one very important fact: Will Jefferson was a married man.

Her face burned with humiliation. Will had purchased her plane ticket to New Orleans, and she knew very well that he'd only booked one hotel room. She also knew what would've happened when she joined him.

Adding to her humiliation was the memory of how angry she'd been with Stan, Olivia's ex-husband, when they'd learned that he'd moved in with Marge. The divorce wasn't even final and already he was sleeping with another woman, involved in an affair. Grace realized now that she was no better than Stan. No better than the men she'd reviled for being unfaithful.

Cliff had guessed what she'd been doing and had ended their relationship. She'd been such a fool. No one had ever treated her better or showed her as much love and consideration as Cliff Harding.

Maybe her problem was that Cliff was simply *too* good. Something inside her rejected his genuine warmth and love. Was it because she felt unworthy? All Grace knew was that she'd done the very thing she'd promised Cliff's daughter she'd never do, and that was hurt Cliff.

She prayed it wasn't too late. She spent at

least an hour gathering her courage to visit Cliff. She'd considered phoning ahead, then decided against it. If he wasn't at the ranch house, she'd just return another time.

She had to face him, had to confess. She wanted Cliff to understand how sincerely sorry she was. Although she didn't deserve his forgiveness, she needed it.

Grace dressed carefully. She chose a jeans jumper and blouse Cliff especially liked. As she got ready to leave the house, Buttercup lifted her head from her pillowed dog bed and watched her every move. Maybe it was a fanciful thought, but she felt as if her golden retriever knew Grace was going to see Cliff. Knew and approved. While friendly, Buttercup was a discerning dog and wasn't prone to accepting strangers, but she'd loved Cliff from the very first.

'I'll be sure to tell Cliff you're feeling better,' she said, bending over to stroke her dog's silky ears. She'd given Buttercup lots of attention during the last few weeks, pampering her in an effort to make up for the neglect.

By the time she walked outside, it'd started to drizzle. Typical March weather. The windshield wipers made lazy swishes as Grace drove the twenty minutes to Olalla and Cliff's ranch.

Although Grace had often visited his ranch, she hadn't been there in at least six months. Turning into his long driveway she was immediately surprised by the number of apparent changes. A dozen horses grazed in the pasture, far more than she recalled from her last visit. A freshly painted white fence bordered the drive; it made for a striking entrance to the ranch. A large two-story red barn had replaced the smaller one.

When she pulled into the yard and parked near the barn, a man she didn't recognize walked out. Raising the hood of her raincoat, she left her car.

'Hello,' she said, smiling. 'I'm Grace Sherman. Is Cliff available?'

The dark-haired man hesitated, then nodded. 'C-Cal Washburn,' he said with a slight stutter. He was attractive—solid and squarely built, with an aura of competence. He appeared to be in his mid-thirties, but it was always difficult for Grace to judge age. His eyes, an intense shade of blue, seemed to look straight through her. It made Grace wonder if Cliff had mentioned her name—and whether or not Cal was going to answer her question.

The front door opened and Cliff stepped out.

'Cliff!' Grace hurried across the yard. Cliff moved aside and held the door for her.

'I hope you don't mind my coming by like this,' she said. The warmth in the house enveloped her.

'Of course I don't mind.' Cliff took her coat from her shoulders and hung it in the foyer.

Grace rubbed her arms. 'It's colder than I expected.'

'Why don't I get us a cup of coffee,' Cliff suggested.

This was going well and Grace began to relax. She followed him into the kitchen, noting improvements in the house as well as the yard.

'How long has Cal been around?' she asked.

'Couple months now,' Cliff said as he stood in front of the cupboard and selected two mugs. He seemed pleased to see her, cordial and polite, but...reserved. She had the impression that her visit had prompted mixed feelings. Which was only natural under the circumstances, she acknowledged.

Cliff poured them each a cup and set hers on the kitchen counter. Grace slipped onto a stool, while he stood across from her, on the other side of the counter.

'How's Buttercup?' he asked.

'Much better. I was terrified when they discovered the tumors. For a while, I thought I might lose her.'

Cliff nodded. 'I'm glad to hear she's on the mend.'

'You and me both.'

The silence that followed was uncomfortable. Cliff didn't make any effort to fill it, so Grace forged ahead. 'I know my visit must be something of a surprise,' she said. She gestured around. 'You've done a lot of work

387

since I was last here.'

'Yes,' he murmured. But he offered no further comment.

Grace stared down at her coffee, wishing she'd thought about what she wanted to say. She stared out the window at the expansive structure. 'When did you build the barn?'

'The contractor started construction the beginning of December.'

'I didn't realize you intended to make such major improvements to the property.'

Now it was Cliff who stared down at his coffee. 'I mentioned a new barn a couple of times.'

'Oh, yes. That's right, you did.' Of course he'd talked about it. She had a vague recollection of it. Anytime they were together she'd been preoccupied, wondering when she could get back home and onto the computer. Grace could only guess how much else she'd missed.

'I mentioned hiring Cal, too.'

'I do remember that.' What she recalled was Cliff's saying he might hire a full-time trainer. She'd obviously been mentally absent during subsequent conversations.

He glanced at his watch—an unmistakable signal that her time was almost up.

'I came because I wanted to apologize, Cliff,' she said quickly. This was difficult. Painful. Embarrassing. But she had to do it. 'You were right—I was involved with someone

388

else.'

His eyes narrowed. 'Married?'

Her face was flushed as she nodded. 'He lives out of state—we only spoke online.'

Cliff sipped his coffee and didn't comment.

She nodded again. 'It's over. Thank God I came to my senses before...before anything happened.' She didn't mention how close it had been. Or that it was only by chance she'd learned the truth about Will. If it hadn't been for Olivia, Grace would have sunk deeper and deeper until she'd been completely swallowed up in the deception. She blinked back tears as she thought about the people she'd deceived— Cliff, first of all, and Georgia. Olivia. Her own daughters. Herself...

'I misled you,' Grace murmured, struggling with remorse. 'You've been nothing but kind, and I abused that. Oh, Cliff, can you ever forgive me?'

'Of course I can,' he said without emotion. After a moment, he added, 'But, unfortunately, I can't undo the past.'

Grace didn't understand what he was telling her. 'I realize that.'

'Do you?' he asked, looking doubtful. He set his coffee mug in the sink, standing there for a moment with his back to her.

'Explain it to me.'

Cliff turned to face her. 'I think I told you this before. I know what it's like to be betrayed. I recognized the signs.'

She hung her head, aware she'd hurt him badly. With everything in her, she wanted to erase the pain she'd caused him.

'Susan had quite a few affairs over the years,' he continued. 'It was a sickness with her, I think. At first I wondered if there was something missing in me, something I wasn't giving her. She was constantly seeking admiration and approval from men. The only way she seemed capable of getting what she needed was through these affairs. Yet she repeatedly told me how much she loved me.'

He smiled then, and it was the saddest smile Grace had ever seen.

'The irony is that I believe Susan *did* love me. For most of our marriage I looked the other way and tried to pretend her indiscretions didn't matter, but I was wrong. They mattered a lot. I held on to the marriage for Lisa's sake. Then before I knew it, my daughter was grown-up, and all at once I realized I was trapped in a relationship that was nothing more than a pretense.'

Grace knew how painful it was for Cliff to discuss the details of his marriage. She also knew what that felt like. Her own marriage had been difficult. For years she'd believed it was something lacking in her that had brought on Dan's dark moods. Only after his death did she learn she wasn't to blame, although she'd accepted responsibility for Dan's unhappiness. Cliff's situation had been quite different, but

Grace identified with his emotions.

'I was hoping the two of us could start over again,' she said, forcing herself to meet his eyes. She so badly wanted to put this behind them and pick up where they'd left off.

He stared at her for the longest moment of her life and then reluctantly looked away. In that movement she read his answer.

'I can't,' Cliff said in a voice so low Grace had to strain to hear him.

'But...' She wanted to argue, but even before she could get the words out she knew it would do no good. His mind was made up and nothing she said or did now would change that.

'I can't go back, Grace. I lived that life once.'

'But I wouldn't—I was faithful to Dan for thirty-four years. I'm not anything like Susan.'

Cliff crossed his arms. He was shutting her out, she thought. He'd rather be anyplace except with her. Still, she held her ground, unwilling to give up on them so easily.

'I'm not saying you're like Susan,' he told her. 'I'm simply saying I can't deal with the feelings I associate with her. The last time I saw you, it was as though every doubt, every negative emotion from my marriage, came flying at me. I don't want to live like that. I can't. I don't want to deal with those emotions anymore.' Lowering his head, he murmured, 'For a while I believed we had something special.'

'We did,' she said. And she'd ruined it.

'Perhaps,' he agreed quietly, 'but I don't feel that way now.' His expression was full of regret. 'I don't think it would be a good idea for us to see each other again. I'm sorry, Grace.'

Her heart felt as though it had leaped to her throat and was pounding its way out. Rather than risk speaking and having her voice crack, Grace nodded. She finished her coffee, then slipped off the kitchen stool.

'I guess this is goodbye.' That was all she could manage.

Cliff nodded.

With only pride holding her together, Grace left the kitchen.

Cliff accompanied her into the foyer and retrieved her coat. He held it for her and she blindly shoved her arms into the sleeves.

Then he placed his hands on her shoulders, gently turning her in his arms. As if he couldn't stop himself, he kissed her. A final kiss. His mouth was moist and warm as it covered hers.

Grace came into his embrace, wrapping her arms around him as she gave herself to the kiss. She sensed his hunger, his desire—and his regret. All too soon, long before she was ready, he pulled away.

He refused to meet her eyes. 'Goodbye,' he said, and opened the door for her.

Twenty-Five

'Are your eyes closed?' Olivia asked, peeking around the sliding glass door that led to the deck of Jack's rental house. Sitting in his hot tub, in plain view of the entire world, was an uncomfortable prospect for Olivia. Jack, however, had refused to take no for an answer.

A misty fog surrounded the hot tub where he sat impatiently waiting for her. It was a cloudy evening, the second Sunday in March. 'My eyes are closed,' he assured her, grinning from ear to ear.

Even from this distance, she could tell he was lying. 'Jack Griffin, your eyes are wide open.'

'Olivia, I've seen a woman in a bathing suit before.'

'But you haven't seen *me!*'

'No, and I'm dying to, so hurry up.'

The patio light was far too bright, she decided. Grumbling under her breath, she tucked the towel more tightly around her and stepped barefoot onto the deck. Although it faced the cove and not the road, Olivia was sure the entire neighborhood would be catching a glimpse of her.

She couldn't even remember the last time she'd worn a swimsuit. This very one, in fact. Years and years ago. James had still been living at home. Justine, too. Her swimsuit was sadly outdated, but luckily it wasn't the kind of material that attracted moths.

'Sooner or later you're going to have to drop that towel,' Jack told her as she took her first tentative steps outside. He leaned back in a relaxed pose, arms spread out across the back of the tub.

'If I see a picture of myself in the *Chronicle,* I swear I'll never forgive you.'

'Hmm, you're giving me ideas.' Jack chuckled as if an embarrassing photograph was indeed a possibility.

'Jack!' Reluctantly she lowered the towel. Feeling as graceful as a walrus, she climbed over the edge of the hot tub and slid into the water. It was warm, soothing and refreshing at the same time. 'Ah,' she sighed involuntarily.

'See? That wasn't so bad, now was it?' he asked.

Olivia moved next to him, sinking shoulder-deep into the bubbling water. Rather than respond, she sighed again, a sigh of pure contentment. She was oh, so glad Jack had urged her to set aside her inhibitions and join him.

'You know, you've got a very attractive body,' he said. 'I don't know why you insist on hiding it.'

Olivia shook her head. 'Do you know how old I am?'

'Yes—and what's that got to do with

anything?'

'Plenty. I've had children, Jack, and my body is far from perfect.'

'Hey, if I wanted to date a twenty-year-old model—' He gave a quick laugh. 'Hell, a twenty-year-old model wouldn't be seen dead with an old fart like me.'

Olivia smiled, too. 'We make a good couple, don't we?' She rested her head against his shoulder.

'Yeah,' Jack agreed. 'We do, Judge O. Especially when we're practically naked in a hot tub together.'

'Jack!' She giggled. She *was* enjoying herself but refused to give him credit; if she did, she'd never hear the end of it.

'Come on,' he said, 'tell me I was right.'

'Would you mind gloating silently?' she muttered, letting her eyes drift shut.

'How's Grace doing?' Jack suddenly asked.

Olivia groaned. She'd been deeply concerned for her friend. 'Better, I think.' Grace had come to Olivia last Saturday afternoon, as upset as Olivia had ever seen her. Despite several attempts, Olivia wasn't able to pry the entire story out of her, but apparently Grace had done something to offend Cliff and he'd decided it would be best if they no longer saw each other.

'Have you talked to her recently?' Jack said.

'I saw her Wednesday night. Why?'

Jack rested his chin on top of Olivia's head.

'I think she might be volunteering for the Humane Society.'

'Oh, yes, she did say something about that.' Olivia approved; Grace seemed to have a lot of time on her hands all at once. She'd always been fond of animals. Buttercup had brought her comfort and companionship when Grace had most needed it. This volunteer position was something she could do to help animals, and perhaps a human or two. Olivia also suspected that Grace saw it as a way of making up for not getting Buttercup to the vet more quickly, not noticing the symptoms sooner. She tried to reassure her friend, but Grace persisted in blaming herself, which Olivia thought unreasonable.

'How'd you know about Grace volunteering?' she asked.

'The way I know about everything. The paper's doing an article about the shelter. When I showed up to talk to the director, Grace was there filling out the paperwork. The shelter does a background check before they accept any volunteers.'

'I think it'll be good for her.'

'I do, too,' Jack said.

Olivia opened her eyes and gazed up at the sky. The clouds had parted and the stars were coming out; it was turning into a spectacular night. Most of her friends were at a fund-raising dinner she'd gladly skipped. She could only imagine what her coworkers would say if they could see the very prim and proper Judge Lockhart soaking in a hot tub. And with a man, yet.

'I wouldn't do this for anyone else, you know,' she told him. She didn't need to elaborate on what she meant; Jack knew.

'I'm glad to hear it.' He kissed the top of her head.

Olivia felt his chest expand and then softly he said, 'I love you, Olivia.'

This wasn't the first time he'd admitted his feelings, but something about the way he'd said it felt different. She leaned away from him and looked into his eyes. 'I love you, too, Jack.'

'Do you mean that, Olivia? Really mean it?'

She nodded. 'I do.'

A sigh rumbled inside his chest. 'I know you don't like to talk about Stan, and frankly, I don't blame you, but I think we should. For the last time.'

'All right.' This sounded ominous.

Jack didn't speak for a moment, and she gave him a nudge with her elbow. 'Your ex-husband made it plain from the day we met that he wanted you back.'

Olivia kissed Jack's chin. 'I know, but he can't have me.'

'He's got a whole lot more to offer you than I do.'

'Such as?'

Jack chuckled. 'You don't really want me to get into *that,* do you?'

'Yes,' she challenged. 'What you don't seem to understand is that my ex-husband doesn't hold a candle to you in a hundred different ways. Okay, he probably brings home a bigger paycheck.'

Jack snorted. 'Probably? No one gets rich in the newspaper business, at least not these days.'

'Are you suggesting money's important to me?'

'No.'

'Then why worry about it?'

Again she felt Jack expel a deep sigh. 'Because I'm attempting to be noble here and you're making it damn hard.'

'Noble?' Olivia wasn't sure she liked the sound of this.

'All right, if you must know, I'm asking you to put me out of my misery and marry me.'

For a wild moment Olivia was too stunned to react. 'Jack, are you proposing?'

'That's exactly what I'm doing. I want us to be together, Olivia. I love you. The way things stand now, all we get are the leftovers of each other's lives—and I want more. I want you to be in my life and I want to be in yours.'

She stared at him, eyes wide.

'I want to be there when you wake up in the morning and at your side when you get into bed at night, and all the in-between times, too.'

This was romantic, and romance was the last thing she expected from Jack Griffin.

'I don't know how to say it any plainer than that,' he concluded.

'Then what was all this business about Stan?' If he told her he'd willingly step aside for her ex-husband, she was going to shove his head underwater, dammit!

'Yes, well, I was going to tell you—' He hesitated. 'No, I won't.'

'Won't what?'

'Won't let Stan have you. I thought I could do it, but as far as I'm concerned, the hell with him.'

Olivia leaned back and rewarded him with a long, breath-stealing kiss followed by a series of short kisses down the side of his neck. 'I didn't mean to interrupt you. Go on,' she urged.

Jack's arms tightened around her. 'I'm never letting you go again, Olivia. I'm only half alive without you.'

She felt a burst of happiness, and her body seemed so light, so buoyant, she thought she could soar straight up to the stars.

Jack took her by the shoulders and turned her sideways so he could look her full in the face. 'Will you marry me, Olivia?'

She blinked back tears and nodded. 'Oh, yes, Jack.' Then she was in his arms again and he was kissing her with an abandon that sent the blood surging through her veins. This was the beginning for them, a beginning that would last the rest of their lives.

*   *   *

A small piece of information had been niggling at the back of Roy McAfee's mind ever since he'd met Hannah Russell. It took him ten days to figure out what it was. Patience almost always paid off; the facts hidden in his memory usually emerged if he gave them time. But now he'd glimpsed the elusive detail and he needed to talk to someone.

Consequently, he showed up at the sheriff's office first thing Monday morning. Davis was sitting at his desk and seemed unsurprised when Roy walked into his office.

'You're up and about pretty early,' Davis said, looking up from the paperwork spread across his desk. 'Anything I can do for you?'

'That depends.'

Davis gestured toward the empty seat.

'I've been giving some thought to our meeting with Russell's daughter,' Roy said as he sat down.

The sheriff steepled his fingers. 'And?'

'You wouldn't still have a list of Russell's personal effects, would you?'

'I do. Mind my asking what you want it for?'

'I'd like to look at it again,' Roy told him.

'Any particular reason?' Davis flipped open a file folder that lay on the edge of his credenza, then left the office for a moment. Roy could hear the hum of the copy machine.

Davis returned, handed him the sheet and

400

sat down again. He reviewed the list along with Roy. 'There were his clothes,' Roy read aloud. 'Nothing unusual there. A good suit, a long dark raincoat and a wide-brimmed hat.'

Davis nodded as he glanced over the items. 'His daughter said he'd taken to wearing the hat after the accident.'

Roy lifted his head. Thus far, everything seemed as it should. 'Anything else catch your attention?'

'His briefcase, of course.'

Roy would've liked the opportunity to search that himself before it'd been released to Hannah.

As if reading his thoughts, Davis said, 'Nothing there. I checked it myself. No secret compartments or anything to indicate it had been tampered with in any way.'

Of course not. That would've been too easy, Roy thought. 'What about the contents?'

Davis smiled, but it wasn't a smile that conveyed amusement. 'He had a crossword puzzle book, a mystery novel and a map of the area, plus a couple of candy bars. For someone who'd traveled this far, he packed pretty light.'

'How about his suitcase?'

Davis frowned. 'Two changes of clothes, as you can see on this list. We turned that bag inside out looking for something that would give us a clue about who he was. I'm telling you right now, there wasn't a damn thing out of the ordinary.'

Roy believed him.

Davis hesitated. 'It seems to me you've studied that list a couple of times in the last few months. Why all the interest now?'

'I've got a feeling.'

'Tell me about your feeling and I'll tell you about mine.'

Roy nodded; that was fair. 'Do you remember, when Russell's daughter was at the Beldons', she mentioned the automobile accident that killed her mother?'

'I remember.'

'She said her father claimed something had gone wrong with the steering.'

'According to the report, the accident investigator found nothing,' Davis reminded him.

'Right,' Roy agreed, but they both knew there were ways to disguise the true cause of an accident. In addition, there'd been a fire, the same fire that had badly burned Russell's face and hands. The blaze could easily have destroyed any evidence of foul play.

'Well?' Davis asked.

'We still don't know what killed Russell.'

'We know his heart stopped beating. What we don't know is why. But then, as the medical examiner said, the guy was in his late fifties, had been to war and back, and survived one hell of a car accident. Maybe it was just his time. He went peacefully, the doc said.'

Roy nodded, but he wasn't buying any of

it. 'As I recall, there was something else in Russell's personal effects.'

'What was that?' Davis asked, looking back at the list. Another smile slipped into place as he slowly straightened and leaned toward his desk. 'A half-full bottle of flavored water,' he said, answering his own question.

'Did Russell's daughter happen to take that with her?'

Davis shook his head. 'She read it on the list, said it wasn't unusual for her father to drink bottled water.' He shrugged. 'I didn't offer to give it to her—don't have it anymore.'

Roy could feel his heart start to pound. 'Don't tell me you tossed it.'

'Nope.' Davis was grinning now. 'I sent it off to the toxicology lab.'

Their eyes met and they nodded at each other in unspoken agreement. 'My guess is, this death wasn't as natural as some would like to believe,' Davis said.

'Why was he killed?'

'Why travel with fake identification? Why come to Cedar Cove in the first place?'

'He came to see Beldon,' Roy said. He was confident of that much.

'Maybe he didn't. Or maybe that wasn't the *only* reason he showed up in Cedar Cove.'

'What other reason could there be?'

Sheriff Davis leaned back in his chair with a self-satisfied look. 'Maybe he came to find out what happened to Dan Sherman.'

Twenty-Six

'I don't need a baby-sitter,' Eddie insisted, defiantly crossing his arms. He glared at Allison, his eyes narrowed, as he silently challenged her to say otherwise.

'Do, too,' Allison retorted. Zach's daughter had never been able to walk away from a dare, especially one issued by her little brother.

'I think we should leave now,' Zach whispered to Rosie under his breath, 'before the kids give us an excuse to stay.'

'Tell her,' Eddie demanded, pleading with his father.

Zach sympathized with the boy, but there were limitations to what he could say and do. 'Baby-sitters get paid, and your sister isn't getting anything to stay home with you.'

'You mean I'm doing this for *nothing?*' Allison cried, but the outrage was all for show and Zach knew it.

Eddie was only partially mollified, but he didn't protest again when Zach led Rosie out the front door. 'The kids'll be fine.'

Rosie agreed. 'I've been dying to see this movie.'

'Me, too,' Zach said as he hurried ahead to open the car door for her.

To his astonishment, she stared at the door and didn't move.

'What?' he asked, slightly annoyed. Granted, it was an old-fashioned courtesy, but Rosie had never objected to it before.

'It's…it's just that it's been a long time since you opened the car door for me.'

Zach felt a little shocked. He knew she was talking about the last year of their marriage, and he supposed she was right. They'd treated each other without considerateness or respect, and the disappearance of small courtesies was a symptom of that.

'It's a nice touch, Zach, it always was. Thank you.' She slipped into the car and reached for her seat belt.

Zach hurried around the front of the vehicle. This was their third 'date.' Their first had been dinner the night Rosie had wept and the children had called him. He still didn't understand what that had been all about, but she seemed to feel better after they'd talked. Even now, almost two weeks later, he didn't remember exactly what they'd discussed that evening; what he remembered was how comfortable it felt to spend time with Rosie again.

In the mess they'd made of their lives, Zach had forgotten one important fact. Rosie had been more than his wife—she'd been his friend. He'd missed the little confidences they'd once shared, the small private jokes, the conversations in bed late at night. He hadn't allowed himself to think about those things

405

until recently, and he realized how much he missed her. How much he missed the way they used to be…

This week the kids were on spring break and Rosie had five free days. They'd already met for lunch on Monday afternoon. On the spur of the moment, they'd decided to take in a show on 'Tightwad Tuesday,' when all movies were three dollars. Popcorn and soda, however, stayed the same price. Rosie was the one who enjoyed popcorn, especially the buttered variety.

The movie, a romantic comedy, had been given rave reviews. While Zach paid for their tickets, Rosie stood in line for popcorn. This was a rare night out for Zach during tax season; most evenings he was in the office until seven or eight.

They chose seats in the back of the theater and toward the middle. He noticed several people glancing in their direction and a few heads moving together in hushed whispers.

'People are talking about us,' Rosie said.

'Well, we *are* divorced,' Zach reminded her with a grin. 'Divorced people generally don't go out on dates.'

'True,' she said. 'Sad commentary, isn't it? We get along better now that we're divorced than while we were married.'

'Yeah.' Zach couldn't deny it. 'At least during the last few years of our marriage.'

'Why did that happen, do you think?'

Zach was saved from having to answer because the lights dimmed and music blared from the sound system. Soon the previews began, about fifteen minutes' worth, with lots of noise and frantic action.

The movie itself was delightful. More than once, Zach laughed out loud. Although he claimed he wasn't interested in popcorn, he ate more than half of Rosie's small bag, which she willingly shared. About halfway through the show, Zach realized they were holding hands, just like they had while they'd dated during college.

When the lights came back on, they remained seated for a few minutes, enjoying the lingering effects of the movie and the music. People started to leave the theater; several nodded at Zach and Rosie. She was right—they'd caused something of a stir. Well, good. Let people talk all they wanted. He didn't object.

'It's been ages since I laughed that hard,' Rosie said, standing.

'Me, too!'

'And even longer since we laughed together.'

Zach could only agree.

Because he was so busy at the office and because it was spring break and the kids were home, they'd decided it would be best if Rosie stayed at the house the entire week. Zach drove her back there.

As he headed toward Pelican Court, they chatted about the movie, laughing again at the antics of the characters and the cleverness of the plot. All too soon, he'd reached the house. Zach wasn't ready for the evening to end, but he didn't know if Rosie felt the same.

When he pulled into the driveway, they sat silently in the car, as if each was waiting for the other to speak first.

'It's still early,' Rosie said. She glanced tentatively in his direction.

It was after ten, and Zach had been in the office since before six. Yet he didn't feel tired at all.

'Would you like to come in?' she asked in a neutral voice, implying that it didn't matter to her one way or the other.

Zach checked his watch, although he already knew the precise time from the digital clock on the car's dashboard. 'Sure,' he said. 'Why not?'

'The kids will probably still be up,' Rosie told him when he came around and opened the door for her. 'Allison stays up till all hours of the night whenever she gets the chance.'

Zach knew that and struggled with it, too. He and Allison had discussed this volatile subject on a number of occasions. His final conclusion was that if his daughter got too tired, she'd learn to adjust. He was saving his big guns for when she started driving.

Zach unlocked the front door and Rosie

entered the foyer ahead of him. Two steps into the house, she stopped abruptly. 'What's this?' she gasped.

'What?' Zach moved around her to find rose petals strewn about. The red petals seemed to take a path away from the door, down the hallway that led to the master bedroom. Talk about blatant manipulation! His children had set up a romantic interlude for him and Rosie. This, no doubt, was primarily Allison's doing, since Eddie, as a nine-year-old boy, didn't have much of a clue about love and romance.

'Everything is suspiciously quiet,' Rosie murmured.

That was when a soft waltz started to play.

'Music, too?' Zach asked in a whisper.

'Romantic music,' Rosie elaborated. 'It's from *Swan Lake.*' She moved into the kitchen and turned on the light. There, in the middle of the kitchen table, was another surprise.

'Wine?' Zach asked, following her.

'Looks that way.'

Sure enough, their children had strategically placed two wineglasses on the kitchen table with one long-stem rose lying between them. A bottle of wine sat in a bucket of ice. Unfortunately, it was a red wine, but Zach wasn't about to complain.

'I believe our children have planned a bit of romance for us,' Rosie said sheepishly. 'In case you're wondering, I didn't put them up to this.'

'I didn't, either, but I don't think it's a bad idea, do you?' He held out his hand to her. 'How long since we last danced?' He had no recollection of their doing so in the past half-dozen years.

Rosie laughed. 'I don't think we ever waltzed.'

'Then it's definitely time to rectify that.' Hand in hand, Zach and Rosie hurried into the family room. He brought her into his embrace and they moved to the classic rhythms of the waltz. Amazing, Zach thought. This seemed so natural.

When the music ended, Rosie flashed him a radiant smile.

Zach could never resist one of Rosie's smiles. Their eyes met in the dim light, and all at once he knew he had to kiss her. He prayed she felt the same way, because waiting a moment longer was entirely out of the question.

They nearly collided in their eagerness. Rosie had her arms around his neck and his were around her waist. Their kisses were wild and wet and urgent, as though it was necessary to feel and taste as much of each other as possible.

With the kissing came something else Zach had forgotten, something that had been buried deep in the mud they'd slung at each other during the divorce. He loved Rosie. He'd loved her as a young man, and, despite everything, he loved her now.

Loved her and wanted her, desperately wanted her.

*   *   *

It was the little things that Bruce Peyton missed most about his wife. Stephanie had died in a car accident almost two years ago, and he'd thought, he'd hoped, he'd be able to adjust with time. It wasn't that he hadn't tried. His friends insisted he date again, and several had set him up with blind dates, but he'd always come away feeling guilty and uneasy. He'd read that a year was long enough to heal substantially from a loss like his. It wasn't true, not for him. He didn't think he'd ever get over her death.

Stephanie had been his only love. Bruce felt lost without her, and so lonely. Jolene, their daughter, kept Stephanie's picture on her nightstand because she was afraid she'd forget what her mother had looked like. That tore at Bruce's heart, but he had no such problem. He carried the memory of her face in his heart. She was with him every minute of every day.

Although he tried, Bruce just wasn't good at little-girl stuff. Right now, for instance, Jolene needed a haircut. Her pigtails fell halfway down her back. Her hair had been cut only once in the two years since Stephanie's death. Not thinking it mattered, Bruce had taken his daughter to the barbershop with him. Seven-year-old Jolene had primly informed him he'd done the wrong thing.

'Girls don't get their hair cut in the same places boys do,' she told him afterward.

Now Jolene was saying she wanted her hair short.

'You're supposed to take me to a beauty shop,' his daughter said when he picked her up at the after-school child-care facility.

'I'll make an appointment,' Bruce promised her. He chose a name out of the yellow pages, a place that promised great cuts, phoned and wrote down the day and time. Monday at four. Then he dutifully arrived at the mall with Jolene in tow.

'Get Nai-led,' Jolene said, sounding out the second word. They stood in front of the shop. His daughter nodded approvingly, and he was relieved he'd apparently made the right choice this time.

Taking her by the hand, Bruce walked into the salon. It was like stepping into an alien world. Women draped with plastic sheets and huge looped curlers twisted about their heads sat in chairs and stared at him as if *he* was the odd-looking one. The smell was none too pleasant, either. He didn't know what these women did to themselves or why, but they had his pity.

Tentatively Bruce walked over to the receptionist's desk. 'I'm Bruce Peyton,' he managed to get out. 'I have an appointment for my daughter.' He leaned against the counter. 'She needs a haircut.'

The woman, who must've been about eighteen, ran her index finger down the appointment schedule. Her fingernail had to be a good two inches long and had something painted on it. He stared hard and realized it was some psychedelic print. Very sixties. But why? He shook his head slightly.

'Here you are,' she said in a chirpy voice. 'She's booked with Rachel.' Looking past him, she shouted, 'Rachel, your four o'clock is here.'

Bruce stepped away from the counter.

'Rachel will just be a moment. Would you like to take a seat over here and wait?' The receptionist gestured to a row of chairs against the wall, all of which were empty.

'Ah, sure.' Bruce sat down on one of the chairs and Jolene sat next to him. He reached for a magazine and quickly replaced it when he saw the lead article was 'Ten Ways to Achieve an Orgasm.' In case Jolene tried to sound out the word *orgasm,* he turned the magazine facedown. Luckily, the latest issue of the *Cedar Cove Chronicle* was available. He grabbed that and hid his face behind the newspaper before anyone could recognize him.

Jolene sat patiently at his side, her ankles crossed, gazing avidly at the ultrafeminine world before her.

413

Less than five minutes later, a dark-haired woman who didn't seem to be much older than the receptionist approached him and Jolene.

'I'm Rachel.'

Jolene scooted off the chair and stood. 'I need my hair cut.'

Rachel smiled and held out her hand. 'I can do that.'

Feeling even more awkward, Bruce stood, too, wondering what was expected of him now.

'You wait here, Daddy,' Jolene instructed him.

Rachel's eyes met his and they shared a brief smile. He had his orders, Bruce figured.

'This won't take more than thirty minutes,' the beautician told him.

'Sure...great.' Bruce sat down with the newspaper, but he soon grew restless. He got up and walked outside the salon and over to the food court. It'd been a while since his last visit to the mall.

He walked around for a bit and then noticed an electronics store. With at least twenty minutes to kill, he decided to ask about MP3 players. Even if he couldn't afford one, it didn't hurt to look.

Before he went into the store, Bruce checked his watch to be sure he didn't inadvertently stay longer than Jolene's appointment lasted. Stephanie had died on her way to pick up Jolene from kindergarten class and his daughter had been left waiting at the school for hours until someone could come for her. She'd been traumatized and, ever since, had reacted to any lateness, any deviation from a promised schedule, with extreme anxiety.

A salesman arrived, eager to show him the latest technology. Bruce had a few questions and they were soon involved in a discussion of the pros and cons of different brands. When he checked his watch a second time, a full thirty minutes had passed. Panic rushed through him as he quickly made his excuses and bolted out of the store. He sprinted across the mall, past the food court and toward the salon.

He could imagine Jolene crying and upset because he'd disappeared. He should've told her he was leaving, should've explained that he was inside the mall not more than a minute away. He should never have left her.

Twice since Stephanie's accident, Jolene had awakened from a nightmare in which Bruce hadn't arrived to pick her up from school. In her dreams she learned he'd died the same way as her mommy. It had taken her hours to sleep again.

Bruce realized he must have made quite a sight tearing into the salon, eyes wild. The entire shop seemed to stare at him.

Jolene broke the spell with a calm, 'Hi, Daddy.'

His daughter sat at a table with her hands outstretched while Rachel sat across from her, painstakingly painting Jolene's fingernails.

Now that his heart had decided to leave his throat and return to his chest, Bruce shoved his hands in his pockets and casually strolled over to them.

'You weren't here when Rachel finished my hair.' She tossed her head to and fro the way women did in shampoo commercials on television. 'Do you like it?'

Bruce nodded. Hair was hair, but he did think his daughter looked awfully pretty. Of course, he'd thought that before she had her hair cut, too.

'I got sidetracked in the electronics store,' he told her.

'That's what Rachel said prob'ly happened.'

The beautician glanced up with the nail polish brush in her hand. 'We lose a lot of men to the electronics store.'

Bruce would bet they did. Given a choice, just about any man would look for an excuse to get out of this women's domain.

'Was she upset?' Bruce asked Rachel.

She glanced up again and smiled. 'Only a little.'

'Rachel said she'd paint my nails. Aren't they pretty, Daddy?'

Bruce considered the bright red polish a moment and then nodded in what he hoped was a satisfactory manner. 'Very pretty.'

'We're almost done,' Rachel said.

'I didn't mean to stay so long.'

'It's not a problem,' she assured him. 'Once

416

I'm finished, we'll need five minutes for Jolene's nails to dry.' She looked up. 'Oh—the manicure is on the house.'

He mumbled his thanks. Five minutes seemed an eternity, but this was what he got for losing track of time. While he waited, Bruce paid the receptionist and added a generous tip for the beautician.

When Jolene was ready, she walked with her arms stretched out in front of her as if she'd seen the *Bride of Frankenstein* one too many times.

'Can I have an ice cream cone?' she asked, gazing across at the food court.

'You can if you promise to eat your dinner.'

'I promise.'

Together—but not hand in hand, since Jolene was concerned about preserving the perfection of her nails—they walked over to Baskin-Robbins and stared into the glass case. Bruce chose vanilla, his favorite. Stephanie had never understood how he could prefer vanilla when he had thirty other flavors to choose from. Jolene was just as predictable. She wanted bubble gum.

They sat at a small table and Bruce watched his daughter lick away at her blue ice cream. He smiled at her complete absorption. She smiled back, and he thought his heart would stop. In that split second, she resembled her mother so much.

Every now and then, Bruce caught glimpses

of Stephanie in their daughter. In the way her eyes flashed with a smile or the way she moved. It never failed to fill him with an immediate sense of loss and regret.

A thousand times or more, he'd gone over that final day of Stephanie's life. It had seemed an ordinary day. Completely routine. If only he'd known… If only he could go back and relive that morning.

He'd gotten up at seven, as usual, showered and dressed. He'd kissed Stephanie goodbye, never suspecting that in less than ten hours she would be forever taken from him and Jolene.

'Daddy…'

Returning to the present, Bruce looked over at his daughter. 'What, sweetheart?'

'I like Rachel.'

'Who's Rachel?'

'Daddy! The lady who cut my hair.'

'That's nice,' he replied absently.

'She's fun.'

'And she does a good job of cutting hair.'

Jolene nodded. 'She wants a husband.'

'What?' Bruce nearly laughed out loud.

'A husband,' Jolene said again. 'I heard her talking to the lady next to her, and she said she's almost thirty. That's old, isn't it?'

'Not so old,' Bruce assured her, hiding a smile.

'She said she wanted to be married before she was thirty.'

Bruce thought that was a rather personal

discussion to be having in a beauty shop, but what did he know about women's—

'I think you should marry her, Daddy.'

'What?'

'You should marry Rachel,' she repeated, as if that was a perfectly reasonable statement.

Twenty-Seven

Maryellen was depressed. She'd been depressed for weeks. She sat in the bleachers at the waterfront park, sheltered from the rain, and sipped hot coffee out of a plastic cup. Leaning forward, she rested her elbows on her knees and stared out over the dark waters of the cove.

Originally she'd planned to meet her mother for lunch, but she'd been stuck at the gallery with a late delivery and had to cancel at the last minute. She didn't have much of an appetite, anyway, and appreciated this time alone so she could think. Lois Habbersmith, her assistant and friend, had seemed to sense this and hurried her out the door.

Maryellen had walked down to the waterfront, which was one of her favorite spots. In the summer the city sponsored Thursday night Concerts on the Cove, and the park and every bit of available space would be filled. She'd always loved the music, the

419

laughter, the atmosphere of infectious gaiety.

This afternoon Maryellen felt little of that carefree summertime energy. She'd lost Jon. It was what she deserved for the despicable way she'd treated him. She'd explained her reasons, but apparently he couldn't forgive her.

That was understandable, she supposed. Her experience with men was limited to one dreadful marriage and a father who'd walked through life in a state of emotional paralysis. There were happy childhood memories, but they were few and far between.

'Lois said I'd find you here.'

Jon's voice broke into her dark musings and startled Maryellen. She nearly dropped her coffee.

'I didn't mean to frighten you.'

'I'm just surprised.' And happy to see him, so happy it was all she could do not to smile and gush and make an idiot of herself. All three of which she'd managed to do any number of times.

Jon walked up the steps and sank onto the bleacher beside her. He didn't say anything for a long while. She didn't, either, and then she couldn't stand it anymore.

'I want to tell you something,' she murmured. 'It's all right, you know.'

'What's all right?'

She held her breath, then blurted it out. 'That you're involved with someone else. I don't have any claim on you and—'

'Who told you that?'

'No one,' she said, not looking at him. 'I figured it out.'

Jon frowned and shook his head. 'You figured wrong, Maryellen. There hasn't been another woman in my life almost from the moment we met.'

She stared at him, not knowing what to think.

He was gazing out at the cove. 'I loved you long before you invited me to that ridiculous Halloween party.'

Now she was sure she'd misunderstood him. 'If that's the case, you have a funny way of showing it.' They'd barely talked in weeks. Their conversations, such as they were, had occurred in passing as he picked up or delivered Katie. It seemed he was continually making excuses not to stay.

'I— You didn't ever want to talk to me,' she said.

'I couldn't.'

'Well, that explains everything,' Maryellen said—with only a little sarcasm in her tone.

'I was afraid if I talked to you, I wouldn't be able to stop myself from telling you….'

'What?' she demanded impatiently.

'I've decided to leave Cedar Cove.'

'Leave?' she cried. He'd just finished saying he loved her! She already knew how deeply he cared for their daughter. Katie needed her father, and the awful truth was that Maryellen needed Jon, too.

'I'm putting the house up for sale first thing in the morning.'

Numb with shock and pain, Maryellen could barely acknowledge his words.

'I've already given my notice at The Lighthouse.'

It was too much. More than she could bear. Each word was like a knife in her heart, the pain intolerable, impossible to ignore. Burying her face in both hands, she laid her head on her knees and burst into tears.

'Maryellen...' His voice seemed faint and far away. Then he placed his hand on her spine, as if she were a small child in need of comfort.

'Why?' she asked, raising her head just enough to speak. 'If you love me and you love Katie? Why would you leave us?' She'd been such a fool. When she'd first realized she was pregnant, she saw Jon as little more than a sperm donor, never guessing how important he would become to her or their child.

Jon didn't answer. She knew what he was doing—the same thing her father had done. Rejecting and hurting those he loved most.

'You never met my father, did you?' she said, struggling to keep the pain out of her voice.

'No...'

'You seem to have a great deal in common

with him. He destroyed the people he loved, too.' Pride carried her to her feet and she stood. 'If you're going to leave, there isn't anything I can say to stop you. The thing is, Jon, I love you, too. I didn't *want* to love you and I tried everything to keep my emotions out of this, but...but it didn't work.'

She took another deep breath. 'I assumed it would be easy to have a baby on my own. Women do it all the time. But it's hard, so much harder than I imagined. You were there for me and for Katie, and slowly, little by little, I realized my mistake. I began to see how important a father's role is to a child. And...to a mother.' She wiped the tears from her cheek. 'Perhaps this is what I deserve, but it sure as hell isn't what Katie deserves. If you walk away from her now, you're a bigger fool than I ever was.' She started to leave, but his words stopped her.

'All right, I'll tell you.'

She frowned at him. 'Tell me what?'

He briefly closed his eyes. 'I've got a record, Maryellen. A prison record. You once asked me where I learned to cook. Well, guess what, it was behind bars. I couldn't tell you for fear you'd take Katie away from me.'

That explained some, but not enough. She lowered herself to the bench again so they sat side by side. 'I'd never do that!'

'I trusted someone else, someone I loved. I learned a painful lesson. It's not one I'm eager to repeat.'

'Another woman?' she asked.

'No, my half brother.' He didn't add any details, and this seemed all he was willing to divulge.

'Why are you telling me now?' she asked. If he was leaving, anyway, it seemed pointless to admit the truth.

He didn't respond.

Maryellen refused to let the matter drop. 'What made me so trustworthy all of a sudden, especially if you're about to drop out of my life and Katie's?'

He had no answer, but that didn't surprise her. Jon rarely volunteered information about himself. It used to be a game she played when he came into the gallery—getting him to chat about himself, learning what she could about him. Even now she knew damn little.

'This might surprise you, but I suspected you might have done jail time,' she said. It was one of the endless possibilities she'd considered late at night, when she couldn't sleep. It wasn't one she'd taken all that seriously, just as she'd dismissed the possibility that he was on the run or an amnesiac or involved in some equally bizarre scenario. Another woman had seemed the most likely….

A scowl darkened his face. 'Not the kind of question you want to ask, is it?'

'What was the charge?'

There was a lengthy silence. 'I was convicted

of dealing cocaine.'

'This is where your half brother comes in?'

Jon nodded. 'The two of us were total opposites. He was the perfect son and I was the starving artist. The disreputable kid. My dad and stepmom favored Jim. He was ambitious, a businessman-in-the-making. He was everything they wanted in a son and I wasn't.'

This was the first time he'd mentioned any family member other than his grandfather and the fact that Katie had been his dead mother's name. His grandfather had left him the land on which Jon had built his house. 'Where's Jim now?'

His face tightened. 'Dead.'

'Oh, Jon, I'm sorry.'

He nodded, but she saw him swallow hard. He set his foot against the back of the bleacher in front of them and slid his hands inside his pockets. 'We lived together, and I was scraping by selling my pictures. I'd take my camera and hike into the forest and get as many shots as I could afford to develop. Jim moved in with me one summer and for a while it was great.'

Maryellen tucked her own hands in her pockets, but leaned closer to him, pressing her shoulder to his, needing to touch him.

'Jim was dealing cocaine. I swear on Katie's life that I didn't have a clue what he was doing. He was in college and his friends were the same upwardly mobile type he was.'

'He was selling to them?'

Jon nodded. 'Fool that I was, I didn't put two and two together. Jim always seemed to have money, always seemed to have whatever he wanted.'

'What happened?'

'One night the police came and dragged us both out of bed. They found the stuff. While I was screaming that it was planted and that we were innocent, Jim was selling me to the cops, saying it was mine.'

Maryellen placed her hand on his forearm, and he gripped her fingers with his own, squeezing hard.

'My brother testified against me, and my father claimed—well, he lied and said I was the one with the drug problem and that Jim had only recently moved into the house and couldn't be involved.'

She closed her eyes, imagining that kind of betrayal. First his brother and then his father, too. 'How could he do that?'

'Dad believed what Jim told him, I guess. He wanted to protect one of his sons—but not the other.'

'Oh, Jon.'

'I haven't seen or talked to my father since the day I was sentenced. I want nothing to do with him. I don't know how I would've survived without my grandfather's support. He did everything he could to help me.'

She understood more and more of what

he'd been through, the experiences that had shaped him.

'Jim died while I was in prison. My father wrote to tell me, but I never wrote him back.' He didn't hide his pain or bitterness.

'How long were you in prison?'

'I was sentenced to fifteen years.'

She gasped. Jon, who loved the out-of-doors, had been locked in a jail cell.

'I served seven of those years, and it was seven years of hell.'

'Jim walked away scot-free?'

Jon looked down at their linked fingers and he squeezed so hard she nearly cried out from the pain. 'He got a slap on the wrist with probation and then died of a heroin overdose the year before I was paroled.'

Maryellen desperately wanted to comfort him, to hold him in her arms.

'Now you know.' His eyes were cold as stones as he held her gaze. 'You can give this information to any court in the land and take my daughter away from me.'

Now she knew why he was putting the land his grandfather had left him up for sale and selling the house he'd built with his own hands. Why he was quitting his job. Leaving Cedar Cove.

'You don't trust me,' she whispered. He was relinquishing everything that mattered to him because he believed he was going to lose it, anyway. Because the minute he lowered his

427

guard, he took the risk that she, too, would betray him.

'I can't.' He didn't bother to deny it. 'The only person I can trust in this world is myself.'

'What about Katie?'

'She's a baby....'

'She's your *daughter.*'

'I love her.'

'But doesn't she deserve to know her father?'

His jaw tightened again.

'Eventually you'll have to trust someone. You can't close yourself off from everyone. Sooner or later, you've got to stop running.'

He didn't look at her, didn't respond.

'I can deal with it if you don't want me in your life, but Katie needs you. Jon, please don't walk away from her.' She wanted to ask the same thing for herself, but wouldn't.

'You know everything now.'

'Yes,' she whispered.

'You won't try to get sole custody of Katie?'

'No,' she said. 'I promise.'

'You probably could, you know.'

'Jon,' she cried in frustration. 'Haven't you been listening to a word I've said? Katie needs you.... I need you. I'm not going to do anything to keep you out of Katie's life. Or mine.'

His eyes narrowed. 'Would you marry a felon?'

'Are you asking?'

He hesitated and then gave a jerky nod. She watched as he thrust his hands back inside his pockets, hunching his shoulders forward.

She blinked hard to keep the tears from spilling onto her face. 'It would be the greatest honor of my life to marry you, to be the mother to your children and—'

'Children?'

'I'm thinking Katie could use a little brother or sister.'

A tentative smile came first and then Jon broke into the most wonderful deep-chested laugh. The sound of it drifted toward the cove, competing with the sharp cry of the seagulls.

Before Maryellen knew it, they were both standing and she was securely wrapped in his embrace. They hugged each other tightly and then he kissed her again and again.

Maryellen raised her face and wept openly as Jon's kisses traveled over her forehead, her cheeks, her chin, moving toward her lips. When their mouths finally met, it was a kiss that spoke of faith and trust and love, and she returned those feelings in full measure.

She was breathless by the time he eased his mouth from hers. 'I want us to get married soon.'

'Yes,' she whispered. 'Promise me you'll never threaten to leave us again.'

'I promise,' he said, and kissed her.

'Promise you'll always love me.'

'Promise.' Another deep kiss.

'Anything else?' he asked, his eyes so full of love it was almost painful to see.

'Lots more,' she whispered. In fact, Maryellen was just getting started.

Twenty-Eight

Home from a Saturday afternoon spent volunteering at the Humane Society Animal Shelter, Grace pulled into her driveway. She enjoyed her work, found real purpose in helping animals. There was such satisfaction in seeing lost pets reunited with their owners and in connecting abandoned or mistreated cats and dogs with people who'd love them.

The vet had a notice about the Humane Society on her bulletin board, which Grace had seen the afternoon she'd taken Buttercup in. She'd decided to respond to the call for volunteers. Buttercup had come into her life at exactly the right moment and Grace wanted others to find the same pleasure.

Her first thought once she'd parked the car was to retrieve her mail. Although she tried not to be hopeful, she couldn't help looking for a response from Cliff. Two weeks earlier she'd written him, reiterating how sorry she was. Although it meant having to swallow her considerable pride, Grace had asked him to give her a second chance. So far, she hadn't heard from him, and now, after two weeks, she suspected she wouldn't.

She walked to the house with Buttercup trotting behind her. The golden retriever sniffed at her legs suspiciously, recognizing the scent of other animals. Buttercup actually seemed a bit jealous and required lots of attention on those Saturdays.

'Did you miss me, girl?' she asked, stroking Buttercup's head. 'Don't worry, there wasn't a single dog there as wonderful as you.'

The phone rang and Grace absently reached for the receiver. 'Hello,' she said, still fondling the dog's ears.

'Grace? It's Stan Lockhart.'

This was completely unexpected. She couldn't imagine what her best friend's ex-husband had to say to her.

'What can I do for you?' she asked coolly.

'I'm in town and I was wondering if I could stop by for a few minutes.'

Grace wanted to refuse him, but didn't have a good excuse. 'Can I ask why?'

'I'm surprised you don't already know.'

'Olivia and Jack.'

'Yes. I won't stay long.'

She reluctantly agreed. As soon as she hung up, Grace hurriedly punched in Olivia's phone number. 'Why do you think he wants to talk to me? I could really do without this,' she complained.

'He probably needs a shoulder to cry on.'

'Let him look elsewhere,' Grace muttered. She had enough problems of her own without dealing with his. As far as she was concerned, Stan Lockhart was a sore loser.

'I don't think it would hurt to hear him out,' Olivia said. 'He's had a shock.'

Yes, he has, Grace mused. For the first time in his life, Stan Lockhart couldn't manipulate Olivia! 'Do you want me to phone you after he leaves?' she asked.

Olivia hesitated. 'Not particularly. Stan's out of my life, and frankly I don't care what he says.'

Grace marveled at her friend. If their positions had been reversed, she'd be sitting by the phone waiting for a report. She'd want to hear all about her ex-husband's regrets.

Fifteen minutes later, Stan arrived, looking decidedly unhappy.

'Come in,' she said, holding open the screen for him.

Stan entered and she showed him into the living room. Buttercup wandered over to sniff him; apparently he passed muster because the dog wandered back to the chair where Grace normally sat and lay down.

'Would you like something to drink?' she asked Stan, only to be polite.

'Do you have any Scotch?'

Yeah, right. Even if she did, she wouldn't offer it to him. 'No, sorry. Coffee or tea.'

He shook his head. 'Nothing, thanks.'

She gestured for him to sit down, which he did on the sofa across from her. 'Olivia's actually going to do it, isn't she?' he muttered.

'If you mean marry Jack, the answer is yes.' The arrangements were in full swing. Seth and Justine were going to hold the reception at their restaurant, following a private ceremony at the gazebo in the waterfront park.

'James and Selina are flying in, she said.'

'Olivia asked if they would.' Grace didn't mean to make him feel worse, but it was important to Olivia that her children be present.

'I thought she'd have one of the other judges perform the ceremony,' he said. 'But apparently not. Who's this pastor friend of hers, anyway?'

'Dave Flemming. He's at the Methodist church.'

'Oh.'

Grace was about to ask if there was a point to his visit when Stan glanced up. 'This is what I deserve, you know?'

Despite what she knew about Stan, Grace felt sorry for him. The news of Olivia and Jack's engagement shouldn't have come as a shock but obviously had. Now his regrets about Olivia would be permanent. There'd be no further chance to make amends, to start over. Oh, yes, she understood about regrets. They were something she'd lived with for quite some time now.

'I made a big mistake myself recently,' she told him.

'You?' He sounded skeptical.

Grace nodded. 'I hurt someone I care about and there's no going back.'

'I feel the same way. I was such a fool. When Jordan drowned...' He paused and stared down at the carpet. 'I went out to the cemetery the other day and visited my son's grave.' He drew a hand along the side of his jaw. 'It's funny. It's been—what, sixteen years? I don't think I'll ever get over it. I still can't believe my oldest son is dead.' He slowly rubbed his palms together, his eyes closed in pain.

'It was as if I self-destructed after we lost Jordan,' he continued, opening his eyes. 'I did the best I could with the mess I'd made of my life after I married Marge, but it was never a good marriage, and we both knew it.'

Grace's heart softened. Although she'd been furious with Stan for what he'd done to Olivia and his two surviving children, she remembered that he'd been a decent father.

'To tell you the truth, I wasn't surprised when Marge decided she wanted out. In a lot of ways, I think she did us both a favor. My first thought when she asked for the divorce was that I'd move heaven and earth to get Olivia back.'

'Jack's a good guy.'

Stan frowned. 'I just don't see the two of them together.'

'That's because you don't want to.'

He gave her a half smile and shrugged. 'I guess you're right.'

'What now?' Grace asked.

Stan shook his head. 'I'd been thinking I might move back to Cedar Cove. But under the present circumstances, I'm not so sure that would be wise.'

Grace knew he was referring to Olivia's coming marriage, and she knew he was conceding defeat.

'Still, Justine and Seth are here and so is Leif,' he added as though thinking aloud. 'I never thought I'd enjoy being a grandfather as much as I do. I missed so much when my own children were growing up, I want to enjoy every second I can with my grandkids.'

'I know what you mean,' she told him. 'I have two.'

His gaze went past her to the fireplace mantel, where Grace kept the latest photos of her grandchildren. 'I can certainly see you in the girl.'

'Thank you.' Grace stared at Katie's picture and was unable to squelch a smile of pleasure. Stan couldn't have given her a greater compliment.

'I never did tell you how sorry I was to hear about Dan.'

Grace blinked quickly and nodded. She wished Dan had lived long enough to know his grandchildren. Tyler and Katie might have made a difference, given him a reason to live. Then again, perhaps not. Dan's life had been troubled, and very little seemed to touch him. He was closer to Kelly than anyone, yet that hadn't stopped him from running away during her pregnancy. In the end, despite everything, death had seemed preferable to the suffering—the guilt and depression—he'd endured in life.

Stan got to his feet. 'Actually, I came to ask if you'd do something for me.'

'I will if I can.'

'I'd like to order a bottle of good champagne for Olivia and Jack on their wedding night.' He slipped his hands into his pockets. 'It would be a bit awkward coming from me, though.'

'Do you want me to take care of it?'

'Would you?'

Apparently Stan didn't know Jack was a recovering alcoholic. 'I'll see to everything.'

'I'd appreciate it.' Stan started for the door, then turned back. 'Grace,' he said, looking at her as if he were seeing her for the first time. 'Would you like to go to dinner with me?'

She was as surprised by his invitation as she'd been by his phone call. 'When?'

He gestured vaguely. 'What about tonight? I know it's last minute and all.' Then, shaking his head, he seemed to change his mind. 'Forget I asked. It's probably not a good idea, anyway.' He reached for the doorknob.

'Stan,' she said, stopping him. She didn't know what had prompted her to do this. But Stan was lonely. She was lonely. And she'd developed a new sympathy for him during this brief visit. She'd seen a little deeper, past the arrogance she'd always associated with Stan.

'Why not?' she said with a smile. 'Let's go to dinner.'

*   *   *

Charlotte Jefferson and her small band of supporters marched single-file down Harbor Street, holding their pickets high. Whenever she could, Charlotte waved her message at oncoming traffic to ensure that the drivers had ample opportunity to read her sign. Several people honked their horns.

Ben Rhodes marched with her. Together they'd attended countless meetings, talked with elected officials and health-care corporations, studied what other municipalities had done. Without results. After all these months, they were no closer to getting a health clinic in Cedar Cove than they were to taking a giant leap and landing on the moon. There'd been several minor attempts to appease them—but it wasn't enough. The time had come to take a stand. To demonstrate!

'Don't look now,' Ben said, bending toward her and whispering in her ear, 'but it looks like we're about to have company.'

Sure enough, the sheriff's patrol car pulled up alongside Charlotte. Troy Davis parked at the curb and climbed out of his Crown Victoria, pausing long enough to hoist up his belt before he walked over to her.

"Afternoon, Charlotte.'

'Hello, Sheriff Davis,' she greeted primly. The sign seemed to grow unaccountably heavier and she lowered it. 'What can I do for you?' she asked, as if it was a perfectly normal thing to see her marching down the main street of town, hefting a protest sign.

'Do you have a permit for this little rally of yours?' He looked past her at the string of fifteen men and women, all regular attendees at the local seniors' center.

'A permit?' she repeated. The truth was, Charlotte hadn't thought she'd need one. At first the demonstration had consisted of only her and Ben. They'd decided to form their own protest and stand silently by the stoplight at Harbor and Heron. However, as soon as word got out, a dozen or so others had asked to join them. Charlotte couldn't refuse her friends.

'Officer, perhaps I could answer your questions,' Ben said, stepping closer to Charlotte.

'I don't believe we've met,' Sheriff Davis said, eyeing Ben suspiciously.

'Ben Rhodes,' Charlotte murmured, gesturing from one man to the other, 'meet the local fuzz.'

Ben chuckled; Sheriff Davis didn't.

'Whose idea was this, anyway?' the sheriff asked.

'Mine,' Ben insisted.

'Now, Ben,' Charlotte said, patting him gently on the forearm. 'Both of us came up with the idea.'

Her friends and allies gathered around. 'And we asked to join her,' Laura said, edging her way closer so that she stood directly in front of Troy Davis's face.

'Yes,' Helen echoed, moving next to Laura, although she was so short she had to tilt her chin up in order to get a good look. Any menacing expression was wasted on the sheriff, who didn't bother to glance down. In fact, it seemed Sheriff Davis was having difficulty keeping a straight face. Charlotte, however, was not amused.

'It's the only way we have of getting heard in this city,' Bess said. She waved her protest sign, nearly clobbering him in the head when she momentarily lost control of the heavy wooden stick.

'Does Olivia know what you're up to?' Sheriff Davis asked Charlotte, ignoring the others.

'My daughter has nothing to do with this,' Charlotte said, although her voice faltered momentarily. Olivia was her one hesitation about this protest. Charlotte knew her daughter objected to her involvement—but

439

what Olivia didn't know wouldn't hurt her.

'We don't feel it's any of the judge's business,' Ben added.

Charlotte thanked him with a small smile. He understood her dilemma and had offered his advice. These days, she often listened to what Ben had to say. He was reasonable and wise in his counsel; he'd proved that over and over. He'd also proved something else, which the others didn't know—that he was an excellent kisser. She blushed at the thought.

'I don't believe I was speaking to you, sir,' the sheriff said.

'Sheriff Davis, that was completely unnecessary,' Charlotte objected.

'Does Olivia know?' he asked again, and the friendliness was gone from his voice.

'She knew about it. She just didn't know *when* I planned to march,' Charlotte answered bluntly.

'So you don't have an assembly permit?'

'There's a logical reason we don't, Sheriff,' Ben said. 'We—'

'I'm sure there is. However, if you don't have a permit, I'm going to have to ask you to disperse and leave the area.'

'We aren't causing any trouble,' Ben said.

'We come in peace,' Laura insisted, sounding as if she'd just alighted from an alien spaceship.

'But we mean business!' Bess's sign flashed back and forth in the sheriff's face.

Glaring at her, he caught the wooden stem with one hand and took it from her. 'Mrs. Ferryman, kindly go home.'

'I was his third-grade teacher,' Bess whispered to Charlotte.

'Officer, I appreciate your problem, but we are on a mission,' Ben started. 'We—'

'I'm on a mission, as well,' Troy Davis said calmly. He held up his hand to attract the attention of the small protest rally. 'I want you all to cease and desist, and go home peacefully. Now.'

'I refuse.' Laura punctuated her comment by pounding the wooden stick against the sidewalk.

'I do believe,' Charlotte said cheerfully, 'that you'll need to arrest us first.'

Sheriff Davis cast an exasperated look at the small group.

'Charlotte,' Ben warned, his voice low and uncertain, 'don't give the man any ideas.'

'Sheriff Davis knows how important a health clinic is to our community.'

The lawman nodded. 'I do know, and personally I agree with you, but the law is the law.'

'Do you think he'll handcuff us?' Helen asked, tugging at Charlotte's sleeve.

Charlotte could see that her friend was wavering. 'Of course not,' she assured her.

'Don't count on it, ladies.' Sheriff Davis released a snap on his belt and brought out a pair of handcuffs. He held them up and dangled them from his fingers for all to see.

Bess gasped and raised her hand to her chest. 'I don't want to be strip-searched.'

'I'm not making any guarantees,' Sheriff Davis said, looking at her as though he had X-ray vision.

Bess shrank back behind Laura.

Charlotte strengthened her resolve and hoisted up her sign once more. She'd come this far and wasn't about to back down now. Ben and her friends would have to make their own decisions. She'd already made hers.

'Five minutes,' Sheriff Davis informed them. 'If you haven't dispersed in that time, I'm afraid I'll have to call for backup and you'll all be arrested for unlawful assembly.'

Charlotte knew what she had to do. She turned to face her dearest friends—Helen, Bess, Laura and the others. She hated the thought of them in a cold, damp cell in the basement of the sheriff's department, but there were times a person had to take a stand. 'The sheriff states that unless we disperse, we're headed for the slammer.'

The group cried out in protest.

'We have five minutes. As for me, I'm staying right where I am. Each one of us should make our own decision.' Having said that, she placed a hand on Bess's shoulder. 'I'll understand if you don't want to go to jail.'

Bess considered her words, and then

seemed to steel herself mentally. 'I'm staying,' she announced, glaring defiantly at the sheriff. 'Troy Davis, I remember you cheated on that spelling test. I never should've voted for you. You aren't to be trusted.'

The small group gathered into a tight knot, buzzing with indecision. To her surprise, it was Ben who raised his hands and spoke. 'Perhaps we should reconsider.'

A chorus of loud protests instantly followed. Ben looked at Troy Davis and shrugged. 'I tried, Officer.'

'Unfortunately, you didn't try hard enough.' The sheriff glanced down at his watch— five minutes must be up—and then without another word, marched over to his patrol car. He turned his head and spoke into the small transmitter attached to his shoulder. He was making good on his threat, Charlotte realized, and calling for backup.

A few minutes later, two patrol cars rolled into view. Charlotte groaned inwardly.

Olivia wasn't going to like this one bit.

Twenty-Nine

Roy McAfee received the long-awaited phone call the second week of April, almost a month after Davis had sent the water bottle found in Maxwell Russell's car to the county lab for testing. He asked Roy to stop by his office as soon as possible.

Within ten minutes of that call, Roy was headed out the front door of his office.

'Was that Sheriff Davis?' Corrie asked, glancing up from her desk as he breezed past his wife.

Roy nodded and reached for his coat. 'Apparently the lab found something.' He'd known they would, and he felt vindicated. Now maybe they could get somewhere with this case.

'The sheriff isn't exactly the most popular man in town at the moment,' Corrie said as she pointed to the latest edition of the *Cedar Cove Chronicle*.

Roy tried unsuccessfully to disguise a smile. The front page of the *Chronicle* had shown a photograph of a disgruntled Sheriff Davis and two deputies handcuffing a group of senior citizens. Roy would say one thing—this small and lively band of retirees had certainly gotten their message out.

'I can't help feeling sorry for Davis,' Roy murmured.

'Of course your sympathies would lie with the lawman, but as far as I'm concerned, Mrs. Jefferson and her friends have a good point.'

'There are other ways of getting the city to provide a health clinic without violating the law.'

Roy should know better than to argue

with Corrie; as usual, she had an immediate comeback. 'The article said Mrs. Jefferson and Mr. Rhodes have done everything by the book and didn't get anywhere, because of the budget cuts. You and I both know what it's like to ram our heads against City Hall.'

'Sheriff Davis was only doing his job.' Frankly, Roy wouldn't have wanted to be the one responsible for escorting a group of old people to jail. From what he'd heard, it had been a madhouse, with several of the ladies demanding lawyers and going on about their constitutional rights. Apparently they'd viewed too many *Law & Order* reruns.

'I should've known you'd side with your friend,' Corrie said. 'How would you feel, though, if that had been your mother or mine?'

He chuckled. 'My mother's been gone for a lot of years and as for yours—'

'Don't even start, Roy McAfee,' she muttered.

But Roy saw that Corrie was trying not to laugh. On impulse, he walked around her desk and soundly kissed her.

Corrie looked up at him. 'What was that for?'

'You're nothing like your mother.'

'Roy!'

'Sweetheart,' he said, pleading innocence. 'I love you.'

Laughing softly, she steered him toward the door.

Roy decided to walk the fifteen minutes to the sheriff's office. His gut told him they were close to uncovering Russell's secrets.

Troy Davis appeared to be waiting for him. He gestured to the chair and then shoved a file at him before Roy even had a chance to sit down.

'What's that?' he asked.

'The toxicology report.'

Roy reached for it and flipped it open. He scanned the first three pages before his eyes landed on flunitrazepam. He raised his eyes to the sheriff's. 'That drug—what is it?'

'Brand name is Rohypnol.'

That was a name Roy recognized. The date-rape drug, as it was commonly called. He'd seen the effects of it during his years on the force. It'd been referred to as 'roofies' when it first hit the streets in the early nineties.

Very clever choice, Roy mused as he read over the report. Not the type of drug anyone would typically use to kill a man over fifty. 'No wonder it took the lab a month to find it,' he murmured, thinking aloud.

'Whoever killed him dissolved it in the bottled water. It's tasteless and odorless—and it's a potent tranquilizer. When it's given in large doses, the obvious happens.'

Roy knew that, too. A large enough dose would have lethal consequences.

Roy set the file on the sheriff's desk. 'All that confirms is what we've both suspected.

Russell was murdered.' Unfortunately, the toxicology report didn't reveal who'd poisoned him or why.

The sheriff relaxed in his chair and steepled his fingers as he rested his hands against his abdomen. He looked directly at Roy. 'It could've been Beldon. He had opportunity.'

Years of police work and intuition said otherwise. At one point, Roy had had his suspicions. There'd still been a lot of missing facts, and he hadn't wanted to cloud the issue with emotion. That was the reason he'd felt he couldn't be Beldon's friend. In the time since, Roy had come to like and trust the other man.

Bob claimed not to recognize his old army friend, which left motive in question. But even if he *had* recognized him, that wasn't cause enough to murder him, in Roy's opinion. 'Frankly, I doubt it.'

Sheriff Davis gave him a hint of a smile. 'I don't see it falling that way myself.'

'Don't forget, the bottle was in the car.'

'Right.'

That didn't automatically clear Beldon, but it suggested Russell had brought the water with him.

'Do you think it could've been a random killing?' Roy asked. There seemed to be more of them these days.

He could tell that Davis had considered the same idea. 'Perhaps, but I think it's unlikely.'

Roy nodded. Too many factors in this case,

including the method used, led him to believe the murder hadn't been a random anything. Whoever they were dealing with was smart. And vicious.

'I don't think this was the first attempt on Russell's life, either,' Roy murmured.

'My thoughts exactly,' the sheriff said. He straightened, leaning toward his desk. 'The car accident that killed his wife sounds mighty convenient to me. I read the report, but there's nothing I can put my finger on. No real evidence.'

The crash had been attributed to driver error. In light of recent events, he wondered. Two of the men who'd been together in the jungle that day were dead and both had died under peculiar circumstances.

'What about Dan Sherman?' Roy asked. 'Are you convinced it was suicide?'

The sheriff didn't hesitate. 'No doubt. He left that letter, too.'

Roy didn't like the route his mind was taking him. Two men were dead, one of them murdered. If Bob wasn't involved—and both Troy Davis and Roy were sure he wasn't—then that led Roy to one conclusion.

'Bob Beldon's in danger,' he said.

Davis sat back. 'Funny you should say that.'

'Why?'

'I had the same feeling myself. I went out to talk to him yesterday afternoon.'

A chill went up Roy's spine.

'I suggested he might want to take an extended vacation while we check this theory out,' the sheriff continued.

'What did he say?'

Troy Davis frowned. 'He's a stubborn man. Bob said he'd done all the running he intended to do. Said anyone who wants to kill him is welcome to try.'

Roy guessed Peggy hadn't been around for that conversation.

Troy shook his head. 'Not only that, he says he *can't* leave. Jack Griffin asked Bob to be his best man, and Bob intends to do it.'

'When's the wedding?'

'First week of May.'

Roy mulled that over and nodded. 'It's been over a year since Russell died,' he said. 'If nothing's happened in all this time, then perhaps nothing will.'

'Perhaps,' Troy Davis returned.

But his tone of voice convinced Roy the sheriff didn't believe it. For that matter, neither did he.

Over the last few months, he'd come to like Bob and Peggy. He'd consider it a personal affront if his friend turned up dead.

*　　　*　　　*

Rosie waited anxiously until she heard the rat-a-tat-tat on the apartment door. Leaping up from the sofa, she hurried to answer it. She

449

was halfway across the living room when the door opened and Zach stepped inside.

As if it'd been weeks since she'd last seen him, Rosie flew into his embrace. Zach wrapped his arms around her waist, half lifting her from the floor. Not a second passed before his mouth found hers. Their kisses were deep and urgent, reminiscent of their college days. The spark that had been missing during the last few years of their marriage was back—and bright enough to start a fire.

When Zach set her feet on the carpet again, Rosie's head was spinning with desire. Forgotten was her intent to discuss so many of the pressing issues that clamored for attention. Instead, all she could think about was the warmth of his touch and the need he created within her.

'Don't you think meeting like this is a little ridiculous?' she murmured.

'Do you?'

'No.' She rose to her tiptoes and kissed him.

Zach kissed her back and all too soon they were in the bedroom—his bedroom. Two days earlier, they'd ended up in hers, and the time before that they hadn't even made it to a bed.

'We're supposed to talk,' Rosie reminded him in the aftermath of their lovemaking. Her head rested against his naked shoulder. They were sprawled on top of the bedcovers, with her arm draped across his waist.

'I know, but when I see you the last thing I

feel like doing is talking.'

Rosie understood perfectly. She was as hungry for Zach as he was for her.

'Did you tell the kids where you were going?' she asked, a little embarrassed that their children might have guessed they'd turned the apartment into a love nest. Even the old-fashioned term made her wince.

Zach chuckled. 'You're joking, right?'

Rosie sighed and rubbed her cheek against his chest, loving the warm feel of his skin. Closing her eyes, she inhaled Zach's scent—distinctively his and almost enough to arouse her all over again. 'I think it's important that we talk, though.'

'I do, too,' Zach agreed, 'but unfortunately I can't seem to keep my hands off you.'

Rosie had to admit she liked this resurgence of their love life—liked it a lot. As for wasting their precious time at the apartment in bed, well, *she* didn't have any complaints.

'The kids aren't blind, you know,' Zach said as his hand made slow, lazy circles on the small of her back. 'They have a fairly good idea who I'm sneaking out to see.'

'Allison said as much,' Rosie told him.

'Okay, so the kids are in favor of our reconciliation,' Zach said, sounding serious, 'but are we?'

'How do you mean?'

'Are we ready to get back together? *Should* we? I love you, Rosie, and you love me.

451

I've always loved you, but even now I don't understand how two people who genuinely love each other could let themselves get divorced.'

Rosie nodded. 'I made a lot of mistakes,' she said soberly.

'So did I,' Zach was quick to admit. 'I don't want to rehash everything we did wrong, but on the other hand, I'm not willing to ignore what happened and then repeat our mistakes.'

'I feel the same way.' The thought of going through that terrible tension again was intolerable. She couldn't live like that, and she knew Zach couldn't, either. Nor could they inflict this nightmare on their children a second time.

'I'd like to continue teaching,' Rosie said. Her contribution to their problems had to do with the fact that she'd volunteered for absolutely every committee, group, field day and task force that came up. She'd developed a reputation as the consummate volunteer, the woman who couldn't say no.

Before the divorce, she had commitments and obligations that took her away from the house most days and every night of the week. It had started when Zach was so busy preparing tax returns. She was lonely and looking for a social outlet, a way to be part of the community. Her volunteering had grown into a time-consuming monster that had threatened to destroy her and her family.

'I always wanted to be the perfect wife and mother,' she whispered, saddened by the memory of her failings.

Zach kissed the top of her head. 'I know.'

'Then I got so caught up in everything, I wasn't any kind of mother at all.'

'Hey, I'm not going to listen to you beat yourself up,' Zach said. 'Especially when I was doing plenty wrong myself.'

His hold on her tightened slightly. 'You didn't wreck our marriage single-handedly, Rosie. I let my ego replace common sense. You were right about Janice Lamond, but I was too blind to see what she was doing.'

'I was so jealous,' Rosie confessed.

'So was I, especially when you started dating that widower.'

She didn't know Zach had been jealous. The warm glow it gave her was childish, but she basked in the feeling, anyway. 'Like I told you, we only went out that once.'

'I thought it was much more, and it confused the hell out of me.' He laughed softly and continued to stroke her back. 'We were supposed to be divorced, and yet the thought of you going out with another man had me seeing red.'

Rosie loved it. 'Well, you can imagine how *I* felt when we were married and I thought you were involved with another woman. *Jealous* doesn't even begin to describe it.'

'It's not going to happen again,' he

promised her.

'I won't get caught up in volunteering again, either,' she said. 'Maybe the occasional short-term thing, but that's it. I know how to set boundaries now.' She took a deep breath. 'I've also discovered that I like teaching—I'd forgotten how much. The hours are great with the kids' schedules, and when I return at the end of the day, I appreciate my home and family.'

'I'll help around the house more,' he vowed.

'Good.' That had been another of their problems. Because she was supposed to be a stay-at-home mother, Zach—and the children, too—had come to rely on her to do everything, to fulfill every need, to be the perfect housekeeper, cook, fixer, scheduler, chauffeur and hostess. To be responsible for everything on the domestic front, in other words.

'I can make dinner two nights a week,' Zach told her. 'I've learned a lot from the cooking channel.'

'I can handle getting dinner ready another three,' she said. Now that Rosie had more time, she'd found out she actually enjoyed cooking.

'Allison's learned a thing or two about helping out in the kitchen,' Zach said. 'I think she'd like being in charge of one dinner a week.'

'That leaves us with only one night open,' she said, thinking that perhaps they could trade off on it.

'One night a week for you and me to go on a date,' Zach said firmly.

'A date?'

'Time for us to be together, Rosie. Just you and me. Do you realize we lived in the same house and barely spoke? We talked, but we were both too busy and too distracted to really listen to each other. You're my best friend, and I've missed you and missed having you in my life. I believe that not spending time with each other is what got us into trouble.'

Perhaps he was right. Perhaps that *was* one of the reasons their marriage had fallen apart. With Zach spending long hours at the office and her filling every spare minute with charity projects and volunteer positions, they'd lost their focus. They'd forgotten about each other; everything else had come first.

Raising herself onto one elbow, she kissed his jaw. 'Have I told you lately how much I love you?'

'You have,' Zach whispered. 'Oh, Rosie, Rosie, it feels so good to have you in my arms again.'

'The kids want us to remarry,' she said.

Until then, neither Zach nor Rosie had said it aloud.

'I know.' She heard the hesitation in his voice. 'How do you feel about it?'

Rosie nestled closer to him. 'Excited...and a little afraid.'

'Me, too,' he said quietly.

They'd both said and done things that burdened the future. Could they maintain this new resolve, continue to nurture their relationship and each other?

'We need to be very sure, Zach.'

'I agree. When we do remarry, and I believe we will,' he said, kissing her again, 'it has to be forever, with one hundred percent total commitment from each of us.' Zach met her eyes, a look of intensity in his. 'We've opened that door marked Divorce and walked through it once.'

She nodded.

'It could easily become a swinging door. With every argument, every disagreement, we can decide we made an even bigger mistake by remarrying. We can turn what seems so right and good now into a living nightmare.'

Rosie understood what he was saying. 'In other words, if we decide to remarry, that's it. There's no going back again. Ever.'

'It's all or nothing,' he said fervently.

Rosie didn't hesitate. She knew what she wanted and that was this man, her husband and lover, back in her life forever. 'All or nothing,' she repeated. 'I want it all.'

'Then, will you marry me, Rosie? In sickness and in health, till death do us part?'

'I will,' she whispered. 'What are we going to tell people?' she asked after a pause.

Zach chuckled. 'We'll tell them the truth.'

'Which is?'

'The divorce just didn't work out.'

*   *   *

'You're a beautiful bride.' Grace wiped a tear from the corner of her eye.

Olivia turned away from the full-length mirror on the back of her bedroom door. She wore a new peach-colored suit, tailored and elegant, and carried a bouquet of pink rosebuds.

Grace sat on the bed studying her. James and Justine would arrive soon and together they'd escort her to the waterfront park where Jack, his family and Charlotte waited.

'Will Jack think so?' Olivia asked, knowing how insecure she sounded. After all these years of living as a single woman, she'd never expected to fall in love again, in love to the point that she was willing to share her home and her life with another man. Until Jack Griffin had come along…

'I think it's so touching that Jack asked Pastor Flemming to perform the ceremony,' Grace said, digging for a tissue in the bottom of her purse. 'I just know I'm going to ruin everything and cry through the entire thing.'

'You won't,' Olivia assured her, although she wasn't nearly as confident about herself. Every time she thought of Jack and how much she loved him, she felt like weeping with joy.

'Oh, Mom!' Justine said, dashing into the bedroom. She brought her hands together in a gesture of reverence. 'You look absolutely *gorgeous.*'

Olivia blushed, then kissed her daughter on the cheek. 'Thank you, sweetheart.'

'Are you ready?' Justine asked. 'The limo's arrived.'

Olivia looked at Grace, and her best friend threw her a bright smile and a thumb's-up. Exhaling unsteadily, Olivia whispered, 'As ready as I'll ever be.'

'James was over at Jack's place, and he's a nervous wreck,' Justine informed her as they walked out to the car.

'Jack?' A few hours earlier, he'd sounded completely under control.

'Eric, Shelly and the boys got here,' Justine went on to explain, 'and pandemonium broke out. One of the babies spit up on Jack's tuxedo. Eric came unglued, but then Shelly calmly cleaned it off.'

'So everything's right with the world once more,' Olivia murmured. It'd been crazy at her house, too. Seth had picked up James, Selina and Isabella at the Seattle airport, and within an hour of their arrival, Selina had announced she was pregnant again. That was when the celebrating had begun.

'Your coach awaits you,' Justine said with a little bow as they reached the sidewalk.

And she did feel a bit like Cinderella going

to the ball. Today marked one of the most significant changes in her life. It was only a matter of weeks since she and Jack had made the decision to marry, but neither was content to delay the wedding. They wanted to be together.

The liveried driver stood outside the limousine, ready to help everyone inside.

'I hope to do something like this for Maryellen and Jon,' Grace said as she stepped into the car with Olivia.

'Have they set the date yet?'

Grace nodded. 'The first Saturday in June.'

'Wonderful,' Olivia said. Weddings seemed to be in the air. Grace's daughter and Jon Bowman had decided to marry; Olivia knew Grace was both delighted and relieved that Katie's mother and father would soon be united.

'Another Saturday you'll have to give up your stint at the Humane Society,' Olivia teased, knowing how much Grace enjoyed her volunteer work with the agency.

Jon and Maryellen's engagement wasn't the only news of a wedding that had reached Olivia. The controversial divorce decree she'd made last year, which had caused such a stir at the courthouse, had turned out rather well. She'd heard from Otto Benson, one of the attorneys involved in the case, that the Coxes were planning to remarry. Olivia was pleased, and wished the couple well. Everything at 311

Pelican Court seemed to be in good shape—a refreshing change.

As the limousine made its way down Lighthouse Road, Olivia looked out the side window at the cove. She loved this beautiful place, this town that was home. She glanced at Grace and smiled. Her friend was adjusting to life as a widow. Maneuvering in unfamiliar territory was never easy; Grace was bound to take a few wrong steps, but Olivia felt confident that all was well at 204 Rosewood Lane, especially now that Grace had found a cause to support. Olivia still hoped Cliff would reappear in Grace's life, but only time would tell.

The limo pulled into the parking lot at the waterfront park. The driver rushed around and opened the door for Olivia, then offered her his hand, helping her out.

It couldn't have been a more perfect day for a wedding. A day of bright sun and fresh spring breezes. The sparkling blue water of the cove sent shafts of reflected sunlight toward the gazebo where Jack stood waiting. Roses, lilies, irises and a dozen other flowers filled huge white baskets, carefully arranged to create a border around the white-painted gazebo.

Her mother was with her friend, Ben Rhodes. Ever since her arrest, Charlotte had been unusually quiet. Olivia was convinced this newfound respect for the law would be short-lived, however. When Charlotte wanted something badly enough, she generally found a way to get it.

Olivia blamed Ben Rhodes for the fact that she'd had to bail her own mother out of the county jail. She was determined to keep a careful eye on him. Olivia wasn't sure the elderly gentleman was a good influence on her mother. Nor did she think it was such a good idea for the two of them to be spending so much time together. She intended to learn what she could about Ben Rhodes.

Jack stepped forward and took Olivia's hand. 'I don't know what I ever did that persuaded you to marry me,' he said as he bent close to kiss her cheek, 'but whatever it was, I can only say I'm grateful.'

'Oh, Jack, that's so sweet.'

He grinned and glanced sheepishly at his best man, Bob Beldon. 'Bob suggested I say that.'

Olivia rolled her eyes. She should have known. Jack was no romantic, but he made up for his lack of finesse in a dozen wonderful ways. She was pleased to see Bob and his wife, Peggy. She didn't know them well, but since Bob was Jack's best friend, she assumed they'd be seeing more of the couple who owned the local B and B.

There'd been some concern about Bob, she remembered, something to do with that dead guy. Jack had been rather vague about it, and for a time he'd seemed uncertain whether his friend would be available for the ceremony. Apparently whatever it was had been resolved, although from the barely restrained tension she felt in the other man, Olivia wondered. Things didn't seem to be quite as they should at 44 Cranberry Point.

The guests gathered in a close circle around Olivia and Jack. Pastor Flemming opened his Bible and smiled up at the two of them.

'Dearly beloved,' he began.

Jack squeezed Olivia's hand, and she returned the gesture. Jack Griffin, newsman and recovering alcoholic, was indeed her beloved, and she was his. Like so many before him, Jack had found new life and purpose in Cedar Cove. She smiled up at this man who would soon be her husband. They were the keepers of each other's secrets...and of each other's heart.